Sylvia
Graubart

HOUSE
OF
DREAMS

BRENDA JOYCE

HOUSE
OF
DREAMS

ST. MARTIN'S PRESS ☙ NEW YORK

www.stmartins.com

Design by Nancy Resnick

Library of Congress Cataloging-in-Publication Data

Joyce, Brenda.
    House of Dreams / Brenda Joyce.
        p. cm.
    ISBN 0-312-26247-7
    I. Title.

PS3560.O864 H6 2000
813'.54—dc21

                                                00-040526

First Edition: September 2000

10 9 8 7 6 5 4 3 2 1

This book is dedicated to
Jennifer Enderlin and Cheryl Nesbit,
two of my best friends,
without whom it would not have been possible.
Much love and appreciation!

PART ONE

THE
SECRET

ONE

BELFORD HOUSE, EAST SUSSEX—THE PRESENT

Just where the hell was her sister?

Cass had spent most of her life in her sister's shadow—Tracey was one of the most beautiful and glamorous women Cass knew—and unfortunately, she had a tendency to run late. Cass was a wreck. Surely today, of all days, Tracey could be on time. Just this once.

In another two hours the house would be filled with Tracey's guests. With Forbes 400 types, their fashion-plate wives, the odd Silicon Valley millionaire, celebrities, dignitaries, the press, two Japanese bankers, a couple of rock stars, an Israeli shipping tycoon, an ambassador, and a sprinkling of dukes, duchesses, and earls. The very thought caused Cass's heart to lurch unpleasantly.

But mostly, Tracey should be on time because she hadn't seen her own daughter in three months even if they did speak on the phone.

Cass stood nervously by the window, staring past the crisply white shell drive and across the green rolling hills of the East Sussex countryside. She was perspiring. Dairy cows dotted the fields spanning the distance between the house and the small village of Belford, which she could just make out as a jumble of pale stone rooftops. The day was gray, the threat of rain imminent, reducing visibility. Even so, she could see the nearest town—Romney, famous for its tourist attraction, an intact castle dating back five full centuries—as it sat on one of the surrounding hills. Cass could also see a thin strip of highway meandering through the countryside. No car was in sight.

"Where's Mother? Why isn't she here yet?" A small voice asked.

Cass's stomach was in knots as she turned to face her seven-year-old niece. "Your mom will be here at any moment, I'm sure of it," she lied. And she thought, *Please, Trace. For Alyssa, for me, just get here!*

Alyssa sat on her pristine pink and white bed, against numerous fluffy pillows, all beautifully embroidered and mostly pink, white, and red like the bedroom, wearing her newest clothes—a short, pale blue dress from Harrods, navy blue stockings, and chunky black suede shoes. Her raven black hair was pulled back with a tortoiseshell barrette, and her face was scrubbed and glowing. She was so pretty, but nothing like her mother—not in any way. "She was supposed to arrive an hour ago," Alyssa said glumly. "What if she doesn't come?"

Cass started and rushed to her niece, who had just verbalized Cass's own worst fears. "She is coming, sweetie. You can bet on that. This is Tracey's black-tie supper, even if Aunt Catherine is hosting the event. You know that. She *has* to show up."

Alyssa nodded, but did not seem convinced.

Cass knew that her younger sister was wild and irresponsible, but she wasn't that wild, or that irresponsible. The evening affair was on account of Tracey's new job with Sotheby's in London. The moment Tracey had asked Catherine if she could hold an event in order to display a very rare necklace to three dozen potential buyers—the crème de la crème of international society—Catherine had agreed. Their aunt rarely refused either one of her nieces. Cass's temples began to throb dully. Tracey would show up—wouldn't she?

Cass could not imagine helping Aunt Catherine to host this event. She was not a jet-setter like her sister. She did not frequent five-star hotels, fly first class, juggle playboys and polo players, or even own more than a single evening gown. She did not go to the weddings of supermodels. Cass's last boyfriend had been a journalist, not a rock star.

"Some people just can't help being late," Cass finally said, forcing a lightness into her tone that she did not feel. "It's a terrible habit," she added. And that much was true. Cass knew that Tracey did not mean to keep people waiting. It just happened. It was less about self-absorption than it was about disorganization and time management. No one lived life the way her sister did.

Still, Cass had been filled with a growing sense of dread all that day. The evening—or her sister's visit—was going to be a disaster. Cass had never felt more certain of anything, even if she could not pinpoint why.

Cass just hoped the premonition of disaster didn't have to do with her filling in for Tracey.

"She's so busy now with her new job," Alyssa said, her dark eyes lowered, her thick black lashes fanning out on her alabaster cheeks. She was the spitting image of her rock-star father, Rick Tennant, who was currently on a world tour and somewhere in the Far East.

Cass hoped that was so. Sotheby's seemed like the perfect job for her sister—she could mingle with the rich and famous, while her employers benefited from her celebrity status and her celebrity associations. Since her marriage, and even more so since her divorce, Tracey had been a fixture on the society pages of most major magazines.

Tracey's marriage to Rick had been over in less than three years. Cass regretted, for Alyssa's sake, that it hadn't lasted. But Alyssa was the best thing that had ever happened to her, and she loved her as if she were her own daughter. In fact, sometimes she forgot that if Tracey wanted to, she could saunter into their lives and whisk Alyssa away without even an explanation. Which, of course, Cass prayed she would never do.

"I hear a car," Alyssa cried, leaping up, her entire face brightening.

Cass was flooded with relief. Alyssa ran to the window, her black hair swinging like a cape behind her, while Cass hugged herself, sighing, because she would not have to play hostess and Alyssa would see her mother after what had become an interminable separation—from a little girl's point of view.

"It's not her," Alyssa said, her tone flat.

Cass stood, her heart sinking, eyes wide. "What?" Where was Tracey!

Alyssa seemed on the verge of tears. Cass took one look at her pinched white face and she reached for her hand. "She's running late. Should we take a walk? It might help pass the time," Cass said.

"I'd rather wait here. I don't want to miss her," Allysa said with a stubborn tilt to her chin.

Before Cass could suggest another diversion, there was a soft knock on the door and Aunt Catherine appeared, holding a silver tray in her hands. Her gaze instantly connected with Cass's, before she entered the room and smiled at Alyssa. "Scones and tea, my dear. You must be famished, Alyssa. You haven't had a bite to eat all day."

Alyssa folded her arms tightly across her chest. "Why does she have to be so late? Doesn't she miss me, too?"

Catherine slowly set the tray down on the Chippendale table in front of another set of windows, one graced by two pink velvet chairs.

Although seventy, Cass's aunt was a tall, statuesque woman who looked no older than fifty. Her reddish hair was shoulder length and worn in a chignon, and she remained extremely handsome, a perpetual light in her blue eyes. Even clad simply in gray trousers, a white blouse, and a darker cardigan, she had the carriage of a very noble, self-assured, and self-sufficient woman. Cass admired her greatly, for her character, her generosity, and the many good deeds she had dedicated her life to. "Of course she does. Our guests will be arriving at seven, and knowing your mother, who needs a good hour or two to dress for this kind of event, she will have to arrive at any moment," Catherine said, smiling.

Alyssa wandered over to the table and stared at the scones. She had been so excited that morning she had gotten sick after breakfast, and Cass had let her stay home from the exclusive all-girls school she attended.

Cass went to her. "Of course she misses you, sweetie. She's your mother. No one is more special to her, believe me. But working for Sotheby's can't be easy; they send her all over the world. I think she was in Madrid just a few days ago. Your mom is probably very tired, sweetie—and really nervous about tonight."

Alyssa looked her right in the eye. "She was in *Vogue* again. With a new man. Does she have another boyfriend?"

Cass blinked. She'd obviously missed that last issue. Actually, she avoided the kinds of magazines and rags her sister usually appeared in. Cass wasn't jealous. It was just oddly hurtful to see her sister on those pages so often, surrounded by household names, looking so perfect. "I don't know," Cass said after a pause, truthfully. Tracey hadn't mentioned a new lover to Cass.

Catherine rubbed her thin back. "Do not fret, dear. Your mother will be here at any moment, and then you can ask her yourself about any new man that might be in her life."

Alyssa bit her lip, looking perilously close to tears.

Catherine said, brightly, "I think everyone in this room is exhausted. I do mean, we have had staff preparing for this evening for two days, not to mention the security from Sotheby's to make sure that ruby necklace is not stolen by some cat thief—those men swarming all over the grounds! Let's take some tea. We'll all feel better, and by the time we're done, I have not a doubt Tracey will be sailing through that doorway."

Alyssa nodded, lips pursed, sitting down in one of the pink velvet chairs, swinging her chunky platform shoes back and forth. As she reached for a scone, Catherine pouring the tea, Cass said, "I'm going to go downstairs and take a breath of air, if you two don't mind."

"I think you should take a long hot soak, Cassandra, and spend some time primping before the mirror for this evening's affair," Catherine said gently.

Cass caught the briefest glimpse of her own reflection in the mirror as she started and turned back to face her aunt. She was wearing not one stitch of makeup, and the Barnard sweatshirt she'd thrown on that morning was as old and faded as her jeans. Her honey blond hair was shoulder length and pulled into a ponytail. Like her aunt, she had strong, even features and good skin. Unlike her aunt, she did not turn heads.

And she knew exactly what her aunt meant—she should take extra care to dress up because one never knew whom one might meet.

"*Moi?* Primp? Would you care to define that for me?" Cass had to smile.

Alyssa even giggled. "I'll help Aunt Cass get dressed," she said. "She can use my lipstick. It would look great on you, Aunt Cass."

Before Cass could accept or decline, Catherine said, "You are far too young to own, much less wear, lipstick, Alyssa." Her tone was stern.

"Actually," Cass cut in, "I thought I'd go over the notes I made last night. I was so tired I feel asleep at my desk, and I want to make sure I can decipher my scrawl."

Catherine just looked at her, her expression a mixture of resignation, reproval, and respect.

Cass fled the room before they could get into an argument about Cass's single-minded focus on her career as the author of historical novels—she'd had four works published in the past six years—and her consequent, serious lack of a personal life—or even the mere pursuit of one.

Cass hurried downstairs in her rubber-soled loafers. They had been over the old tired argument a dozen times—she should get out more, date more, she should be married, she should have her own kids. Catherine just didn't understand. Taking care of Alyssa and her work was just about all she could handle. There was only so much time in every day.

A housemaid smiled at her as she hurried past, down a dim hall with stone floors, her mind torn between thoughts of Tracey's arrival and her departure, the desire to protect Alyssa from all of life's disappointments, both large and small, and her own inner voice, which agreed with her aunt entirely. Five years ago, when she had packed up her life and moved with Alyssa from her small apartment in New York City to Belford House, she'd given up her pursuit of a personal life and hadn't dwelled much on it since. There had been no choice to make. Alyssa had needed her from the day she was born, and the moment Tracey and Rick had decided to divorce, it had been clear to Cass that if she didn't raise the small child, no one else would. She hadn't had the means to be a single mother, and moving in with her aunt had been the perfect solution. There were no regrets.

Cass stepped through a pair of doors that opened on one side of her aunt's flower gardens, the driveway to her left and just within the range of her peripheral vision. She swung her head around and hesitated, noticing a black Citroen in the driveway. Her sister drove an Aston Martin. Or rather, her driver did. Tracey had made out very handsomely in her divorce settlement.

It was too early for any guests to have arrived, and just as Cass was pondering that notion, she realized that someone was standing in the gardens on her right, his back to her. For one moment she wondered if he was one of the security men from Sotheby's. He was tall, dark haired, and well dressed in tan trousers and a black sport jacket. The tan trousers gave him away as something other than security, because the security men wore all black. Cass approached, clearing her throat, about to ask him if he needed help—or was even in the right place.

He turned.

Cass felt a flash of recognition even before his eyes met hers. She stumbled, for one instant lost in confusion.

Just what in God's name was Antonio de la Barca doing in her aunt's flower gardens? She did not know him personally, but he was the kind of man a woman would never forget, not having met him even once. Not that they had actually, really met. He was a professor of medieval studies, of international renown, tenured in Madrid, and Cass had attended a lecture series that he had given at the Metropolitan Museum in New York City seven years ago. She recalled the series so well: Medieval Myth, Fact or Fantasy, a Mirror to Our World. She had been researching her third novel at the time, and his course had been just after Alyssa's birth but before her sister's quickie divorce.

"Señora, I see I have startled you. Please, forgive me," he said, his smile slight. He had an intriguing Latin accent.

Cass tried to recover her composure. "I wasn't expecting anyone to be out here," she managed, her heart racing madly. This was absurd.

Why was she so surprised to see him? Obviously he must be there to attend the dinner party. It was now clicking in her brain that the necklace that was the highlight of Sotheby's next auction was a period piece, dating back to the sixteenth century. Article after article had been written about the stunning find. Perhaps he had even appraised its historical value.

"A servant assured me that I could take a walk in the gardens without disturbing anyone, but I see I have disturbed you. Again, my sincerest apologies." He was wearing tortoiseshell eyeglasses, which hardly detracted from his strong, attractive Spanish features. His gaze was at once assured and questioning.

Cass knew she was blushing. He did not seem to remember her, but of course, he would not. Even if she had asked dozens of questions after each and every lecture. Her gaze slid to his hands, but they were tucked in the pockets of his trousers. He'd worn a wedding ring seven years ago, and the gossip among all of the women attending the lectures had run rampant, because supposedly his wife had simply disappeared without a trace the year before. Cass recalled the ceaseless speculation—was it even true? Had she run away? Or had some unspeakable horror befallen her? Of course, no one had had any answers. But it had certainly made him even more of a romantic figure in the eyes of the women attending the lecture series. Just about every woman there had been madly in love with him.

Cass included.

"I'm being a terrible hostess," Cass finally said, finding her tongue. "You must be here for the evening's dinner party. My aunt is Catherine Belford. I'm Cassandra de Warenne."

For one moment he studied her, not accepting her hand. Cass wondered if she had said something wrong, and then the moment passed— her hand was in his grip, which was firm and cool, and he bowed ever so slightly. "You're American?" he asked with some surprise.

Her accent was a giveaway. "My mother was American, and actually I was born in the States, but when she died, my aunt took us in. I was eleven at the time. I've spent so much time here, I consider myself at least half British." Cass knew she was speaking in a nervous rush.

He removed his eyeglasses, tucking them into the interior breast pocket of his impeccably tailored navy blue sport jacket. "You went to Barnard?"

Cass suddenly realized, with no small amount of horror, how she was dressed. Unfortunately, she could feel her color increase. "Yes. I graduated ten years ago," she said. "I took a year off, then went back for my master's."

"I've lectured several times at Columbia," he said with a smile. "I know both colleges well. They are fine schools."

Cass shoved her hands, which were damp, into the pockets of her jeans. Did she sound like an idiot? Or a blushing schoolgirl? "Actually, I attended your lecture series at the Met a few years ago."

He just looked at her, his expression difficult to read.

Cass felt like taking back her words. Should she have admitted that she remembered him? "You *are* Antonio de la Barca?"

"Forgive me again." He raked a hand through his jet black hair, hair that was even darker than Alyssa's. "I do not know what is wrong with me today." He shook his head, as if to clear it. Then he stared. "Yes, I did give that lecture, seven years ago." Something crossed his face, an expression Cass found difficult to read. "A great institution," he murmured, and he turned slightly, staring toward the rolling hills and Romney Castle. Cass realized it was drizzling.

She ignored it. She also ignored the slight twinge she felt because he didn't remember her at all. "It was a wonderful lecture, Señor de la Barca. I enjoyed it immensely."

He faced her, their eyes meeting. "Are you a historian?"

She hesitated, debating telling him the truth. "I majored in European history at college," she said. "My master's is in British history. And now I write historical novels." She kept her hand in her pockets.

His eyes flickered. "How interesting," he said, and there was nothing patronizing in his tone. "I would love a list of the titles you have published."

"I'd be happy to give one to you before you leave," Cass said, wondering if he would really read one of her books, then worrying about any inaccuracies he might find. "Are you here to see the necklace?"

He nodded, eyes brightening. "A sixteenth-century piece? The way it has been described, it would be worth a king's ransom—and would have belonged to someone exemplary. If the piece is authentic, which clearly it must be, as Sotheby's does not make such grievous errors, then I am more interested in discovering who might have originally owned it than anything else." He smiled at her.

"It's stunning," Cass said eagerly. "Of course, I've only seen the photos. Those rubies are cut so slightly and so primitively that the average person would assume them to be glass. I can't wait to actually see the piece tonight."

He was nodding. "Rubies were very rare in the sixteenth century," he said, his gaze directly on her again. "Only the most wealthy and powerful possessed rubies. This necklace might have belonged to a queen or a princess. That the Hepplewhites discovered it in their possession is rather amazing."

"Can you imagine if Lady Hepplewhite had thrown it out as she first thought of doing, assuming it to be a costume piece?"

He was smiling, shaking his head. Cass was smiling, too.

"I'm writing a novel set during Bloody Mary's reign," she said impulsively. "It was a fascinating period in time, and Mary has been so stereotyped and so gravely misunderstood."

Both of his dark brows lifted. He stared. "Really."

Cass bit her lip. "I can't help it. My imagination runs away with me. That necklace could have been a careless gift handed down by Mary to one of her favorites. She was very loyal and generous to those in her household."

"Yes, it could have been." Their gazes locked. "Or it could have been a gift from her father to just about anyone—one of his wives, one of his daughters—or perhaps his son Edward passed it along in a similar manner."

"It would be very interesting to trace the lineage of the necklace," Cass mused.

"Very interesting," Antonio de la Barca agreed, his gaze still focused entirely on her.

There was something in his tone that made Cass tense. She could not look away, and now she remembered talking to him after a lecture and being as mesmerized by the brilliance in his hazel eyes. The brilliance and the intensity.

She had to take a step backward, away from him. Even if he was a widower, he was way out of her league. Besides, she had learned her lesson years ago. Eight years ago, to be exact—just before Alyssa was born. When you fell in love, all good judgment flew out the window, and the result was tragic. Having had her heart broken once and forever was enough. The man who broke it was a college love affair—but it had apparently been more important to her than it had to him. She knew she had moved past the heartbreak. She just never wanted to go there again. "It's raining," she said, to break the moment, which had somehow seemed far too intimate and even awkward.

He glanced up at the sky, smiled slightly, as the skies opened up and it began to pour. "Indeed it is," he said.

"C'mon," Cass said, turning to lead him inside.

But he was shrugging off his designer sport jacket and draping it over her sweatshirt-clad shoulders. Cass did not have time to gape. Talking her elbow very firmly, he hurried her back inside.

Once out of the rain, Cass handed him his nearly soaking jacket. "I hope you haven't ruined that."

"It hardly matters," he replied.

Cass hesitated, aware of the darkening shadows of the late afternoon, and as suddenly aware of the fact that this particular guest was several hours early. What was she to do with him?

Clearly her thoughts were written all over her face, because he said, "I am meeting Señora Tennant here, but apparently she is somewhat late."

Cass stiffened. *He's meeting Tracey here?* "Tracey is my sister."

He started. "She never mentioned that she had a sister. I was assuming you to be her cousin."

How did de la Barca know her sister? "No, we're sisters, even if we look nothing alike," she said slowly. A new sense of dread, very different from the one that had been haunting her all day, was filling her.

Why was he meeting Tracey? Before Cass could even begin to sort out what was happening, Alyssa came pounding down the stairs, crying out in excitement that her mother had finally arrived.

And the front door swung open behind them. Cass heard it just as she felt a gust of cold, wet air, but she was looking at his hands now, which were hanging by his sides. He was wearing a very bold ring with a bloodred stone on his right hand, but the slender wedding band she had seen seven years ago was gone. Well. He had not remarried. And that explained everything, she thought grimly. His involvement with Tracey had nothing to do with the sixteenth-century necklace. Cass knew it the way she knew she would have an awful time that evening.

"Hello, everyone!" Tracey cried from behind Cass.

A huge weight settled on Cass's shoulders, and she turned.

Tracey stood in the doorway in a pair of beautifully tailored white pants, an exquisitely cut short grayish white jacket with Chanel buttons, and a pair of high-heeled white boots. Her long, pale blond hair was loose, the dampness causing it to curl about her face and shoulders. She looked as if she had just stepped off a catwalk, or out of the pages of *Vogue.* Which, considering Alyssa's earlier comments, apparently she had.

Tracey was classically attractive. Her features were perfectly even, her eyes blue, her skin unblemished. She was one of those women who looked as good without makeup as they did with it. And while there might be more beautiful women in the same room with her, Tracey was always the most striking. She was the one who turned heads. Because she was model-thin and close to six feet tall. She also lived in drop-dead designer clothes. No one made an entrance like her sister did, Cass thought sourly. She realized she was hugging herself.

"Cass, how are you?" Tracey smiled, apparently not having noticed Alyssa, who stood on the lowest level of the stairs, clinging to the banister. She hugged Cass hard, but Cass hardly noticed. How the hell had her sister and de la Barca met? How?

Tracey's gaze became questioning. "Cass?"

"Hiya, sis." Cass managed a smile.

Tracey beamed at her, then turned to face Antonio de la Barca. The smile she sent him told Cass all she needed to know. They were lovers. This was nothing new—so why was she surprised? Dismayed?

"I see that the two of you have met," she said happily. "Don't tell me you're already dressed for supper?" she teased.

"Ha ha," Cass said, watching Tracey kiss Antonio on the cheek. At least she was spared the real thing. How *had* they met? *When* had they become lovers? And why, Goddamn it, did she care? Tracey changed men the way she changed her wardrobe—which was seasonally, at least. Cass was used to it—she expected no less.

Although if she were brutally honest with herself, she could admit how nice it would be to have an endless stream of boyfriends.

But she wasn't Tracey. She just couldn't settle for good looks and good times.

Tracey pulled on her ponytail. "Why are you so grumpy? I was only kidding, sis. In fact"—her smile widened—"I brought everyone presents!"

Cass stepped back a bit. "How have you been? You look great, Trace. I guess Sotheby's agrees with you."

Tracey beamed, which only made her lovelier. "A lot of things are agreeing with me lately," she said, her gaze locking on de la Barca. She stopped, spotting Alyssa with her nose between the bars of the iron banister. "Darling, come here!" Tracey cried.

Alyssa slowly stood, her face as red as a beet. "Hello, Mother," she said, her brown eyes wide and riveted upon Tracey's snow white figure.

Tracey pounced on her, embracing her once, hard. Cass watched. She watched Alyssa's body remain straight and hard and tight, and she watched Tracey's smile fade and finally vanish as she straightened, a look of hurt in her blue eyes. Alyssa climbed up the stairs a step, a similar look of hurt in her near-black gaze. In the next instant Tracey recovered, the cover-girl smile firmly in place as she turned and rushed to Antonio, looping her arms in his. "I see you've met everyone," she said too brightly.

It was hardly noticeable, but he disengaged their arms. "I have met your sister, but I have not met your daughter," he said somewhat quietly. His smile was brief.

Cass's antenna went up. Trouble in paradise? Something was up, and she had to know what.

"Alyssa, come meet my boyfriend, Antonio de la Barca. Tonio, this is my beautiful daughter, who is seven, I might add."

Alyssa finally came down the stairs. "I saw your picture in *Vogue*. With my mother."

Antonio stooped so that he was not towering over her. And he smiled and it was wide and genuine, marking him as a man who liked children. "Your mother is the kind of woman that photographers wish to photograph. I have no doubt that one day you will be the very same kind of woman."

Cass fell in love with him in that moment. The sudden, shocking depth and intensity of feeling immobilized her. It was the kind of feeling she'd had once before—a sensation of absolute free-falling, a headlong plunge, into the abyss of emotional space.

Cass had gone there once before and barely survived. She stared at her sister, her niece, and the stranger in their midst, paralyzed.

Antonio continued to smile at Alyssa. Very slowly, very slightly, Alyssa smiled back.

And Cass could not move. She could not even think, she could only feel. She was stunned. Terrified.

He was so gorgeous and so Old World, so masculine, so intelligent . . . Jesus.

And he was her sister's.

Which was just fine.

This could not be happening, she thought.

"I have a son," Antonio continued, "only three years older than you. Maybe one day you will meet him."

Alyssa's eyes brightened. And when she spoke, it was clear to Cass that she was doing all that she could to sound detached—but her tone was breathless. "What is his name?"

"His name is Eduardo, and he lives with me in Madrid, just a few blocks from the Plaza de la Lealtad. We live near a beautiful park, El Retiro, where many children play soccer and Rollerblade in the afternoons." Antonio straightened. Tracey was wearing four-inch heels. At that moment they were the exact same height.

"I would love to go to Madrid," Alyssa breathed.

It suddenly clicked in Cass's very befuddled and stunned mind why Tracey had sent Alyssa several postcards from Madrid. Now she knew why Tracey had been channel-hopping. And she had a very unladylike but very New York City thought. *Shit.*

Cass tried to get a grip. She tried to recover her composure. She did not know de la Barca, not at all, and it was insanity to think that she had just discovered some kind of profound feeling for him.

She was not falling in love.

No way. Not now, not ever, not today.

"Well, one day I am sure you will," Tracey said, moving into the center of the tableau. "Look at what I have brought you, darling," she said, digging four packages out of her Vuitton duffel bag and handing them all at once to Alyssa.

Alyssa clasped her hands in front of her, staring down at the gift-wrapped boxes. "Thank you, Mother."

"You have to open them!" Tracey cried. Then, "Aunt Catherine! There you are, and just in time. I have something for you, too!"

Catherine was coming down the stairs. She was smiling, and Tracey flew into her arms. They embraced warmly, and then Tracey handed her a small box that could only be from a jeweler.

Cass went to Alyssa, trying to avoid looking at de la Barca. "Do you want to take the gifts upstairs to your room and open them privately?" she asked softly, for Alyssa's ears only.

Alyssa nodded. Tears had formed on the tips of her lashes.

Cass wanted to hug her, hard. Suddenly she wanted to turn and shout at Tracey that all the gifts in the world could not make up for her absentee style of motherhood, that gifts could not buy love. She wanted to shout, *Wake up! I know you love her, but show it, Goddamn it! Spend some time here, with your family!* But she said none of those things. Alyssa's control was fragile, at best. And now, so was her own.

Wouldn't de la Barca want an intellectual woman?

"Oh, you have to open the pink package, you'll just love it!" Tracey cried, rushing forward and handing it to her daughter. It was one of the smallest packages present. In the same breath Tracey delved into her duffel and produced a long flat box for Cass. She smiled. "And don't you dare say no."

Cass knew it was clothing. Her sister had incredible taste in clothes, was the chicest person Cass knew, but Cass wasn't Tracey. She didn't wear miniskirts and she didn't wear stiletto heels. Of course, she was only five foot three. She wouldn't even be able to walk in the kind of shoes Tracey wore. "Thanks," she said.

"Are you all right?" Tracey asked with concern.

"Absolutely," Cass said, imagining that her smile was stretched wide and thin.

Catherine suddenly said, "Oh, Tracey, dear, how lovely."

Her tone was odd. Cass looked up to find Catherine holding a stunning Elizabeth Locke pin, a large peridot stone engraved with the figure of a woman, set in a matte gold bar with a diamond chain. But she wasn't admiring the pin. Her brow was furrowed, and she was staring at their visitor. Cass realized she had forgotten to introduce him to her aunt.

But before she could do so, Tracey was speaking in a gay rush. "I was walking down the street when I saw it in the window and I just knew it was perfect for you," she said, smiling happily at her aunt.

"I wish you hadn't," Catherine said very softly, for the hundredth time, her gaze now on her niece. But then it veered back to de la Barca, and her aunt's expression made Cass concerned.

Alyssa had opened her pink parcel, and now she sat down on the second step of the stairs, clutching something to her chest.

Tracey turned eagerly. "It's a collector's item, darling. Her name is Sparkee. Isn't she just the cutest?"

Alyssa bit her lip, nodding. "Thank you, Mother."

Cass realized she was holding a Beanie Baby. Alyssa adored the small stuffed animals and had been brokenhearted when they had all been retired last year. Tracey had probably found the little toy in an auction, or even on the Net. She had gone to great lengths, clearly. But Cass could not focus on mother and daughter now. "Aunt Catherine? Are you all right?" Her aunt seemed oddly stiff with tension.

"We haven't met," Aunt Catherine said quietly.

"Forgive me, but I am intruding—and that is the last thing I wish to do," Antonio de la Barca said as quietly.

But Tracey was swooping down on her aunt, having looped her arm in Antonio's again. "How could you intrude, darling? Aunt Catherine, this is Antonio de la Barca, from Madrid. Tonio, my aunt, Lady Catherine Belford."

Cass started forward. Her aunt was immobile, as if afraid to move, the color having drained from her face. "Aunt Catherine? Are you ill?" she asked with alarm.

If Catherine heard her, she gave no sign. She stared at de la Barca, her expression strained. She could not seem to take her eyes off him. "You resemble your father," she said thickly.

He had been reaching for her hand, and now he froze. "You knew my father, Lady Belford?"

Slowly Catherine nodded, and something terribly sad flitted through her eyes.

"Many years ago," Catherine said. And suddenly her face crumpled with the onset of tears.

"Señora?" Antonio asked, alarmed.

"Oh! I just remembered—I need to ask the caterer something." Catherine turned, almost running, and quite shoving past Tracey.

"Aunt Catherine!" Cass had never seen her aunt act in such a manner before.

Tracey was also wide-eyed.

"Why don't you show our guest to his room," Cass said. She didn't wait for a reply. She hurried down the hall after Catherine, pushing open the door to the kitchen.

Inside it was a flurry of activity, as the caterer and her staff were busy making the last-minute preparations for a cocktail hour and a supper that would serve forty. Catherine stood by the end of the center aisle, hunched over it, leaning upon it, her back to Cass. She was shaking.

Cass did not understand. She rushed to her aunt, slipping her arm around her. "What's wrong? What has happened?" Cass cried.

At first Catherine couldn't speak. She could only shake her head wordlessly, continuing to tremble.

"Aunt Catherine, talk to me, please," Cass begged. One of the staff handed her a tissue and her aunt accepted it, dabbing at her eyes.

"I never expected this," she whispered. "After all these years. Cassandra, we must get that man out of this house—and out of Tracey's life."

Cass was incredulous. "Why?"

"Why?" Catherine turned on her, and Cass was shocked to see both pain and fear in her aunt's wide eyes. Catherine was shaking. "I will tell you why, Cassandra. I killed his father."

TWO

"What is wrong with Auntie Catherine?" Alyssa asked. She was perched on the canopied bed in Cass's bedroom. The room was stone floored, but numerous multicolored Persian rugs covered it. The walls were painted a lovely deep hue of salmon, almost matching the tawny marble mantel over the fireplace. There was a seating area there, which Cass often used, but not as much as she used the huge eighteenth-century secretaire in one corner of the room, where her laptop was set up.

"I'm not sure," Cass said, clad only in a pair of panty hose and a bra. Cass remained stunned. Catherine had not explained her astonishing statement. Instead, she had dashed out of the kitchen, leaving Cass standing there in absolute shock.

Cass was very close to her aunt. Catherine was her best friend in the entire world, as well as her surrogate mother. Cass's father had died when she was three; her mother had died when she was eleven, and Catherine had taken the sisters in. Catherine had no children of her own. Quite early in her marriage, her husband, Robert Belford, had suffered a massive and debilitating stroke. For all intents and purposes, Cass and Tracey's aunt was their mother.

Catherine was, to Cass's mind, an amazing woman. She had not only raised the sisters herself while caring for her invalid husband, she had devoted herself to a good dozen charities throughout her life. She was a pillar of the community and an exemplary human being. She was a giver, not a taker.

She could not have killed a man.

I killed his father.

Cass felt ill. She told herself that there was an explanation, and that Catherine had not been speaking literally.

But what if she had? What had happened, and when had it happened? Clearly Antonio de la Barca knew nothing.

Cass grimaced as she recalled the way her sister had clung so possessively to him earlier in the foyer.

"Aunt Cass, are you plotting a new scene?"

Alyssa cut in to her thoughts and Cass blinked. "Not really," Cass said.

"You had this funny look on your face. You had better hurry, Aunt Cass, or you'll be the last one to arrive at the party," Alyssa said gravely. "I think you should wear that red dress Mother bought for you."

"I don't think so," Cass said. She had to get dressed, but she could not seem to focus on the task at hand. Her mind was swimming . . . images of her aunt competing with images of Antonio de la Barca and Tracey.

"Mother looked beautiful in that outfit, didn't she? She is so beautiful." Alyssa's sigh was admiring and wistful.

Cass heard herself sigh, also. How was she going to get through this evening now? Her headache intensified. It had not escaped her notice that Antonio was sleeping in Tracey's bedroom. "She's always stunning, sweetie. That is nothing new."

"I really like her new boyfriend." Alyssa flushed. "I hope she marries him."

Cass just stared at her, her insides churning unpleasantly. "And why is that?"

"He has a son—I'd have a brother. And maybe we'd be a family again," she said hopefully. "All of us, Aunt Cass. Wouldn't that be wonderful? All of us together?"

Cass could think of nothing worse. "Honey, if your mother marries, I don't think I'll be welcome in her new home. It just doesn't work that way." She was beginning to perspire, she realized.

Alyssa was startled and dismayed. "But why not? I can't live with them if you're not there, too!"

Cass had been about to open the closet; now she paused. She had never seen Tracey look at any of her other lovers the way she'd looked at de la Barca. Tracey was in love. And why not? De la Barca was a catch.

Cass closed her eyes, ill. Men fell head over heels in love with Tracey—every single one of them. She was the one to walk away and break their hearts. De la Barca was probably smitten at this very moment. Tracey could probably walk down the aisle with him tomorrow if she wanted to. And de la Barca was a family man—he loved children. Cass already knew he was a great father. It was so obvious. They would take Alyssa away from her . . .

"Aunt Cass? What's wrong? Did I say something to upset you?"

Cass fought for air. She knew she had to shut off her thoughts or she would never make it through the evening. She turned, opening her closet, but instead of seeing the clothes hanging inside, she kept seeing Tracey walking down the aisle in a wedding gown. Damn it. Maybe Catherine was right. Maybe Antonio and Tracey should not be together, because maybe that might lead him to a truth Catherine did not want revealed. A truth that could destroy her aunt, and even the entire family.

Cass stared at the dress she held in her hands without seeing it. What was she thinking? If her aunt had killed a man, then she had committed a crime, hadn't she? Had it been covered up? Had the police been involved? What about Antonio's family? Did they know?

But what if it had been self-defense?

"Aunt Cass!" Alyssa cried sharply.

"I'm fine." Her words sounded clipped and far too high in pitch to her own ears. She was losing it. She was allowing her incredibly fertile imagination to run away with her. She had to get a grip. She didn't have the facts. She had one shocking confession—a confession that might not even be accurate.

But how could her aunt make such a mistake?

"You're not wearing that red dress Mother bought you?" Alyssa exclaimed as Cass pulled a knee-length black sheath off the hanger. "Aunt Cass, that dress is ugly."

Cass sat down hard on a royal blue damask ottoman. "Shit." She had to speak with Aunt Catherine. Sooner, not later. The problem was, they had a house full of guests, and Cass couldn't imagine finding a moment to speak with her before the next morning.

"Aunt Cass!" Alyssa was bug-eyed.

"Sorry. The American in me," Cass apologized. Suddenly she felt despondent. "I'm too short to wear red. Too short, too curvy, too everything." She didn't tell Alyssa that, in the back of her mind, some stupidly vain and foolish part of her dreaded making a fool of herself in front of de la Barca. Not that it mattered. He was in love with her sister. She could go to the black-tie affair stark naked and he wouldn't even notice. Not with Tracey around.

It had always been that way, too, ever since they were small children.

Cass had thought she was used to the fact that her sister got all the attention. Apparently she wasn't as resigned and habituated to the circumstance as she had believed.

"Aunt Cass, you're pretty, and you'll be beautiful in that dress." Alyssa was so earnest.

"You are prejudiced, but thanks," Cass said, meaning it. She stood and unzipped the back. Then she realized it smelled like mothballs.

Suddenly Cass wanted to cry. Her life was nearly perfect. It really was. She had her aunt, her niece, her wonderful work, and she had Belford House. Yes, a husband who was a best friend as well as a lover, and another child or two, were missing, but between raising Alyssa and her research and work, not to mention her daily horseback rides, she hardly had time to even think about that, much less the future.

But tonight she wished she had known in advance that Tracey was coming with Antonio de la Barca. She would have been psychologically prepared, and she'd have bought a new black dress, too.

And she wished, with all of her heart, that Catherine had been grossly exaggerating when she had said that she had killed Antonio's father.

Before Cass could step into the dress, there was a knock on the door and Catherine entered, clothing in her hands. "Cass, I want to apologize for my terrible behavior earlier," she said, her face lined with worry.

Cass forgot all about her own cares. She sat up ramrod straight, mesmerized by the look in her aunt's eyes and the secret they now shared. "Your behavior wasn't terrible," she said carefully, her pulse drumming. "There is nothing to apologize for. We need to talk about this, Aunt Catherine."

"There's really nothing to say." Catherine grimaced, glancing away. Unable to look her niece in the eye? Then, "I know you're not going to wear that beautiful Halston, are you?"

Cass shook her head.

Catherine didn't hesitate. "I picked this up for you last week. I don't know why . . . I was shopping for a new gown for myself, but when I saw this, I just felt it was right for you." She laid a pair of black jersey pants with slit legs on the bed, followed by a beaded black top. "It's simple but elegant and it will show off your figure to perfection, Cassandra," she said.

"How could I not like this?" Cass whispered, fingering the beaded top. "This is beautiful. And the black makes me feel safe."

Catherine smiled at her. "Maybe one day you'll discover the excitement of feeling unsafe," she said softly.

Cass reached out to hug her, hard, feeling overwhelmed once again. "I don't think I'm genetically predisposed to dangerous living, Aunt Catherine." But now she wondered about her aunt as a younger woman. Had she been involved in something dangerous? Illegal? Something that had put her in a situation where she had killed Antonio de la Barca's father?

Catherine laughed. But her eyes were tearing; she was still distraught. She turned away so Cass would not see.

"I like the red," Alyssa announced firmly. "On my birthday you have to wear the red."

Cass smiled, but it was forced.

"I had better get ready as well," Catherine said. She paused at the door. "Cassandra? Forget what I said. I'm a tired old woman, and sometimes, well, the past is as clear as a bell, far clearer than just yesterday. At other times I am hardly sure of what I am thinking. I was exaggerating, dear. It's a long story . . . There was this accident . . . this tragic accident . . . I've blamed myself. And it's not important now, Cassandra." And she smiled, but the smile did not reach her eyes, and the light there held a question. Would Cass believe her?

This time Cass did not even attempt to smile back.

Because her aunt was lying and Cass saw the lie in her eyes.

Tracey studied herself in the bathroom mirror. She was wearing a pale blue gown that was sheer enough to see through, the top and the back plunging dangerously low. The two tiny straps were exquisitely beaded, as was the one hip-high slit. She wore a flesh-colored undergarment with it, which she had purchased with the gown.

Tracey knew she was beautiful; today, however, she did not look her best. So she had carefully concealed the circles under her eyes, as carefully applied shadow and smoky liner to her eyes. With her fair coloring, less makeup was always more, and she was very careful as she added a touch more blush to her high cheekbones. She wanted to be radiant; she wanted to glow. And she wanted to see hunger in Antonio's gaze when he glimpsed her in the brand-new Versace evening gown.

Tracey stared. She looked tired. And there was no mistaking the worry in her eyes.

Everything was going wrong, every possible thing, but it was always that way when she came home.

She should have never decided to hold this affair at Belford House. What had she been thinking?

Tracey inhaled, trembling. Her temples throbbed. She had been hoping to have a magnificent supper party to launch the auction of the ruby necklace—that was what she had been thinking. And her aunt's fabulous family home had seemed like the perfect place—a setting that could not be replicated at any London club or trendy restaurant.

Tracey looked down at the flute of champagne on the sink. She had no intention of partying that night. Her intention was to stay sober, to be a magnificent hostess. The flute was half-empty. Tracey hesitated.

Why not? she thought.

Because she was so scared. And her fear had nothing to do with the black-tie supper affair, even though she wanted that to go well, even though she wanted Sotheby's to be pleased.

Why not? She had to calm her nerves.

To hell with it, she thought, and she drained the rest of the glass. One glass would not hurt her.

For one instant, Tracey was soothed, and then the glow vanished almost as quickly as it had come. Fear took its place. She was acutely aware of Antonio in the bedroom, dressing. She turned to stare at her profile. Her stomach was as flat as a board. As she smoothed her dress down, she could see the two sharp points of her hip bones.

If only she hadn't come home.

Her bathroom door was ajar, and she heard Antonio moving about. The sickness inside her abdomen grew. He was angry with her, but she did not know why. He had been cold to her ever since she had arrived. And this was just what she needed now, on this important night, which had already gotten off to a completely rotten start. What had she done?

What hadn't she done?

Tracey gripped the flute. Alyssa hated the Beanie Baby, Cass hated the dress, Catherine was disapproving because she had spent so much . . . She could never please them, no matter how she tried, and it hurt. It hurt so much, she hated coming home. It hurt so much! Why could she never please them, never do anything right? She knew she was a rotten mother, while Cass was so perfect at it. She knew they all judged her and found her lacking—even her own daughter. *God. Hell. Bloody hell.* She also knew damn well that she hadn't been back to Belford House in three months. They all thought she didn't know. She wasn't stupid. She had a calendar. She knew, all right. She'd never been gone this long before, and it made her hate them, sometimes, and it also made her hate herself.

I can't take this, she thought desperately.

Alyssa loved her aunt more than she did her own mother.

Antonio was in the next room, and he was guessing the truth. She had seen it there in his eyes.

Tracey wanted to cry, but now was not the time. She faced her flawless reflection in the mirror and reminded herself that most women would die to be in her shoes—to be model-gorgeous, to have a perfect body, to be a celebrity of sorts, to be wealthy, to have Antonio. But did she have him? And if so, for how long?

Sick with fear, Tracey stared at herself. Last weekend he had been distracted, absorbed. As if he was losing interest in her . . .

She reminded herself that they had had great sex.

On the other hand, she knew the signs. And although she didn't know him that well—he wasn't like any of the others—she knew him well enough. He'd been hard to seduce in the first place, harder still to nab as a steady, and now he was regretting everything.

Just one more. Why not? Otherwise I just can't handle any of this.

Abruptly she poured another glass of champagne, her hands shaking wildly. Men did not leave her. She always left them . . . first. Before they could fully understand the truth. That her beauty was only that, beauty. And that inside, there was nothing but gaping black holes of misery and loneliness.

She sipped the champagne, eyes closed. Ignoring another inner voice that told her not to. *Bloody hell.* She would screw the hell out of Antonio—he would never leave her. When she was ready, she would be the one to walk away. She was always the one to walk away. Always.

No one ever left her. She left them.

She had somehow finished the glass of champagne. Tracey stared at the flute in her hand, her vision blurring with tears. Panicked, she worried about running her mascara. The panic escalated. The problem was, she couldn't imagine not having Antonio in her life. She was seriously smitten—she hadn't felt this way about anyone other than her ex-husband.

She heard him moving about in the other room as he finished dressing. The guests would be arriving at any moment. There were only minutes to spare. Plastering a smile on her face, she left the bathroom, walking very carefully in her strappy silver sandals with their extremely narrow stiletto heels. It was now or never, do or die. Because she would never make it through the evening without reassurance.

Antonio stood in the middle of the bedroom, adjusting his black bow tie, clad in his black tuxedo pants, his white dress shirt, and a black cummerbund. His expression was one she instantly recognized; he was lost in thought, miles away. She never could understand why he was always thinking so much. He was the most intriguing man she had ever met. And he was kind.

She'd never had a kind boyfriend before.

Rick had slapped her around. So had the others.

Tracey paused to watch him, her heart melting. "I have something for you," she whispered. She knew he could never resist her.

He turned, clearly startled. Then his gaze slid over her.

She slowly pirouetted for him. "What do you think?"

He did not smile. His set facial muscles did not relax. "I think you are lovely, as always." And he turned away.

Her eyes widened and she stared. He didn't even care that she was practically naked in the most beautiful designer gown she had ever seen! Abruptly she walked up behind him, her pulse pounding with dread. "Tonio, please talk to me," she began.

He turned slowly. "We should go downstairs. Your guests are arriving. You are the hostess even if this is your aunt's house."

"Don't be angry with me," Tracey said softly, pressing closer to him. "What have I done to displease you?"

He set her away. "I was embarrassed when I met your sister. You never mentioned her."

Tracey stiffened. This was about Cass? "She never came up."

He stared and his expression was impossible to read. "You failed to mention the very existence of your sister, and that she would be here, but that I can abide. But what I cannot abide, what I cannot understand, not for the life of me, is how you could not tell your daughter that I would be here—or tell me that she would be here."

Tracey was frightened. Antonio doted on his son, and she could sense where this might lead. "Tonio. I did tell her." She hadn't meant to lie. The lie had popped out. "But she must have forgotten—either that or she didn't hear me."

He stared at her. "I was under the impression that your daughter lived with you in Hempstead Heath."

Tracey felt paralyzed. His tone was filled with accusation. Accusation—not love, not desire. And she thought, *He sees the truth.*

Desperately she smiled at him, reaching for him. The panic blended with new fear. It was so raw.

His hands settled on her waist—holding her away. "I've known you for three entire months. But I am entirely confused. When have you last seen your daughter? Or have I misunderstood? She does live here—with your aunt and sister?" There was dark disapproval in his eyes.

Tracey blinked at him, and slowly she stepped away. She felt dizzy—she needed a drink. *Just one more.* "I didn't lie," she said.

"I am at a loss."

Tracey felt as if she were spinning, spinning, rapidly around. How could this be happening? Now, when she had finally fallen in love with someone good and kind, instead of a self-serving prick like Rick and all the others? Her instinct was to flee. "Antonio," she whispered, on the verge of actually rushing away to hide in the bathroom.

He caught her arm gently. "I'm sorry," he said, his gaze softening. "Don't cry. You will ruin your mascara and we must go downstairs."

Tracey felt the tears moistening her eyes. "I come to see her whenever I can," she tried. And it was the truth. "I really love her." And that, too, was true.

He softened. "Of course you do."

She tried to tug her hand free, but he wouldn't let her go.

"Your daughter needs you," he finally said, slowly. "I saw it this afternoon, the way I can see now that you wish to be far more than you are."

A tear fell. Tracey was horrified. "Of course she needs me," she said, her smile stretching wide. "I'm her mother and she's my child. Did I tell you I'm taking her skiing in December? Just the two of us, a mummy-daughter holiday." She smiled again, oddly breathless. She had no plans to go skiing with Alyssa. But that was why she was such a rotten mother, wasn't it?

"That is a wonderful idea," he said, studying her. "Where are you going?"

"Saint Moritz," Tracey said quickly, inhaling harshly. "Maybe you and Eduardo can join us?"

He gave her an odd look. "I do not think so. I wouldn't intrude on your time alone with Alyssa." Something passed through his eyes, frightening Tracey. Because she thought it might be pity.

She nodded quickly, clinging to him. "What was I thinking? I am so nervous about tonight that I cannot even think clearly! Every year we go away, just the two of us." Another inadvertent lie.

He brushed his knuckle across her smooth, alabaster cheek. His eyes roamed her face. It was a moment before he spoke. "It is never too late to make up for one's mistakes, Tracey. Not while there is the promise of tomorrow. Let me give you that advice, because I have experienced vast regret, firsthand." He smiled a little at her then.

In spite of his smile, Tracey remained queasy with fright. The panic would not abate. She was losing him. Tracey felt tears welling up in her eyes.

His brows lifted. "I have upset you, and I did not mean to. We should go downstairs. There are five limousines in the drive."

He was kind even now, when he no longer liked her. She should leave now. Not say another word. Just go, run, fast and far. Leaving would be safe. *Oh, God.* What should she do?

Leave. Stay. Run. Stay. Pretend. Go. Madrid.

Tracey inhaled. Maybe now was not the time to tell him her plans. That she would see the auction through, then quit her job, moving to Madrid.

"Tracey." He had come up behind her, his large palms cupping her shoulders. "You are still upset. I beg your forgiveness." He turned her around to face him. "Let's go downstairs, *querida*."

Tracey saw it then in his eyes. He was going to leave her. Soon. And she finally faced what she had known deep in her heart all along. He was only at Belford House because of the damned ruby necklace. Last weekend had been the end for him. "Please," Tracey whispered, a word she had never used before, not this way.

He was startled. His eyes slid over her face. "We'll talk about this later," he finally said.

Tracey's mind was spinning—she could not think clearly, she could only feel. What if she became the kind of mother Cass was? The kind of mother Antonio expected her to be? Wouldn't that change everything?

Why hadn't she thought of this before! She would take Alyssa to Madrid with her. "Antonio."

He paused.

Tracey smiled, and it was a mask, one hiding her fear and panic. She slipped into his arms, pressing fully against him, cheek to cheek, while sliding her long thigh between his, up hard against his groin. Her gown parted up to her hip, revealing that she was wearing nothing beneath the nude slip. "I love you, darling," she said. "We still have a few minutes before we have to go downstairs." And smiling, she pressed more fully against him.

One by one the guests wandered from the salon into the dining room to view the ruby necklace. It was the table's centerpiece. The table was long and narrow, covered with white linens, Waterford crystal, and Christofle silver, seating twenty on each side. Low floral arrangements consisting of white orchids floating in translucent pink bowls of scented water adorned each half of the table; in the center, on a pedestal, nesting in royal blue velvet, was the triple-tiered necklace.

Cass entered the room, aware of four security men in black suits hovering about. A couple was leaning forward eagerly to see the piece, and Cass waited for her turn to approach, keeping a discreet distance between them. Nevertheless, she heard the woman say, "I know this is a fortune in rubies, but it is so mundane. It looks like something a tart might wear, purchased from the ground floor of Sloane's. I don't know, Roger. I just don't know."

"I am in some agreement," Roger said. "After all, half the value is the piece's historical association—so it would be a bloody shame to take it apart in order to correctly cut and set all the rubies."

Cass could hardly believe her ears, and she watched them drift away.

"Now, that would be far more than a shame, it would be a sin," de la Barca murmured in her ear from behind.

Cass almost leapt out of her skin. She had avoided coming into contact with him as she sipped a glass of champagne with the other guests. As she knew no one, she had felt quite out of place, lingering by herself with Alyssa, but she had been acutely aware of him from the moment he had entered the salon—alone. Tracey had arrived ten minutes later, and Cass had then spent the next few moments trying not to notice the fact that Tracey had never been more stunning—or more flushed with happiness.

She was very stiff as she turned to face de la Barca. "It would be the worst travesty," she agreed, "and I hope that the person who buys this piece doesn't do such a terrible thing."

He smiled at her, his gaze sliding just once and briefly over her hair, which was rather thick and hanging straight to her shoulders; her face, which was devoid of makeup except for mascara, lip gloss, and a touch of blush; and her beaded top. "I will pray with you," he said. "No sweatshirt tonight?"

Cass flushed, but he was smiling, and a reluctant smile formed on her own lips. "I did not have a choice," she said.

He laughed. "You are lovely, señora."

"Please, call me Cass. There's no need to be formal."

Their gazes slipped together and as quickly slid apart. "Shall we?" He gestured.

Cass nodded eagerly and they turned and approached the ruby necklace. Cass gasped. In that instant she could imagine it adorning the neck of Mary, Henry Tudor's daughter who had briefly reigned as England's Catholic queen. The necklace was stunning. Each tier of rubies was set in gold. The first tier boasted tiny drops, the second larger ones, the third the largest. But hanging from the last tier was a ruby the size of Cass's thumb. And it was nested amongst a border of tiny, glittering diamonds. "How wonderful," Cass whispered, her heart beating madly, riveted by the sight.

Antonio de la Barca was silent.

Cass twisted to glance up at him and was stunned to find him unsmiling, eyes wide and fixed. If she did not mistake her guess, he had not even heard her; he was stunned. "Antonio?"

"*Por Dios,*" he breathed.

It was as if he had forgotten that they stood beside each other, mere inches separating them. Cass wet her lips. It was impossible for her not to be acutely aware of him as a man, and a damned great-looking one at that. The wool sleeve of his tuxedo jacket brushed her bare shoulder. And he smelled as good as he looked. She was suddenly insanely jealous of her sister.

Antonio straightened, glancing down at her. He did not smile. His expression remained stunned.

"Do you know something about this necklace?" she asked, unable to tear her gaze from his, completely diverted now from her thoughts about Tracey.

He hesitated. "Yes. Yes, I think that I do."

Cass straightened. "What? What is it?"

He hesitated again. "I believe this necklace—or one very similar to it—was worn by one of my ancestors."

Cass felt her eyes widen. "But how is that possible? You are Spanish and this necklace was found by Lady Hepplewhite at her home in

Highridge Hall. Which, as you must know, dates back to the fourteenth century."

He nodded. "I know all of that. One of my ancestors was briefly married to an Englishwoman. Her name was Isabel de la Barca. She died sometime before 1562, when my ancestor took his second wife."

Cass was about to make a comment about his knowledge of his own family tree, when Catherine said, her voice quiet, "No."

In unison they turned. Dread crept along Cass's spine as she saw how her aunt was staring at Antonio. There was no mistaking her fear. Or was it revulsion?

"No," she said again. "Her name wasn't Isabel de la Barca. It was Isabel de Warenne. She was the earl of Sussex's daughter, back in the middle of the sixteenth century."

Cass stared at her aunt, a prickle of excitement rising within her in spite of her worries. "De Warenne?" Cass asked breathlessly. "Any relation of ours?"

Catherine finally looked at her. "Yes, but not directly. She had no children. We share the earl's father as our common ancestor."

Cass was amazed, not that Catherine knew so much about the family's history, but that she revealed it offhandedly, and she was amazed at the coincidence they now found themselves in. "Our families intermarried in the sixteenth century," Cass gasped, facing Antonio. She almost grabbed his hands but managed to restrain herself. "Do you know what the odds of that are?"

He smiled at her, as if swept up by her excitement. "Quite unlikely. There is a portrait in my family home, and the necklace Isabel is wearing in it is remarkably similar to this one."

"I'd love to see it," Cass said without hesitation. It was a vast understatement. She would die to see it.

"It would be my pleasure to show it to you," Antonio said, his gaze on hers, and Cass felt the moment that their eyes locked.

And as she stared into the brown and green flecks of his irises, she had visions of traveling to Spain, to his ancestral home, to view a portrait of the ancestor who had linked their families once, centuries ago.

"No. Cassandra is not going to Spain."

Her aunt's voice was so harsh that Cass flinched before facing her. "What?"

Catherine flushed. "How can you go to Spain? You are in the middle of a deadline."

Cass stared, realizing what her aunt was up to. She did not want her involved with Antonio de la Barca, just as she did not want Tracey involved, because of the secret of the past. Because Antonio might discover what had happened to his father. If the matter were entirely closed—or entirely innocent—Catherine would not be so stricken. "I am in the middle of a deadline," Cass finally allowed, with a quick smile at Antonio. She did not tell him she had an entire year to finish the book she was working on, and she was also dismayed. How she wanted to go to Spain, to this man's home, to see the portrait of Isabel de Warenne, her ancestor.

If Antonio was disappointed, Cass could not tell. "I suppose I could photograph the portrait," he said, studying them both. "And send the photographs to you."

Catherine did not reply. So Cass said, "That would be great," with an enthusiasm she did not feel. But now she was determined to get to the bottom of Catherine's secret, and to go see the portrait for herself without opening up any cans of worms. "Has the portrait been evaluated?" Cass asked. "Do you know when it was painted? And by whom?"

Antonio smiled, perhaps at her fervor. "Actually, no. But as I said, Alvarado de la Barca remarried in 1562. So the portrait was painted before that. She seems quite young, eighteen, maybe, if I recall correctly. I haven't been back to the house in a number of years."

Cass found that last statement a bit odd, and she thought she saw a darkness flitting through his eyes as he spoke. But she might have imagined it, because now he smiled a bit at her. "Where is your family home?" she had to ask.

Before he could reply, Catherine's voice rang out. Loudly. Oddly. "She died in 1555."

Cass stiffened, turning to gaze at her aunt in surprise. "What?"

Catherine was extremely pale. "She died in 1555. Isabel. She was a heretic, and they burned her at the stake."

Cass stared at her aunt, who stared back, her eyes wide, blue, burning—almost unseeing, almost fanatically. And Cass was filled with dread. She shuddered.

What a terrible way to die.

THREE

Cass quickly moved over to Catherine, putting her arm around her. Her mind was spinning, racing. "The year 1555 would be the last year of Mary's reign. A number of heretics were burned at the stake."

"Yes, they were. Even more heretics were burned in the empire," Antonio said.

Cass knew he referred to the Hapsburg Empire, inherited by Mary's husband, Philip II of Spain. "What a terrible death." She shivered. She felt sick to her stomach just thinking about it. "But didn't nearly everyone who was Protestant when Mary came to the throne profess outwardly to being Catholic? Why was Isabel singled out for heresy, I wonder?"

Antonio stared at Cass, and Cass thought she saw a new respect in his eyes. "Only fanatics were prosecuted, as a warning to the rest of the populace," he said. "I did not know about Isabel's fate." He regarded Catherine. "However did you learn of her death? And are you certain of it?"

Catherine pursed her mouth, her eyes blurring with tears. "I had forgotten," she whispered almost inaudibly. "For a while."

More alarmed than ever, wondering if her aunt would make herself ill, Cass tried to change the subject. "Have you had a chance to see that stunning necklace yet?" she tried lightly, hoping to distract her.

But Catherine seemed riveted by Antonio. "Every time I look at you, I see him. I am so sorry..." Her voice broke. She cleared it. "He was researching your family's history," she said. "Here at the British Library. I am so sorry."

And Cass, looking at her, hearing her, had to close her eyes. The plea for forgiveness was all too apparent. A terrible sadness began to weigh Cass down. Could this really be happening? Had her aunt killed Antonio's father, or had it been an accident? And surely her aunt didn't intend to confess to something that had happened thirty years ago? "We had better get back to our guests, Aunt Catherine." She managed a small smile at Antonio while tugging on her aunt.

"I was only four years old when he died," Antonio said suddenly, causing both Cass and her aunt to turn. His gaze was unwavering. "I have so few memories. My mother remarried two years after his death—and never speaks of him. I was hoping, maybe, when you have the time, that you might share your memories with me." His eyes were brilliant, demanding, intense.

Cass grew more alarmed. That would be a terrible idea! "I'm sure my aunt would love to sit down with you and reminisce when she's feeling better. She's fought a flu all week," she added as an afterthought. And she flushed, hating the white lie.

Suddenly Catherine spoke. "We met here in London. I was on the board of the British Museum, where he was also doing research." She smiled. "We met at a function for the museum. And quickly discovered the two ancestors which we had in common." But Catherine was crying now. Tears had slipped from her eyes.

Cass gave Antonio a warning look. "Aunt Catherine, you are not well," she said firmly—she would brook no protest. "Maybe you should lie down for a few minutes before returning to the party."

Catherine finally tore her gaze from Antonio. "I am sorry," she whispered, sagging against Cass. "I am not well. I know we have guests, but I must go upstairs. Cassandra, I am exhausted."

"I'll take you right up," Cass said quickly. And she was relieved, because she did not want her aunt conversing with de la Barca. "Will you excuse us?"

"Of course," he said. "I only hope that you will feel better tomorrow, Lady Belford."

"Cassandra? I am having difficulty breathing. It is too stuffy and warm in here," Catherine said.

Alarmed, Cass realized how much paler her aunt was becoming. But her aunt's statement was odd, because the dining room remained oddly chilled. And Cass became even more alarmed, because Catherine kept touching her throat, and she was taking deep heavy breaths through her mouth. "To bed," Cass said quickly. "And I will bring you some chamomile tea."

"Cassandra." His accented voice halted her in her tracks. She glanced over her shoulder at Antonio. "I'd love to continue this conversation about our families," he said.

She hesitated, and her passion for the past won out over her better judgment and her fear. She had to smile. "So would I."

They walked across the room. "No, Cassandra," Catherine said, low and husky, so Antonio would not hear. "His father was obsessed with the past. Clearly he is, too. Why else would he be here? I have asked so very little of you." Her gaze was wide, even wild. "Leave this subject entirely alone, stay away from Señor de la Barca, and please, try to get him out of our home. And then, just forget about this entire night."

Catherine was no longer making any sense. Cass stared at her aunt, almost gaping, and saw not an elegant older woman in a black Oscar de la Renta tuxedo with a diamond and pearl pin, but someone old and so terribly tired, someone frail and failing. Suddenly her aunt's wrinkles were striking, when Cass had never noticed them before. Suddenly her blue eyes seemed watery. Suddenly she seemed every bit her age. She was an old woman, and Cass had never realized it before.

Cass put her arm around her. Tears slipped unbidden down her cheeks. "I'll do my best," she lied. She was not going to boot Antonio out. She could never do such a thing. Or could she? If he left, it would be a relief—as far as safeguarding her aunt's secret went. "It's late. It's been a rough day. Don't worry about anything now, Aunt Catherine, except getting a good night's sleep." She could not force a smile, but she hugged her aunt, hard.

Catherine nodded wearily, leaning against her niece. "Thank you, Cassandra. Thank you. I knew I could trust you."

Trust. What a significant word, Cass thought, suddenly weary. As Cass guided her aunt from the room, she finally glanced back at Antonio.

Their eyes met.

And then they both looked back at the necklace simultaneously—as if on cue. And this time, when their eyes lifted and met, it was in silent communication.

Come hell or high water, Cass knew she was going to Spain to see Isabel's portrait.

"You are such a blessing, Cassandra," Catherine said, clad in an ivory, red, and gold Japanese kimono, her red hair loosened now and hanging about her shoulders. They were in Catherine's lavishly appointed bedroom. "Why don't you call The Golden Hart and see if they have a room for Señor de la Barca?"

Cass stared. "Aunt Catherine," she said slowly, "this is so unlike you. How can we ask him to leave? He's Tracey's guest. Maybe it would be better to just let this play out; he'll be gone tomorrow anyway."

"I thought you understood," Catherine cried.

Quickly Cass went to her. "Aunt Catherine, do you need a glass of water?"

Catherine shook her head. "I need a gin and tonic and an aspirin."

Cass bit her lip. "I'll get you the drink if you really want it." But she did not move. "Aunt Catherine, I'm going crazy with worry. You didn't really mean what you said earlier, did you?"

Catherine met her gaze. Then she turned her back on Cass, walking over to the bed but not getting into it. "I made a mistake," she said softly. "I shouldn't have said a word. And now I am not going to discuss the subject. Not now. Not ever." She turned, and her face was set.

Cass's heart drummed. She had to know what had happened, but she was also frightened for her aunt's health and did not want to push her now. "Were you lovers?" she asked.

Catherine's face changed. She began to shake her head no, and then she covered her face with her hands. "He loved his wife, but even more than he loved her, he loved the past. I loved Robert, I have always loved Robert. Eduardo and I were friends—drawn together by his work." She did not continue.

Cass could fill in the blanks. They had begun as friends and had ended up in bed.

Catherine rubbed her brow. "I had erased this part of my life from my mind. I wish Antonio de la Barca had never come into our lives!" she cried with vehemence.

Cass stared at her aunt, who was so pale. She hesitated, then asked, "Do we have to worry about criminal prosecution, Aunt Catherine?"

Catherine looked at her. And she said, "The police said it was an accident."

Cass's heart turned over. What was the meaning of Catherine's words? Her tone had been strange—as if the police had been wrong.

"You said it was an accident, too," she whispered, her throat constricted.

Catherine suddenly reached for her small beaded evening bag, and she pulled a tissue out and dabbed her eyes. "I need that drink, Cassandra. Please."

The bedroom door opened and Tracey rushed in; Cass took one look at her sister's tight expression and she knew that fireworks were imminent. She rushed to her. "Trace," she began. Hoping to warn her sister to lay off because Catherine was not well.

"What have you both done?" Tracey cried, hands on her hips. "My God! How could you!"

Catherine straightened.

Cass intercepted her. "Whatever you are upset about, this is not a good time. Catherine isn't feeling well. Let's go." She grabbed Tracey's arm, but her sister did not budge. "Supper's about to be served. We need to go downstairs."

Tracey was flushed, and she shook Cass off. "Antonio said he's leaving. He said he has somehow upset Aunt Catherine, and that it would be better if he stayed elsewhere tonight. He's going back to London!" Tracey regarded Cass with such a look of disbelief it was almost comical. But Cass also saw the genuine hurt in her blue eyes. "I can't believe this!"

Cass bit her lip. "I'm sorry," she began, meaning it. "You can see him in London—"

"I won't have it! This is *my* affair. *My* night. *My* life." She looked at Catherine. "And my boyfriend. How could you be so rude to him!?" she cried.

Cass stiffened. "Are you sure his leaving is our fault?"

Tracey's eyes darkened. "Just what the bloody hell are you implying?"

Before she could respond, Catherine stood. "Tracey, you must trust me, this is for the best. Let him go. You cannot be involved with him. Terrible things will happen, I am so sure of it—and I am so afraid for you, for all of us."

Tracey's eyes widened; so did Cass's. "Not be involved with him? I love him! I'm going to marry him," she declared. She turned to Cass. "I don't know what you're thinking. But you and Aunt Catherine did or said something to make him decide to leave. *I* had nothing to do with it."

Cass felt her heart skipping a series of beats. Was Tracey being literal? Were they engaged? An image flashed through her mind, of Tracey and

Antonio together on their wedding day. Cass could not shove it aside, for Alyssa was with them, as the flower girl. Cass stared. "You're getting married?" She could hardly get the words out.

"Well, we haven't exactly made plans," Tracey began, and Cass didn't really hear the rest of her sentence, she was so relieved.

They would not take Alyssa away from her.

"Cass? Are you even listening? I love Antonio," Tracey was saying. "But you always take Aunt Catherine's side."

"Tracey, I understand," Cass said quickly, unable to believe how shaken she had been, and all for no real reason. "Look, I'm not always taking Catherine's side, but maybe it's better if Antonio doesn't spend the night here. Catherine really isn't well."

Immediately tears came to Tracey's eyes. "You want to boot him out, too? If he leaves, I leave," Tracey cried, suddenly furious. "Aunt Catherine, this is absolutely unfair."

Cass grew angry. "Tracey, can't you cut Aunt Catherine some slack?" she asked. "Does everything always have to be your way?"

Tracey gaped at her. "Always my way? Nothing is ever my way! I come home and get pounced on by all of you, the moment I step in the door. Nothing I do is ever right."

"What?" Cass gasped.

"No." Catherine stood. She was trembling. "Stop it. The two of you. Stop it now. And listen to me. Tracey, I do not want you involved with that man. *I won't have it.*"

Tracey gaped. Even Cass blinked at their aunt and did a double take.

"I will not have it," Catherine said firmly. "For all of our sakes."

A huge silence fell over the room.

And Cass looked from her unyielding aunt to her astonished sister. In that moment the only thing she could think of was when Tracey had come home one day at the age of fifteen with a thirty-year-old boyfriend who drove a red Jag and wore alligator boots. Catherine had tried to talk some sense into her, but to no avail. Tracey had dated the man for a good six months anyway. And Catherine had never issued an ultimatum.

Until now.

But Catherine's guilt in a man's death, accidental or not, had not been an issue then, either.

"You won't have it?" Tracey finally echoed.

"I will not. I have raised you as if you were my very own daughter, and if you have any respect for me, any love, you will respect my wishes in this matter," Catherine said very firmly. "You will let him leave. And you will not see him again."

Tracey stared at her, speechless.

Cass felt as if she were in some surreal dream. "Aunt Catherine," she interjected gently, "let's drop this subject for the moment. What do you say?"

"I'd rather not," Catherine said firmly.

Cass felt as if she were conversing with an utter stranger. Was this actually her aunt speaking?

"Forget it," Tracey said to Cass, harshly. "There's nothing to discuss, and that is that." She flung a last, furious look at her aunt and stalked from the room, her bare pale blue gown swishing open about her legs.

Cass went to her aunt, placing her hand on her shoulder. Now she truly understood the feeling of dread she had had all day. Cass was so upset she could not imagine going downstairs to join their guests— much less surviving the evening.

Catherine barely looked at her. "Dear, please get me that drink," she said in a barely audible whisper.

"Coming right up," Cass said as cheerfully as possible. And giving her aunt one last worried look, she left the room.

Catherine waited until she was gone. And when she could no longer hear her niece's footsteps, she went to the door and closed it. Then she went to an armoire, opened it, and knelt beside the lowest drawer. It was hidden, and a secret latch let it spring free.

She withdrew the old, faded, leather-bound book carefully, held it to her breast, and fought tears of rising panic.

It was her private journal.

The last entry had been noted in July of 1966, just hours after Eduardo de la Barca's death.

She had never destroyed the diary; she had been oddly, insanely, unable to. And she had always regretted it.

She prepared to destroy it now.

It was well after midnight, and Cass stood in the foyer against one wall, half-hidden by a huge marble table and a large seventeenth-century clock, arms folded tightly across her chest. She was still clad in her evening clothes, and all of the guests had left. Except for one.

He was coming downstairs. She heard his footsteps, but that wasn't how she knew it was he. Even had there been other guests about, she would have known. There was something about his presence that made her tense with expectation.

He came into the dim, flickering light of the foyer. Their gazes met and held.

Feeling uncomfortable, Cass looked away. "Thank you for being so understanding," she said.

"It is not a problem. I only hope your aunt feels better tomorrow." Cass looked up. "So do I."

His gaze was searching. "Will you call me and let me know? I would appreciate it."

Cass nodded. "Do you have a card?" Her pulse was racing, stupidly.

He smiled at her as he handed her one. "The last thing I wished to do was to upset this household or my hostess."

How much did he guess, how much did he sense, and how much had he heard? "It's the flu. She'll be back to herself in no time."

He didn't smile. His stare was scrutinizing. "You are very close to her," he said.

"She raised us, Trace and me," Cass said simply. "She is more than my surrogate mother. She is my best friend."

"She seems like an admirable woman."

"She is."

A silence fell, hard and awkward, between them.

"Well, I think the night was successful. I know a few guests appreciated the necklace," Cass tried. Oddly, she did not want him to go. Not yet.

"Yes." Then, "The piece belongs in a museum. I intend to try to convince Sotheby's to offer it privately first to several institutions."

Cass's eyes widened. "Is that possible?"

"Here in Europe, yes. The auction houses never do such a thing in your country."

Cass couldn't smile. A slight noise made her glance toward the stairs, but she saw nothing and no one. "I guess Tracey's asleep?"

He hesitated. "She was not gracious about this situation. She is very upset."

Apparently Tracey had changed her mind about leaving. Cass suspected Antonio had made her stay. She was impressed. "Tracey's my little sister," Cass said, unable not to defend her. "She's always been a bit spoiled. It's not her fault. Her beauty has allowed her to get away with things the average person never could." Cass shrugged. "It's always been that way."

"Sometimes beauty can be detriment and not an asset," he said.

Cass was so surprised that she stared. He was also staring. She heard the clock behind her ticking loudly in the night.

He finally smiled, slightly. "It was a pleasure meeting you, Cassandra. And any time you wish to discuss the sociopolitical consequences of the cult of Saint James upon the Spanish people and Christendom, I would be glad to comply."

Cass felt her mouth drop open. He remembered her. Not only did he remember her, he remembered a brief intellectual debate they had had on the subject of one of Spain's most important patron saints, all those years ago at the Met.

He bowed and strode past her, into the night.

Cass watched him go, smiling.

"I thought you might be able to stay a few days, instead of rushing back to London like this," Catherine said the following day.

Tracey was packing her garment bag, clad in a black pleated mini-skirt, a thick beige sleeveless sweater, and black, knee-high riding boots with odd little flaps on the calves. Her legs were bare, her skin flawless and glowing. But her movements were abrupt and angry. "I never said I was spending the weekend. Besides, is there any point in staying?" She straightened to stare at Catherine.

And Catherine's expression was filled with hurt and dismay. "We would love to have you," she began softly.

"Last night was a bloody disaster," Tracey cried.

Cass was also present, standing tensely by the foot of the bed. "Tracey, if you have to go this morning, at the crack of dawn"—and that was an exaggeration—"couldn't we at least talk this out first? So there are no hard feelings?"

"No. I really have to go. So much to do." Tracey smiled at them. It was brittle. Hurt was also reflected in her blue eyes—along with an anxiety Cass hadn't noticed before.

It suddenly occurred to Cass that her sister was chasing after Antonio. That for once, she was so infatuated that, like most lovers, she was nervous and filled with doubts. And in spite of herself, Cass felt for her then. "The auction's ten days away," Cass tried. "It would be so great if you didn't rush off."

Tracey began zipping up the garment bag. "It would have been great if Tonio hadn't felt compelled to leave last night."

Cass went over to help fold the large Val-Pack and place it on the floor. "Look, I agree. Last night didn't go that well. I mean, I think the guests all had a great time, but we certainly had it out. I'm sorry, Trace."

Tracey straightened, hands on her hips. "Are you? I think you took Catherine's side for another reason. Because you are jealous."

Cass froze. "What?"

"You heard me." Tracey stared.

Cass started to tell herself that she was not jealous, then she gave it up. Of course she was, just a bit. It was natural. A woman would have to be blind in order not to be jealous of her sister as far as Antonio de la Barca was concerned. "If I acted out of any desire, other than the one to protect Aunt Catherine, I apologize," Cass said quickly—and instantly regretted her choice of words.

Tracey shrugged. "I am having dinner with him tonight before he returns to Madrid." She smiled.

Cass managed a halfhearted smile in return.

"Tracey, we have to speak," Catherine said firmly, her arms folded tightly over her breasts.

Cass knew what was coming, but she pretended not to. She carried the heavy bag to the door. Maybe it was for the best if Tracey did leave. The tension was becoming unbearable.

Tracey faced her aunt with a too innocent look. "About?"

"I think you know."

"I haven't a notion." Tracey smiled, a bit too sweetly, a dead give-away.

"You must listen to me very carefully," Catherine said slowly, her coloring paler than usual. She seemed to be choosing her words with care. "There is a cloud hanging over the de la Barca family. A cloud of tragedy and death. And . . . there is a history between our family and Antonio de la Barca's. No good has ever come of the families being involved. Please, do trust me, Tracey. Do not see him again."

Cass stared at her aunt, considering her words. Before Tracey could protest, Cass stepped quickly between them. "What kind of history, Aunt Catherine?" Cass tried to meet her aunt's gaze, but Catherine wouldn't allow it.

Catherine busied herself with straightening the cushions on a settee. "Over the centuries, our families have been entangled, Cassandra—time and again. In business, in love, in war, in politics. And it has always turned out badly for everyone involved." Still Catherine did not look at her.

Cass stared. What wasn't her aunt telling her? "How badly?" Cass asked. "As badly as Isabel being burned at the stake for not being a true-blue Catholic?" She did not add, *As badly as Eduardo being tragically killed?*

Catherine started, paling. "Let's not even bring her up."

Cass was on alert. "Why not? You love our family history as much as I love history, period."

Catherine shook her head. "No good can come of it," she said.

Before Cass could ask whether no good could come of discussing their ancestor or no good could come of Tracey's involvement with Antonio, Tracey cut in. "What nonsense," she said. "This is madness. Who cares about the past? I'm going to Madrid at the end of the month—and I intend to spend most of the summer there."

Even Cass whirled. "What about your job?"

"I'm leaving. I've thought about it and decided that I do not suit Sotheby's."

Cass just stared, not really surprised. And she did not doubt that Tracey's decision had little to do with Sotheby's and everything to do with Antonio de la Barca.

Catherine came forward, taking Tracey's hands. "Oh, darling, don't leave. You are so perfect for Sotheby's. You have class and elegance and a high profile which they need—"

"I belong with Antonio, Catherine. I can't manage a long-distance relationship, with an entire sea between us. I can't bear it when we are apart." Tracey turned her back on them to walk into the bathroom. The door was wide open, the lights on, and she picked up her makeup case.

"Please, Tracey, just this one time, listen carefully to me. I know too well what I am talking about," Catherine pleaded.

Tracey stared, holding the makeup case. "You don't know. Antonio is marvelous—I've never known anyone like him before. I'm not going to let this one get away from me. I meant it when I said I'm going to marry him."

Cass heard herself say, "You know, Trace, a good marriage is built on a foundation of shared interests. You and Antonio don't seem to have very much in common."

Tracey stabbed her hand at her. "I knew you would take her side. What in bloody hell would you know about marriage, relationships, or, for that matter, even men? You've had one relationship in your entire life, and he wasn't even in love with you."

Cass felt as if she had been struck.

"Point made," Tracey said coldly.

Before Cass could dare think through her thoughts, Catherine's cold voice interrupted her.

"If you go"—Catherine slowly turned, her chest heaving with the effort her words were costing her—"I am disowning you."

Tracey turned white. Cass thought she lost all of her own coloring, too. "Catherine. You don't mean that." She knew her aunt was mistaken. She knew Catherine was speaking hysterically. She could not mean to disown the niece she had adored for an entire lifetime.

But she had never seen her aunt's expression so severely set.

My God, Cass thought, unable to breathe. *She means it.*

"I don't need your damned inheritance. Go right ahead and disown me." Tracey was furiously bitter.

"Tracey!" Cass cried. "You don't know what you're saying!" Cass looked from her rigid aunt to her equally rigid sister.

Tracey said, chin high, "And not only am I going to Madrid, I'm taking Alyssa with me."

FOUR

Please don't cry, Aunt Cass."

Cass jerked up from where she had been lying on her bed, not exactly crying, but tears somehow slipping from her eyes. She was in a panic, thinking about Tracey taking Alyssa away, and no matter how she tried, she could not seem to think clearly. *Hadn't she always known that this would happen?*

That one day Tracey would march into Belford House and take Alyssa away?

But that wasn't what was happening, she tried to tell herself. It was only a summer vacation, for God's sake!

Now she tried to smile at her worried niece and she failed.

Alyssa rushed forward, and Cass flung her arms around her, holding her hard and tight. "I'm a big, fat ninny," Cass whispered unsteadily.

"You are not a ninny," Alyssa said adamantly. "They'll make up, I know they will." She smiled hopefully, but her big brown eyes were filled with concern.

Cass stroked her hair, glad Alyssa incorrectly thought her tears had been caused by the fight between her mom and her aunt. "Of course they will." But she was thinking, *What if?*

What if Tracey stayed in Spain—and did not send Alyssa back?

No! She must not anticipate the very worst! How could she even think such a thing?

But Cass was so sick. How could she not consider the worst? What would she do if Tracey decided to become a full-time mother? Alyssa was the daughter Cass had never had. She could not survive if she was taken away. Should she fight her over custody? But how could she do such a thing, when it would tear the sisters apart forever—and destroy her niece? She tried to tell herself again that Tracey was so unpredictable, so changeable, that all this would blow over in a matter of days. Why, knowing Tracey, tomorrow she would change her plans entirely, decide to meet de la Barca in the south of France, without bringing Alyssa along.

She was neither soothed nor reassured.

There is a cloud hanging over that family.

No good has ever come of the families being involved.

Christ. Was Aunt Catherine right? Was this the result of some centuries-old curse or something?

Cass was the writer of fiction for several good reasons. As Tracey had succinctly pointed out she didn't have much of a real life. But more important, she adored the past, and she had an overactive imagination. Making up stories was the easiest thing in the world for Cass. Now her imagination was kicking into overdrive. On a certain level, Cass knew she was hysterical and overreacting. That she was inventing a scenario that might not be the truth. But she could not reduce the panic within her. She could not step back from her own worst fears.

"Then why are you crying?"

Alyssa's small, sweet voice cut in to her thoughts. Cass stared. "It hurts me to see them argue," she finally said. How she hated lying to her niece.

"I hate it, too." Alyssa sat down on the bed beside Cass. "But, Aunt Cass, Auntie Catherine is wrong. Mother only wants to take me for a holiday to Spain." And her eyes sparkled.

Cass blinked. And as she realized that Alyssa was excited about the prospect of taking a trip with her mother, something inside of her twisted painfully. Was she being selfish as well as hysterical? Tracey had never taken a trip with her daughter. *It was only a summer vacation.* Alyssa was smiling now. Cass managed a smile in return, and she stroked her niece's hair. "It's very complicated, honey. Aunt Catherine's merely worried. After all, you've never traveled with your mom before. But you're right. A holiday with your mom, why, this is long overdue." The sick feeling inside did not abate. The panic did not go away.

Alyssa nodded eagerly. "And you'll come, too."

Cass started. It hadn't been a question. And her instinct was to agree—why not? Hadn't Antonio invited her to Spain to see the portrait? But she said, slowly, "Honey, Tracey wants to take you, not me. Just the two of you. I wasn't invited."

Alyssa had stopped smiling. "But it's not the two of us. Her boyfriend will be there, and his son. And I'll miss you. You have to come!"

Wouldn't that be the perfect solution? Cass thought. She would be present during the summer to make sure Tracey did not intend to keep Alyssa; she could see the portrait; and while she wasn't thrilled at the idea of spending time with the two lovebirds, she could take care of Alyssa properly, since Tracey did not have a clue as to the wants and needs of a seven-year-old child. "Your mom hasn't invited me," Cass said finally.

"But you can tell her that you have to come." Alyssa stared. "Aunt Cass, I can't go without you."

Cass swallowed. It was the perfect solution. What did she have to lose?

Everything, she thought grimly. "Okay. I'll drive out to see Tracey today."

Cass sat ramrod-straight inside her two-door BMW, pulled up at the curb. The quaint, tree-lined street was jammed: Hempstead Heath was an extremely popular neighborhood, especially with artists, musicians, and the nouveau riche. The outdoor cafés and tables on the block were filled with the young and the hip; equally chic pedestrians were window-shopping numerous boutiques. And on the opposite side of the street was a series of mansions and villas, behind stone walls and wrought-iron gates.

Her heart was pounding and the air seemed constricted in her lungs and chest. Cass got out of her car, feeling as if she had aged a decade in the past twenty-four hours. And from what she had seen that morning just a few hours ago as she had showered and dressed, she had. She closed the sedan's door and walked to the crosswalk. She was in a daze, as well as exhausted, and she didn't wait for the light before crossing. Fortunately, there wasn't a lot of vehicular traffic, but a driver blared his horn at her just the same.

Cass really didn't hear. She could only hear one voice, one thought, there in her mind. She couldn't let Tracey take Alyssa away. She *had* to go with them to Spain.

The gates to Tracey's mansion were open. A garage abutted the lime-stone Tudor-style house, and the doors were open—Tracey's black Aston Martin was visible inside. Cass hoped that meant she was home. And if she wasn't, she would wait.

Trepidation filled her. She walked up the white shell drive. Blooming gardens surrounded the house, but Cass hardly noticed. She rang the bell. Reminding herself to stay calm, no matter what.

Cass knew her sister. If Tracey saw how frightened she was, how she was unraveling, she would somehow use Cass's weakness against her. If she yelled and screamed, Tracey's determination would only increase. If she was clever and gentle, she could convince Tracey that bringing Alyssa along without her would only interfere in her private life.

A servant told her that Mrs. Tennant was in residence, and asked her to wait.

After a few minutes, Tracey came downstairs, clad in a pair of jeans and a skimpy top that somehow had *designer* written all over it. "Cass?" Her tone and expression were wary.

Cass tried to breathe evenly. So much was at stake. "Hello, Tracey. I had to come speak with you."

Tracey stared, her expression not softening. "All right. Come in."

Cass managed a smile, following her sister into a huge, mostly white, very modern living room. Tracey and Rick Tennant had bought the six-bedroom house together, just after their marriage, and Tracey had managed to keep it after the divorce. "Tracey, I am sorry about the fight."

Tracey grimaced. "Did you hear what she said to me?"

"She didn't mean it," Cass said quickly.

"Yes, she did. She meant every word. But then, she never really liked me. You were always the perfect one, the one who could do no wrong. You were always her favorite."

Cass stared in surprise. "That's not true! You were always the apple of her eye, Trace. The picture-perfect angel in blond pigtails."

Tracey laughed harshly. "Oh, please." She fingered a huge crystal ashtray on a living room table.

Cass didn't know what to say. "I don't understand how this has happened. I don't think Catherine is well. I am sure she will come to her senses in no time."

Tracey looked up and shrugged. "I don't care if she is going bonkers. She hates Antonio—but I love him. And that is that."

Cass turned away, stared at the gardens outside, then turned back. "You know, you're right. I am a bit jealous, and I am sorry, really sorry, for it."

Tracey's eyes widened.

"I mean, he is a great guy and it's obvious. I wish you the best, Trace."

"That's why you drove out here today? To wish me the best?" Tracey was disbelieving.

"I'm really upset by that fight. I didn't mean to take sides. I didn't realize that sometimes I stick my nose where it doesn't belong. It's really hard, Trace, being the glue in this family. We seem to need glue. I'm just trying to help." Cass meant every word. She was the glue in the family. The mediator, the peacemaker, the go-between. It was never easy, but maybe, sometimes, she shouldn't interfere. But she was only trying to help.

Tracey stared. "You're just too nice sometimes," she finally said. "Sometimes I wish I were more like you."

Cass looked up. "You're kidding, right?"

Tracey shrugged. "I know I'm too wild. It must be a genetic defect."

Cass's pulse raced. "Look at me. Always with my nose in a book."

They smiled tentatively at one another.

"So when are you leaving?" Cass asked, not breathing.

"I've booked tickets for the eighth. And frankly, I don't know when I'm going to come back," Tracey said.

Cass's heart felt as if it had lurched to a stop. She found it difficult to breathe—Tracey had just admitted what Cass was afraid of. "Tracey, Alyssa starts school the last week of August. On the thirtieth, to be exact."

Tracey waved at her. "I hadn't thought that far ahead. Don't worry, she won't miss school."

Cass felt the tension riddling her body. Should she believe her? *No good has ever come of the families being involved.* Cass could practically see Tracey and Antonio, with Alyssa between them, strolling down the block of some quaint Spanish village, just like a real family. "Tracey, have you thought about what it will be like, taking care of a child all by yourself for most of the summer? I mean, you can't go out to dinner with Antonio and leave the kids behind by themselves. Whenever you want to go out, you will have to hire a baby-sitter."

"I'll hire a nanny when I get there. Full-time. I already thought about it, Cass," Tracey said with a smile.

Cass was alarmed. "You have to check the person's references thoroughly. You have no idea how rotten some nannies are!"

"You're really worried," Tracey said, appearing somewhat amused.

And Cass felt her eyes grow moist. "I love her so much. And we both know you're not good at taking care of her. Little kids need so much. They can act and sound like adults, but they're children, with frightened, needy hearts that crave love and attention."

"I'm not changing my mind," Tracey said flatly, unsmiling. "Alyssa is coming. She'll have a great summer. Eduardo's a very nice boy. I'm certain they'll be friends."

Cass stared, sweating. "I could come. I could take care of the kids while you and Antonio do whatever it is that the two of you like to do."

Tracey looked at her, eyes wider now, and then she laughed, shaking her head. "No. I don't think so. The whole point is for Antonio to see that I can be a good mother. If you come, he'll see how great you are with kids and how lousy I am. No bloody chance." She shook her head again.

Cass crossed her arms. "I knew there had to be an angle," she said recklessly, ignoring the voice within her that told her not to take this tack. "So this is what this holiday is about? Using Alyssa to shore up your relationship with your boyfriend?"

"I am not using Alyssa," Tracey said fiercely. "And who said anything about shoring up my relationship? Antonio is in love with me, in case you haven't noticed."

"So what's new?" Cass retorted. "He's only number one hundred and fifty-six. Or is it two hundred and fifty-six?"

Tracey paled. Then her face turned red. "Get out."

Cass jumped. "I'm sorry. That was uncalled-for. It's just—"

"No. You meant it. You are so hoity-toity—as if you're better than me because you're just like Aunt Catherine, an aging old maid who's practically a virgin. God, it's so sad! What is there to be proud of?"

Cass stepped backward, her heart pumping hard now. Her fists clenched. "Maybe I'm proud to be Alyssa's real mother, being as her biological mother is too busy scoring new lovers to bother with her very own daughter."

"Just get out, Cass, before I have you thrown out," Tracey flashed out dangerously.

Cass did not move. "What gives you the right to come into our lives and wreck them? What gives you the right to decide how Alyssa spends her summer? She doesn't want to go without me, Tracey. She told me just this morning. I've raised her ever since she was two. You should at least ask me my permission before you make plans for her."

"Ask your permission?!" Tracey was incredulous. "I don't think so!

What gives me every right is the fact that I am her mother, and not just biologically. I don't recall that you've adopted her. Do you?"

Cass felt as if she had been struck. "You know you can't care for her. You don't have any sense of responsibility. This isn't right."

"Good-bye, Cass. I'll call the house to let you know when my driver is picking *my* daughter up." Tracey turned and started to leave the room.

And for the life of her, Cass couldn't move. She said, "I don't know how you can look at yourself in the mirror."

Tracey froze. Then she turned around. "It's really easy, Cass. Really easy—as easy as it is looking at myself on the society pages of all the top magazines." She smiled. "How do *you* do it? I mean, are you a size ten now? Let's see, at five foot three, that would make you, what? Ten pounds overweight—or is it fifteen? Or twenty? Have you taken a good look at yourself recently? You look forty, Cass, at least. Oh, but you must already know that. Why else would you lock yourself away at Belford House, writing books nobody gives a shit about, that nobody actually buys, while playing nanny to my daughter?"

Cass slapped her across the face.

Tracey jerked back, crying out.

Cass could not believe what she had done, but never had words hurt more. Never had the truth hurt more. And for a moment, both sisters stared at one another, equally stunned, equally angry.

"Maybe I should adopt her," Cass heard herself say hoarsely.

"Just you try," Tracey responded furiously.

Their gazes locked, and Cass's only thought was, *How has this happened?* She had come to make peace, not to threaten Tracey with taking her daughter away from her.

"Thomas!" Tracey shouted. A huge man in black pants and a white polo shirt appeared in the doorway. "Please escort Ms. de Warenne to her car," She said.

Cass didn't move as the bodyguard came and stood beside her. "Trace," Cass tried.

But Tracey had left the room.

Cass was escorted out.

By the time Cass arrived back at Belford House, it was well into the evening. High clouds covered the night sky, and a cool breeze washed up from the beach. Cass parked her BMW by the garage and walked up to the house, approaching it from behind. There a flagstone terrace looked out over the Sussex countryside, with views of a series of gradually descending hills, crisscrossed with stone walls and interspersed with glades of shady trees. Even at night, there was enough light from the village and the town of Romney to make out the rolling hills; during the day one could espy the occasional wheeling seagull, wandering too far inland from Beachy Head.

Cass was in a state of shock.

And she was furious with herself.

Instead of solving the problem Tracey posed, she had made it worse. Tracey was going to Spain, with Alyssa, and she had firmly rejected Cass's offer to come. But it was far worse than that. The sisters had come to blows and Cass had threatened to fight Tracey for custody of Alyssa.

And she hadn't meant it. Dear God, she hadn't. Or had she?

Cass closed her eyes and thought, unwillingly, *If worse came to worst, I could take Tracey to court and I would win. No matter what it took.*

Cass's eyes flew open; she was aghast with herself. How could she be thinking such a thing? She needed a drink. But more than that, she needed a crystal ball with which to predict the future.

"Cassandra? Is that you?"

Cass looked up. The two terrace doors leading into the house were open, and Cass saw her aunt appear between them, backlit by the house's interior lights. "Yes." She trudged across the terrace, refused to meet her aunt's questioning eyes, and stepped into the small paneled study where a fire danced in the hearth.

"What is it? What has happened? I have been so worried—where have you been?" Catherine asked.

"Where's Alyssa?" Cass asked. Desperation overcame her.

"In her room. She's reading," Catherine said. "You went to see your sister, didn't you?"

Cass hadn't told anyone where she was going. "That's right." She went to a dry bar and uncorked the port. Her hands, she saw, were trembling slightly as she poured herself a stiff drink.

"I can see from the look on your face that it did not go well."

Cass drank, felt tears sting her eyes as the port burned her stomach, and she said, "I blew it."

Catherine laid her palm comfortingly on Cass's shoulder. Cass shrugged it off.

"What happened?" Catherine asked.

"I hit her." Cass finally looked her in the eye. "I slapped her right across the face and now she's going to take Alyssa away—and I don't even know if she will come back." Cass felt herself beginning to lose it then. She had to fight for self-control. But there was no control, not of any kind. Their lives seemed to be unraveling in front of their very eyes.

"Oh God. It's already beginning, isn't it?" Catherine whispered, wringing her hands.

Cass flinched, and when she looked at her aunt, she felt an astounding degree of vehemence toward her. "Don't start with that mumbo jumbo now!" she nearly shouted. "Don't even begin to suggest that this has anything to do with de la Barcas and de Warennes and one of our infamous ancestors!" She could feel herself shaking, and she saw her aunt recoil. *No good has ever come of the families being involved . . .*

"You just don't know," Catherine said simply.

"I know that you started all of this!"

Catherine turned white. "This isn't about me—and I think you are starting to understand that."

"I'm sorry!" Cass cried, reaching for her aunt, who slipped away. "I'm sorry—but how could you disown her? How?"

"I intended to protect her," Catherine said weakly, sinking down into a chair.

"To protect her? There is nothing to protect her from, except herself. If she wants to have a fling with—or even marry—Antonio de la Barca, that's her business! She is an adult—even if she is a screwed-up one!"

"We must protect her, Cassandra," Catherine said wearily. "We must."

Cass stared. Her aunt's earlier words continued to replay in her mind, haunting her. There was no way Cass would buy in to what her aunt seemed to believe. "This isn't about two families being involved, with tragic consequences. No. This is about Antonio de la Barca's father. Somehow you were involved in his death. So it's not Tracey you are trying to protect, is it? You're trying to protect yourself."

Rising, Catherine staggered backward, and Cass felt as if a part of her was outside of herself, watching her do this to the woman who had raised her like a mother, the woman she loved as both her mother and best friend. She wanted to stop her tirade, the accusations, the anger, she did, but she could not. Not when Alyssa was being taken away from them.

Cass stared at the pale, ravaged face of her aunt. "What happened?

And don't you dare tell me that you refuse to talk about it! I have every right to know! Tracey intends to marry Antonio!" Cass was shouting. She was also crying. "He is hardly stupid! And he's a historian. Don't you think he'll figure this out, sooner or later? What if he wants justice? Revenge?"

Catherine crumpled into a chair. She hid her hands behind her face. She muttered, "Hasn't it occurred to you that his father's death was just another part of the whole terrible pattern?"

"There is no pattern!" Cass rushed to her. Her instinct was to grip her small shoulders, shake some sense into her. Instead, she caught herself, horrified with all that was happening, truly horrified with herself. But she could not stop now. She knelt in front of her aunt. "I beg you. I am begging you. I want to save this family from whatever might come. If Antonio de la Barca is a threat, I have to know precisely why he is a threat—and don't tell me it has to do with the centuries-old past. I want my child back, Aunt Catherine. *I want my child back.* But I can't fight for her in the dark like this. *Did you kill him?*"

Catherine dropped her hands from her face, her eyes wide, pale, watery. Their gazes met, held, locked.

Cass waited.

"It is complicated," Catherine finally said.

First disbelief, then anger, engulfed Cass. And she was so stricken that she could not move. She was shaking.

Behind them, the phone rang.

Neither aunt nor niece moved.

Cass fought for composure, realized she was panting. "I am not giving you a choice," she warned.

Catherine straightened with her innate dignity as the phone ceased ringing. "Do not speak to me in such a manner, Cassandra. I am your elder, your aunt."

Cass remained kneeling; her aunt remained seated and ramrod-straight. Cass was about to tell her that she was being selfish—words that would wound her to no end. And she knew she should not speak them, she did, but again, she was out of control. And just as the words were about to roll off the tip of her tongue, one of the housemaids appeared in the doorway and said, "Ms. de Warenne. You have a caller."

Cass barely looked up. "Take a message, please." She stared at her aunt, who now stared down at her gnarled, veined hands. A huge sapphire ring, set with diamonds, given to her by Robert on one of their anniversaries—their twenty-fifth, Cass thought—sat on her left ring finger.

The maid hesitated. "It's Ms. Tennant and she says it is urgent."

Cass leapt up as if struck. She gave her aunt one last look and rushed to the phone on the small, leather-inlaid desk in the corner of the study.

Cass tried to clear her mind. She tried to shove aside the panic and fear and think rationally as she picked up the receiver, but it was impossible. Cass felt faint. "Trace?"

"Yes," her sister said, her tone as cold as ice.

"Trace, I am so sorry about—"

Tracey cut her off. "My lawyer's name is Mark Hopkins. My driver will pick Alyssa up tomorrow. Please pack most of her things. Mark will be in touch with you and Catherine." And she hung up.

"Tracey!" Cass cried. She hit the talk button frantically, but the only response was a dial tone. And as she gripped the phone, redialing desperately, for one moment she almost thought she saw the walls beginning to come down around her, in slow, slow motion. Of course, it was her imagination—the walls were not undulating before her very eyes, they were rock-solid. It was her life that was caving in on her.

The phone rang. And rang. And rang. Until Tracey's answering machine came on.

"Tracey!" Cass cried. "I know you are there. Please, please, pick up! Please!" But her sister did not answer the phone.

Cass tried her cell phone, with the same results. Then she tried her house again, and again, and then the cell, and finally she sat down in the chair beside the desk, the receiver slipping from her hands, and she began to cry.

"This is only the beginning," Aunt Catherine said slowly, standing next to her now.

Cass looked up through her tears and said, bitterly, "Yes. This is only the beginning." Even though she knew that they were not speaking about the same thing. "How can you cling to your selfish self-serving explanations, knowing that tomorrow Alyssa is leaving, maybe forever, and that Tracey's lawyer will be contacting us?"

Catherine looked as if she would collapse at any moment. She said, "He was hit by a car, in a tiny village in Spain, one you have never heard of. Pedraza."

Cass blinked. Her aunt had spoken in the tone of a robot. She had been wounded terribly. Cass flinched but said, "So it was an accident after all." It was too late for relief.

Catherine wasn't even looking at her. She was staring past her, or through her, into the wall—or into the very far reaches of the past. "Hardly."

Her temples pounded so hard she could hear the beat of blood inside her own head. Cass somehow shook her head. "What you have described is an accident."

Catherine just smiled at her, sadly. "I deliberately lured him in front of the car. I wanted to destroy him."

FIVE

Cass walked into Belford House, numb and exhausted. Alyssa had been picked up that morning by Tracey's driver. Cass hadn't told her niece what was happening—because she was hoping desperately that all of this would blow over. Alyssa thought she was off for a week or two with her mother; still, Cass was never going to forget her little face as she settled in the back of the Mercedes sedan. She had been ready to cry, but bravely fighting her tears.

It was raining heavily outside—it had been raining all day long—and the gloom felt like a shroud on Cass's shoulders. She hadn't worn a slicker, and she was soaked. Slowly she walked through the foyer and wandered down the hall.

What am I going to do now? she kept thinking. It was a litany, there in her mind.

"I already miss you, Aunt Cass," Alyssa had said, her lip trembling.

Cass's heart had broken then and there. She had somehow controlled her expression, reaching into the car to hug her one more time. Wondering if it would be the last time. "Have a great holiday with your mom," she had said, trying to keep the choked-up sobs out of her tone.

"But why can't you come? And why am I going now?" Alyssa had cried.

"You know your mom, always changing plans," Cass had said with false cheer.

Alyssa had nodded and the door had been closed and Cass had stood there in the mist and rain, watching the car driving away, until she was staring at nothing but an empty stretch of road.

She hadn't wept. She had jumped onto her horse and ridden all over the countryside, sick inside, so sick that she had finally thrown up. And now it was raining, and she was wet and cold and exhausted, while Harry, her hunter, was warm and dry and feasting on mashed bran.

She knew she must focus on her work, that work would be her salvation, but she was filled with panic and grief, and sitting down at her laptop was an impossibility now.

What if this doesn't blow over? What if Alyssa doesn't come back? Ever?

Panic seized her. Cass tried to turn off her thoughts. *No good can come of the families being involved* . . . She entered the library grimly, going to one oversized window, staring blindly out at the wet, gray Sussex countryside. Night was falling. She should have never let Alyssa go. She could have found a way to outwit Tracey. This had nothing to do with Antonio de la Barca coming into their lives.

She hated her sister. God, she did.

And the sudden hatred shocked her. Cass pulled her shoulders back, stiffened her spine, and trembling with the chill that was within her soul, not just her body, she walked down the corridor until she saw one of the maids. She did not hate her own sister. "Any messages? Any calls?"

"I'm afraid not, Ms. de Warenne."

She really hadn't been expecting or hoping for a call from Alyssa, but the lawyer hadn't called, either. Cass was relieved. She was so relieved she felt faint, and the world around her began to blur and gray.

"Ms. de Warenne?"

Cass managed to look up at the elderly woman she had known since she was eleven years old—a kind local woman with grown children and teenaged grandchildren who refused to call her Cass or even Cassandra. "Yes, Celia?"

"Lady Catherine has taken to her bed. I'm afraid she isn't well. You've been gone all day, and I tried to call Dr. Stolman, but she would not hear of it. Maybe you should go check on her, as she shoos me out every time I try to enter her room."

Celia's plump face was creased with both age and worry. Cass felt drained, she had nothing to give, and certainly nothing to give to her aunt. It was still so very hard not to blame her for all of this. But she nodded. "Okay."

"And, Ms. de Warenne? Maybe you should be getting out of those wet, muddy clothes. It won't help Miss Alyssa if the both of you come down with pneumonia."

Cass looked into Celia's concerned brown eyes and started to cry. Soundlessly.

"She'll come back," Celia said, laying her palm on Cass's back. "I have nary a doubt."

Cass fought the tears and nodded as she pulled away from Celia, wiping her eyes with her fist. "I'll go check on my aunt," she said automatically. If only her sister weren't such a loose canon. But she was, she'd always been unpredictable, and wishful thinking wasn't going to change that fact.

Cass paused as she opened the door to her aunt's bedroom. All the lights were off except for one lamp beside her bed, and her aunt lay there, unmoving. Tension heightened within Cass. And with it came worry.

If her aunt was sleeping, she did not want to wake her up. Slowly, trying to be as quiet as possible, she entered the room. And suddenly the temperature seemed to drop drastically inside. Cass froze.

What was going on? Why was the bedroom so cold? There was even a fire roaring in the hearth. Puzzled, Cass approached the canopied bed.

And as she did so, more and more tension seemed to build within her.

This is just the beginning . . . No good can come over of it . . .

Cass shook her mind free of her aunt's words. Catherine was not lying still, she was tossing and turning restlessly, probably in the midst of a dream. Suddenly Cass paused and strained to see as she glanced all around her.

But what was she looking for?

She did not know; she only knew that something felt terribly wrong.

"What's wrong," she muttered aloud, "is that my aunt is ill and this room isn't even warm. She will catch her death."

Cass readjusted the thermostat, which did not seem to be working properly, then went to her aunt's bedside. As she touched her shoulder gently, Catherine's lashes fluttered and she blinked at her. "Tracey?"

Abruptly Cass froze, because even through her aunt's jersey nightgown, Cass could feel that she was running a high temperature. Very alarmed, she touched her aunt's face—her skin was burning.

"Tracey," Catherine whispered.

Cass didn't want to worry her now. "Tracey's just fine." She turned on another bedside light, opening the drawer in the night table. She found her aunt's telephone book and quickly dialed up their local doctor, who still made house calls when necessary. She left a message with his service, hurried into the bathroom, located aspirin, and returned to her aunt's bedside.

"Where is Tracey?" Catherine moaned.

Cass was at a loss. And then she decided to lie. "She hasn't left for Spain yet, Aunt Catherine," Cass said, sitting beside her. "You have to sit up and take some aspirin."

"No," Catherine said weakly. "Cassandra, I am going to die."

Cass cried out. Then, "Aunt Catherine, don't talk that way!" Tears suddenly filled her eyes. If her aunt died, she would never recover. A piece of her heart would be gone forever.

"Too late," Catherine whispered harshly. "She's here."

Cass stared, wondering if her aunt was delirious. But then Catherine said, "I am so ill, Cassandra, so ill." Tears slid down her cheeks.

Cass decided she would take her aunt directly to the emergency room. "Aunt Catherine, you have to sit up," she tried, sliding her arm under her, holding back panic.

"I cannot," she whispered. "I hoped to win, but I cannot."

Cass was motionless. Catherine was delirious, she decided. She reached for a glass of water, holding her aunt in a sitting position. "Come on, Aunt Catherine, you can do it." She was sweating herself, she realized, even though it was ice-cold in the room.

"Cassandra, I haven't told you the truth."

Cass froze.

"Not entirely," she added, her eyes closing.

"Now is not the time." Very determinedly, Cass forced two tablets into her aunt's mouth, then pressed a glass of water to her lips. She was rewarded when Catherine finally swallowed. Cass set her back down against the pillows, briefly immobilized with relief. But her relief was short-lived.

"The truth." Catherine would not let it go. "Oh, God." She struggled to sit up again.

Cass had no choice but to help her. "I don't care what the truth is," she said, meaning it. "I only want you well and this family back together again."

Catherine shook her head, forcing her eyes open. "Isabel. I am speaking about Isabel."

"Isabel?" Cass cried, incredulous. Her aunt wanted to talk about their ancestor now? Cass's temples throbbed. It crossed her mind that things had gotten worse and worse ever since the damned black-tie affair. Cass didn't really want the comprehension, she didn't really want to know any more, but she had to. She had to listen. "What? What about Isabel?"

"She has come back."

Cass stared. It was a reflexive reaction and she said, "There's no such thing as ghosts, if that is what you mean."

"Come back, to win."

Cass was regarding her flushed, feverish aunt, reminding herself that anything she said was undoubtedly insensible, when Catherine looked her right in the eye. "She's here," she said.

And her eyes changed. The unfocused light vanished, and in its place were blazing intelligence and frightening intensity. Cass jumped off the bed.

And when she looked back down at her aunt an instant later, her eyes were closed, her face was peaceful, and Cass knew there was no way she had seen such a . . . what? How could she even describe the expression she had thought she had seen?

If she dared to try, she would label it as savage.

Or murderous.

I wanted to destroy him.

Cass stared at her aunt, who seemed to be sleeping peacefully now. Her face had relaxed. The look of hate-filled rage was gone.

If it had ever been present.

Cass felt tears form behind her eyes. She was exhausted herself. She had imagined that indescribable look. She must focus now on getting medical care for her aunt, because if anything happened to her, given the events of the past few days, Cass knew she would never forgive herself or her sister.

Suddenly she felt overwhelmed. She sank back down on the bed beside her aunt, reaching for her hand. Alyssa was gone, Tracey had snagged Antonio de la Barca, her aunt was seventy years old and stricken with pneumonia, if she did not miss her guess, and Cass was supposed to do what? Save her aunt's life and save her from a public embarrassment at the least and criminal prosecution at the most? Fight Tracey tooth and nail for the return of Alyssa? Jettison Antonio de la Barca from their lives? Bury a secret she had never asked for knowledge of in the first place?

Just how the hell could she accomplish all of that? She was one single woman, and a flawed one at that.

The telephone rang. It was Dr. Stolman, and Cass quickly filled him in. He instructed her to take her aunt's temperature, which she did. It was 102. He told her he would call for an ambulance and that he would meet her at the hospital.

Immediately Cass went to the door and called for Celia. While the maid was gathering up a few things for her aunt, Cass returned to Catherine's side, sitting down and clutching her hand, very frightened now.

The minutes ticked by endlessly. Cass was mindless with fright. She kept telling herself that everything would be all right. It was a mantra, one she chanted silently, again and again—one she did not really believe.

If only they could rewind time the way they could rewind a tape, she thought. If only they could start over . . .

"Everything is ready, Ms. de Warenne. Why don't you go gather up a few fresh clothes for yourself?"

Cass hardly heard Celia. But she said, "I'm staying here. Where are they?" And then, for lack of anything else to do, she screwed the cap on the bottle of aspirin and replaced the telephone book she had used in the night-table drawer, where it belonged. And as she did so, she noticed the blue leather book within.

Cass hesitated, because the book was old and hand-bound, the leather jacket worn and faded. There was no title on the cover.

She could not help herself. She picked it up, opened it—and was paralyzed.

It was obviously a journal. And the very first entry was dated 1964. Cass could hardly breathe. Because she recognized the handwriting as her aunt's.

Catherine's words haunted her mind. *I lured him in front of the car. Deliberately. I wanted to destroy him.*

Cass trembled. She suddenly, without debate, flipped open to the very last entry—July 15, 1966.

And names leapt off the pages at her.

Casa de Sueños.

Pedraza.

Eduardo de la Barca.

Isabel de Warenne.

Cass slammed the journal closed, shoved it back in the drawer, and leapt off the bed. A moment later the paramedics were ringing the front door.

"I wonder why Antonio didn't meet us at the airport," Alyssa asked, standing beside her mother in the dim shadows of the hallway of a turn-of-the-century apartment building.

Tracey was frazzled. Their flight had been delayed for two hours, time that she and Alyssa had spent in the VIP lounge with little to do other than chat. The problem had been that Tracey didn't really know her own daughter, and all of the subjects that interested Alyssa were foreign to her, even her friends. The longer Alyssa had gone on, the more inept Tracey had felt. The longer they spent together, the more Tracey kept comparing herself to her perfect sister. Cass would be enjoying the delay. She would be all smiles, all good cheer. Tracey had begun to regret bringing Alyssa with her to Madrid. What if Antonio saw how incompetent she was as a mother? She had wanted to impress him, and now she was worrying that the opposite would be the case.

But there had been no choice. Her aunt and her sister had made this trip inevitable.

Tracey felt all of the hurt and anger welling up in her as she thought about how Cass and Catherine had taken sides, once again, against her. And to make matters even worse, maybe she should have waited a few days before traveling. She was exhausted; she didn't feel well. She felt weak and shaky.

"Mother? Are you well?"

Her daughter's voice jerked her back to the present, and Tracey had to take a couple of deep, soothing breaths. "Yes." She smiled at Alyssa, but it was forced. "Actually, he isn't quite expecting us. We're surprising him."

Alyssa almost gaped at her mother.

And Tracey was angry, because there was a judgment in her daughter's reaction to her, too. "He will be thrilled to see us," she assured herself as much as Alyssa. He would be thrilled, wouldn't he?

Alyssa flushed and looked down.

If Tracey did not know better, she would think that her seven-year-old daughter thought that it was incorrect to appear without an invitation. Had Cass already instilled such values in her? Tracey knocked again, her stomach upset with tension, perspiring now in her short summer skirt and paper-thin cashmere tank top. God, Spain was so hot. But then, she already knew that.

She glanced at her watch. Antonio should be at home. Classes had been over for one week now, and knowing him, while he would be immersed in research of some sort or another, at this hour he would be having a late lunch with his son.

She had never met such a devoted father before. In a way, he was just like Cass.

It flitted through her mind that they deserved one another. Tracey did not like that thought, not one bit. She reminded herself that Cass was hardly his type.

There was no answer, and after a few minutes had gone by, Tracey began to realize that no one was home.

She felt her temper rising, "Just great," she muttered. "Now what am I going to do? Sit on the floor and wait?"

"Mother?"

For one moment, Tracey had forgotten that Alyssa was standing beside her. "What is it?"

Alyssa flushed. "I need to use the bathroom."

"Oh, great!" Tracey cried. Now she was regretting the fact that Antonio had never given her a key to his apartment. God knew he should have. She had certainly spent enough time there. And the memories that flooded her, in that instant, were all of their torrid lovemaking. She began to relax. Her wavering confidence began to return. Antonio was a *man*. A very passionate man. She could manage him, of course she could.

The elevator whirred behind her, and Tracey spun around, hoping it was Antonio. But his neighbor, a middle-aged woman, stepped from the elevator instead.

"*Señora, buenos días,*" she said, glancing curiously at Alyssa.

"Hi," Tracey said. Then, "Have you seen Señor de la Barca today? Do you know if he's at his office at the university?"

Her eyes widened slightly. "Señora, my English no is good. *Señor no está en la universidad. Está en Castilla.*"

Tracey didn't speak Spanish, but she got the gist. "He's in Castile? In the north? At his country home, Casa de Sueños?" she cried, distraught and disbelieving.

"*Sí. Señor fue a Castilla.*"

"What?"

"Ahh—went . . . *ayer. Ayer.*"

Yesterday. Antonio had gone to the country yesterday. Tracey just stared, unable to believe her damnable luck.

Alyssa tugged on her hand.

Tracey almost snapped, "Not now," but the older woman was smiling kindly at them both. She inhaled. His country home was an hour north of Segovia. He'd showed her once on a map. What was the name of that little town it was outside of? Damn it! Pedamo, Pedaso, no, Pedraza. Tracey was certain that was it.

"Can my daughter use your bathroom, please? *El servicio? Por favor?*"

A moment later Alyssa was entering the woman's apartment, while Tracey was making plans.

The following morning, Cass sat at the desk she worked at in the library. It was covered with books, several of which were open. She was taking notes, but she couldn't concentrate.

By now, Tracey and Alyssa should have been in Madrid for several hours. Cass had contacted Mark Hopkins earlier, with great trepidation. He had been extremely closemouthed, but at least he had admitted that mother and daughter had flown abroad the night before. He had not raised the subject of a custody battle, but he had said that he would be in touch.

Cass shoved the biography of Mary Tudor aside, aware of a headache lingering just behind her temples. As she did so, the photograph she had tucked into the back of the book started to slip out.

Cass took out the color print of the sixteenth-century ruby necklace, staring at it without quite seeing it. Should she be relieved that Hopkins hadn't called her and hadn't raised the topic that she dreaded? Should she dare to hope that Tracey had been bluffing when she'd said her lawyer would call? Tracey hadn't actually specified just why her lawyer would be calling, but then, whom was Cass fooling? They had been fighting over Alyssa. And what about her aunt, who remained ill with a bacterial infection? Catherine was on antibiotics, but her fever remained high, at 100 degrees. For a woman of seventy, that was serious. What if her aunt died?

Cass was filled with worry, panic, regret, and guilt. She regretted their arguments. She still didn't understand how so much vehemence had blossomed between them, when they'd only shared warmth and camaraderie until then.

And Cass kept hearing Catherine in her delirium. At least she had not been delirious again.

Cass found herself staring down at the photograph she held in her hands. This had all started, hadn't it, when Antonio de la Barca had appeared at their home? Or had it started decades ago, when his father had been killed, accidentally or not, by an automobile in some town called Pedraza?

Or had it begun centuries ago?

Cass was dismayed by her last thought.

No good can come of the families being involved . . . You are starting to understand . . .

Her aunt's words echoed disturbingly in her mind. Cass's headache increased. Centuries ago, one of her ancestors had been, apparently, burned to death at the stake. An important woman, the earl of Sussex's daughter, a noblewoman married to a Spanish nobleman. Cass had done a bit of research. The de la Barca heirs were the counts of Pedraza. A number of heretics had been burned at the stake toward the end of Mary's reign. But most of those who had suffered such a death had been fanatically Protestant. Had Isabel been a religious fanatic? But then how had she married a Spaniard, who would obviously be devoutly Catholic?

Suddenly Cass could envision a lovely woman in period Tudor dress—in chains and manacles. She was used to her imagination running away with her—in fact, she expected it—so her flight of fancy hardly surprised her. But her sudden compassion did. Poor Isabel. If she had really met such a tragic fate.

Suddenly Cass wondered if Antonio was lobbying various museums, hoping to make a museum sale privately for the ruby necklace. She studied it critically now, wondering if Isabel had worn it, and if Isabel was really her ancestor—which would mean that her family was indeed connected with the de la Barcas. And what if Isabel had had children? Then Antonio's family was very distantly related to hers. Cass stood up abruptly, entirely perturbed, setting aside the necklace.

Tracey and Antonio, Catherine and Eduardo. Then she thought about her own reaction to Antonio.

This is nonsense, she decided angrily. Even though she was a romantic and the kind of woman to believe in destiny, there was no destiny here. Catherine might think so, but it was all terrible coincidence.

Cass folded her arms. Uneasily she stared down at the photograph. The problem was, she did believe in destiny and fate. She always had, and it was a theme in her novels, one she had repeated time and again. Were there a few too many coincidences present here?

Catherine had said that Isabel had died in 1555—the last year of Queen Mary's reign. How in the hell would her aunt know, or even remember, that?

The very last entry in her aunt's journal had mentioned Isabel. Cass shivered. She was so cold, and it was a coldness that began in her very bones.

Cass suddenly glanced around at the library where she usually worked, a room that she loved. The walls were painted a moss color with a satin finish, the ceiling was pink with a gold starburst in the center, the wood-work and wainscoting were all gilded, and every piece of furniture in the room had its own treasured past. The past. It was a part of the present, a part of all their lives; it had always been that way.

But it had never felt more present, or stronger, or more imminent, or even more urgent, than now.

"Ms. de Warenne?"

Cass was so engrossed in her own mental rampaging that she jumped at the sound of Celia's voice. "You scared me." Her heart was thundering.

"I beg your pardon. Lady Belford's fever has broken. She's awake, and she's asked for you."

"Thank God," Cass cried, overcome with relief. It would only take her half an hour to reach the hospital. *Thank God!*

"And you have a phone call," Celia added.

Cass hadn't even heard the phone ring. "Would you please take a message."

Celia looked her in the eye. "It's Ms. Tennant."

Cass froze. And then she leapt forward, dashing to the phone. She was breathless as she picked it up, and she could hear her own deafening heartbeat. "Trace?" she cried eagerly.

"Hi, sis," Tracey said with some hesitation.

Relief washed over Cass again and again. Catherine was recovering, her sister had called. "Thank you for calling. Tracey, I am sorry about our fight. How is Alyssa? Is she okay?"

"Alyssa's fine." There was a pause. "Are you really sorry?"

"Yes, I am," Cass said quickly. "I'd do anything to make it up to you!" And she meant it.

"I'm sorry, too," Tracey said, and her tone grew hoarse. "I didn't mean all those terrible things I said."

"Neither did I," Cass cried, gripping the phone so tightly her hand hurt.

"We're marooned," Tracey said. "Cass, we need help."

Cass was immediately alarmed. "Marooned?! Where are you?"

"At the Ritz, in Madrid. Cass, I need your help."

Cass finally absorbed Tracey's dramatic statement. Being stuck at the Ritz was hardly a hardship, but she said quickly, "How can I help?"

"Antonio went up to Castile. I can't get a damned driver on such short notice, can you believe it? Tonio's country home is a good three hours from here. I have a great idea. Why don't you take the next flight to Madrid, which is at eight this evening, and we'll all go up to the north together first thing in the morning?"

Cass stared blindly at the phone. "What?"

"There's an Air Iberia at eight. Out of Gatwick. It's only noon. If you leave by two, you can make it. I need you to drive, Cass. Otherwise we have to wait until Monday to get a driver. And you can spend the weekend with us. That's what you wanted in the first place, isn't it?"

Cass didn't have to think about it. "Of course I'll come," she cried eagerly. "You book that flight while I pack! I will make that eight P.M., Trace, I swear it."

"Cass, I already booked the flight for you, and your return as well."

For one second Cass digested the implications of Tracey's statement, especially that of her return being finalized after the weekend. And then she shoved those thoughts—and the discontent they would bring—far aside. "Can I speak to Alyssa?" Cass asked eagerly. It was sinking in. They were no longer fighting, even if things weren't perfect. She was going to join her sister and Alyssa in Spain, even if for only a short time. She'd be able to shore up their truce, and make certain Alyssa did come home when the summer was over. And Antonio de la Barca, who had invited her to see Isabel's portrait, would be there as well.

Cass suddenly sank down in the chair. And Aunt Catherine's fever had broken. Everything was going to be all right. She realized she was trembling. This had all been much ado about nothing.

"Alyssa's napping," Tracey said. "I'll have you picked up tomorrow. Call me when you've checked in at the airport."

Cass agreed, and the sisters hung up. Then she just sat there, thanking the heavens above for this turn of fate and refusing to think about Catherine's secret. Thank God Tracey hated driving, and refused to get behind the wheel of a car.

Then Cass thought about her aunt, who was awake and asking to see her. After instructing Celia to pack a bag for her, Cass jumped into her BMW. She made it to the hospital in exactly twenty-three minutes; traffic had been light.

The lights were on in her aunt's private room, as was the television. The volume was low. Her aunt was propped up on pillows in bed, but her eyes were closed. Cass didn't know if she was resting or if she had fallen asleep again. As quietly as possible, she closed the door and approached her.

She touched her forehead, which was cool. More relief surged within her and she sank down beside her aunt on the bed. She loved Catherine so much, and she wouldn't have been able to bear it if anything had happened to her. Cass could not face her deepest thoughts. Catherine had become sick from the stress of the turmoil and conflict that their family had been plunged into. Because Cass had gone to battle herself, instead of being the peacekeeper.

Never again, Cass vowed.

"Cassandra?" Catherine whispered.

"I'm here. And you've been sick, Aunt Catherine, but your fever's broken now, and you are going to be fine." Cass smiled at her.

Catherine smiled slightly back.

"And Alyssa is fine. Tracey called. They're both fine and we've made peace. Everything's going to be all right."

Her aunt's eyes opened and she looked at Cass. "Nothing is right."

Cass was startled and then dismayed. "What?"

Catherine screwed her eyes shut. A tear slipped free anyway.

Cass did not want to distress her aunt now. "Everything is fine," she said too brightly. "In fact, I am on my way to Spain to join Tracey and Alyssa. See? Things could not be better."

Catherine's lids flew open. "Don't go!"

Cass stood, very disturbed. "I have to go, because I need to take care of Alyssa and make sure that she comes home."

Catherine shook her head weakly. "Is that your intention? To holiday with them in Castile?"

Cass was grave, her aunt had guessed her intentions. "Yes. Let's talk about happier subjects, Aunt Catherine. I'll bet you can come home tomorrow."

But Catherine would not be deterred. "I am so afraid for you, for Alyssa, for Tracey," she said. She reached for and gripped Cass's hand. "At all costs, do not go to Castilla. Do not let Tracey and Alyssa go. Just go to Spain and bring them home. Promise me."

Cass inhaled. "I would if I could, but you know my sister, Aunt Catherine. She's in love and dead set on meeting her boyfriend. I can't stop her."

"But you have to! You have no idea, Cass, no idea of what will happen if you go, or she goes, there."

Cass was uneasy, but she smiled. "You're right. Aunt Catherine, what are you trying to say? What do you think will happen if we go to Castile? Look, maybe there have been a few tragedies when the de la Barcas and the de Warennes have been involved, but it was just coincidence. I am certain of it."

"You are wrong," Catherine said flatly. "And I know that you know, in your heart, the truth. Because I know who you are, Cassandra. You are a romantic and a fatalist. I've read every single one of your books! I know how your mind works. And I know your heart."

Cass's unease increased. She could not respond. Because if she dared to cease the denials, her aunt was right.

Catherine had clutched her hand. "Everything was fine between me and Eduardo until we got to Casa de Sueños. Everything was just fine until then."

"What do you mean?" Cass asked warily.

"We weren't even lovers before then," Catherine said. "We were friends and associates, we respected one another, we adored our respective spouses! I joined him there to research *her* life! We were so enthralled with our pursuit of the ancestor we seemed to share. But within days, we went from being lovers to detesting one another—to trying to hurt one another. We became savages—and then he was dead."

Suddenly Cass understood. Her aunt had never recovered from the trauma of Eduardo's death, which was why she could not be rational about the de la Barca family. How relieved she was. Of course, her aunt needed therapy. Cass intended to make certain that she got it. "I will do my best to get everyone to come home," she said, to appease her aunt. But it was a tiny white lie.

She was going to Spain—and she had every intention of going to Antonio's ancestral home in Castile. In fact, now that the most recent crisis had passed, she was aware of just how excited she was, excited and impatient. Cass realized she was smiling. The historian in her could not be kept at bay.

And as for the woman in her, well, Antonio wasn't available, he was out of her league, and the woman in her would have to be ignored.

But Catherine was staring. "I cannot believe you would even try to deceive me," she said quietly. "Oh, God. You will go, and nothing I say or do will stop you."

At a loss, no longer smiling, Cass said, "Please don't worry. Everything will be fine."

"No. Nothing will ever be fine again."

PART TWO

THE SUMMONING

SIX

CASTILLA—THE FIRST DAY

Are we lost?" Alyssa asked.

Cass tried to smile in the rearview mirror. But there wasn't another car on the road, and the last village they had passed through had been a jumble of old stone buildings, none with glass windows, set down in the middle of the rugged desolate terrain they were cruising through. Had Cass not seen a sign boasting ASAR AL HORNO, she would have thought the place to be a ghost town. As it was, the damned village wasn't even on the map.

And now she understood the phrase *la tierra muerta*. The dead land.

For the past hour, they had driven through rough, barren, rocky terrain that clearly could not support agriculture or much of anything else. But not moments before that, the land had been flat, fertile, green fields, while the walled medieval town of Pedraza had been set amongst beautiful rolling hills.

Pedraza. It had been so quaint. Cass found it hard to believe that Eduardo had died so tragically there—the victim of a car accident. And it had been an accident. No matter what Catherine had claimed, now that Cass had had some time to reflect, some time to relax, putting a distance between them, she was convinced that her aunt was blaming herself for something that was not her fault. Because she remained traumatized, and perhaps not just by the accident. Maybe she had never gotten over the guilt of the affair.

"I thought that old woman in Pedraza said the castle was right up the road," Tracey said with annoyance.

Cass was grim—and glad for the interruption to her thoughts. "That's what I thought. But neither one of us speaks Spanish, so maybe we misunderstood. Maybe we should have gone right at the last intersection outside of Pedraza."

"I don't think so," Tracey replied, her tone terse.

Cass abruptly stopped the car, squinting through the windshield in spite of the sunglasses she wore. "Can I see that map?"

Tracey handed it to her, not that Cass felt it would do any good. Unbelievably, Tracey had neither directions, an address, nor the phone number of the de la Barca house. But the house wasn't far from Pedraza, she had insisted, and the villagers there had nodded enthusiastically, pointing the way, at the mention of de la Barca and Casa de Sueños.

Casa de Sueños. Cass knew enough Spanish to know that Antonio's house was named House of Dreams. It was not just an unusual name; Cass thought it incredibly, yet somewhat eerily, romantic.

Tracey was already stepping out of the car to light up a cigarette. It was horribly hot out, but in her midriff-baring top and short white skirt, she looked amazingly cool. Cass glanced at her—she wouldn't mind a little help with the map—but Tracey avoided her eyes. It had been that way since her arrival at the hotel in the middle of the night.

The tension between them remained, and it was inescapable. So much for their truce.

Grimly Cass tried to locate where they were on the map. Outside, Tracey continued to puff on her cigarette, with obvious annoyance and even impatience. Cass felt the flaring of her own temper, because if this was anyone's fault, it was her sister's.

Alyssa leaned over the backseat. "Even if we are lost, this is an adventure, isn't it? And we're all together now." She smiled, at once worried and relieved.

Cass turned to her and couldn't resist hugging her hard. "It is an adventure," she said gaily. "And I bet that castle is right around the corner."

Tracey tossed her cigarette aside.

Cass looked up and saw her sister regarding her and Alyssa far too intently. More tension grew in Cass. She released her niece. "It's not marked on this map," she said.

"Hi ho," Alyssa said, pointing through the side window. "What's that?"

Cass turned to look in the direction she was pointing, squinting. "What is it that you see, honey?" she asked.

"A building. I'll bet that's the castle where we're supposed to turn," Alyssa cried excitedly.

Cass couldn't see anything, but she fervently hoped it was. "Let's go see," she said with a smile.

Tracey returned to the car after grinding out the cigarette. Cass shifted into gear, while Tracey tried to find a radio station with decent reception, and failed. "Christ, I thought it would become cooler the farther north we went. Bloody stupid of me."

Cass didn't reply as Alyssa cried out, "There, there, I told you!"

Cass finally saw the stone castle. "Thank God," she said, accelerating. The two round towers and rotting walls were the exact same shade as the surrounding ground, and perched as it was on a higher bluff, and backlit by the high afternoon sun, she could have driven right by it without ever noticing it. "You have eagle eyes," she told Alyssa, who was beaming with pride.

"Finally!" Tracey said excitedly. "Go left, Cass. We go left at the castle ruins."

Cass obeyed. As they drove past the castle at a more sedate pace— the last thing they needed now was a flat, for the road was rutted dirt and filled with stones—she craned her neck for a better view. "I have to date that," she said, more to herself than anyone. "It could be four-teenth century."

"Forget the castle, Cass. There it is, I see the house," Tracey cried, relief in her tone.

Cass redirected her gaze and saw, rising up out of nowhere, high stone walls and iron gates. Not far from the gates, she could see a long, two-story stone house with a tiled roof, one end a square tower, with three other, smaller buildings beside it. A few tall trees graced the house, and wildflowers seemed to be blooming in the grassy, overgrown front yard. The land rolling away from the house was mostly flat and barren, but in the distance she could just make out the shadowy outlines of distant mountain peaks.

Cass stopped the car in front of the gates, which were closed. She jumped out, while Tracey waited in the car, and saw no sign of either a buzzer or intercom; worse, the property looked deserted. Cass was perplexed as she glanced around, wishing she saw either a car parked outside the house or some sign of human activity.

"What is it?" Tracey called from the car, rolling down her window.

Cass hesitated—the gates didn't seem to be locked. "I hope we're in the right place," she said. And just as she was about to push them open, she heard an approaching vehicle.

Cass spun around, watching as an older-model Jeep raced up the road from the direction in which she had come. The dust-covered vehicle had no top, just a roll bar, and Cass had a perfect view of the driver. Immediately her mouth went dry, and the greeting she had secretly rehearsed escaped her mind.

The Jeep halted beside the Renault. Antonio was wearing dark sunglasses, but his gaze was clearly directed at her. Cass tried to relax, decided it was impossible, plastered a smile on her face, and strolled toward him as he climbed out of the Jeep. She was about to offer up a very casual greeting, when Tracey leapt from the Renault with a cry, flinging herself at him. Cass halted in her tracks.

She watched them embrace, then quickly turned away. She had already known that this weekend wasn't going to be easy. Not as far as her sister and Antonio were concerned. But she had refused to dwell on it. Now she felt the tension within her increasing. Damn.

"Surprise!" Tracey cried gaily.

He removed his sunglasses, and Cass turned back just in time to see the shock on his face. He hadn't been expecting them. Utter mortification filled her.

"What in God's name possessed you to come here?" he asked, his gaze swinging now to the car and its single remaining occupant.

"Isn't this a wonderful surprise?" Tracey said quickly, still smiling widely and pressing against him.

Cass wanted to throttle her sister until she gained some sense. How could she do this? She had no time to think things through, however, for Antonio had turned toward her. "Cassandra." He smiled then, but briefly. "Forgive me. Forgive my lack of manners. I am not used to surprises such as this one."

"I had no idea," Cass said, remaining mortified.

He looked directly at her again. Cass knew her cheeks were heating. How could Tracey have such nerve even if he was her lover?

"Darling, life cannot always be planned," Tracey said, but her smile was faltering, as if she had lost some of her self-confidence. Her blue eyes were wide, the picture of slightly wounded innocence. "You told me you would love to have Alyssa come visit, and look, she is here.

We've spent hours and hours trying to find this place! You are in the middle of nowhere! We are so hot, tired, dirty, and thirsty!"

"Had we planned this holiday, I could have given you directions," he said wryly. "What about the auction? You must have a tremendous amount to do."

Cass wondered how Tracey would explain that.

"The stress was making it impossible for me to eat and sleep," Tracey said quickly, smiling. "My physician advised me to let someone else handle the auction."

Cass realized her mouth was hanging open and she shut it.

Then to Alyssa, Antonio said, "*Buenas tardes, señorita.* I am sorry that I was not prepared to greet you more properly. Come. *Vamos aquí.*"

Alyssa was stepping from the car, and from her blush, Cass knew she felt awkward and uncomfortable, too. "I do hope we are not imposing."

"You could never impose, *querida*," Antonio replied with another smile, this one more genuine. Cass saw that he was recovering his composure.

Alyssa smiled again.

"This will be the very best holiday, I promise everyone," Tracey said seriously. She spoke to Antonio and Alyssa, clearly excluding Cass.

"I'll open the gates. It will be but a moment," Antonio said.

Cass watched him stride away and push open the gates. He was wearing a faded blue polo shirt, at the throat of which she had glimpsed something gold, khaki shorts, heavy socks, and well-worn hiking boots. He might come from an old and noble Castilian family, but he didn't resemble a blue blood now. In fact, he didn't look like a professor of medieval history, either. A passerby might assume him to be the foreman of some farm or bodega, she decided, or even a mountain guide.

They all climbed back into the Renault. As Cass drove slowly after the Jeep, she could not restrain herself and she said, "How *could* you?"

Tracey faced her. "Don't you bloody pick on me!"

Cass gripped the wheel, hard. She forced down the retort that she so wanted to make and remained silent.

"Besides, he's my boyfriend and I know exactly what I'm doing," Tracey said, a steely edge to her tone.

Cass shot her a glance. She was grim. There was no point in arguing; the deed was done. "You're right. You know him a lot better than I do," she said. But she didn't really believe it. Antonio de la Barca was not a simple man. Cass was quite certain there were many layers there—and that her sister didn't have a clue.

Cass parked beside the Jeep in the shade of several trees, in front of the house. A headache had arisen out of nowhere. Their host was waiting for them, and he remained silent as he led them inside. Cass avoided his eyes, wishing she could act more naturally around him. While Tracey started oohing and aahing over how lovely the house was, how quaint and how very Spanish, Cass paused, instantly wondering where Isabel's portrait was.

Nothing will ever be fine again.

Cass refused to listen to her aunt's nonsense. She began to shiver. It was dim with shadows inside, and blessedly cool. She hugged herself, allowing her eyes to make the adjustment from the sun's blinding glare to the house's darkness. It took her a moment, while Alyssa slid her hand into the crook of her arm. Then she pressed close to Cass.

"Aunt Cass?" Alyssa whispered, sounding nervous.

Cass slid her arm around her, as she realized just how run-down the property was. They were in a large, stone-floored hall with extremely high ceilings, mostly devoid of furniture, the flagstones underfoot chipped and broken, the stuccoed walls coarse, timeworn, weather stained, and flaking. Cass glanced up at dozen swords hanging on the walls, along with a shield containing a coat of arms. There was also a wall-sized tapestry depicting a pastoral scene which was faded and torn but exquisite nonetheless.

Her pulse was pounding a bit now. But not exactly with excitement. She adored history in any shape or form, but oddly, she was filled with trepidation.

Cass grimaced. Of course she was anxious. Her aunt had done a number on her, apparently. And she and her sister were at odds, and the stakes were so terribly high. The stakes were Alyssa—and maybe even Antonio de la Barca.

Cass froze, unable to believe her last thought.

The stakes were Antonio de la Barca.

"Aunt Cass? Why is this house so cold and dark?" Alyssa whispered.

"These houses are built to be this way," Cass responded, automatically whispering back. She was stunned by herself. What was wrong with her? She was going to have to readjust her thinking, she decided. Before she got into serious trouble. She had no intention of ever competing with Tracey for a man.

Chilled thoroughly now, but from the inside, not the outside, Cass glanced around.

The house was built around a courtyard. A pair of doors opened onto it, and Cass glimpsed a broken limestone fountain, boasting the headless sculpture of a nude man, who was also missing one arm. It was not running water. A decrepit balcony ran along the entire second story around the interior courtyard. Cass did not think it would be wise to lean against the railing. She saw weeds poking out from the cracked and scarred red slate tiles underfoot outside.

"I don't know if I like it here, Aunt Cass."

Cass glanced down at her niece, intending to reassure her, but her words died before she could speak them. The house was lovely, even if it was terribly run-down. Her aesthetic eye told her that. She was a historian and she could appreciate the Spanish architecture and furnishings with their slight Moorish accent. But she really wasn't crazy about it either.

"Cassandra?"

Cass realized her host was trying to address her. She had been so immersed in her musings and surroundings, she hadn't heard him at first. She smiled a bit guiltily. "Your home. It's . . . overwhelming."

Their eyes met but did not hold. "I agree. At first there is something quite overwhelming about *la casa*." He shrugged in a very European manner, but he did not smile. He glanced around. "Actually, I haven't been here in many years—and we only arrived a few days ago. I had forgotten the feeling of this house, just as I had forgotten all the treasures within it."

"We?" Tracey asked quickly, stepping closer to him.

Cass wondered why he hadn't been to his ancestral home in years. She couldn't help thinking that it has something to do with his missing wife. Perhaps being here without her was just too painful.

Antonio explained that he was here with Eduardo and Alfonso. Cass had no idea who the latter was, and she assumed he had referred to the very historic feeling of the house. Or did he refer to something else, something less tangible?

She was finally putting her finger on what disturbed her, and what was undoubtedly disturbing Alyssa. The house was not inviting, not in any way. It was so cold, so dark.

But before her imagination went wild, she reminded herself that it was not inviting because no one had lived in it or maintained it for years and years.

"When was this place built?" she had to ask, rolling her neck to try to work out some of the tension—which just kept escalating.

"In the early fifteenth century, although the tower, where the chapel is, dates back a century earlier," he said, smiling slightly at her.

Cass inhaled. And she wondered if her ancestor Isabel de Warenne had lived there. "And the castle?"

His eyes seemed to sparkle. "It was a military fortification that remained in the hands of my family for many years. Most of the existing structure was built in the fourteenth century, but upon earlier foundations. As you probably know, there was a great need for military fortifications here in Spain, right until the end of the reconquest. But even after that, sometimes, nobleman fought nobleman, or more likely, bands of roaming outlaws." He smiled, as if the idea enthralled him. "However," he continued, "my family fell rapidly out of favor with the royals, and by the late sixteenth century the castle was run-down with neglect, having been unoccupied for close to a century." His gaze held hers. "It was an amazingly rapid fall from grace."

"Why?" Cass asked eagerly, all other thoughts momentarily forgotten. "What happened?"

Tracey stepped between them. "We've been traveling all day and the two of you are going to discuss history?" She turned and looped her arm in Antonio's. "Tonio, I have missed you," she said softly, leaning forward to kiss his mouth. In her flat sandals, she had to rise up on tiptoe to do so.

Instantly Cass turned away, refusing to watch the intimate moment. She smiled down at Alyssa, but now it was forced. Perhaps to comfort herself, she took Alyssa's hand.

"Let me introduce you to my son and show you to your rooms," Antonio said. "Eduardo?"

"I'm here, Papá," a small voice said from the other side of the hall, standing at the corner of one corridor.

Cass turned with a smile of greeting, wondering how long he had been standing there in the shadows of another hallway, when her smile failed her. No one had warned her that Antonio's son was in leg braces and crutches. She gripped Alyssa's hand more tightly, to forestall any exclamation of surprise. She wondered if Eduardo had been the victim of polio.

"Eduardo, we have guests."

Cass heard the softness and love in his tone and shot him a look. He was smiling at his son, who was very agile on his crutches, and he hobbled quickly forward.

As Antonio made the introductions, it took Cass two seconds to realize that Eduardo did not like her sister—but that was hardly unusual, because he would think her a threat to his own mother. Eduardo called her señora, inquired politely about their trip, and then refused to look at her again.

"Eduardo." Tracey was overly enthusiastic, rushing to the small boy and pecking him on both cheeks. "It is *soo* wonderful to see you again."

Cass winced. Her sister was hardly the Pied Piper when it came to children, and her forced efforts were painfully obvious. She wondered if Antonio was fooled. "Hi, Eduardo," she said, stepping toward him. "I'm Cass. I hope you don't mind sharing your father with all of us."

He met her eyes, startled. "In my country," he said in perfect although heavily accented English, "there is no such thing that you have spoken of. My home is your home."

"Thank you," Cass returned. "My niece is seven. How old are you?"

He glanced at Alyssa. "Ten."

"Maybe you can take Alyssa exploring," Cass suggested.

He met her gaze. "Exploring?"

"Well, this house is certainly worth exploring, don't you think? And then there's the castle—I'd even join you guys, if you'd let me." She grinned.

He stared at her and then turned to look at Antonio for permission. "We'll see," Antonio said, unsmiling.

Cass hoped she hadn't overstepped her bounds. But certainly he wasn't overprotective of his son because of his handicap, or was he? She hoped not. From what she had seen, Eduardo could move very well indeed. "Well, I hope to do some exploring tomorrow, jet lag and all. Maybe you and Alyssa can tag along."

Eduardo bit his lip and glanced at his father again.

"I think that's a great idea," Tracey cut in.

Cass could guess why she was so approving. "Maybe we could even take a picnic lunch to the castle," Cass enthused.

Antonio stared at her.

"*Papá, por favor,*" Eduardo pleaded.

Cass bit her lip. The gist was clear—Eduardo wanted to come.

"Cassandra, why don't we discuss tomorrow's agenda at some other time?" Antonio said somewhat grimly.

"Am I being too bold?" Cass asked bluntly. For the first time, she had the nerve to look him in the eye.

"You are very bold." But he seemed to smile.

"It's an American thing," Cass said lightly, unable to glance away. "If the castle's out, maybe we can picnic somewhere else, or maybe I can even take the kids to lunch in Pedraza." Not that she really wanted to go back there.

He finally softened. "Perhaps."

Cass realized that he continued to stare at her, and she finally flushed and tore her gaze away. She looked from Eduardo, who was clearly hopeful, to Alyssa, who hadn't said a word, but whose eyes were shining with expectation. She tried not to look at Tracey, who was going to read her like a book if she wasn't very careful. "How about a siesta?" she asked her niece. "I'm beat from all that driving."

"I am a bit sleepy," Alyssa admitted.

"Okay. Let's follow our host. Eduardo, want to mosey along?"

He seemed startled. "Mosey?"

"American slang. It means follow along in a leisurely manner."

For the first time, he smiled. He looked exactly like his father, Cass thought; he would one day be an extraordinarily attractive man. "I'll mosey along," he said in his heavy Spanish accent.

A moment later they were walking down a hallway that ran parallel to the opposite corridor, the interior courtyard outside and between both halls. Windows and doors lined the long hall, giving Cass a clear view of both the courtyard and the opposite side of the house. There was no furniture in the courtyard, none beneath the balcony on the other side. The neglect was a shame. Cass wondered how impoverished the de la Barca family was. It wouldn't be unusual for an old titled family, and he certainly couldn't make very much from his profession as a professor.

It crossed her mind that the ruby necklace might belong to his family—and that they could use the income.

At the end of the corridor, they went upstairs, and Antonio opened the door to a dark bedroom with a magnificent if not timeworn canopied bed. "Cassandra, you may use this room. Alfonso and I will bring your bags in shortly."

Cass stepped past the threshold and her host, acutely aware of him as she did so. She glanced around—the room was lovely, the walls whitewashed but faded, stiff gold floor-length draperies closed over the windows, exquisite but threadbare, once colorful Persian rugs on the stone floors, the bed done up in shades of peach, blue, and gold, a mélange of stripes and paisley patterns. A tawny-hued marble mantel was over the fireplace. Above that, in an old, gilded frame, was a portrait of a stern-looking man in period dress. Cass rushed over to it.

"An ancestor of mine."

Cass hadn't heard him come up behind her and she jerked, half turning to meet his gaze. "Late sixteenth century," she shot. "Look how high that neck ruff is, and look at the shape of the belly—it was called a peascod," she cried. She heard Tracey sigh with exasperation and ignored it. "Paned trunk hose, fur-lined cape. Oh, God, look at the stones on that cross he's wearing. Wow."

Antonio laughed. "I am in complete agreement with you," he said.

Cass felt absurdly pleased that she had impressed him with her knowledge.

"My sister is a bookworm," Tracey said flatly. "All she does is read, when she is not writing, always about the past. She *loves* the past." It wasn't exactly a compliment.

Cass felt somewhat deflated, but hardly wanted to defend herself by getting into a debate about the details of her lifestyle.

"Reading is one of the finer things in life," Antonio said, unsmiling, his back to Tracey. "And I am enthralled with the past, sometimes more so than with the present."

Cass looked at his strained countenance. He had just defended her, while setting Tracey down. Cass glanced at Tracey, who appeared taken aback.

"The two of you have something in common then," Tracey said, going to Antonio and standing so close to him that she touched his side and he had to look at her.

"Indeed we do." He turned back to Cass. "He is Alvarado de la Barca."

The change of subject was abrupt, but Cass knew exactly what he meant, and she whirled to stare at the Spaniard in the portrait—the man who had married Isabel de Warenne. "Oh, God," she whispered, the hairs rising up on the nape of her neck. And she had a distinctly bad feeling.

Antonio smiled slightly at her. "Her portrait is in the opposite hall," he said.

Cass met his regard. "I can't wait to see it," she said, undeniably excited.

"I look forward to showing it to you," he returned.

"Antonio, was she a fanatic? Was that why she was burned at the stake?" Cass had to ask.

"Do we know for certain that she was burned at the stake—and that she did die in 1555?" he returned. "I would prefer to verify your aunt's claims."

Cass faced him fully. "Before I left home, I grabbed a box of pamphlets and brochures I bought when Alyssa and I toured Romney Castle a few years ago. The de Warennes were the earls of Sussex in the sixteenth century, and that was their seat. I didn't have a chance to go through the material because I was in such a rush. But we may find some mention about Isabel there."

"What are the two of you talking about?" Tracey asked.

Cass had briefly forgotten that her sister was present; indeed, for a few instants she had forgotten that anyone else was even in the room, other than herself and Antonio.

Antonio said, "My father spent the last few years of his life compiling information about my family's history. The library here is a treasure trove—although nothing has been categorized or filed. I have only just begun to delve into his files and notes."

Cass met his intense hazel eyes one more time. She hesitated, and said, slowly, "How old were you when he died?"

"Four."

Cass had thought that was what he had said before. "How did he die?" Her heartbeat was so loud now. Surely everyone in the room could hear it. And her tension was so high she was sweating buckets. Of course, should anyone notice, they'd think it the summer heat.

"It was a tragic accident," he said as slowly. "He was hit by a car."

Cass nodded, feeling like a liar and an accomplice. Relief almost swamped her. She should have never tested him to see what he knew.

"Actually," Antonio said, his tone oddly casual, "I went to the *policía* the other day."

Cass blinked at him, praying she had misheard. "What?"

"Returning here made me more than curious," he said, and now his gaze was on her, green and amber and golden, pupils black and wide. "I wanted to understand how it happened. You see"—he did not smile, but continued to regard her with such intensity that Cass was breathless—"my mother would never speak of him after his death. Not even of the accident. She was very bitter."

Cass thought she managed to bob her head up and down in the

parody of a nod. Of course his mother would have been bitter—if she had learned about her husband's affair with Cass's aunt.

"There was a woman with him there, that day, the day that he died."

Cass froze. Incapable of movement, of taking a gulp of air, of anything at all. And she thought, *No*.

"Yes," he said calmly. "It was Lady Belford. Your aunt was with him when he died. In fact, he died in her arms."

SEVEN

Belford House—the Same Day

The faces leered at her, grotesquely altered by memories and the passage of time. But she knew them, she did. Eduardo, his two sons, his wife. And Isabel . . .

Catherine woke up with a cry. And for one instant she did not know where she was, for one instant she thought she was somewhere cold and frightening and dark, and the sickly sweet scent of violets was everywhere.

But then her eyes adjusted to the dimming daylight and she made out the familiar outlines of her bedroom—a room that had been her sanctuary ever since she had first come to Belford House as a very young, naive bride. She had been dreaming about the past, a haunting nightmare she had not had in decades, but which she now had every night since that damnable black-tie affair. She sat up, pushing off the covers, still trembling and breathless.

And when she finally stood, filled with sorrow and stricken with fear, she glimpsed her ravaged reflection in the mirror across the room and she was shocked by her appearance. She was no longer the young, beautiful girl with stars in her eyes who had wed a much older man; she was no longer the mature, self-assured woman who had made a terribly immoral choice, then committed an unspeakable crime. Nor was she the elegant, older woman hiding an unbearable secret who was aunt, mother, and great-aunt to her nieces and grandniece. Suddenly she was old and ancient beyond description.

Eduardo's favorite saying rang in her ears, so much so that she could hear his patrician voice with its tantalizing foreign accent. *What is past is prologue.* How often had he told her that?

She thought about Tracey and Eduardo's son, and tears ran down her cheeks.

There was a desk in the corner of her room. Catherine slowly made her way toward it, aware now of being chilled through and through, in spite of the fire that blazed in the hearth, in spite of the heavy wool robe she wore. At her desk she eased herself down into one of the Louis XV chairs, and then she reached for the phone.

"Lady Belford! What are you up to, out of bed, roaming about, with you as weak as a newborn kitten?" Celia cried from the doorway.

She *was* as weak as a newborn kitten, and Catherine closed her eyes, wondering what Celia's reaction would be if she told her the truth, as she had told Cass. Catherine was never going to forget the look on her niece's face when she had confessed to Eduardo's murder. The look had been one of disbelief—followed by shock, and horror.

The very same look had been on Eduardo's face, in those last seconds when he realized what she had done and that he was dying.

Celia had come over and Catherine looked up. "Call the airlines. Book flights for me. I must go to Spain."

Celia was astonished—justifiably so. "Lady Belford! No disrespect intended, but I must speak my mind!"

Catherine thought, wearily, *When ever have you not spoken your mind?* Celia had come to work for her shortly after Robert's terrible stroke.

"You have been very ill, and now is not the time to go traipsing off after your nieces and Alyssa. Trust me. All will be fine."

Catherine felt far older than her seventy years just then, but she had always been a strong woman, and she drew on all of her strength now. "I am going to Spain. Even if that is what she wants. And either you shall book my flights, as well as a driver, or I shall. I will leave—as soon as possible."

Celia gaped at her.

Catherine finally looked up.

And Celia must have seen the resolve in her eyes, because she grimaced. "At least the fever is gone," she said. "I'll make the calls from another room, then." And as she walked out, Catherine heard her grumbling to herself.

Catherine did not care.

She was old, and now she knew she was going to die much sooner rather than later. Because the past was prologue, and she was going to Spain, to prevent the very worst from happening, to save her family. And no one was going to stop her, not loyal Celia, not the *policía,* and not a woman who had been dead for 445 years.

May 3, 1966

These past weeks have been the most exciting of my life. Eduardo and I have worked side by side without interruption, piecing together the puzzle of Isabel de Warenne's life. I have come to admire him immensely. Eduardo is brilliant, but unlike many brilliant men passionately devoted to their careers, he has never sacrificed his family for his work. However, I begin to suspect that his wife fails to understand him as she should. Having met her several times, including recently for a lunch we all shared, I begin to feel that she is jealous of our relationship.

It is a shame. She has nothing to be jealous of. Eduardo and I have become close friends in our pursuit of Isabel de Warenne, but nothing more.

I understand him too well. A liaison is as foreign to him as a language like Chinese. And even though Robert and I have not had relations since the stroke, nor could I live with myself if I took a lover.

Together we have accomplished more than he ever could alone, or with the help of one of his students. We have over one thousand pages of documented notes.

He has invited me to his home in Castilla. To Casa de Sueños, where Isabel's husband once lived—where she, perhaps, also lived. I am aware that I should have refused, because of Maria. But how could I refuse? When I cannot wait to set foot in his home, when every instinct I have tells me that the answers we seek lie there?

As I write this most recent entry, my plane is descending, about to land in Madrid. In a few more hours, I will be in Castilla. I am as impatient as a young girl. I just cannot wait. Our first order of business, we have decided, is to explore the family crypt in the hope of finally locating Isabel's tomb.

CASA DE SUEÑOS—THE FIRST NIGHT

Cass closed the dusty armoire, which creaked in protest, and smiled at Alyssa. "Ready for that siesta?" she asked. They had just finished unpacking a portion of their things. For Cass, the task had been performed almost mindlessly. Antonio's words continued to ring in her ears, and all she could think was, *What does he know?*

Did he know anything at all other than the fact that her aunt had been with Eduardo when he died? Surely he did not suspect that foul play had befallen his father? But why else would he have responded— and looked at her—the way that he had?

"I am really tired," Alyssa admitted.

Cass propelled her toward the bed, in a state of exhaustion herself. Most of it, she knew, was emotional. "While you nap, I'm going to explore this house," she said. She felt compelled to locate Isabel's portrait. But what should she do about Antonio now that he knew—or suspected—that her aunt was involved in his father's death?

What could she do, other than react to whatever he threw out next?

Alyssa paused, not climbing onto the high bed. "Aunt Cass, I don't want to stay here alone."

Cass had to face her niece. But even as she did so, she could sense what was coming. The bedroom had a dark and uncomfortable feeling to it. "Why not?"

Alyssa folded her arms across her flat chest. "I don't really like this room," she said slowly.

Cass met her gaze. And she couldn't help glancing around their bedroom. It was a charming room. She knew that. But it was so unbearably still inside.

Suddenly she realized that she wasn't really thrilled with leaving Alyssa alone in the room, either.

"This place is too old, it's creepy," Alyssa whispered, not moving to get into bed.

Cass looked at her, then scanned the room. She had partially opened the four sets of draperies, and even though it was almost seven in the evening, bright sunlight was streaming into the room. Through the parted curtains she could glimpse the stark terrain stretching away from the house. She could even make out the castle's twin towers. On the other side of the room, there were views of the courtyard and the opposite wing of the house. And while the room and the furnishings were old, everything was undeniably beautiful. Except . . . except what?

Something just wasn't right, something was amiss. The whole house was so still and dark and cold. It was almost as if the house was just waiting for something to happen.

Which was absurd.

Cass scanned the room again. Her gaze landed on the portrait hanging over the fireplace, and she tensed immediately. Isabel de Warenne's husband did not appear to be a pleasant man. His face was stern and set; Cass had little doubt he had been both a difficult and a narrow-minded man. It was his portrait that was disturbing, she decided. *He* was disturbing.

Alyssa followed her gaze. "He's creepy. He looks like a mean man."

Cass patted her head. "Honey, I couldn't agree more, but it's only a painting." Poor Isabel. Cass shivered. However had she managed to marry Alvarado? Their cultural and religious differences alone would have doomed the marriage, much less the nature of his personality.

Cass shivered again.

"Can't I come with you?" Alyssa asked, a plea in her tone.

"No." Cass was quietly firm. "Jump into bed, and I'll be right back." She dismissed her apprehensions as ridiculous. "We are both overtired," she said. "That is all."

Alyssa's face was filled with anxiety as she did as Cass asked. Cass removed the covers, except for a gold sheet. And she stroked Alyssa's hair, just once. "I'll open the windows. Maybe there's an evening breeze."

Cass opened two windows. When she turned, her niece was soundly asleep.

The sight of the sleeping child made her smile, love welling up inside her breast. Thank God she had come to Spain to join Tracey and Alyssa. Thank God they were through the worst. Cass knew she would have to do something to make sure an incident like this one never happened again. But what?

Fight her sister for Alyssa.

Cass should be Alyssa's mother. Tracey did not deserve to be the mother of her own child.

Cass froze.

She was stunned. How could she have had such terrible thoughts? Where had such thoughts come from?

She had never contemplated taking Alyssa away from Tracey. Because in spite of how difficult Tracey could be, in spite of how irresponsible and inconsistent, she was Alyssa's mother. And she was also her sister and Cass loved her. Cass never wanted to hurt her. They were family, for God's sake.

Cass turned away, frightened, wishing she had never identified her thoughts. And as she left the room, unease pricked at her again. For some damn reason, she hated leaving Alyssa alone.

She turned back, hesitating. But sunlight was streaming into the room, dust motes drifted in the air, and Alyssa was smiling slightly as she slept. Cass turned away.

In the corridor, Cass paused. Tracey had been given a bedroom next to the bathroom they would share, and her door was solidly closed. Cass didn't know whether her sister was inside, and she didn't really care. She suspected Tracey and Antonio would do a lot of bed-hopping because of the need for separate rooms—which Tracey hadn't seemed particularly happy about. It wasn't her business what they did behind everyone's backs, and she refused to dwell on it.

She wanted to see Isabel's portrait. In fact, the more time this weekend she spent brooding over Isabel, the less time she would be able to contemplate her sister's relationship with Antonio. He had said the painting was on the other side of the house.

Cass walked quietly down the corridor to the spacious landing on top of the stairs. She found the opposite hallway, which ran parallel to the one she had just been in. All of the doors lining the hall were closed; one side of the corridor had windows overlooking the balcony above the courtyard. As Cass walked down it, she was disappointed, because there were no paintings hanging anywhere at all. Had she misunderstood?

Someone stepped out of the shadows.

Cass cried out—but it was only Tracey. She had just stepped out of a room, and like Cass, she was startled. Then Tracey said, with some anger, "You frightened me! What are you doing prowling around up here?"

Cass's own heart beat too rapidly; she had practically jumped out of her skin. "You also gave me a fright," she said. "I'm exploring."

Tracey eyed her, coming closer, still in her miniskirt and tiny top but barefoot, her hair down. It was disheveled. "Outside of Antonio's bedroom?" she asked pointedly.

Cass stood utterly still. She realized then what Tracey had been up to with their host, but really didn't want it shoved in her face and down her throat. Being there with them was hard enough. "I was hoping to find Isabel's portrait."

"Right," Tracey said, reaching into the pocket of her skirt and withdrawing a cigarette pack and a lighter. "Right." She lit up.

Cass felt her frayed temper flare even as she tried to tell herself to walk away until she was well rested; no good could come of this conversation, and the weekend had only just begun. "At least you waited until your daughter was asleep," she heard herself say. And the moment she spoke, she regretted it.

Tracey stepped closer. "Don't judge me." And for one instant, the light in her blue eyes was utterly hateful.

Cass was so shocked by the hatred she saw that she stepped instinctively backward. And when she blinked, Tracey was standing there, looking annoyed and put off, but there was no hatred on her face, no vehemence in her eyes. Cass realized she was shaking. Had she just seen what she had thought she'd seen, or had she imagined it? "I'm not judging you," she said carefully. "I don't care what you do. As long as it doesn't impact on Alyssa."

"Of course. My daughter. My daughter and Saint Cassandra." Tracey crossed her arms tightly, still clenching the cigarette.

Cass stiffened. "Let's not fight. It's been a hellishly long day. We're both tired—"

"Crap!" Tracey said, tapping her foot. "What is wrong with wanting to make *love*? Especially when you're in *love*? I am sick to death of your holier-than-thou attitude! I just can't take it anymore!"

Cass recoiled. It was a moment before she could speak. "I don't want to fight, I didn't come here to fight—"

"No, you came here to drive us to the country."

Cass blinked. She fought her base instincts, and lost. "Actually, I came here to rescue you from the crisis of being stuck at the Ritz for the weekend."

Tracey smiled. "Saint Cassandra to the rescue. Always doing what is right."

"I'm hardly perfect—in any way," Cass said, trying to keep her tone calm. "But I hate to say this, I am not the one with the attitude. I am not the one holding a grudge. I came here hoping to put that horrible fight behind us. Why can't we do that?"

Tracey inhaled with anger on her cigarette. "Is that what you really want?"

"Of course," Cass said automatically, but her earlier thoughts echoed in her mind—she could fight her sister for Alyssa . . . Tracey did not deserve to be the mother of her own child.

And then there was Antonio. Why should Tracey have him, too?

Cass didn't want that last thought, didn't want to even admit to it, face it, or anything else, but it loomed large, uncontrollable in her mind. Her heart sank. She was unable to control her own mind, her own feelings, and it was frightening.

"I think you came here for another reason entirely," Tracey said flatly, exhaling a plume of smoke upward into the air.

Cass was still. "Really? Well, whatever you are thinking, it is wrong."

"Why were you really up here, then?" Tracey pressed. "And don't tell me after all of the driving we did today, you came upstairs to look at some moldy old painting! Could it be that you were in search of Antonio?"

Cass felt her heart lurching. "You're nuts," she finally said.

Tracey stepped closer, her eyes intent on Cass's face. "Your feelings are obvious. Every time you look at him, it's obvious. You are going to embarrass yourself, Cass." And it was a warning with too many layers to count.

Cass stared, dismayed and becoming angry. "I don't have feelings for him."

"You eat him up alive with your eyes. Every time he looks at you, you blush! Talk about being gaga over a guy!" Tracey realized her cigarette was about to burn her fingertips. She hesitated, glancing around, but there was no ashtray there in the middle of the hall. She carefully stubbed it out on the baseboard. Cass could only stare.

Her ears were ringing. Her face was burning. The truth hurt.

"Cass." Tracey straightened, her tone calmer. "Do you really think all of your babbling about that Isabel de Warenne will snare him?" She shook her head. "You might entertain him, but that's about it. He's the man I intend to marry and I love him. But you're my sister, and I care about you, too. And I don't want to see you hurt, or making a fool of yourself. I mean, your feelings are really obvious, and Antonio is hardly stupid."

Cass shifted, feeling as if she had just been blindsided. "Thanks for the advice, sis," she managed stiffly. "But I'm not interested in your boyfriend, not that way. I find him brilliant as a scholar, period. I know I'm not his type. Just like I know he's yours."

"I think I'll take that siesta now," Tracey said. Her look was meaningful. "I'm exhausted."

Cass folded her arms and stared. Thinking, *Okay, rub it in—you bitch.*

And then she recoiled, and although the physical act was to step back and away from her sister, her horror was directed at herself. She had felt such a surge of hostility and vehemence toward her own sister that it had almost been like hatred.

What was happening to her?

How could this be happening?

It was happening because Antonio de la Barca stood between them. Just as Catherine had warned.

"Coming?" Tracey asked, with a brief smile—as if their entire conversation had never occurred.

And suddenly Cass found herself walking down the corridor with her sister. She felt dazed, numb. And she couldn't help wondering, what if her aunt was right?

"You know, Cass, if you don't mind some more advice, I think you need to get laid." Tracey was cheerful.

Cass looked at her, even more dumbfounded. Had she just heard what she thought she'd heard? "What?"

"I don't know how anybody could live the way you do," Tracey said, very pleasantly. "You know, Spanish men are something. They really are. Why don't you have an affair while you're here? It would be good for you, I can guarantee it." She smiled.

"No, thanks," Cass managed, wondering if she had entered the Twilight Zone. Very determinedly she studied her feet as they moved one after the other. "Remember? I'm only here for the weekend." But she could not shake an image of her aunt now, pleading with her not to go to Castilla, and not to let Tracey and Alyssa go, either.

They paused in front of Tracey's bedroom door. "Cass, you're thirty-two going on ninety, destined for spinsterhood like Aunt Catherine. But it's not too late to change." Tracey touched her. "You're my sister. I want you to be happy. I really do."

Cass managed a brief, brittle smile. "I'll think about it," she lied.

"I'll see you at supper, then." Tracey hesitated, then hugged her, hard. Then she slipped into her room. Cass found herself staring at the closed door.

Thirty-two going on ninety. Destined for spinsterhood.

Making a fool of herself.

Entertaining Antonio . . . babbling on.

And for a moment, Cass just stood there grimly. This, she thought, would be *the* weekend to remember.

It was almost midnight. Alyssa was sleeping, and Tracey's door remained shut—although Cass felt quite certain that she was not inside. Cass was hesitant as she made her way downstairs, her slides clicking loudly on the stone floors. The night outside was thick, dark, and starless, without any breeze. She was tense. Far tenser than made any sense. She could not sleep.

Supper had been a miserable affair, with her refusing to look at their host—afraid she would blush if she did so even though by now she was feeling that she had been thoroughly manipulated by her sister. If so, it had worked. She was determined to stay as far away from Antonio as was possible. It had put a damper on the evening—and a damper on the entire weekend. Tracey, of course, had chattered away for most of the meal, in very high spirits apparently, and the two children had seemed to get along well. Antonio hadn't said much. He had appeared tired. Uncharitably, Cass could imagine why.

The house was so dark.

Cass shivered. There were wall sconces lining the corridor and the stairs, but their lights were small and flickering. And the house was so quiet. There was no sound of air conditioners or fans, no TV, no radio, and there weren't any exterior noises either—even at Belford House, one could hear the occasional car on the road, the barking dogs, the whickering of a horse or a cowbell. It was almost eerie.

At all costs, don't go to Castilla . . .

Oh, balderdash! Cass thought with exasperation. As much as it hurt to admit it, her aunt was irrational when it came to the subject of the de la Barcas. That made sense. Nothing else did.

Cass paused in the central hall by the entryway. She slowly looked around. And one by one, the hairs on her nape rose.

She glanced around again, but she was alone. Why was she so nervous? Everyone in the house was asleep. There was no reason to be nervous or uneasy; Cass had never been afraid of the dark before, and she wasn't afraid of the dark now. Except that she almost felt as if someone or something was lurking around the corner or in the shadows, about to jump out at her.

"Christ," she muttered irritably.

She thought about Alyssa, sleeping soundly upstairs. Once again she'd felt uneasy when leaving her there, even though she knew her anxiety was unfounded. It occurred to her that she could turn around and go back upstairs; she could pick up a book or go on-line and surf the Web. She'd brought her laptop with her; she never traveled without it.

Finally Cass continued down the next hallway. She had one weekend in Castilla in which to explore. She was a history nut to begin with, but her curiosity about the history of her family and its connection to the de la Barcas had been thoroughly aroused in the past few days. The mystery of Isabel de Warenne remained in the forefront of her mind. And since the weekend wasn't turning out the way she had expected— not that she'd had very much time to ponder it—she might as well satisfy her own burning curiosity rather than dwell on Tracey's torrid love affair or Catherine's involvement in Eduardo's death. Or the fact that Antonio had actually taken the time and made the effort to go over police files that were thirty years old.

Cass shivered again, this time her heart sinking with sickening intensity. Her game plan was to focus on the past—the far past, as in the sixteenth century—and avoid any and all references to her aunt and Antonio's father if he ever broached the topic again.

The first step was to view Isabel's portrait. Maybe she had misunderstood Antonio. Maybe the portrait was in the opposite corridor downstairs, not upstairs. Cass suddenly faltered.

The last door in this wing of the house was open, and the room beyond was well lit. It was a library—bookshelves lined the one wall Cass could glimpse—and Antonio was bent over a huge desk. She stared at him for one instant, thought, *Shit*, and turned abruptly around.

But not before he glanced up, seeing her.

Cass hesitated, about to flee, and he said, "Cassandra?"

Cass swore to herself again. He was now the last person she wished to see—right? Slowly she turned around.

He was standing.

Cass heard her heart drumming. She hesitated, and said, "Hi."

He smiled, moving to the doorway. "I thought everyone was asleep."

Somehow, Cass drifted forward. "So did I." She couldn't help wondering what he was working on.

He just stared.

Cass actually felt herself begin to blush. Christ—her sister had been right!

She looked away, anywhere but at him, and took a quick inventory of the room. Bookcases lined two walls, crammed to overflowing not just with books, but with folders and papers. Another wall held a large fireplace with a black marble mantel; his desk was freestanding. The walls were painted moss green, the ceiling, boasting circular star-patterned plaster in its center and panels with various motifs, pink and gold. Most of the furniture was shabby and tired, and two sets of wide doors opened onto the grounds in front of the house.

He had been working. The desk was covered with notes, open books, and more notes. There was a glass of brandy on it, as well.

"I hope I'm not interrupting."

"Of course not." He removed his tortoiseshell eyeglasses. "Would you care for a drink?" he asked.

Cass almost gaped. "I . . . actually, I was hoping for a glimpse of Isabel's portrait."

His eyes brightened. "How remiss of me. I offered you a viewing at your home in Sussex, but in the confusion of your arrival today, I completely forgot about it. I apologize."

Cass stared. "Antonio, I'm the one who is sorry." The words spilled forth unbidden. "I had no idea we were arriving without an invitation."

"I am aware that you were not involved in your sister's scheme," he said simply, a slight, wry smile on his mouth.

He had made that so easy. Cass stared. He was wearing a small but substantially wrought gold cross on a chain on his chest, and it had caught her attention.

"But now that you are here, I truly wish for you to enjoy your stay in Castilla," he said.

Cass met his hazel eyes, which seemed black in the night. "I do not think I have ever met anyone as polite as you. You should toss us all out on our backsides."

He laughed, the sound warm and rich, washing over Cass like melted chocolate. "Cassandra. I never say what I do not mean."

Cass looked away. His eyes were just too intense. "What are you working on?"

"I am trying to compile the history of my family—as my father attempted to do."

Cass looked up slowly.

He turned casually away, fingering the papers on his desk. "It will take me months to file all of his notes and records." He turned. "Shall we?"

"Shall we?" she echoed.

"Her portrait is upstairs." And with his eyes lighting up, he went to his desk and picked up what Cass saw was a photograph of the ruby necklace. "Come." He smiled, inclining his head.

Cass preceded him out of the library and into the corridor. She glanced at his profile as she fell into step beside him. "The portrait. The portrait of Isabel de Warenne," she asked eagerly. "Do the necklaces match?"

His smile was brief, his gaze as brief but penetrating. "You will judge for yourself."

"I can't wait," Cass said, meaning it.

They had reached the landing on the second floor of the house. It was the same hall where she and Tracey had fought just a few hours earlier. She followed him halfway down the corridor, then paused behind him as he pushed open a door. And Cass followed him into a night-darkened room.

He hit the wall switch, but nothing happened.

Cass didn't move—it was almost impossible to see—as he groped his way around what had to be a bed. She heard another switch clicking, but no light came on.

"I'll have to get a bulb," he said, moving past her in the dark. "I'll be right back."

Cass's eyes widened—she almost told him to wait, she'd go with him—but he was gone.

Her tension mounted dramatically.

Which was absurd—she was only in a pitch black room. Cass was about to retreat to the hall outside, when her every instinct went into overdrive.

She paused. Straining to hear; straining to see.

Which made absolutely no sense, for there was nothing to see, and certainly nothing to hear, unless it was a mouse. Right? There was no reason for her to feel alerted or alarmed.

But she was alarmed, and nervous as all hell, and the room was far cooler than she had realized—or had the temperature just dropped? Cass hugged herself. Her eyes began to adjust to the darkness, while unease continued to creep along her spine. The bed, another canopied affair, began to emerge from the shadows. The room felt large; she felt isolated and alone. Cass suddenly became aware of something else—she sniffed the air. A very faint floral scent was present.

She realized she did not like this room, even though she hadn't seen it. She did not like it at all. Cass was about to walk into the hall; instead, she did not move at all.

Something was *very* wrong, but what?

The room was freezing cold, but the air was thick and stuffy. So what? Actually, the atmosphere was more than thick, it was heavy, but then, the Castilian night had felt heavy and oppressive all evening. Her imagination was running away with her. That had to be it—nothing was different or wrong. Just like nothing was wrong with her own bedroom upstairs.

On the other hand, maybe something was wrong with this entire damned house.

She wanted to walk out, but her feet seemed to be cement blocks. And suddenly the floral scent was there, wafting around her, thick and sickeningly sweet. And so terribly overpowering.

Suddenly panicked, Cass stepped out of the room. But alone in the long hallway, with the wall sconces casting flickering lights and dancing shadows, she did not feel relieved or relaxed. In fact, her shoulders were as stiff as a board. Tension pounded along her neck and invaded her shoulders. She could hardly move them, she could hardly breathe.

"You coward," she tried to whisper, but she couldn't seem to get enough air and her words were a hoarse croak.

Where the hell had that perfume come from?

Vents, was her first thought. But her room, and Tracy's, were on the other side of the house, the courtyard between them. They were the only women in the house. And neither one of them wore sweet perfume.

Suddenly Antonio was approaching, lightbulb in hand. "Actually," he said, when he came closer, "I put bulbs in the other day. They must have been old or defective." His gaze became searching. "Are you all right?"

Cass wet her lips. "I'm behaving like a wimp. That room made me nervous," she admitted somewhat reluctantly.

For one moment he regarded her, and then he said, "It's not a pleasant room."

Cass gaped as he walked back inside. Then she rushed after him. What did that mean?

An instant later, one beside lamp came on.

Cass glanced quickly around, expecting all of her silly unease to vanish. It did not. In fact, it heightened. And she really saw nothing of the room, not the huge bed, not the Oriental rugs, the chairs and settee, the small writing desk. Her gaze slammed to a halt on the portrait hanging over the fireplace.

"Isabel de la Barca," Antonio said, his tone hushed.

Cass didn't move.

She stared.

She stared at Isabel de Warenne.

The woman in the portrait, a young woman with alabaster skin and red-gold hair peeking out from beneath her headdress, stared right back at her.

"Oh, God," Cass breathed, trembling and forgetting all of her fears.

"My sentiments exactly," Antonio murmured from the other side of the room.

It was one of the most stunning works of art Cass had ever seen. Whoever the artist was, he had captured this woman so strikingly that it was as if she were there on the canvas, vital and alive, real flesh and blood. And then Cass realized that the striking blue eyes holding her own were filled with sadness.

"She's incredibly unhappy," Cass breathed in a whisper.

Antonio spoke in a whisper, too. "There is also an accusation in her eyes."

Cass finally stepped closer. Isabel had been beautiful in a very classic way. Her face was oval, her cheekbones high, her mouth full. And her dress was exquisite—red velvet, Cass thought, with a high, white neck ruff, puffed, slashed sleeves, a narrow, cinched-in waist. Her gaze shot to the necklace of rubies hanging around her throat. Dark red on pale white.

It was the same.

It had to be.

"Yes," Antonio said softly, finally coming to stand beside her. He began to hand her the photograph, but Cass waved it away.

"It was hers," Cass said excitedly, unable to tear her gaze from the portrait.

"She wore it for this portrait, at least," Antonio murmured softly. "I used a magnifying glass to compare the photo and the painting."

Cass found herself gazing into those haunting blue eyes again. "What do you know about her?"

"I have no dates on her. What I do know is this: Alvarado married his second wife, Elena, in 1562, and they had three sons."

Cass was still mesmerized, and now she realized she was perspiring ever so slightly. "If my aunt is right, if she was burned at the stake in 1555, there is a record somewhere. More importantly, I want to find a de Warenne family tree for the sixteenth century. As the earl of Sussex's daughter, she would have to be included in it." The woman in the portrait could not be much older than twenty—maybe she was only seventeen or eighteen. Then Cass realized that they were still whispering. "Why are we whispering?"

He smiled briefly but did not laugh. "I do not know. Awe, perhaps. This portrait is dated. Again, the magnifying glass. The artist is Dutch, I think, someone I have never heard of, Vandeerleck, and just below his name is the year 1554." He looked at her.

A whole bunch of information was clicking inside of Cass's mind at once. She seized his arm, vaguely realizing that she had never touched him before. "If she died in 1555, that was one year more or less, after this portrait was finished. My God. Look at how young she is!"

"I have had those sentiments exactly," he said.

"We must find a genealogy," Cass said.

"There are other ways. If she was accused of heresy, there would have been charges and a trial."

"And records," Cass said grimly, hoping that this young woman had not suffered such a tragic fate.

"Elena was a great heiress. Wealthy as well as titled. I am descended from her and Alvarado, by the way."

Cass knew he was about to make a point.

"It's possible Isabel was disposed of in another way." He shrugged.

"What do you mean, disposed of? Do you mean, locked away? Like, shoved off into a convent somewhere, or the tower of an old, outlying estate, and left there to wither away and die?"

"Alvarado wouldn't have been the first nobleman to get rid of an unwanted wife that way," Antonio said calmly, his gaze holding hers.

Cass stared, then turned to look back at Isabel. "If she knew he was planning such a fate, no wonder she is so anguished, and you're right, there is an accusation in her eyes." And she thought about Alvarado's portrait, hanging in her own bedroom. Had two people ever been more mismatched? Spanish and British, Catholic and Protestant, middle-aged and young. Cass's compassion for her ancestor knew no bounds.

Cass suddenly hugged herself; she had to. She wasn't feeling very optimistic about Isabel's fate, whatever it might have been. "Sussex was a Protestant before he joined the public uprising which helped put Mary Tudor on the throne. But many nobles did just as he did, throwing their lot in with her when it became apparent she would actually succeed Edward, and they outwardly conformed to the Catholic religion. But only a dozen or so were actually tried for heresy and condemned to the stake."

He smiled at her. "You do know your history."

Cass flushed with pleasure. "Obviously you do too."

They smiled, then they both turned simultaneously to stare at Isabel's portrait in silence. Suddenly the room was so quiet Cass could hear Antonio's slow, even breathing, and her own, which was more labored than his. She shivered again, but no longer because it was cold. She almost wanted to glance behind her, to make sure they were alone. And suddenly she was certain that Tracey was standing there in the doorway, spying on them. Cass whirled; she was wrong. The threshold was empty.

Cass turned back to the portrait. There had been tragedy in Isabel's life, she decided; it was written right there in her eyes for anyone to see. "Was this her room?" she asked.

"I don't know. But I would guess so. The master bedroom is next door."

His room—the room Tracey had come out of earlier, barefoot and disheveled. Cass realized she was still hugging herself, and she released her arms. "Maybe," she said slowly, "that's why this room feels so . . . strange. So dark and unpleasant. So . . . intense. Because she lived here, maybe even died here, and she was so unhappy here."

He did not laugh at her. "The room is strange, as you have said. I have felt disturbed every time I come inside here." He paused, then said, "Eduardo won't come in." Their gazes met.

Cass could not look away, and even while she was very aware of being alone with him there in the disturbing bedroom, in the thick of the night, she grew very uneasy. She couldn't help glancing all around, but of course, the room was only that, an old room with old, tired furnishings. Something was nagging at her, though, and she couldn't pinpoint what it was. It was something else that her aunt had said. "Do you smell that? Is it violets?"

"Yes." His gaze was piercing. "Alfonso probably used an air freshener this afternoon when he was informed that you had arrived."

Oddly, Cass was very relieved. She laughed. "God, for a moment I was stupidly thinking it was the dead woman's perfume." And the moment she had spoken, she ceased laughing, stunned, because she hadn't been thinking that—where the hell had the words come from?

Antonio didn't quite smile at her. "We do not have quite the same fondness here for ghosts which you British do."

Cass wished he had smiled. As lightly as possible, suddenly determined to leave the room, and quickly, she shrugged, saying, "You know us Brits. A ghost in every manor, two in every castle." Determined to leave, she found herself ensnared by Isabel's blue eyes again, and suddenly she frowned.

Cass walked a few feet to the right, turned and faced the portrait. Isabel stared directly at her.

Unable to breathe, Cass walked to the left to the very far side of the room, then turned. Again she was pinned by Isabel's haunting stare. "Her eyes," she cried, low. "Good God, no matter where you are in the room, her eyes follow you."

"I noticed that," Antonio said quietly. "This artist was brilliant, I would say. Wouldn't you?"

Cass didn't know whether she was amazed or shaken, but she quickly returned to stand beside Antonio. She was about to ask him if he was ready to go, when the room was suddenly cast in blackness.

Her heart rate accelerated wildly.

He touched her hand. "It's either a faulty bulb or faulty wiring. No one's lived here for thirty-four years, Cassandra." His tone was reassuring, as if he guessed her thoughts.

"Of course," Cass said. But she didn't like the sensation she was finally identifying, a sensation that had been nagging at her ever since they had entered the room. It was the sensation of being watched. The sensation of not being alone.

Which was truly absurd.

Because they were alone; she had checked out the room a dozen times in the last five minutes.

He took her arm and they crossed the room. Later Cass realized it was a reflexive gesture on his part, but as they stepped through the door, he hit the light switch, as one would do to automatically turn off the lights when leaving.

The bedside lamp came on.

Cass faltered, almost falling into Antonio's arms. He righted her, and for one moment she looked up into his face, feeling not just surprise, but shock—and a frisson of fear.

He must have seen and understood the look on her face, because he steadied her and said, "If I am to stay all summer, I will have to have an electrician to the house. The wiring is clearly faulty."

The wiring, of course. He turned off the lights and they stepped into the hall. Cass watched him firmly close the door. She knew she should not be shaken like this. But the house wasn't just huge, it was very old, and it hadn't been lived in for years. "You know," she said slowly, her heart drumming in her chest, aware that she should not bring up her aunt, but unable to stop herself, "my aunt begged me not to come here."

He faced her, his gaze searching. "Indeed."

Cass was hugging herself. "She isn't thinking clearly these past few days. She fell ill just before I left and was briefly hospitalized."

"I'm sorry. I am glad that she is recovering. What did she say?" he asked.

Cass couldn't smile when she wanted to be light, joking. "She said . . ." She hesitated. "She thinks our families share some kind of terrible destiny. That any involvement between your family and mine leads only to tragedy." And finally she laughed, but the sound was hoarse and distorted.

She expected him to scoff at her. He did no such thing. He stared.

Cass's smile faded. "My aunt fell ill. And Tracey . . ." She took a breath. "We have been fighting terribly, but it's not because a de la Barca is in our midst."

He said, "That is interesting."

"It is?"

"My mother has some odd notions, too. Not that she will talk about them."

Cass became more uneasy. "What kind of odd notions?"

His gaze held hers. "She thinks Isabel is here."

Their eyes met.

"My mother will swear to it on the Bible, and she is devout."

Cass felt her mouth form a humorless smile. "Well, I suppose it's possible. I believe in that kind of stuff." She added, "Sort of." Then, "There's probably a slew of your dead ancestors lingering around this place. Maybe that's why this house feels so dark and unhappy and strange." She couldn't help glancing up and down the corridor—as if expecting to see a ghost. Fortunately, she did not.

And then it hit Cass, hard, what her aunt had said just before she had been hospitalized. She'd said, "She's come back." And she had been speaking about Isabel.

Cass felt a terribly frigid sensation cross over her, like a veil of ice-cold air.

"I doubt my mother is being accurate." Antonio cut into her thoughts. "She is an old woman," he said, staring. "Like your *aunt*."

Their gazes collided. Cass said quickly, "Maybe we should call that electrician sooner rather than later?" Because he had inflected on the word "aunt."

He smiled, and it was grim. "My mother also hates your aunt. Were you aware of that?"

Cass's knees buckled. She blinked at him and could not think of a single thing to say. But the blow was coming and she knew it.

"In fact, she hates your entire family," he said. *"With a vengeance."*

EIGHT

CASA DE SUEÑOS—DAY TWO

"What a glorious day," Cass cried as she climbed out of the rental car with the two children, having just parked in front of the ruins of the castle. "Do you need help, Eduardo?" she asked, as if it were the most natural question in the world. But of course, watching him adjust his crutches and maneuver his legs from the car to the ground concerned her. Her impulse was to rush over and help.

"*No, señora, gracias,*" he said gravely, pushing himself up on the crutches. Alyssa was waiting patiently for him, and she swung his door shut when he had climbed out.

Cass opened the hatchback and took out two blankets and their picnic basket. She slammed it closed, unsmiling. She'd hardly slept a wink all night. Was Antonio playing cat and mouse with her?

Cass didn't want to think about the last few words they had exchanged. Such thoughts only ruined the beautiful day. In fact, in the light of such a day, most of her fears of the night before seemed ludicrous.

"This castle really belonged to your family?" Alyssa was asking, her tone hushed with awe.

Eduardo smiled with pride. "*Sí.* For hundreds of years. It was used to fight the Arabic people."

"Arabs were in Spain?" Alyssa asked, puzzled.

As Eduardo gave her a rudimentary explanation, Cass set down the picnic items, taking her camera out of her shoulder bag. She wandered away from the car, gazing up at the first tower, and the incomplete wall that ran from it to the second tower, refusing to think about her next encounter with Antonio de la Barca. It was a perfect day for a picnic, a perfect day for the children to enjoy themselves—a perfect day for her to enjoy herself.

There wasn't a single cloud in the extremely blue sky. Although it was hot out, a dry breeze caressed Cass's skin. The road she had arrived on was partially in view, but it was unpaved, not a single car was on it, and it was easy to ignore. And just behind the castle was a huge stand of fir trees, a startling act of nature. Cass was just beginning to realize that she liked Castilla. There was something compelling about the desolation, the starkness, something compelling and grand. It was too bad she was there under such strange and stressful circumstances. One day, she promised herself, she would return for a real holiday.

Cass began taking pictures.

"Aunt Cass? Can we go inside the castle?" Alyssa called.

"Wait for me," Cass instructed, slinging her camera over her shoulder.

"I am fine, señora," Eduardo said seriously.

Cass had promised Antonio she'd be very careful when they had been leaving. But Eduardo's eyes were so earnest and hopeful, and as he moved as agilely as a squirrel on his crutches, in spite of his braces, she realized that he longed to play as another child might. She hadn't asked, but she was fairly certain that he had suffered from polio as a young child. It was a terrible shame.

"All right," Cass decided impulsively. She watched the two children cross a plank set over the ditch that surrounded the ruins. And it was just that, a ditch, for it was only five or six feet deep and could not be considered a moat by any stretch of the imagination. Cass thought that natural erosion had created it.

She couldn't help wondering if Isabel had ever bothered to visit these ruins.

Isabel. Antonio's mother believed that she was haunting Casa de Sueños. Or did she believe that Isabel was haunting the de la Barca family? Her aunt had made a similar statement. *She's come back.* Of course, her aunt had been suffering from a very high fever when she had uttered those words. Still, it was very odd that she should be writing about Isabel de Warenne in her journal.

Cass had done some math. Antonio had been four years old when his father died—he was now thirty-eight. Eduardo had died in 1966.

And Catherine's last journal entry had been July of 1966.

Cass didn't particularly like the direction in which all the bits and pieces of information were pointing. She would be very distressed should she learn that Eduardo had died that July. And she didn't know whether to be glad or dismayed that she had not read her aunt's journal. In truth, she was afraid of what it might contain.

But even if the entries were incriminating of her aunt, one could still assert that her aunt was so traumatized by Eduardo's death even then, thirty-four years ago, that her ramblings were irrelevant.

Now, standing before the fourteenth-century ruins, Cass couldn't help wondering if Antonio's home did harbor some of his ancestors. Haunted houses were a fact of life in England, and Cass had certainly visited her share. It would explain why the house was so unfriendly and so daunting, so cold and so gloomy. Besides, the villa was so old. How could it not house an entity or two?

The house was uncomfortable, but that was as far as it went. All of her aunt's dire warnings regarding the de la Barcas and Castilla were insensible ramblings. Period.

The children had paused in the arched entryway on one side of the tower. Cass watched them suddenly disappear behind the rotting stone wall, before her very eyes.

Suddenly Cass was seized with uncertainty and fear.

This was not, she decided, a good idea. If anything happened to Eduardo, Antonio would never forgive her—and she would never forgive herself. Every instinct she had was now screaming at her, *Stupid, stupid, stupid!* And her fears had nothing to do with lingering spirits. She rushed to the picnic basket and blankets, then hurried after the children. It would be so easy for Eduardo to trip and hurt himself.

The moment Cass crossed the dry moat and entered the ruins, she saw them standing in the center of what had once been the great hall. Relief made her pause and sigh. From now on, she would keep them in sight.

Cass glanced curiously around. Pieces of stone were visible here and there on the ground, poking up from the dirt—sections of floor and one small mound of what had been either a wall or a column. Then she realized that Alyssa and Eduardo were not moving.

"Kids? Everything okay?" They were staring through a gap in the far wall, their backs to Cass. She was mildly alarmed.

In unison they faced her, their small faces pinched and white.

Her alarm escalated. "What is it?" Cass cried, rushing to them.

"Aunt Cass, someone's out there," Alyssa whispered.

Cass faltered, instinctively drawing both children to her, turning to look through the gap in the wall. What she saw was the stand of firs, but her mind was racing. There was no other car in sight. The closest village was twenty minutes away, by car. Who could be out there, and why? And how had he, or she, gotten there? She did not like being alone with the two children if a stranger was lurking about.

She did not like it one single bit.

"I don't see anyone," she said tersely. "Are you sure you saw someone?"

They both nodded. "A person went into those trees very quickly," Eduardo said. "As if she did not want us to see her."

"I thought it was a man," Alyssa said. "A short, fat man."

"My eyes are very good," Eduardo said simply.

Cass's pulse raced. She stared at the stand of trees but saw no movement, and no sign of any human being. "Guys, is it possible you imagined someone out there? It wouldn't make very much sense for someone to be all the way out here without a car."

The two children looked at one another. "The villagers often use bicycles," Eduardo said. "Or they walk."

Cass tried to recover her calm. "Well, whoever it was is long gone now. Shall we explore? Or shall we eat first and explore later?" She smiled at the two earnest faces turned up toward her, but she was worried and trying to hide it. What if they had seen someone lurking about?

"Eat," Alyssa said with a shy smile at Eduardo.

"Eat," Eduardo said, smiling at Cass.

Cass did a double take. If she did not miss her guess, her niece had a crush on Antonio's son! It was sweet, and she smiled as she spread out the blankets. Then her pleasure vanished. She couldn't help glancing back toward the stand of firs as everyone sat down. But there was no movement, none at all.

Relax, she ordered herself. *Relax and enjoy the peace and solitude, because when you go back to the house, it won't be half as peaceful.* And she wasn't thinking about the weirdness of the night before, or Isabel or any other de la Barca ancestors, but her sister and their host.

Cass helped the children, handing them plates, followed by chunks of fresh bread, smoked pork, cold hams, sausages, and a variety of delicious cheeses.

"Do you like Pokémon?" Eduardo asked Alyssa.

Alyssa's eyes went wide. "I love Pokémon. I have ninety-three cards. I got Drowzee the other day."

"I have two hundred and two cards," Eduardo said. "But I am older than you."

Alyssa's eyes were shining.

Cass tuned out, her gaze immediately going to the gap in the wall, which she was purposefully facing. No one was out there. The children hadn't seen what they'd thought they'd seen. So why were the hairs on her nape crawling? Why couldn't she relax? Abruptly she stood up.

A hawk wheeled overhead. She could not admire it in its flight.

Cass unslung her camera. "I'm going to take some shots of this castle," she said, "and eat later."

The children were now immersed in a discussion of the traits of Charmander and Gengar. Cass angled her camera, taking a variety of shots of the walls, the towers, the crenellated tops of the towers, the arch. She squatted, hoping to get in a long shot of the wall and the second tower. She climbed up a set of steps and took shots of the views from the wall where she now stood. Finally she was satisfied.

Cass hopped off of the wall, returning to the children, who had finished their lunch.

"Now can we explore, señora?" Eduardo asked hopefully.

"Sure," Cass replied. It was hard to smile back. And she had to glance over her shoulder one more time, but of course, no one else was present among the ruins that day.

Antonio was apparently waiting for them when they returned. His gaze went right to his son. Cass saw relief fill his eyes. And he smiled at them all. "How was your picnic?" he asked.

"Muy bueno," Eduardo said with an answering smile.

"The children had a great time," Cass told him.

His gaze settled on her face. "And you? Did you enjoy yourself?"

Cass hesitated. Then, "I had a great time, too." She looked away, then back. "I got some wonderful shots of the ruins."

He stared, and Cass had an inkling that he knew she was holding something back.

Eduardo said, "We saw someone in the trees, Papá."

Antonio looked at his son. "At the ruins?" He was incredulous.

Cass interrupted. "The children think they saw something," she said. "But no one was out there, it was their imagination."

He nodded. "Time for a siesta," he told his son. Then he glanced at Cass. "Your aunt called." His gaze narrowed. "She sounded distressed."

Cass nodded, immediately grim, avoiding his gaze. It was suspicious—Cass was certain. Catherine's unease would only heighten her own tension. Still, she had to return the call and reassure her that all was well. "I'll call her later. Alyssa, it's siesta time for you, too."

But Alyssa was already yawning, a victim of the heat and jet lag. "That's fine, Aunt Cass."

"Cassandra."

Cass paused in midstride. She was never going to get used to the way he spoke her full name with his melodic voice and sensual accent. "Yes?"

"While the children nap, perhaps you might join me in a little investigation?" His gaze searched hers.

Her pulse raced. "What kind of investigation?"

"I want to check the family crypt. The lady in question must be buried there, and we can at least learn her dates."

"I'd love to go," Cass said so quickly that he laughed.

"I'll meet you here in half an hour," he said. "If that is fine with you."

She needed a shower; she would have to rush. "It's more than fine," she said. Then, "Where's Tracey?"

Before Antonio could speak, Tracey stepped into the hall from the corridor that led to their rooms. "Right here," she said, her look as hard as steel and as cold as ice, and directed at Cass.

Cass was taken aback. "We had a great picnic," she said.

Tracey's smile was brittle. "I'd like to go to the crypt, too. Count me in."

And in that split second Cass knew she did not mistake the sheer hatred she witnessed in her sister's eyes. But then the instant was gone. Tracey had turned her attention to Antonio.

Cass could not breathe.

Oh, God.

Tracey saw her as a threat.

But then, shouldn't she? Not because Cass could actually steal Antonio away, but because she'd had those terrible thoughts about doing so.

"Half an hour," Antonio was saying. "I suggest you wear closed shoes."

"No problem," Tracey said, strolling over to him and wrapping one arm around him. She was wearing short shorts, studded thongs, and a tiny T-shirt. Most men would be going bananas around her. For the first time, Cass realized that Antonio was not returning her affection; instead, he stepped aside.

Cass had no idea what that gesture meant. She fled.

"This was once a thriving monastery," Antonio said. "It was finally abandoned about sixty years ago, not due to lack of religious devotion, which my country has in excess, but for economic factors." He parked in what had one been the car park of the monastery, glancing at Cass in his rearview mirror.

"How interesting," Tracey said brightly—too much so. Cass knew she was bored and pretending interest in their expedition.

"I thought you didn't know very much about this area," Cass said as they all stepped out of the Jeep. A few old stone buildings faced them, the largest a rectangular one, windowless. There was a well to her right, and some abandoned farming equipment.

"I've been reading my father's files and research material since I arrived at the house earlier in the week," Antonio told her. "He was a brilliant man, but like most brilliant men, he was very disorganized. I wish he'd filed everything methodically."

"That would make our search so much easier," Cass agreed.

"What search?" Tracey demanded as they walked past the wall of the long, rectangular stone building with its sloping roof. Gravel crunched underfoot.

Cass wished she'd phrased her words differently.

"Since when are the two of you searching *together*?" Tracey asked again.

A cemetery was ahead, numerous weather-stained marble and granite headstones rising up out of the grassy earth, a mausoleum with a temple pediment in their midst. Cass was aware of her pulse beating somewhat erratically. Their mission had seemed intriguing when they'd discussed it in theory—suddenly Cass realized what they were about to do. *Good God,* she couldn't help thinking. Were they really going to go inside a crypt?

Antonio said, calmly, "I have asked your sister to help me research. After all, she shares my love of the past."

Tracey looked from him to Cass with wide-eyed disbelief.

Cass sighed inwardly, not in the mood for further conflict with her sister. "It's just research," she muttered, irritated. She eyed Tracey. "And only for the weekend. Remember, I'm going home on Monday."

Tracey did not visibly relax.

"You're welcome to stay," Antonio said.

Cass turned to look at him, surprised.

"I could use your help," he said.

"She's leaving," Tracey said firmly. She appeared determined, and confused. The look of confusion in her eyes made her seem young and vulnerable. "She's made her plans." She looked back and forth between them again.

They entered the overgrown cemetery in silence. A few misshapen trees guarded the perimeter of the plot, and the grass brushed up against Cass's knees. It was very still around them, still and silent. She wished a bird would sing, at least. "Who's buried here?" she asked, her voice sounding loud and abrasive to her own ears.

"Noblemen. Monks. Lesser family members." His gaze found and held hers.

Cass found it difficult to look away. She thought he could sense her slight unease. When he smiled at her, she turned to quickly study one magnificent marble stone, years of dust and grime marring what otherwise would be a smooth white surface. Seventeenth-century dates were etched on the stone, with an inscription she could not read. "A de la Barca," she murmured.

"This is madness," Tracey said, hugging herself. "Wandering around a damned cemetery."

Antonio did not reply, leading them through the graves, he and Cass pausing to read the dates and inscriptions on the stones they passed. They finally paused outside of the mausoleum, a building that now seemed imposing. Four thick columns supported the pediment, a series of stone steps led up to the front door—and a huge padlock was on the lock.

"It's locked," Cass cried—hearing warring notes of relief and disappointment in her tone.

Antonio grimaced. "I should have guessed. Of course the crypt would be locked, in order to discourage vandals." He frowned.

"I have a great idea," Tracey said, tugging on his arm. "Let's drive into Pedraza for a cool drink and some tapas."

No one answered her.

Cass was torn. What if the answer they were looking for was inside that mausoleum? And she didn't want Antonio to think her a coward. She inhaled. "Maybe we can jimmy the lock," she said, and with determination, she walked up the dirty marble steps.

"My thoughts exactly." Antonio was behind her. His breath feathered her ear. This was not, Cass knew, a good time to start noticing small details like that.

Cass grabbed the padlock and pulled as hard as she could. It broke so easily that she went flying backward, landing on one of the lower steps and tumbling back to the ground below.

"Are you all right?" Antonio rushed down the steps, kneeling beside her, his large hands closing over her shoulders, which suddenly seemed ridiculously small.

Cass looked into his eyes, saw the concern there, realized how she must appear, and started to laugh. "Eureka," she said.

He laughed, too, shaking his head. Then he held out his hand. Cass took it, and he helped her to her feet.

Then she dropped his hand and turned to face Tracey. Two bright spots colored her cheeks. The sisters locked gazes. Cass meant to soothe her as Antonio moved away, but she said, "I can't help it if we both love the past."

Tracy's jaw tightened. "You sure can't."

Cass wished she'd said anything else. Why had she thrown fuel on the fire?

"Let's go inside," Antonio suggested as if he had not noticed the growing tension between them.

They entered the mausoleum, which was cast in pitch black darkness. Antonio turned on the flashlight he was carrying, but the small beam did not illuminate anything other than a very small circumference of perhaps a foot or two. Cass began to shiver. It was not just dark inside, it was damp and cold, and very, very musty.

"No one's been down here for years," Cass muttered, espying a pair of tombs on her right. "I hope this is not considered a violation of anyone's rights."

"We are fine," Antonio said, excitement in his voice.

"You are both insane. Who would want to go down here with a bunch of dead people?" Tracey cried nervously.

"Trace, everyone down here is dead and buried." Cass smiled reassuringly, even though her sister could not possibly see her face clearly. And now was not the time to think about the strange sensations she'd had last night, or about the house being haunted—if Antonio's mother was right—or to wonder whether Isabel was the one lingering about. Tracey was right. They were nuts.

"There's no such thing as ghosts," Tracey muttered, clearly hoping to believe her own words.

"Ssh," Antonio said, wandering past the first two tombs. They were magnificent: stone effigies of the dead sculpted atop the stone crypts.

Cass stared, shivering. And then the historian in her got the best of her. She had research to do, a tomb to find. Cass had a very small penlight in her purse, which she took out. She followed Antonio past more tombs, eyeing the engraved dates as she went. "This is fascinating, if a wee bit nerve-wracking," she finally said to Antonio's back.

He was far ahead of her, and she and Tracey hurried to keep up. "This section is filled with seventeenth-century tombs," he said eagerly.

Cass came up behind him. She couldn't help but be excited herself. And it wasn't as bad as she had thought, being down there in the crypt. Not once she started to get used to it. "If she was married in 1554, and she was twenty, max—and my bet is she was younger—and she was not burned at the stake, if she lived until fifty or so, she died at the turn of the century." Oddly, she did not want to speak Isabel's name.

"I have already thought about that. If she did die before Alvarado's marriage to Elena—" He stopped. "*Dios mío.* Here they are."

Cass almost slammed into his back; she found herself gripping his waist from behind, peering around his broad shoulder—which she was not even eye level with. "Who? Alvarado and . . . ?" She trailed off.

"Alvarado and Elena," he breathed.

Tracey came to stand beside them, saying nothing.

Cass felt an absurd disappointment; she had thought it was Alvarado and Isabel he was referring to. Antonio flashed his light over both tombs, and Cass instantly saw that the sculpted effigy of Alvarado was truly a likeness of him. Although forbidding in appearance, he had been an attractive man. He had been born in 1528, he had died in 1575. Elena had been much younger than he, Cass saw, and she had died earlier; her dates were 1544–1571.

Cass trembled. "She was a child bride. Didn't you say they married in 1560?"

"In 1562." He shone the light around. "She must be here. But where?"

Cass followed the light, reading names and dates. "Maybe she outlived them both. Maybe you were right. Maybe he sent her off to a convent somewhere, or another estate, and she died and was buried there."

"Or maybe she was burned at the stake and no one cared to gather her ashes and bury her properly," was Antonio's disturbing response.

"I hope not," Cass muttered. And her own tiny penlight went out.

Cass tried to snap it back on, but it would not work. "Hell," she said. "So much for freebies."

"Hello? Who cares about that woman? I think we should go. I don't like it down here," Tracey said, pressing up against Cass. Cass could feel her sister trembling, but then, in her tiny shorts and T-shirt, she was pretty bare.

"I hate to say this, I wouldn't mind leaving myself," Cass said. "Antonio, you're in the mid fifteenth century. She's not here."

"You're right. She isn't here." His tone was heavy with disappointment.

"It's okay. We'll find her. We need to make a dent in all of your dad's paperwork," Cass said reassuringly. Then she thought of her use of the word "we."

"You're right. There's so much to do." He turned and his eyes held hers. "I really appreciate your help, Cassandra."

Cass found herself staring, not seeing him clearly, and unable to smile. "It's a pleasure, actually." The words came out of their own accord. They were, barring the unusual circumstances, the truth.

Then, "Shall we go?" Antonio abruptly removed the light from the last tomb.

"You bet," Cass said.

Antonio met her eyes, and this time their gazes held.

And Cass finally had to face the fact that when he looked at her, her heart raced, her knees went weak, and her insides turned to jelly. *Goddamn it.*

"Did you know that my aunt and your father were lovers?" Tracey said loudly.

Cass whirled. Aware of Antonio stiffening, his head jerking around. Her sister's smile was nasty.

And Cass knew she hadn't misheard—but how the hell did Tracey know?

Tracey folded her arms and faced them both. Her expression was ugly. "I overheard Aunt Catherine telling *you* all about it, Cass." She smiled at Cass. The smile was cold, menacing. "What an interesting, no, *fascinating* conversation the two of you had."

Cass's heart had briefly stopped. Sweat trickled down her temples. "Trace, please, don't." How much had Tracey heard? How much did she know? Surely she wouldn't sacrifice Aunt Catherine in order to hurt her and Antonio?

"They were lovers." Tracey looked at Antonio. "Right here, at Casa de Sueños."

Antonio stared at her. Cass took one quick look at him and saw he had gone unbelievably pale. Without thinking, she reached out, found his hand, and held it, hard. "I'm sorry," she whispered. "I am so sorry."

He was speechless.

Then Cass looked at her sister. "I don't believe you could do this," she said very coldly.

Tracey shrugged. "Aunt Catherine has quite the story to tell. Doesn't she, Cass?"

Cass felt the rigid tension in Antonio's hand before he pulled it free. All of her suspicions were founded—Tracey had heard everything. Cass was certain. And she wanted to throttle her sister, for being no different from a spoiled child seeking attention the only way she knew how to get it. But more than that, she had to stop her from revealing anything else. "I wouldn't know," Cass lied. "I think we should get out of here. Antonio?"

His gaze swung from Tracey to Cass herself. "I suspected they were lovers," he said slowly, staring at Cass. "I suspected as much once I found out your aunt was here when he died. When I found out how much my mother hated her."

Cass was still. "I am sorry," she said again, helplessly.

His gaze was hard. "What is it that you have not told me?"

Cass stiffened. And as she debated a reply, her pulse rioting, she heard the door to the mausoleum slam shut above their heads.

And they were left standing amongst the tombs in the heavy darkness.

NINE

CASA DE SUEÑOS—THE SECOND AFTERNOON

The door!" Tracey cried with panic. "What if we're locked in?"

Cass stood beside Antonio. Knowing her eyes were wide, and registering the same panic that was in Tracey's tone, she turned to him. It was hard to make out his features in the dark. "Was that the door?" Her voice did not sound like her own; its pitch was too high.

"I think so. Be calm. We're not locked in." His own tone was flat and firm and infinitely reassuring.

He was already moving past them, the way they had come in. Cass was briefly immobilized, thinking, *Someone shut the door.*

Just like someone had been lurking about the castle a few hours ago?

"Someone shut the door," Tracey whispered, suddenly standing beside her while echoing Cass's very own thoughts. "And we're trapped down here with bloody dead people."

Cass opened her mouth to deny it, to tell her it was the wind. But there was no wind, and they damn well knew it. "Don't curse the dead," she said.

Cass and Tracey looked at each other. Her sister's face was a paler shadow in the darkness of the crypt, except for her eyes, which were strikingly white. And then they rushed after Antonio.

He was at the top of the steps, pushing the vault's door. Cass almost swooned with relief when she saw it slide open. She and Tracey shared a glance again—then they dashed up the stairs and outside.

Antonio was standing there waiting for them, scanning the surrounding countryside. He did not smile at them. "Ready to return to the house?" he asked, closing the door. "Tomorrow I will put a new padlock on this."

Cass realized that her heartbeat was still thundering inside her chest. She was also scanning their surroundings—no one was to be seen. And there was only one vehicle parked in front of the monastery. "Not a soul in sight," she muttered.

Antonio's gaze swung to her and it was sharp.

Cass realized what her choice of language had been.

"Who shut that door?" Tracey demanded as they hurried down the steps and away from the mausoleum.

Cass glanced at Antonio as they moved rapidly through the cemetery. He did not respond. "Well," she said, as lightly as possible, "maybe a sudden gust of wind blew up."

Tracey gaped at her, halting in her tracks. "And you're an intellectual? Not only isn't there a breeze, that door is heavy. Very heavy. It would have to be pushed closed, and you know it."

Cass didn't know what to say. She didn't even know what to think. But Tracey was right. Someone had closed that door; there was no other explanation. Cass's footsteps slowed and she started glancing around once again.

"Let's not dally," Tracey muttered, outpacing her. But she was looking back at Cass—and she walked right into a small, knee-high headstone. She cried out.

Cass turned as Antonio helped her to right herself. Tracey stepped back from the smaller gray stone, brushing her hair away from her face. Her hands were trembling, Cass saw.

"Are you all right?" Cass asked, coming over quickly.

"Just a bruised shin. Let's get the hell out of here. This graveyard gives me the shivers."

"*Por Dios,*" Antonio said, shocked.

Cass turned.

He was leaning over the stone. "Cassandra." Excitement had replaced the shock in his voice.

And Cass knew. "Is it Isabel?" she cried.

"Come." He did not look away, squatting now.

Cass knelt beside him. The epitaph was engraved in Spanish, but the name Isabel de la Barca and the dates 1535–1555 were eminently visible. "Oh my God!" Cass cried, so excited now that she did not care that she was leaning against Antonio.

He did not appear to notice. And he read, his voice oddly resonant now,

"HERE LIES ISABEL DE LA BARCA
BORN 1535 DIED 1555
THE NIECE OF JOHN DE WARENNE EARL OF SUSSEX
AND WIFE OF ALVARADO DE LA BARCA COUNT OF PEDRAZA
A HERETIC AND WANTON WOMAN GOD SAVE HER SOUL
MAY SHE REST IN PEACE."

Cass could not move.
Antonio also remained motionless.
And then, slowly, their eyes met.

GATWICK AIRPORT—THE SAME AFTERNOON

What was she doing? Catherine thought, clutching Celia for support. The two women were in a queue, slowly moving up the aisle of a Boeing 747, looking for their seats. For the first time ever in her life, Catherine was using a cane. She was still so weak.

What *was* she doing? It wasn't too late to change her mind and turn back.

"Here we are, Lady Belford, here's our seats," Celia said cheerfully. She had insisted on coming with Catherine. In return, Catherine had insisted that she did not need an escort or a companion. But in the end, she had capitulated, not having either her usual determination or strength of will.

And Celia, of course, was now cheery to no end. She was not the type to remain reproving for very long.

Catherine took the window seat in business class, settling down with relief.

But the sense of relief was only physical. Trepidation filled her. She was overwhelmed by it.

"Are you all right, then, Lady Belford?" Celia asked, having taken her seat beside her.

Catherine's smile felt faint. She nodded. "Thank you, dear."

Celia smiled back, but worry was reflected in her warm eyes.

I am too old for this, Catherine thought, sighing. *I am too old to take*

on such conflict, I am too old to confront the past. What in God's name has possessed me?

But the moment those thoughts had formed, she knew.

She knew, and it wasn't a "what" but a "who." She closed her eyes as one of the pilots began speaking over the intercom system. She did not hear a word he said.

Instead, the past became the present, as image after image swept over her, crystal-clear and breathtakingly vivid.

Living memories.

Memories of flesh and blood.

Memories she'd wanted to forget, but they were unforgettable.

And unforgivable.

The plane began to taxi down the runway.

June 6, 1966

Guilt fills me to no end.

His wife is not here. She was not here when I arrived. Her jealousy led her to take the two boys to her mother's in Sevilla. She will not answer or return Eduardo's calls.

He is downstairs opening up a bottle of Rioja as I write. How has this happened? How did we become lovers—that very first night I arrived here at the villa? And how is it that even now, filled with shame and guilt, I lie in his bed, thinking of him, tasting him, wanting him?

So terribly that it hurts?

And I love my husband. In spite of his condition, I have never strayed. It never occurred to me to do so. I do not know how I did so now.

And I am not in love. Not with Eduardo, at least. For I love my husband. I do.

The guilt, the shame, the lust, are all there, in my mind, tormenting me, whirling, round and round, like a carousel, spinning, making it almost impossible to think clearly.

Yes. No. Stay. Go.

I am afraid.

I am afraid of myself and my passions. I am afraid because, for the first time in my life, I have no integrity, no ethics, no self-control, no sense of wrong and right. And I am afraid of this house.

Sometimes I think I am beginning to be afraid of her.

For in the past week, as we have delved deeper into the life of Isabel, as we have begun to piece together the events that led her to her fate, I have begun to notice an uncanny resemblance between her and myself. I have not dared mention it, but when I look in the mirror, I no longer see myself. I see her.

And Eduardo sees her too. For last night he awoke in the middle of the night, and he called me Isabel.

The Jeep bounced wildly over the road. Cass sat in the back, hanging on to her seat by gripping the side of the Jeep; Tracey was in the front beside Antonio, her long hair whipping about wildly.

Here lies Isabel de la Barca . . . heretic and wanton woman . . . God save her soul.

Cass remained stunned. They had stumbled upon her grave; she had died in 1555, probably at the stake, and she had only been twenty years old.

Antonio hadn't said a word since leaving the cemetery either.

Cass leaned forward, and because the Jeep was open, she had to shout over the roar of its engine. "Can you believe it?"

She did not have to elaborate. "They did not even bury her with her husband," he said, glancing briefly at her in his rearview mirror.

"She was only twenty when she died," Cass shouted. "No wonder she is so sad in that portrait." Cass wondered if Isabel had sensed what her fate was to become. That would also explain the depth of her sorrowful expression.

God. How lonely and scared she must have been.

Twenty was so young.

"The two of you never cease to amaze me," Tracey shouted, turning briefly to stare at Cass. "We were almost buried alive in that bloody house of the dead, and all you can think about is a woman who died centuries ago?"

Cass sobered, some of her elation fading. Tracey was right. "Antonio, maybe the children really did see someone out by the ruins earlier today," Cass said, her hand now on the back of his seat. "The castle isn't that far from here, is it? Even on foot?"

"No," Antonio returned with another rearview glance at her. In the mirror, briefly, their eyes met. "It's not."

In the bright daylight, maybe because he wore a pale blue polo shirt, his eyes appeared strikingly green. *Way to go, Cass,* she thought with annoyance that was directed at herself. Now was not the time to think about his eyes. "Are there homeless people around here?" Cass asked as the wrought-iron front gates of the house appeared ahead of them, and beyond, the house and its adjoining chapel silhouetted against the starkly bare, rocky terrain.

"Of course," Antonio said. "But they do not stray from the village and the towns."

Cass looked at Tracey's back. "Well, I guess we have our answer. Someone must have strayed."

Tracey turned to stare at her. And suddenly the oddest light came into her eyes, changing them, lightening them, brightening them. Making them unrecognizable. And she smiled at Cass.

The smile was challenging and superior. It was as unrecognizable as her eyes.

Cass did not understand. Her pulse rioted. And an instant later, when she glanced at her sister again, doing a double take, the strange expression was gone.

Cass's relief was short-lived.

Tracey said, "We've gone and pissed bloody Isabel off, we've raised the dead, that's what I think."

Cass almost fell off her seat.

Tracey followed Antonio through the house. "I need to speak with you," she said.

He did not answer her, entering the library.

Tracey followed him in, wishing she hadn't said what she'd said back at the crypt, desperately. She hadn't wanted to hurt him; she loved him. She had screwed up, hugely. What was wrong with her?

Tracey was close to tears. The entire point in coming to Spain was to revive their flagging relationship. So far, nothing appeared to be going the way it should, or the way she had expected. She had thought that seducing him the day of their arrival would have set things to right, but it hadn't. Not at all.

Tension continued to creep over her. *This is all Cass's fault.*

She watched him walk over to the doors that opened onto the front grounds of the house. He just stood there, with his back to her, gazing out at the ugly brownish terrain.

She was losing him, surely but slowly, and it seemed that everything she said and did was pushing him away. She had finally fallen in love, but she kept saying the wrong things, she kept doing the wrong things—and the result was only to expose herself. She kept exposing the truth—and it was ugly.

Tracey squeezed her eyes shut. She could still flee—she should flee—but somehow, she loved him even more now than she had before, and she did not have the strength to walk away. She was so scared, because she really didn't have the courage to stay, either.

If only she could get rid of her sister.

She blinked. It *was* all Cass's fault, she thought, stunned by the workings of her mind, but get rid of her? Cass was leaving on Monday. Maybe she should even send Alyssa back with her—since having Cass here with her daughter was only highlighting her own imperfections as a mother. Tracey despaired, wringing her hands. She just did not know what to do. This time there did not seem to be any easy way out of her dilemma.

How had this happened?

"Antonio? I am so sorry for what I said back there in the crypt." Tracey was contrite.

"Are you?" He turned and stared enigmatically. Suddenly Tracey realized she had no idea what he was really thinking—or feeling.

Tracey wet and bit her lip. She knew she should tell him she had made it up, and lying had never been extremely difficult for her before, but now, oddly, her tongue refused to turn over the words, her mouth refused to part.

"My father loved my mother very much. In fact, he adored her." Antonio stared at her. "That is the one thing of which I have no doubt."

Tracey could not seem to speak. She could only think, cursing inwardly.

"But I also knew he was having an affair with your aunt. Although she never admitted it at the time of his death, I read the police reports very carefully, and there were too many clues." He grimaced.

"I wish I hadn't brought the subject up." Tracey walked over to him and laid her hands on his arm, leaning against him. "I apologize. I just—"

"You don't stop to think," he said, pulling away. "You are reckless."

Tracey froze. Her heart had stopped in midbeat. And when it began again, she felt the hurt beginning, and it was the seed of something huge and unbearable.

No one, no lover at least, had ever stood before her, cataloguing her imperfections, complaining.

Only she herself did that.

He walked away from her.

"No!" Tracey cried, still stunned. Tears suddenly filled her eyes.

"I'm sorry." He turned and held up a hand, as if to forestall her. "Tracey, I think it best if you leave on Monday as well. You should not have come in the first place."

She could hardly breathe. She could hardly comprehend what he was saying. She could only stare in disbelief.

"I have work to do, and I have to check on Eduardo." He was about to leave.

Tracey did not move. Her mind, her heart, everything felt numb. She said, unthinkingly, "Eduardo? Work? I'm trying to talk to you!"

He flinched.

Tracey also flinched, for she could not believe the viciousness in her tone. What was wrong with her? What *was* happening? She rushed forward. "I'm sorry. Antonio, forgive me. I love you. I don't know what I was just thinking! Just give me a few minutes, please, to prove it to you." She reached for him.

He gripped her wrists, not allowing her to touch him. "No."

She reeled, shocked by his adamant tone and his equally adamant expression.

"Please don't send me away," Tracey heard herself say, reaching for him. "I need you. I need you now more than ever."

He cut her off. "It's over." His face hardened. "What happened yesterday was a mistake."

"A mistake?" She was shocked, and suddenly she was so angry. "You weren't complaining when I was giving you the blow job of a lifetime, Tonio."

"I have work to do," he said, dismissing her. And he walked away from her, going to his desk.

She stared at his perfect profile as he flipped through some folders and notes. And then she stormed over. And even while she knew better than to lose her temper, her tongue began—and it would not stop. "I am standing here, barely clothed, in love with you, and you want to stick your nose in a book? What kind of man are you?" she taunted.

He ignored her tirade, actually sat down at the desk, and as he reached for a legal pad, a photograph fell out of it.

The ruby necklace, the one worn, perhaps, by her ancestor Isabel.

And images flooded Tracey, of Antonio and Cass stooped over the grave together, of them standing shoulder to shoulder in the mausoleum, of them whispering together in the dining room at Belford House as they regarded the necklace on display.

"This is about Cass!" she cried.

The chair was a swivel chair and he spun around, shoulders drawn up hard and tight. "I beg your pardon?"

"This is about my sister, Miss Bookworm, Miss Earth Mother, Miss I'll Do Anything to Get Your Attention, Antonio, isn't it?" Tracey began to shake violently. When had she ever been this angry? She could not remember a single time.

"This has nothing to do with your sister," Antonio said. And this time he stood abruptly and exited the room, leaving her standing there by herself.

But Tracey hadn't heard him. She could only think, *Cass. Damn Cass.* And she clenched her fists hard and harder still.

This had gone too far.

Cass had gone too far.

Cass was about to go upstairs to wake Alyssa when her sister appeared on the other side of the great hall. Cass hesitated because Tracey was staring at her. "Is something wrong?" she asked slowly.

Tracey said, "Yes."

"Tracey? What is it?" She came forward quickly. And dread unfurled within her.

"What have you done?" Tracey asked harshly. Her blue eyes were brilliant.

Cass realized that her sister was angry. "What happened? I haven't done anything."

"No?" Tracey said. Then, "Stay away from him."

Cass halted in midstride. "What?" She'd never heard such a dangerous tone in her sister's voice before. "What are you talking about?" But she knew exactly what—and whom—Tracey was talking about.

" 'What?' " Tracey cried mockingly. " 'What are you talking about?' You're trying to steal Antonio away from me. Don't you bloody deny it."

Cass had stiffened impossibly. "I'm not. That's absurd." But . . . wasn't she?

"You're lying," Tracey said, advancing on her.

Cass stepped back, stunned. "I would never interfere in your relationship, and if you and Antonio are having difficulties, don't blame me."

The words weren't even out of Cass's mouth when Tracey pushed her hard. Cass reeled backward, against the wall. She was in disbelief. And then she was afraid.

Because her six-foot-tall sister towered over her, grabbing her by her shirt now. "Isn't this why you wanted to come to Spain in the first place? To make me look bad?"

"No, it's not. Tracey, stop," Cass cried.

Tracey pulled Cass off of the wall and flung her hard in the other direction. Cass was hurled back toward the center of the hall, and she hit the stone floor on her hands and knees. And then she heard Tracey coming.

Cass crouched, looking up. She hadn't realized just how strong her sister was. "What are you doing?" she shouted at her. But it crossed her mind that Tracey had lost all self-control, that she was briefly, temporarily, insane.

"I hate you," Tracey cried, kicking her.

Cass tried to roll away. But Tracey's foot made contact with her jaw just the same, and even though she was wearing sandals, it hurt. Cass gasped, her hand flying to her face, suddenly realizing the danger she was in.

She was no match for her sister, who was so much bigger than she. Who was enraged and out of her mind.

And Tracey pressed forward, in on her. "Did you hear me?" she raged.

Cass stared at her, shocked, afraid. She did not know whom she was looking at. She had never seen her sister this way before. In fact, Tracey didn't really look like Tracey. She looked like some strange, enraged woman.

"I have always hated you," Tracey cried down at her.

And Cass met her eyes and she believed her, and maybe it was then that something in her died. "But we're sisters," she whispered. *"You're my sister."*

Tracey stared at her, and she looked at Cass's cheek—Cass imagined a welt was there—and suddenly the angry, ugly light in her eyes began to fade.

Cass slowly stood up. One of her knees was bleeding. "You're my sister. I will always love you, Trace, no matter what you say or do."

Tracey's expression slowly changed. The anger vanished, and only bewilderment remained. And then horror came. She backed away, her gaze never leaving Cass. "Oh, God," she said. "Oh, God, what have I done!"

Cass hugged herself, tears suddenly welling up in her eyes. "You beat me up," she repeated. "How could you kick me?"

Tracey backed away, shaking her head. "I don't know. I'm so confused—I can't think—I'm sorry, I don't know!"

Cass tried to suck down air—she had forgotten to breathe. It was only then that she realized how violently she was beginning to tremble.

But Tracey continued to shake her head, having lost all of her color, and she turned, rushing out the front door of the house.

Cass thought she was crying, but she could not be sure.

It struck her that she should go after her, but she did not move. The vicious scene replayed in her mind. Cass closed her eyes. In those few violent moments, Tracey had wanted to kill her.

Cass was certain of it.

Cass found Alyssa tossing restlessly as she entered their bedroom.

She had recovered some of her composure, but only by telling herself very firmly that Tracey had merely lost her temper. That she had not wanted to harm her own sister—much less kill her. *That* was absurd. In spite of their differences, they loved one another. Cass had imagined the vicious, brutal intent.

Coming to Spain had been a mistake.

Trying not to dwell on that thought, Cass hurried to her niece, who appeared to be caught up in the throes of an unpleasant dream. Alyssa was making small, whimpering sounds. "Wake up, sweetie," Cass said, stroking her forehead. Her jaw still ached from where Tracey had kicked her. "Wake up, Alyssa. You're having a bad dream, that's all."

Alyssa's eyes popped open. Wide-eyed and frightened, she stared unseeingly at Cass. "No!"

"Honey, it's me, your aunt Cass."

Alyssa looked at her, and she sighed loudly. "Oh, Aunt—Aunt Cass! You're hurt!" she cried, fully awake now.

"I'm fine, it's just a bruise," Cass said.

"It looks terrible," Alyssa said. "What happened?"

Cass did not reply. She was still in shock, she realized, and no amount of rationalizing or deep breathing was going to help. Tracey had appeared very unbalanced, if she dared to be frank with herself. "I fell. Don't worry," Cass reassured her niece.

"Aunt Cass, your knee is bleeding," Alyssa pointed out with a seven-year-old's interest in gory details.

"I guess that was some fall, huh?" she said with a false smile. "I'm fine, honey." She put her arm around her niece. To distract her, Cass asked, "So what were you dreaming about? I came in and you were making lots of noise. Bad dream?"

Alyssa bit her lip, nodding. Now she moved closer to Cass, while glancing fearfully over her shoulder, behind them. "Aunt Cass, I had *such* a bad dream. I don't like it here. I want to go home."

Cass stared, not really all that surprised.

"I hate this house the most!" Alyssa burst out.

Cass was taken aback. Her niece was not wildly emotional. Cass worried, in fact, because generally she was so self-contained for a child. But there was nothing self-contained about her now. Cass had never before seen her so agitated.

Cass slid her arm around her, and even as she did so, she thought about her encounter with Tracey and her pulse quickened. *Coming to Spain was a mistake.* She knew it with certainty now.

"Why do you hate it here, honey?" she asked carefully. She was quite certain the answer would have to do with the growing tension between her and her sister. Children were the first to pick up on those kinds of family dynamics. Thank God Alyssa had not seen Tracey push her around and kick her.

"Aunt Cass, do you believe in ghosts?" was Alyssa's answer, and she was whispering.

Cass's heart skipped a beat as she picked up the child's pink jeans at the foot of the bed. "Of course not," she lied. Why would Alyssa even ask such a question?

As clear as a bell, she could hear the thud of the door to the mausoleum when it had slammed shut.

Alyssa folded her skinny arms tightly to her chest. "I don't, either," she said firmly.

Cass smiled at her niece. It was forced and cautious. "Honey, what made you even ask?"

"I don't know." Alyssa sounded genuinely bewildered, but she remained worried. "Maybe because this house is so big and so old. And so cold." She shivered. "Aren't you cold, Aunt Cass? I'm always cold in this place. I really hate it here. I know my mother wants to stay, but do you think we could go home?"

Cass's pulse leapt. "I'm scheduled to return on Monday. Maybe your mom will let you come home with me." She knew she shouldn't, but she was manipulating the child. So she added, "I'd love for you to come back with me, honey. But it would be up to your mom. This is a holiday just for the two of you."

Alyssa nodded, not appearing very happy.

And Cass, recalling what had just happened in the hall downstairs, could not face the thought of leaving Alyssa behind with her mother. "You know," she said as lightly as possible, holding out her jeans, "Belford House is old, Alyssa, and you're happy there."

Alyssa stared at her before slipping on her jeans. "Belford House is different," she said.

"Why? Why is it different?"

Alyssa hesitated. "It *feels* different, Aunt Cass. It's such a *nice* house. It's *happy*. And I don't have bad dreams there like I do here." Tears finally filled her eyes. "I don't want to sleep alone, Aunt Cass."

"It was only a dream," Cass soothed, stroking her hair. But the oddest notion had just crossed her mind: Hadn't she heard somewhere— maybe on a talk show with one of those supposed mediums—that children were far more apt to see "entities" than adults? And wasn't Alyssa right? This was an unhappy house. "And I'm sleeping with you, remember?"

Alyssa was grim. "I don't want to take a siesta tomorrow if you're not there."

"All right." Cass took her niece's hand and they walked out of the bedroom. "Do you want to talk about the dream you had? Would that help?"

"I don't know. But it was so real. There was this beautiful lady, and she kept whispering things in my ear. She was so beautiful, but she really scared me, she was so mean and hateful."

Cass stared, Isabel's image instantly coming to mind. She told herself not to be ridiculous, there was no connection between Alyssa's dream and her ancestor. Alyssa might have overheard them talking about her, but she had never seen her portrait, and surely she hadn't been dreaming about her. "Well, you're awake now, and it was just a dream." She paused. "We all have very odd dreams, Alyssa. Usually they don't mean anything."

"This lady was dressed like the women in one of those movies you like so much, Aunt Cass. Why would I dream about her?"

They faced each other. "What was she wearing?" Cass asked cautiously.

"A long red dress with a huge skirt, and this white ruffled collar. Her dress had big puffy sleeves, and she had a necklace on, just like the one from Sotheby's that my mother brought to our house."

And Cass could not believe what she was hearing. She reminded herself that Alyssa had seen the ruby necklace when it had been on display during the black-tie supper. Cass had showed it to her herself. And Cass had certainly taken Alyssa to plenty of museums—Alyssa had seen sixteenth-century dress on mannequins and in artwork many times. But she had also seen earlier and later period dress. *No,* Cass thought. *This is just a coincidence.* "What did her face look like?" she asked very slowly.

"She was very fair, her eyes were very blue, and her hair wasn't blond, but it wasn't red either," Alyssa said earnestly. "Aunt Cass, why are you so surprised?"

Cass could not reply. She could only regard her niece, thinking, *How is this possible? Why would Alyssa have a dream about Isabel de Warenne? Could the dream be some sort of mental telepathy? Was Alyssa picking up on Cass's fascination? Because Alyssa had never even seen Isabel's portrait.*

Isabel has scared her to death.

"Do you know who this lady is? Do you know her name?" Cass asked.

"No, but I don't want to dream about her ever again," Alyssa said firmly.

Cass inhaled. "What are you saying? That you've dreamed about her more than once?"

Alyssa nodded tearfully. "I dreamed about her last night, too, Aunt Cass. And I'm afraid. *I'm so afraid to dream about her again.*"

Cass was motionless. It was a moment before she could move, and then she gripped her niece's hand. "Well," she said roughly, "it's only a dream."

"I know," Alyssa said. Then, "I'm hungry."

But Cass had halted. And even as she spoke, she did not really want to know. "Alyssa. You said she was whispering in your ear. Do you remember what she said?"

Alyssa paled. "Yes."

Cass stared, not liking the look in her dark eyes. "Honey?"

"It's the same thing. She always says the same thing. She says, 'I will be your mother now.' "

Cass left Alyssa with Eduardo in the kitchen, under the supervision of Alfonso, drinking chocolate milk and chatting about movies they'd recently seen. She was growing anxious. It was half past seven; Tracey had not returned. She had walked out of the house about one hour before.

In the great hall, Cass went to the front door, opened it, and looked out. Antonio had obviously parked the Jeep in the garage, and only her rental car was out front. The driveway stretched a short distance to the front gates, which were open. Both the drive and the road beyond were absolutely deserted. The rough, barren terrain stretched away as far as the eye could see, finally joining the shadowy outlines of a distant mountain range and the cloudless blue sky. And finally, the heat was lessening. The sun remained strong, but was just beginning to lower itself.

Where was Tracey? Where could she have gone? And what should Cass think about Alyssa's dream?

Nothing, Cass told herself firmly. It was only a dream, and as such was meaningless.

At all costs, don't go to Castilla . . .

She's come back . . .

I killed his father . . .

Cass walked back into the house. She felt oddly unnerved. She had come to Spain to patch up her relationship with Tracey and bring Alyssa home; instead, Tracey had recently attacked her, and Cass was more interested than ever in Antonio de la Barca—against all ethics and all better judgment. Cass realized that she had an intense headache. And what about the fact that her aunt had confessed to involvement in the violent death of a man three decades ago while in Castile, and the behavior of her sister just an hour or so ago? Tracey had been violent, irrational, and dangerous. Was there a connection?

Cass shook herself free of her thoughts. There were no parallels to be drawn; she was being overly dramatic, as was her nature.

She had her camera slung over her shoulder, but before she took some shots of Antonio's home, she thought it wise to ask his permission. A moment later she found him in the library, hunched over his desk, his tortoise shell frames slipping down his straight nose.

She hated interrupting him. He was clearly engrossed. "Antonio? Knock, knock." She smiled at him. And instantly wondered if Tracey was right.

On some subconscious level, was she trying to steal Antonio away from her sister?

He looked up. "I have found—" He stopped. Immediately he was on his feet. "What happened?" he asked grimly.

Cass looked up and met his hazel eyes. She could not look away.

And she thought for one moment, that Tracey was right. She wanted this man, she would do anything to get him, and it was so very wrong.

"What happened to your face?"

"I . . . walked into a door." Cass flushed, stepping back. She must never let her mind go there again.

He gave her a disbelieving look.

Cass wet her lips. "Would you mind if I photographed your house?" Her heart was hammering madly. He belonged to her sister more than ever after that incident in the great hall. She must stay in control.

He stared at her bruised face for another moment. "Of course not."

"Great," Cass said. She walked over to the windows, looking outside. Tracey was still not in sight. Where could she be?

"What's wrong?"

"Have you seen Tracey recently?" she asked worriedly.

"About an hour or two ago."

Cass knew he was staring at her; slowly she faced him. Their gazes leapt together, and as quickly leapt apart. "Tracey and I had a huge fight. I wish I knew where she was. I wish she wasn't wandering around outside—it's so unlike her."

He stared with growing concern. "We also fought," he finally said.

Her antenna went up. No wonder Tracey had been so hateful—she was so good at laying blame everywhere else but on herself. "Oh?"

He just glanced at her, clearly not about to tell her the details of their argument. But now he was walking over to the window and scanning the grounds outside.

The scene in the crypt replayed then in her mind. She went over to him, touching his arm. "Antonio."

Their eyes met.

"My sister's a mess," she said unevenly. "A complete mess, but . . . she's not a bad person. She really isn't."

"She needs to grow up," he said, his gaze steady and direct. "She cannot always have her way, and she must learn to manage with disappointment. She is a child. Temperamental and reckless, spoiled." He turned to look outside again. Something dark flitted through his eyes.

Cass couldn't agree more with what he had said. But how could he be dating her if he felt that way about her? And clearly he was now beginning to worry about her disappearance. "I'm so sorry about what she said in the crypt."

He stiffened. "She wanted to hurt me. Which I can understand, actually. What I do not understand, though, Cassandra, is you." He faced her fully.

Cass tensed. Why had she brought this subject up?

"When were you going to tell me the truth about your aunt and my father?"

She hesitated. "I didn't see the point. I didn't want to hurt you. You were so young when you lost your father, and I am sure you cherish the few memories of him that you have."

His gaze was piercing. "What is it that you're still not telling me?"

Cass shook her head, her heart going wild. She did not want to be put on the spot like this, not now, not by him. "Did Tracey say anything else?" she had to ask.

He turned away. "No."

He wasn't being honest. She was certain. Her gaze strayed outside; soon it would be twilight. She glanced at the tall, centuries-old standing clock: 7:45. "Should we go look for Tracey?"

He was picking something up from his desk. And when he turned back to her, Cass knew. She just knew what he held in his hand.

Their gazes locked.

Cass felt ill.

"A copy of the police report. It makes very interesting reading," he said.

She felt paralyzed. "I'll bet," she managed.

"Although the police determined that my father's death was an accident, the case was hardly black and white."

Her ears started to ring.

"The driver of the car which took my father's life insisted that it was not an accident."

TEN

Cass remained paralyzed.

Antonio kept staring into her eyes.

She managed, "What? Not an accident?"

"I would like to talk with your aunt. I have a great many questions to ask her." He paced away after tossing the report on the desk.

And Cass knew she must protect Catherine at all costs. She rushed after him. "I'm sure she'd be glad to talk to you the next time you are in England," she lied frantically.

"You are miserably inept when it comes to dishonesty," he said flatly.

Cass blinked.

"Don't lie to me," he said less harshly, his gaze moving over her features slowly, one by one.

She had the urge to confess, then cry. "I'm not. I mean, I am not a liar—it's not my nature."

"That is more than obvious." Their gazes held.

She wet her lips. "Don't make me say something that I am not at liberty to say," she tried.

His brows came together in an expression of puzzlement.

Cass felt as if she were pleading now, and maybe she was. "Can't we let the past rest—where it belongs?"

"Is that really possible—for either of us?" His answer was spoken as honestly, and as softly.

Of course it wasn't. They were both fascinated, mesmerized, and compelled by all things old and ancient. "I think I should go look for my sister," Cass said, to escape.

He stopped her in her tracks. "*Suicide.* As if my father would actually commit suicide."

She faced him, stunned.

He turned away, but not before she saw the grief, confusion, and disbelief in his eyes.

She was relieved for her own sake, for Catherine's sake, but for him, she hurt. "Is that what they think?"

He didn't look at her. "It's what the driver said, time and again. That my father walked directly into the path of his car, that it was deliberate, that he wanted to die."

She was trembling. She was being given the opportunity of a lifetime, yet somehow she just couldn't seize it. And she hated lying to him yet another time.

"Why would my father want to die?" Antonio asked plaintively.

Cass stared up at him. She bit her lip, wondering if he could hear her deafening heartbeat. And she gave in to the urge to comfort him the way she would Alyssa or any other human being in need. She approached him and laid her hand on his shoulder from behind. "Antonio, maybe we will never know the truth. Maybe we shouldn't know the truth."

He slowly turned. "I do not think I can accept that," he said, again searching her face with his gaze.

"This is terrible," Cass said, meaning it. The urge to come clean and tell him what Catherine had confessed nearly overcame her then.

"Yes, it is. And not only is it terrible, I am just beginning to comprehend the amazing coincidence of de la Barcas becoming intimately involved with de Warennes, time and again, over the centuries, with no good ever coming of it."

For some reason, standing there so close to him, in the room now darkening with shadows, she almost felt that it was their involvement that was on his mind, even as intellectual and platonic as it was. And she thought about Isabel and Alvarado, her aunt and Eduardo, and now Tracey and Antonio.

Cass closed her eyes. *Tracey and Antonio, or me and Antonio?*

"Cassandra?"

Her eyes opened, and an eternity was built into the ensuing heartbeat and their locked gazes. And Cass knew, she just knew, that he was wondering the exact same thing.

And he tilted up her chin, leaning forward, and before Cass could really understand what he was doing, his lips moved over hers. Cass felt the floor beneath her feet tilt. She gripped his arms, clinging, exultant—nothing had ever been this right!

His hands closed on her waist. And suddenly the barest of kisses quickly changed; suddenly lips were parted, locked, sucking hard, and tongues dared to touch. Suddenly Cass was enfolded in his arms, her small body tucked thoroughly against his.

And Cass was overwhelmed by every inch of his hard, muscular body, by the feel of his frame, his strength, his touch, his taste. Even his smell was dizzying her with urgency . . .

And as abruptly, the kiss ended. Antonio pushed her away; Cass could barely comprehend what was happening.

They could only regard one another, wide-eyed and breathlessly, and Cass could not decide who was more surprised, Antonio or herself.

Cass felt her cheeks grow hot. Still she could not breathe. She remained in shock. Her sister's boyfriend . . . "I . . . I had better go look for Tracey before it gets any darker." Her words came out in a rush.

"Cassandra," he said, slowly. There was a flush on his face as well. He looked dumbfounded.

Cass trembled, clutching her Minolta to her chest. Was he already having regrets? While she was trying not to give in to elation and all kinds of hopefulness?

"I think we should talk. Now."

Cass didn't know what to do, what to think. She was afraid. "I think we should look for Tracey."

He seemed grim and he finally glanced at the clock. It was eight o'clock. Outside, the sun was setting, and while Cass could not see it directly, the sky was darkening and stained with bands of pink and orange. Antonio suddenly walked to the window. "I don't want her wandering out there after dark," he said. "Perhaps she is already back."

. Her heart continued to behave like an African jungle drum. Cass stared. There was an innuendo to his words that she did not like, not at all. "I doubt she went far," Cass said desperately. "She never drives, both cars are here, so she's on foot."

His jaw flexed. And this time, when he tried to meet her gaze, she was the one to look away.

She was an idiot, Cass thought, hurrying to the door. He was worried about her sister—she had just seen it written all over his face. How could she have ever let a moment like that happen? *Damn, damn, damn.*

This was far more than inappropriate. Cass shivered. If Tracey had wanted to kill her before, it would only be worse if she ever learned about this brief, mistaken moment of passion.

Cass shivered again.

Antonio caught her arm from behind, halting her. "Don't run away. I must explain myself."

Cass wanted to pull away, but she could not seem to move. "What is there to explain? You and I, we got carried away. Somehow. You're in love with my sister."

His eyes widened. "Is that what you think?"

Cass nodded. "Every guy she's ever dated has been head over heels. Men. They can't get past the perfect face, the perfect body, the perfect hair." She shrugged.

"I am not in love with your sister," he said flatly.

Cass stared, wondering whether she should believe him.

His jaw flexed again. "Our relationship is over," he said, his gaze excruciating direct.

Cass was speechless. It was over?!

"We have nothing in common. I was aware of our differences from the moment we met. It should have never started."

Cass hugged herself, absolutely breathless. "How did you meet?"

"At the Palace Hotel in Madrid. I was meeting an associate for drinks; your sister was with a friend." He shrugged.

Cass really didn't want to know more.

Suddenly he swore in Spanish. "This is so awkward," he said.

Cass was motionless. What was awkward? The subject—or the growing attraction between them? The fact that they had kissed?

He paced, raking a hand through his hair. Then he stared at her. "You are more of a mother to Alyssa than Tracey is. How long has this gone on?"

Cass found it hard to reply. "Since Tracey's divorce. Since Alyssa was two."

"I admire you, Cassandra," he said. He did not smile at her.

Cass was already stunned. Now it felt as if his words had somehow knocked the air right out of her lungs. *He admired her.* Antonio de la Barca admired her. She knew she should get a grip, rein herself in; he had been Tracey's lover, not hers, but Christ, never in her wildest dreams would she have imagined a man like this telling her that he admired her. She shrugged. "My life is Alyssa and my career, my aunt, and Belford House."

He smiled briefly. "We seem to have parallel lives."

Cass could only stare. They did have parallel lives, in a way. "I guess so." How lame.

His smile faded. "What just happened . . ."

"It's okay," Cass cried. Suddenly she needed air. She was off balance; she needed time to think and regroup. But mostly, to think.

He was through with Tracey. Did she dare?

Dare.

It was the tiniest voice there in her mind, but Cass heard it.

Of course you dare.

The voice was stronger now, even unsettling.

"No, it's not okay. I am under some duress, but even that is an inadequate excuse." He paced again, but only to the window. Night was falling. The sky was a dark, rich shade of inky blue, and a star was winking down at them. The clock wasn't far from where he stood. It was now 8:15.

"I apologize for my behavior," he finally said, facing her. "You are my guest, sleeping here under my roof. It was inexcusable, given the complicated circumstances, to put you in such an untenable position."

Cass forced what she hoped was a very bright smile onto her face. "Apology accepted," she said too lightly.

His gaze was piercing.

Cass avoided it by looking away.

"However, there is something I want to ask you."

Cass nodded, fidgeting now. "Shoot." She was aiming for flippancy. Like it didn't matter that their kiss was a mistake. Like she totally did not care that he admired her. God, right now she felt like strangling Tracey.

Tracey, who stood in her way.

And the extent of her sudden hostility toward Tracey astounded her.

"You share my passion for the past. The amount of research my father has done is incredible. I realized the moment I arrived here that the first order of business is to file everything. It would take months should I endeavor to do so alone."

Cass hadn't realized there was so much material, but he was right. "You should file everything. It will make all future research so much easier to do."

"I want you to stay," he said abruptly. "I could use your help."

She started.

"I think if the two of us work together, we could organize the library within thirty days."

Cass continued to stare. She was overwhelmed—there was nothing she would like more than to work with him, side by side, day by day, cataloguing his father's research, she realized. God, they could even reconstruct the intriguing yet oh-so-tragic life of Isabel de Warenne. "How can I?" she finally asked.

"Is it your deadline or your sister which stands in the way of your accepting my offer?" he asked.

She bit her lip. "I have almost a year left on my deadline, and when I'm inspired, I'm fast. It's Tracey. And what about Alyssa? Alyssa would have to stay with me." She couldn't believe she was even considering his stunning proposal. And Alyssa hated Spain. She wanted to leave— and Cass had practically promised her that they would leave together on Monday.

"That is hardly a problem," he said, and now he was smiling warmly. "Eduardo could use the company; he could use the friend."

Cass's heart turned over so hard and so fast that she was dazed with the realization that she was a goner. One kiss, one professional proposal, and she was a complete goner. She was head over heels for this man, and to deny it any longer would be absurd. *Shit*, she thought. *Shit. Now what?*

Dare.

"Think about it," he said.

Cass looked up at him. She was almost ready to blurt that there was nothing to think about, of course she would stay. But she wasn't a fool. She was a sensible, thinking, responsible adult. If she stayed— jeopardizing her relationship with her sister—she would also wind up with a broken heart, and undoubtedly a whole lot of egg on her face, as well.

And then there was Alyssa. If Tracey decided to play hardball, she could lose Alyssa forever.

"I'll give it some thought." Cass turned hurriedly away before he might try to persuade her again. "Let's try to find Tracey," she said, cutting him off. "You search the house—I'll go outside." Not giving him a chance to respond, she bolted from the room.

Cass finally saw her sister sitting beneath a short, stubby tree behind the cottage and garage. Darkness had finally fallen. Too many stars to count had emerged in the yawning blackness of sky overhead. She paused, not really seeing Tracy's hunched-over form, wishing she had responded to Antonio's proposal in a more dignified and composed manner. How could she have run out like that? If he hadn't realized before, by now he must know how she was feeling about him. Cass felt like a fool.

She walked slowly toward her sister, suddenly dreading their encounter, and worse, suddenly so angry because this wasn't fair. Cass and Antonio had so much in common, and what did Tracey have in common with him other than the drop-dead good looks that they shared? "Tracey," she called out grimly.

Tracey did not look up.

And suddenly Cass felt a frisson of fear. Tracey was so still, so unmoving, that she could have been a statue. Cass broke into a run. "Tracey!"

Her sister, who sat with her legs outstretched, her back to the tree, staring straight ahead, did not respond. As if she hadn't heard Cass, or as if she were dead.

An image of Isabel flashed through Cass's mind, whispering in Alyssa's ear. *I will be your mother now.* Cass didn't want to recall that odd message now—she didn't want to even think of it as a message. What was wrong with her? "Tracey!" Cass shouted.

There was no response.

Cass sprinted forward, finally reaching her sister. It took her one instant to realize that although immobile, Tracey was very much alive. Warm and almost catatonic, but breathing, alive.

"Trace?" Cass squatted, removing her hand from in front of her sister's nose where she had felt her faint breathing. Her sister still hadn't acknowledged her, she still hadn't moved. Tears stained her face, as did some small specks of dried blood. Her white shorts were filthy, both bloodstained and dirty; dust and dirt covered her legs. Cass saw an ant crawling on her thigh. She swatted it off. Her sister didn't even blink. "Trace!" She grabbed her shoulders, shaking her. What was happening?

And Tracey looked down, more tears sliding down her cheeks. "Everything I do is wrong."

"No, that's not true," Cass cried, pushing her blond hair behind her ears. "Honey, please get up, you're sitting in the dirt and there are bugs." Relief overcame Cass. Tracey was fine; nothing was wrong. Everything was just fine.

"I am so fucked up."

Cass inhaled, hard. "No, Trace, you're not fucked up, this is just . . . this is a mess, we're all in a mess, together, although God only knows why." Cass took her arm. "Please get up. Let's go back to the house, let's get all cleaned up, and then you and I, why, we'll sit down and chat over a good, stiff gin and tonic."

"I don't know what's happening," Tracey whispered, still not looking at Cass. "I was so angry. I've never felt such blackness before." She started to shake.

And their violent argument of that afternoon flashed in its entirety through Cass's mind. "Tracey, it's over. You didn't mean it. I know you didn't mean to hurt me. We're sisters and we love each other, right?" Cass felt desperation overcoming her. "I'm sorry, too. Maybe you're right. Maybe I am sort of halfway in love with Antonio, but I swear, it means nothing, really, and I would never try to come between you guys." In that moment, Cass meant it, with all of her heart and all of her being, but damn it, she was now lying too. And she knew that as well.

"What should I do?" Tracey cried, finally looking at Cass. "He's booting me out. Sending me away. He doesn't want me anymore because he knows the truth."

Cass stared, aware that she, too, was now trembling. She was confused, because Antonio didn't know the truth. "Let's talk about this in the house," Cass whispered, regretting their kiss, his proposition, and worse, her own damned feelings. Regretting everything. Guilt was an ugly thing.

She shivered and had to glance behind them, but they were alone. "It's too dark out here, and it's getting cold." The house seemed to stare at her from a distance, the windows, lit up from within, like hollow, vacant eyes. "Let's go back."

Tracey stared at her, her eyes riveted on Cass's face. "I did that," she whispered.

Cass touched the welt on her jaw, which she had forgotten about. "It doesn't matter. It was a mistake. You didn't mean it."

"Don't you understand? Why won't you understand? I did mean it, Cass. *I did mean it*," she said.

Cass stared. Unease slithered up and down her spine.

Tears filled Tracey's eyes. "I'm scared, Cass. I'm so scared!"

Somehow Cass pulled her to her feet even though her body was stiff, unmoving, like lead weights, and she wrapped her arms around her and held her, hard.

"Everything's going to be all right. I promise. As soon as we get home. Because that's what we need to do, you, me, and Alyssa, we need to go home." And Cass meant it, fervently.

To hell with Antonio's proposal.

This place was bad news.

Cass was suddenly certain of it; she had never been more certain of anything before.

Cass left Tracey preparing to shower before supper once she felt reassured that her sister was recovering her composure. She was absorbed in her thoughts as she walked downstairs. Was Tracey having some kind of nervous breakdown? Her emotional fragility worried Cass.

Don't you understand? I did mean it.

Cass powered on her laptop, stiff with tension, replaying the last conversation with her sister in her mind, again and again. A moment later, she was on the Web. She began a search for sites dealing with ghosts.

She could not help herself. She needed information. Because there was no way she could continue to ignore the fact that every time she went into Isabel's room, she felt extremely disturbed. The entire house was disturbing. Cass was prepared to accept the idea that Casa de Sueños was haunted, although she refused to equate that event with all of the odd things that had happened since their arrival. Cass knew she was going to unearth a lot of nonsense, but if she sifted through it carefully, she might also unearth some interesting facts about the supernatural.

And as she began scrolling through the list of sites, she was aware of something nagging at her. She was uneasy—and she assumed it was her sister's strange behavior that was disturbing her.

To Cass's dismay, there were thousands of Web sites dealing in one way or another with the subject of ghosts. She stared in dismay at her screen. For God's sake, a sight about satanic practices had come up.

Cass realized it would be very hard to weed out seriously researched and scientific information from all the garbage. She stared harder at her screen, going down the list, when the words in front of her became blurred and distorted before becoming normal again.

Cass froze. It had happened so quickly, in the blink of an eye—had she imagined this, too?

Because computers did not have static.

Computers did not behave like television sets from twenty years ago.

And then it happened again. The word *ghosts,* typed into the search box, stretched, wavered, stretched again, as did every image on her screen. And in the next instant, her screen went blank.

Cass stared in disbelief, because it was as if she had powered off. She pressed the space bar and the Enter key a few times, in case she had gone into the suspend mode, but her window did not reappear. She powered on. The screen lit up.

"What's wrong, Aunt Cass?"

Cass didn't turn. "This is so weird. My laptop just went off—it's never done that before." Then she began to worry. Undoubtedly she had a technical problem. The last thing she needed, now or anytime, was a breakdown. "Damn it." She dialed up to the Web again, but before she could connect, the screen went pitch black again.

Cass jumped to her feet while Alyssa wandered over.

"It's okay," Cass said reassuringly, and of course, it was okay—her two-year-old laptop needed repair, obviously, but Cass couldn't help thinking it so odd that it had gone on the blink.

Don't go jumping off the deep end, she told herself. But she wasn't soothed. To the contrary, she just stood there staring at the dark screen, thinking about Isabel's haunting blue eyes. And suddenly, in her mind, Cass could see Isabel clearly—and her gaze was filled with belligerence.

It was unnerving.

Cass reminded herself that Isabel's eyes, in the portrait, were filled with sorrow. Still, she could not shake the hostile expression from her mind's eye. And hadn't Antonio said he found her gaze to be accusing?

Cass grimaced, more determined now than ever to find out more about Isabel. Suddenly she froze.

Here lies Isabel de la Barca . . . the niece of John de Warenne earl of Sussex.

Cass blinked. "But she was the earl's daughter," she said aloud. "Wasn't she?"

A sound behind her caused her heart to skip erratically. Cass whirled. Her door was ajar. "Antonio?"

There was no answer.

"Maybe we should go downstairs," Alyssa said uneasily. Then, "Aunt Cass!"

Cass whirled. And she was faced with a sight she had never before seen: her laptop was on, but it looked like a television screen filled with black and white static when no reception was possible. She stared at the glowing screen.

"Aunt Cass? Someone's here," Alyssa whispered with fear.

Cass turned, reaching for her—thinking the worst—when she distinctly heard a car door slamming outside.

That was when the fragrance of violets registered.

For one moment, Cass's mind went blank with shock. In the next instant, she decided, grimly, that the answer had to do with ventilation and nothing else.

Someone began pounding on the front door.

Both Cass and Alyssa jumped.

Cass squinted down at the illuminated dial of her watch. It was about nine-thirty. Who in God's name could that be?

"Aunt Cass?" Alyssa pressed closer to her as someone continued to bang urgently on the front door.

"There's nothing to worry about," Cass lied, her heart a traitor to her own cause. The scent of violets was stronger. Cass couldn't think about it now. She thought about the fact that there were two children in the house, one of whom was crippled, and a very old man. With her next breath, she chastised herself for even thinking of the need to defend themselves. "C'mon," she said, as the banging continued.

She grabbed Alyssa's hand and they hurried down the hall, Cass grim, deciding she would have to call her computer consultant in London first thing in the morning. Obviously a chip or something had gone haywire on her machine, and he would have some kind of incredibly brilliant explanation for the static—if that was what it was.

The banging had stopped. Cass and Alyssa entered the great hall just in time to see Antonio opening the front door. A second later a tall man with dark blond hair entered the house, his tie askew, his pinstriped gray suit rumpled.

"Gregory," Antonio cried, his eyes wide. "What are you doing here?"

Gregory responded in a spate of Spanish, throwing his arms into the air.

Cass was overcome with relief. Clearly they were friends, and she suspected they were more, cousins or brothers, for their features were so similar. "It's okay," she whispered to Alyssa.

But Alyssa's smile was feeble.

Antonio gripped the man's arm. "Calm down. *Tenemos invitados,*" he said, gesturing at Cass and Alyssa.

Gregory glanced at her, but briefly, before facing Antonio again. "I have had the worst feeling all day," he said heavily. "I called your office, your house, repeatedly, but of course, you are here, and I did not know, so there was no answer."

"I am here, and all is well," Antonio said calmly.

Cass doubted that. And then she realized just what she was thinking—something was wrong, and she felt it in every fiber of her being.

Gregory, a very attractive man with tousled, dark blond hair, did not smile. "You never come here. Who would have guessed! I finally tracked your secretary down—I found her home number in your desk in your apartment." He was growing angry now.

"It did not occur to me to report my agenda to you," Antonio said quietly. "May I introduce our guests?"

Gregory finally looked at Cass, and then at Alyssa. He smiled. "I apologize. I have been distressed." His smile was brief. "You must be Tracey Tennant. I am Antonio's little brother, Gregory." His smile flashed, and it was wry.

Cass flushed, having never been mistaken for her sister before. "I'm her sister, Cass de Warenne, and this is her daughter, Alyssa," she said.

"Forgive me my mistake," Gregory said. He came forward to shake her hand and pat Alyssa's head. Then he looked back at Antonio with concern. "Is everything all right?" he asked.

"Everything is fine," Antonio said firmly. "I'm sorry you drove all the way out here when you could have called instead."

Gregory stared. "What do you mean? Your secretary told me that I must come."

Antonio also stopped. "I beg your pardon?"

Cass looked from the one to the other, growing uneasy.

"Your secretary told me that I must come, and immediately," Gregory said, flushing.

Antonio stared and shook his head. "There must be a mistake. She would not say such a thing. I never suggested that you should join me here. I never even thought it."

"She was very clear," Gregory said. "The summons was very clear."

Cass wondered at his odd terminology.

"Well, you are here now, so why don't we plan to enjoy the weekend?" Antonio smiled with a shrug. "It's been a long time since we were here together, eh?"

"That is an understatement," Gregory said, appearing unhappy. "I still cannot believe that you really decided to take a holiday here, of all places."

Cass did not move. What did he mean? What was amiss? She

watched the two brothers start down the corridor, Antonio telling him about the research he was doing. Alyssa tugged on her hand. Cass continued to stare.

Gregory's words echoed. *The summons was very clear.*

"What is it, Aunt Cass?" Alyssa whispered.

And suddenly Cass felt eyes on her back. She whirled—but no one was there.

Cass could not relax. For in that moment she *knew* she was being watched.

"Oh, God," she cried, gripping Alyssa's hand so tightly that Alyssa cried out. Was Aunt Catherine right?

Was this house haunted? Were the two families destined to suffer tragedy together?

"Aunt Cass." Alyssa tugged her hand. "She is summoning us all to this place."

Startled, certain she had misheard, Cass looked down. She cried out, jerking away. Because she saw not her niece, but glowing eyes set in a face stretched taut with malevolence.

The face smiled and it was frightening. And as Cass stared at the face of an adult woman set on her niece's small body, it returned to normal. Cass blinked, and was met with Alyssa's childish countenance once more.

Cass could not seem to get any air. Had she just seen what she thought she had seen—and had she just heard what she thought she had heard? Or was she going crazy? "What? What did you say?"

Alyssa said, the picture of innocence, "She is summoning all of us together, and soon Auntie Catherine will arrive."

Cass gasped as Alyssa turned away, following in Antonio and his brother's tracks.

"But Aunt Catherine isn't coming," Cass whispered.

Alyssa did not seem to hear her.

She fought to think clearly, but it was impossible, especially as she now stood alone in the huge great hall, where the lights were few and dim. Cass remained aware of the barely there whiff of violets now, and she managed to think, sluggishly, *Isabel is here. My aunt is right, and she is somehow here, and responsible for everything—either that or I am the one who is a nutcase.*

Suddenly Cass did not want to be alone in the hall—or alone anywhere in the house. She rushed down the corridor, after Alyssa and the two brothers. And when she reached the library, she was greeted with a warm and cozy scene that should have been comforting: Antonio was making drinks, Gregory beside him, the two children were seated on one sofa sharing a book, and a huge fire danced in the fireplace. Cass could not relax.

She realized that Gregory was regarding her a bit too closely. Automatically Cass shot him a smile. He smiled back.

He had seemed unnerved when he had first arrived at the house. Now he seemed cheerful, relaxed.

The summons was clear.

She is summoning all of us.

Was it possible?

Cass sank down on a moss green silk sofa with big, multicolored, tasseled pillows. Her mind felt dazed, but even so, it raced. Every odd occurrence that she had witnessed since her arrival yesterday went round and round in her brain, like a mental carousel. And that expression on Alyssa's face . . .

"Martinis?" Antonio asked cheerfully.

Cass was wide-eyed. Why was his mood so upbeat? Was it because of his brother's arrival?

Antonio was handing her a glass. He was smiling, as if it were a perfect world.

Cass stared up at him. Maybe she was going crazy, because everyone seemed contented, normal, while she was the one in the throes of a growing hysteria. In fact, she almost felt as if she were watching a surrealistic film. "Does this evening feel strange to you?"

He continued to smile. "Only my brother's appearance is odd, and that is because it was so unexpected."

The fire danced merrily in the fireplace. The children giggled together over something one of them had read. The men were sipping their drinks. Cass glanced warily around. Why was she the only one to be alarmed and uneasy? She set her drink down. Didn't anyone else feel the tension that had fallen over them all like a huge, dark cloak? "But why would your secretary instruct him to come here?"

"Undoubtedly they misunderstood one another."

The lights in the room suddenly dimmed, before brightening.

Cass stood up, alarmed.

"It is only the wiring," Antonio told her. "Are you all right, Cassandra?"

She stared at him, wondering what he would say if she told him that Alyssa had changed before her very eyes just moments ago, that she had spoken about a summoning, that Cass thought that odd fragrance was a dead woman's perfume. . . . The list was endless. "Maybe it's not wiring," she said slowly. "My laptop went on the blink earlier, and I can't figure out what happened."

"It's been a long day," Antonio said, smiling at her once more.

He was not a smiley kind of guy. Cass felt as if she were looking at a stranger—it was Antonio's face, his body, but not his character.

He turned back to his brother. Cass watched them chatting quietly, and then she looked at the children. And Alyssa seemed oblivious to her previous fears, listening to Eduardo as he read aloud as if it were story time in school. What were they reading? Good God—it was "The Legend of Sleepy Hollow."

Upstairs, directly above them, something thumped.

Cass almost jumped out of her skin. "Did you hear that?" she cried.

Antonio returned to her. "Why are you so nervous? Old houses make noise. Surely you know that."

"That was Isabel's room," Cass said.

Gregory moved to stand beside them. "I heard something as well. Is Alfonso upstairs?" he asked. He seemed less relaxed than his brother.

"Alfonso is in the kitchen," Antonio returned.

Suddenly Cass wondered where Tracey was.

Gregory had moved back to the beautiful gilded cart that served as a dry bar and was making another shaker of drinks. Cass went to her niece. "Alyssa," she whispered, so the brothers would not hear. "What did you say to me back there in the great hall?"

Alyssa blinked at her as Eduardo paused in his reading. "I don't remember," she whispered back. Then, "Why are we whispering, Aunt Cass?"

Before Cass could reply, Antonio turned abruptly away from his brother. "I have good news," he said to her.

"Really?" Cass asked, wishing Antonio had been with her when Alyssa had appeared transformed into someone else. She wished there had been a witness so she wouldn't be doubting herself. But she was doubting herself. She could not have seen what she thought she had seen. Her imagination was playing tricks on her.

He pulled over a tufted beige ottoman and sat down. "Cassandra, I have found a family tree, clearly made in my father's own hand." His eyes sparkled. "It was scribbled in pencil, but legible enough."

Cass had to sit up straighter. All of her worries were forgotten. "What have you learned?"

"I will show you," he said, smiling slightly now. He stood and went to his desk, and when he returned, he handed her several pages of paper.

Cass's heart was pounding. And her hands were shaking as she took the pages from him and spread them out on the sofa, sliding to the floor on her knees. Antonio knelt beside her.

She was about to go to the first page but had to stop. Cass's eyes widened, because the last entries were "Catherine de Warenne, born 1930, died?, married Sir Robert Belford, born 1912, died?," followed by an entry for the births and deaths of her own parents.

"My father died in 1966," Antonio said softly, his breath feathering her ear.

"Two years before I was born," Cass said as softly. Which explained why her own birth had not been recorded.

Her pulse was pounding so loudly now that everyone must hear it. Cass had to look at Antonio, and their gazes locked.

"Go to the first page," he whispered, his eyes bright.

She flipped the pages. "Isabel," she breathed.

And everything they had wanted to know was right there, legibly printed in Eduardo's handwriting. Isabel de Warenne had been born in 1535 and she had died in 1555—no surprises there. She had married Alvarado de la Barca a year before her death. If they had had a child, which was unlikely, it was not recorded. Cass used her finger and scrolled up and immediately understood what had happened.

"She was the earl's daughter," she breathed. "But he died in 1543 and his brother inherited the title."

"Yes," Antonio said.

His tone was strange. But Cass did not look at him this time, because the extent of a terrible tragedy was right there in front of her eyes on the written page. "Oh my God," Cass whispered. "They all died. Her father, her mother, her brother—they all died in 1543."

"Yes," Antonio said. "They all died."

ELEVEN

Even in her skirts, she could run faster than her brother, Tom, who was only two years older than she. Laughing, Isabel outdistanced her ten-year-old brother, ignoring the cries of Lady Caroline. The surf broke at her feet. The Sussex coastline was green, idyllic, and beautiful, the hard-packed beach covered with gleaming crushed shells, rushing the rolling dunes and the fertile, flowering Sussex hills. But Isabel had grown up in East Sussex, and although not immune to the beauty around her, she ignored it, the way she ignored her nurse, who continued to call for her and her brother. Reaching the big dilapidated ball, straw poking from its broken hide, she seized it, the effort causing her to fly across the sand and land hard on her face, the ball clutched tightly in her arms.

A mouthful of sand did not disturb Isabel, who merely spit hard to rid herself of grit and grain. A moment later her brother was on top of her, landing there with an indignant *whoop!*, and they were shouting and laughing and screaming as they wrestled for the ball.

The breaking waves finally washed up over them, and they both shrieked in unison, because even in the summer, the sea was so terribly cold. Overhead, gulls circled and cawed in bright, sunny summer skies, looking for their dinner.

"Isabel! Thomas! The two of you, ill-bred urchins, heed me this moment!" Their furious cousin was shouting, her cries louder now.

There was something in her tone that caused Isabel to stop laughing, and as she sat up, covered in sand, her brother did the same. She saw from his suddenly puzzled expression that he had heard the note of alarm and panic in Lady Caroline's voice as well. Isabel met his gaze. They were both vividly blue eyed, but otherwise, there was little resemblance between them, as Tom took after their father, the earl of Sussex, a big, dark man, and Isabel their mother, the countess, who was slender, fair, and red haired. She took his hand, her heart lurching. "She is a popinjay," she whispered. "Always so afraid, and taking to wing without ever a thought twice."

Thomas stood and pulled her to her feet. His swarthy face was sober now. "She is undoubtedly distraught because we are late." He shared another, significant glance with her.

And Isabel's heart lurched unpleasantly. Their parents had gone to court for the king's wedding to Catherine Parr, his sixth wife, and were expected back that day. Just before her father the earl had left for court, he had lashed her for her mischief and her wild, boyish ways. Isabel had promised to behave in the most exemplary manner befitting a Christian lady, and wrestling in the sand with her brother would not help her cause. She was afraid of another whipping.

Fortunately, the earl hated the lash as much as his children did, and the punishment never lasted for very long.

"Do not worry," Thomas advised, slipping his arm around her thin shoulders. " 'Tis my fault this time, and I will advise his lordship of it."

"No, do not," Isabel said, aware of unshed tears suddenly filling her tone. "I do not want you to suffer the lash, too."

"I do not mind," Thomas said kindly. " 'Tis easier for me because I am a man."

Isabel had to give him a look. "Not yet, Sir Fool. You do not even have your spurs, so how can you be a grown man!"

They started down the beach, toward Lady Caroline, who was waving frantically at them. Isabel was certain now that their parents had returned to Romney Castle, and her steps slowed. "Father told me, as I am the heir, I am a man, no matter my age." Thomas was firm. "And I must never forget that one day I will be earl, one of the most important peers in the realm, thus I must always act according to my station in this world." He sighed then, heavily.

Isabel understood, and she squeezed his hand. "Do not ever regret your blessing, Tom. You could be no more than a baker's brat. Instead, you are one of the most highborn."

"No, I do not harbor regret," he said promptly.

But Isabel knew him as well as she did herself, they were so very close. She knew he loved playing ball more than fencing with his master, that he preferred hawking to Latin and Greek and mathematics, and that he dearly despised the teachings of the likes of Plato, Plutarch, Cicero, and Seneca, which he claimed he could not fathom in the least. And Tom simply had no use for subjects that had become popular because of King Henry's penchant for them—alchemy, astronomy, astrology. He did not know how lucky he was, Isabel thought wistfully. While he spoke three tongues, albeit not fluently, she was adept at pricking her thumbs while straining over her needlepoint. He rode astride while hawking; she falconed in the ladylike position of sidesaddle. What she would not give for a tutor who would enable her to study four or five languages, add and subtract numbers with ease, decipher the treatises of philosophers from Ancient Greece and Rome— instead of learning by heart passages from the Bible and *On the Instruction of a Christian Woman*. The earl had been swift to state, many times, that a woman need only obey God and marry well, and Isabel's education was based on that premise. She wondered what her father would say—and do—if he knew she frequently eavesdropped on her brother's lessons and that she could work her way through a passage from Socrates.

"Lady Caroline appears more distraught than usual," Tom said suddenly, wiping sweat from his brow. "What can be amiss?"

Isabel was wondering the very same thing, when suddenly she realized he was heavily flushed—and still sweating profusely, which was strange. And a few odd little spots that looked like blood pricks had broken out on his round cheeks. But before she could respond, Lady Caroline was swooping down upon them.

She was a plump widow of nineteen, huffing and puffing for breath. "The Lord have mercy on us all," she wept.

Isabel faltered, realizing that whatever was happening, it was hardly so simple as her being caught by her powerful father in shared mischief with Tom. "Cousin Caroline, what transpires?" she managed, a whisper of dread.

"The earl has returned from court. Dear God, may He have mercy on us all!"

"Lady Caroline," Tom snapped, "what has passed?"

Her gaze was wild and tear filled. "Your mother is taken with the sweating sickness!" Caroline cried, her round face ashen.

Isabel stared.

And she pictured her beautiful, redheaded mother, Lady Margaret, as she had last seen her, just weeks ago, in purple brocade and flashing sapphires, a gold headdress hiding most of her flamboyant hair, a warm, beautiful smile on her lips, and her newborn babe, Isabel's infant sister, Catherine, named after the new queen, in her arms. She pictured her proud father beside them, beaming in spite of his desire for another son. And then other images flashed into her mind, of the houses in the village where the sickness had worked its journey of death. Of the shuttered windows and doors barred shut, of the required sign—wisps of straw and a white slash—marking every household where the sickness had struck.

"No," Isabel said, suddenly reeling with dizziness and fear. "No, 'tis a mistake!"

But it was not a mistake.

The sweating sickness had come at last to Romney.

By the time they reached the castle, set high on the hill, overlooking the bay below where Isabel and Tom so frequently played, Tom was beginning to cough.

As they dashed through the courtyard, Isabel realized how oddly silent and still the bailey was. Usually it was a hive of activity, filled with dairymaids and stableboys, knights and pages, men at arms and watchmen, as well as local merchants eager to sell their produce and wares. Horses, donkeys, and oxen mingled with cows, dogs, and the occasional sheep. But now only two men were hurrying about their business, rushing past Isabel, Tom, and their cousin as they crossed the bailey. Tom coughed again.

Isabel turned to look at him as they raced into the great hall. His face was flushed the shade of beets. She froze.

"I am fine," he whispered hoarsely.

Isabel knew too much about the sweating sickness, and fear seized her. The first signs were often a cough, the fever, and head pains, and within hours—before even being able to return home to loved ones, sometimes—the victim was dead. "Tom," she cried, seizing his arm.

But he jerked away. "Do not touch me!" he cried. And then he grabbed his head, moaning.

In sheer horror, Isabel watched her beloved brother grapple with his head pain.

From behind, Caroline gripped Isabel, dragging her away.

"No!" Isabel screamed, struggling to break free. "No! Let me go to my brother, please!"

"You cannot," Caroline gasped, both of her stout arms locked around Isabel. "He's got the sickness, too, dear God!" She inhaled. "Master Tom! Upstairs to your room and be hasty about it. To bed with you, do you hear me?"

Tom nodded, unable to stand upright, doubled over with pain.

"He needs me, let me help him!" Isabel screamed.

Caroline slapped her hard across the face. "Do not think to be a brat now! Our lives depend on it!"

Isabel hated her. In that instant she hated her, when she had only loved her up until then. "I want my father," she demanded furiously. "I want his lordship. Where is he? He will set you in your place, he will!"

"He be pacing outside the countess's chambers," Caroline retorted.

"Then that is where I am going. Release me now, Lady Catherine," Isabel commanded, still struggling to wrest herself free.

Thomas fell to the floor at their feet.

Both Caroline and Isabel were stunned, for an instant unable to do more than stare. And then Isabel realized Caroline had ceased her vigilance. She squirmed free of her captor, rushing to her brother, bending over him. But before she could even turn him onto his back, Caroline had seized her by her hair and was dragging her back again. Isabel shrieked with pain.

"Leave him be!" her nurse ordered frantically.

"Let me go," Isabel shouted, as frantic. Then, to her surprise, Caroline did just that.

Her ears were ringing from the pain of having her hair nearly ripped out of her scalp. She dashed back to her brother, kneeling over him, aware now of the tears starting a ceaseless slide down her face. She turned him over, and saw more blood spots broken out on his face. "Oh, Tom," she said, sobbing now. "Do not die, you cannot! Tom!"

His lashes fluttered, but he did not respond. And he was burning like fire to her touch.

"Where is everyone?" Isabel shouted, glancing around wildly. "I need a servant to put him abed!"

"There is no one here who will do it," Caroline cried, standing a dozen feet distant, "for fear of contagion."

Isabel was suddenly frantic. She did not fear contagion—if Tom died, she wanted to die, too. She would care for him, but she needed to get him into his bed. Her father! No one would dare disobey the earl!

Isabel raced through the hall and upstairs, expecting to find her father outside her mother's apartments. Instead, she saw two of her mother's ladies, huddled together, sobbing. Isabel ran to them. "Cecelia," she cried, wrenching on her arm. "Where is the earl? How is my mother? Where *is* everyone?"

Lady Cecelia Farqhuier blinked at her through red, swollen eyes. "Your mother is burning with fever and oozing with sores." She wept anew. "The earl has taken to his own bed. Lady Mary and Lady Jane are dead. They died this morning within minutes of one another."

Isabel stared, in shock now. Two of her mother's ladies in waiting, dead. Her father, in his bed? "Father?" She could hardly get the word out.

"The sickness has taken, him, too."

Isabel backed away, disbelieving. "No. 'Tis impossible."

Lady Anne looked at her through her tears with profound sorrow. "Go see for yourself, then."

Isabel continued to back up, shaking her head in negation. Her father the earl was the most powerful man she knew. When he spoke, men listened; when he walked, the ground did tremble. He held the king's ear, was a ranking member of the council, and was, like his liege lord, both feared and revered. Although in his late forties, he remained a big, boisterous man, who still enjoyed and won jousts, who still relished hunting, and who still turned many ladies' eyes. Isabel had always feared her father as much as she respected him. She could never recall a time when he had been wrong.

He could not be ill. Not her powerful, handsome, brilliant father. Not with the sweating sickness, which showed no mercy to its victims. For no one survived.

Suddenly a priest walked out of her mother's rooms.

Isabel's eyes widened. Privately Lady Margaret held to the old faith, but very privately and very secretively, and the earl chose to look the other way. Isabel's heart turned over again and again with dread. What was Father Joseph doing in her mother's apartments at this time of day, dear God? For anyone to see? If word of this got back to court, her mother could be tried for heresy and treason. "Father?" she tried, deep inside herself already knowing the answer.

He genuflected. "Dearest Isabel," he said gravely. "I am so sorry, but your mother walks with the Lord now, and know you that she is at peace."

Isabel found it difficult to breathe. Her mother, dead? And she had not even been able to say good-bye? "No," she whispered, her heart starting to shred and hurt so painfully she had to clasp her palm to her unformed breast. "No." She felt herself begin to tremble violently.

The priest smiled sadly at her. "She was a devout and good woman, and rest assured that she finds Heaven a wondrous place. She is with the Lord now, Isabel. Where she must finally be."

Isabel shook her head, thinking, *No, No, No,* as the two ladies burst into loud, keening sobs. Then she turned and ran down the hall, but it was empty. Not a single lord stood outside her father's chambers, and Isabel did not understand.

Or did she?

They were either all dead, or afraid of death.

Isabel bit her lip, her heart pumping painfully, tears salty on her lips, and she pushed open his door. A huge form lay unmoving on the massive, canopied state bed. "My lord?" she tried. Her tone sounded raw to her own ears.

There was no response.

And Isabel was terrified.

Too much so to go forward to find out if he still lived—or if he had also died.

She turned and fled, rushing back downstairs, only to find the great hall empty, except for Tom, who lay where she had left him.

Isabel collapsed beside him, already knowing the truth, already knowing that her father was dead, too. "Tom," she wept, "you cannot die. You cannot leave me, I need you, do not die!"

There was no response, not even the barest flutter of his thick lashes, and through her tears, Isabel realized he seemed terribly still. But her vision was blurred and askew because of her tears, and she blinked furiously, to improve her sight, determined to see him breathing, living, alive. Her vision cleared. He was so still. But surely he breathed?

More dread—more terror—seized her.

Isabel lifted a shaking hand and held it over his mouth.

No breath feathered her hand.

She tried again, her hand shaking uncontrollably now, determined to feel his warm, moist breath on her flesh.

And she felt nothing.

Desperately Isabel ripped open his tunic and shirt and laid her ear to his burning chest. There was no movement beneath her cheek, no rise and fall of his rib cage as he breathed, and worse, there was no heartbeat, nothing.

He was dead.

And when her uncle, John de Warenne, arrived three days later for the funerals, her infant sister and Caroline were dead, too. But Isabel had survived.

She did not know why.

TWELVE

I would suspect the plague."

His voice sounded so far away. Cass had to close her eyes, trying to block out the image of a pretty little girl standing in an empty medieval courtyard, simply stunned by the loss of her entire family.

No, not her entire family. Her uncle had survived. Her uncle had become the earl of Sussex when Isabel's father had died.

She opened her eyes to find Antonio regarding her with concern. "How tragic," she whispered. "If it was the plague, that should be easy to find out."

"Tomorrow," he promised her.

Outside, a wind had picked up. The gusts rattled the window panes.

Cass held his gaze, Isabel's image coming to mind again as a small child. "She was an orphan," Cass said grimly. "She was the earl of Sussex's niece once her father died. Sussex probably became her guardian; I imagine he must have arranged the marriage for her."

"I would think so," Antonio said, his gaze riveted on her face. "Isabel must have had quite a dowry to attain the match. Are you all right?"

Cass was facing him, aware that his enthusiasm had been replaced by concern for her. She still felt shell-shocked. And she was surprised by her reaction to the facts they had just discovered.

She was becoming too concerned with Isabel's life. Or was it compelled?

"Cassandra?" They knelt side by side; his shoulder pressed against hers. "Something is bothering you. What is it?"

The light from the fire illuminated his clear, slightly golden skin, his hazel eyes. Cass took her first sip of the martini. It was cool, bitter, and dry. She had just realized how close to her he was—and Tracey would be walking in at any moment.

Cass stood up abruptly, aware of her guilt. "She had a tragic life from beginning to end. I mean, she lost everything when she was eight—and she died at the stake twelve years later. I'm overwhelmed."

"I can see that." His gaze held hers as he also stood. "Perhaps this helps to explain the coldness of this house."

She stared. "Do you believe in ghosts?"

"I'm not sure," he said truthfully. "There is vast charm in doing so, is there not?" He smiled slightly.

Cass had to smile a bit, too. "Yes, it is romantic," she agreed. "I am somewhat confused," she confessed. "Wouldn't Isabel have had to convert to Catholicism in order to marry Alvarado?"

"Yes."

"Then how could she have been tried for being a heretic?"

"In the course of history," Antonio said, "in the course of *our* history, the converted were often the first scapegoats of the Inquisition."

"I hadn't realized," Cass said. "But for some reason, I had assumed she died in England. But maybe you're right, maybe she died here." Cass shivered. "Well, if she is haunting this house, it is understandable. I would too, if I were in her shoes."

"Do you think she is haunting this house?" Antonio asked, his regard unwavering.

Cass met his eyes. "I don't know," she said slowly. Then, "I hope not. But . . ."

"But what?"

Before Cass could blurt out everything that was on her mind, Gregory said, "You have finally met your match, Tonio. A woman as obsessed with the past as you." He smiled at them both.

Cass looked at his handsome face and saw that the smile was false, that it did not reach his eyes. She was taken aback. And she wondered if he did not like her.

And in that single instant, the look he gave her was piercing and malevolent.

Cass stepped back, backing right into Antonio, who steadied her. When she faced Gregory again, he was smiling and the epitome of masculine, easygoing charm.

Cass could not breathe. Had she just seen what she thought she had seen? Had he just given her a look of deep, unrelenting hatred? And if so, why?

For God's sake, they had just met!

Cass was shaken. She moved away from Antonio, and it was then that she felt her presence, before she even saw her. She slowly looked up to find Tracey standing on the threshold of the room.

Cass stiffened, an image of her sister, in a miniskirt, her feet bare, stealing from Antonio's bedroom pervading her mind.

And that was followed by another image, of her sister almost catatonic beneath the tree.

And suddenly Cass hated Tracey. It was Tracey standing between her and Antonio, it was because of Tracey that she would have to refuse Antonio's proposition and return home, it was Tracey who could— and might—take Alyssa away from her at any moment.

And the depth of her hatred astounded Cass.

"Hello," Tracey said somewhat hesitantly. She smiled at Antonio, then Cass, and finally she glanced at Gregory.

His eyes were wide. His instant admiration for her sister was obvious—Cass had seen such a reaction too many times to count.

Cass turned away as Antonio made introductions. She was shaking. And she hated herself for her jealousy. Why was she being reduced to such base emotion? She was good old dependable, sensible, responsible Cass! She was the family-oriented one, the dutiful niece, the supportive sister, the maternal aunt. She was the peacemaker!

She walked away from the group to stand in front of the fire, to stare into the dancing flames, aware now of the headache that had formed behind her temples. And for one instant, Isabel smiled at her from the midst of the flames.

Cass cried out, leaping away from the fire.

Antonio rushed to her. "Did you get burned?" he demanded, eyes wide.

She gripped his arms, staring unseeingly into his face, seeing instead Isabel, smiling—and not prettily. Cass flung a look backward at the hearth. The fire crackled merrily, innocently, within its confines.

She was shaking like a leaf.

"Did you get burned?" Antonio was asking again, holding her upright.

Cass felt her world tilt and spin.

"Is she all right?" That from her sister—her damnable sister.

"I think she might faint." Gregory.

Cass had never fainted a single time in her life, and she wanted to tell them that, but before she could get the words out, her world spun into shades of gray and black, while the windows rattled and the wind roared, and then the darkness was complete.

The plague.

Do you believe in ghosts?

She is summoning all of us together.

Cass felt nauseous. Their voices—Antonio's, Alyssa's—echoed in her mind. And then she really heard their voices, just as something grossly malodorous went up her nostrils. Cass coughed, eyes flying open.

Antonio was bending over her, holding smelling salts. He started to push them toward her again, and Cass turned her head away. "I'm fine."

"You're not fine." His tone was terse. "You must be exhausted."

"She's never fainted in her life, I don't think." That from Tracey, who stood beside Gregory, the two of them at the foot of the sofa.

Cass tried to sit up, but she was still a bit dizzy and she collapsed.

"Lie still," Antonio said sharply.

Cass's eyes flew to his because there was no mistaking his tone. He was concerned for her welfare—extremely so.

Something turned to mush inside of her heart. "I'm okay," she said, aware of the quaver in her tone. "I don't know what happened . . ." And she froze.

She had seen Isabel in the fire.

"Aunt Cass?" Alyssa's voice sounded, filled with childish fear.

No, Cass thought frantically. She had not seen Isabel in the fire. She was obsessed with Isabel, and her imagination was playing terrible tricks upon her. "Honey, I fainted. I'm overtired. But I'm fine."

Alyssa slipped around Antonio, and Cass reached out to take her hand.

"No more martinis," Antonio said firmly. As he spoke, the phone rang. "Alfonso will get that." He slid his arm beneath Cass's back and he helped her to sit up.

Cass was acutely aware of him, and she felt herself flush. She glanced at Tracey. Her sister was staring. Nothing had changed.

Or had it?

Gregory was also staring.

Alfonso appeared on the threshold of the room. He was a spry man of sixty with a head of thick white hair. "Señora," he said to Cass. "*Teléfono*. Señor?" He spoke to Antonio. "*La cena.*"

Cass knew Antonio was about to tell the houseman that he should take a message, and she struggled to her feet. Somehow she knew it was her aunt, whom she had forgotten to call. A moment later she had the phone in her hand. Antonio touched her shoulder; everyone was leaving the room. "Supper is served," he said quietly. "We will be in the dining room."

Cass nodded, returning her attention to the call as everyone filed out. "Aunt Catherine?"

"I am so glad . . . you." The connection was terrible, filled with an echo and static. "Worst trouble," her aunt said, sounding far away.

"I can hardly hear you," Cass cried, gripping the phone. "Can you hear me? Is everything all right?"

"Very well," her aunt seemed to say. She continued to speak, but Cass could not make out another word.

"Aunt Catherine, I can't hear you!" Cass cried loudly. "We're losing this connection. Can you hear me?"

Her aunt spoke again. Cass heard, "Flight . . . Madrid."

"Aunt Catherine?" She stiffened. It felt as if someone had set two heavy boards on her shoulders, which were weighting down her entire body. Cass realized the lights in the library were wavering. Or was that just shadows? She couldn't possibly be fainting again, could she? "What did you say?"

"Castile," her aunt seemed to shout. "Tomorrow!"

And Cass froze, forgetting to breathe. In that instant she understood. Her aunt was in Madrid and she would arrive in Castilla tomorrow.

And soon Auntie Catherine will arrive . . .

"No!" she shouted. "Aunt Catherine, don't come, we'll be home in a few days . . ." She stopped. The line had gone dead.

And as suddenly, the lights in the library went out.

Cass was motionless. She continued to clench the phone as she stood there in the blackness, her heart pounding with undue force, dread washing over her in nauseating waves.

Her aunt was coming to Casa de Sueños.

First she, Tracey and Alyssa had come, then Gregory, and now Aunt Catherine . . .

"Stop it," she told herself, slowly hanging up the phone. She groped for the lamp and tried the switch, but the lights did not come on. The fear escalated. Cass reminded herself that the wiring was faulty; this was a very old, very poorly maintained house. She turned and bumped into a chair, pain shooting up through her knee, and suddenly she felt eyes upon her.

Cass was frozen, incapable of movement, straining to hear, her skin crawling. The sensation of being watched did not diminish. Cass whirled. "Isabel?"

For she could smell her now, the scent of violets wafting closer and closer still. Cass had no doubt to whom the perfume belonged. "Isabel?" She did not feel like a fool; she felt like a terrible coward. She was trembling, her pulse pounding with alarming force. "Are you here?"

The fragrance was overpowering now.

A log fell in the fireplace.

Which was hardly unusual, but now Cass flinched. Warily she scanned the room. Cass faced no one, just a roomful of furniture and paintings. She backed up slowly, glancing around again, but she was completely alone.

Her shoulder was touched by something soft.

Cass cried out, jumping, turning, but it was only a billowing section of drapery. Still, she could not breathe evenly.

Then she realized all the windows were closed, there was no air conditioning in the house, but the damned curtains had moved.

They had moved.

She is here, Cass thought, desperately.

And then, *No one is here! Don't be ridiculous!*

But she stared at the curtains, which were still now. "Isabel? What do you want? I'm not your enemy. I'm your friend. What do you want?"

Cass didn't know what she expected, but there was no reply. She shivered.

"Cassandra?"

Cass whirled at the sound of Antonio's voice. He was standing on the threshold, holding up a candle. Its light was very steady—because the air in the house was so still.

"Who are you talking to?" he asked.

Cass was now aware of the perspiration covering her body in a fine layer of moisture. She maneuvered past some chairs and tables, toward him. "Antonio, I have changed my mind." She kept her voice low. She reached him on the threshold of the room and felt a vast relief. She had to restrain herself from pressing her body close to his.

"In regard to?" he asked.

"To your question—do you believe in ghosts."

He stared at her. And he said, "I am certain the faulty lighting is due to a lack of maintenance and repair, not to her."

Cass stared at his face, which was cast in shadow but illuminated by the candle he held. "Do you smell that floral scent?"

There was no hesitation. "Yes."

Cass wet her lips. "It's her scent. It's her. Isabel."

At least he did not laugh. He said, "I am calling an electrician to-morrow. The entire house is out. Gregory and Alfonso are searching for the fuse box."

Cass grimaced. "Is there a basement?"

"Of sorts," Antonio said.

She grew rigid. "In castles, the dungeons are below ground. I never thought about it, but—"

"This was a fortified manor. You are correct. Dungeons are below."

"Just what we need," Cass said. "By the way, the phones are also dead."

He touched her elbow, still holding up the candle. "We'll eat by candlelight," he said.

Cass didn't think she could summon up any appetite. *Summon.* Damn it all, the word was engraved on her mind now.

As they stepped into the corridor, Antonio said, "But maybe the time has come for me to be honest with you." He paused.

Cass waited expectantly.

"I think I have felt her, too."

Their shoulders brushed as they approached the dining room, which was now alight with candles. The effect wasn't soothing, because the shadows danced. And it certainly wasn't romantic. "What do you mean, you have felt her, too?" Cass whispered.

"I think a presence is very strong in that bedroom upstairs. I had hoped I was imagining it." He may have blushed. It was hard to tell. "That room feels heavy. It's thick and dense. Unhappy even." He shrugged.

Cass paused to stare at him. "This entire house is unhappy. But then, she must have been terribly unhappy when she came here."

"Well, if she is haunting Casa de Sueños, it is probably with good cause, but it also is fairly irrelevant," Antonio said. "Undoubtedly her ghost has been here for four hundred and forty-five years." He smiled briefly, his gaze searching hers.

They were standing just outside the dining room. Cass was aware of Tracey watching them as she sat alone at the table with the children. Both Eduardo and Alyssa were also intent. "I'm worried," she finally said in a whisper so the children would not overhear. "Aunt Catherine's on her way here, and that means all the de Warennes and de la Barcas will be present, with the exception of your mother."

"I do not get your meaning," he said slowly.

Cass inhaled. "What if we're all supposed to be here for a reason? And what if that reason has something to do with the past? With her? Tragedy seems to result whenever the two families come together. We're certainly all together now." Then, grimly, "I imagine that Isabel hates your family."

"Isabel is dead." Antonio was grave. "I have been thinking a lot about that extraordinary coincidence, actually, myself."

Their gazes locked.

"Found it, but it won't do us much good," Gregory said, striding to them, a flashlight in hand. "You need some upkeep on this place, Tonio. Fuses are blown left and right—I've never seen such a thing before."

"We don't have any fuses anywhere?" Cass asked, alarmed.

"Alfonso has been looking," Antonio said. "Why don't we sit down and try to eat something?" He touched Cass's shoulder, guiding her toward the dining room, when the flashlight in Gregory's hand went out.

Gregory cursed in Spanish, flicking the button repeatedly. Then he looked up at his brother. "I don't believe it. Do you have batteries for this?"

Antonio stared at the powerful flashlight, which had gone dead. "I don't know."

Gregory groaned.

Cass glanced into the dining room at the worried faces of the two children. Then she did a double take, riveted by Tracey's expression. Something seemed so odd. Her face was so—relaxed. "It's all right, guys. Tomorrow we will have all the power back," Cass said cheerfully. But she was thinking about her laptop, the lights, the flashlight, and that weird static on her screen. She was thinking about that face she had seen in the fire—even though she was now convinced that had been her imagination. Still, there was a growing possibility that Isabel was haunting them.

No, there was a growing *likelihood*.

But did it really matter?

After all, Isabel was a sad and tragic spirit. What could she really do?

Tracey suddenly stood up. "Yes, everything is all right."

Cass went on alert. Her sister's manner *was* strange—almost too calm, too tranquil. Cass didn't like it. Not when she couldn't help recalling Tracey's odd behavior when she had found her in some kind of trance earlier that day. "Trace?"

Tracey smiled at her. "I'm not hungry. I'm tired, I'm going up to my room."

Cass watched her walk casually past everyone, growing more disturbed by the second. Suddenly she didn't like her sister going upstairs by herself—not one bit. She rushed after her. "Can't you wait? In twenty minutes Alyssa and I will come up, too."

Tracey gazed into her eyes, her own regard the picture of innocence. "What's wrong, Cassandra?" she asked. "Are you afraid of the dark?"

"A little," Cass admitted. "Especially on a night like this."

Tracey smiled. "I love the dark," she said. "Good night." She turned and glided into the great hall.

Cass watched her go. And it was only when Tracey had turned the corner that she realized that her sister never called her Cassandra, and that she had always been afraid of the dark.

Alyssa was gripping Cass's hand tightly as they all said good night to one another in the great hall. Cass's heart lurched unpleasantly as Antonio, with Eduardo in hand, Gregory beside him, went down their respective corridor on the other side of the house. She stared after them. The night felt oppressive. Worse, it felt menacing.

At least the wind had died down.

But now the silence felt unnatural. It was deathly.

"It's so quiet," Alyssa whispered. "Aunt Cass, do we have to sleep up there?"

Cass quickly smiled down at her niece as they made their way by candlelight down the terribly dark, shadowy corridor. That hall alone was enough to give her goose bumps. Their footsteps sounded too loud on the wood floors. She wanted to glance over her shoulder repeatedly.

Tonight, she knew, she would never sleep a wink. And no matter how she chided herself, she just could not relax. "Where else should we sleep?"

"I don't know," Alyssa said helplessly.

Upstairs was as quiet as below. Tracey's door was firmly closed. Cass's insides curdled as she walked past; she hated the idea of her sister sleeping alone. She debated checking in on her, but one look at Alyssa's pinched, white face made her change her mind. Her niece needed all of her attention now.

She had left their bedroom door wide open, and now they walked inside. And Cass froze.

The screen of her computer stared at her, glowing with light, a DOS prompt blinking.

Alyssa either understood or felt her tension, because her hand tightened in Cass's.

Cass stared, unable to move, barely able to think. She had closed the laptop. She had turned it off. And the rest of the power was off in the house, wasn't it?

She whirled and hit the light switch on the wall, but no lights came on.

Then it dawned on her that her laptop was running on its battery. But she had closed the lid. Hadn't she?

"What is it?" Alyssa cried nervously.

Cass began to sweat. She was not going to draw a very stupid conclusion. As Antonio had said, so what if Isabel was around? Undoubtedly she had haunted his house for 445 years. It was hardly a big deal; half of the castles and manors in England were supposedly haunted, as well.

Ghosts did not open laptops and turn them on. There was a reasonable explanation.

"I don't want to sleep here," Alyssa announced with desperation in her tone. "I don't!"

Someone touched her from behind. Cass cried out, whirling.

It was only Alyssa. But the abrupt movement had made her candle go out.

"Now we have no light," Alyssa cried, choking on tears.

"We can't sleep with a lit candle, sweetie." Cass meant to be cheerful. But a droplet of sweat was trickling down one temple. Now she did not want to turn off her computer—it was the only light they had.

She looked slowly around their room, but could only see distorted shapes and shadows. "I have a great idea. Let's take a blanket and some pillows and sleep downstairs . . . in the library." She would feel better sleeping on the same side of the house as everyone else, she thought— and hoped. And if any room could be considered cozy, the library was it.

"Okay," Alyssa agreed eagerly.

A moment later they were on their way.

"So how do you plan to do it?" Gregory asked Antonio as they left Eduardo tucked in Antonio's bed.

Antonio pushed open the door to another bedroom farther down the hall. "Whatever do you mean?" They were speaking quietly in Spanish, so as not to wake the sleeping child.

Gregory smiled at his brother, folding his arms over his chest and pausing in the doorway as Antonio set a lit candle down. "Your girlfriend is exquisite—but she's not your type. Not at all."

"You are right."

And Gregory smiled. It had been obvious to him from the moment he first walked into the house, and it had only become more obvious as the evening had worn on. "In fact, knowing you as well as I know myself," he said, "I would say you are somewhat fond of Cassandra." In spite of how he felt about returning to Casa de Sueños, the personal dynamics unfolding before his eyes were rather interesting.

Antonio eyed him. "Why do you take pleasure in my intimate affairs?" he finally asked—without rancor.

"Because I am seven and a half minutes younger than you." Gregory grinned. "I live vicariously through you," he joked. For he was the one with the endless stream of girlfriends and the weekends in the south of France, not his brother. Then, sobering, he clasped his shoulder. "Because it has been a long time since I saw a smile in your eyes," he said.

The twins' gazes met and held, and for one brief moment they were both thinking about the same woman—Antonio's wife. Antonio quickly looked away.

"Get some sleep. You've had a long day." Antonio turned, holding his own candle. Then he paused. "Oh, by the way. Cassandra and I are friends, and that is all."

Gregory nodded, not missing the fact that his brother would still shut down should the subject of Margarita even begin to arise. But it was nice to see him even remotely interested in the kind of woman he should be dating. "What a bind," he said lightly. "Sisters. Hmmm."

"*Buenas noches,*" Antonio said firmly, practically shutting the door in his face.

Gregory laughed then, tossing his suit jacket on the bed, glad to see that Alfonso had brought his overnight bag up to the room. As he stripped off his tie, his good humor instantly vanished. Whatever had possessed him to return to his old home? He hadn't been back since the summer his father had died.

All the pleasure he had felt at seeing his brother and nephew again, and all of the relief he'd had at learning that they were fine, disappeared. He hated Casa de Sueños, the place of his father's death. Sometimes he thought he hated it even more than Antonio did.

Too well, as if it were days ago, not thirty-five years, he remembered being a small boy and hiding in his mother's armoire, hiding from . . . what? Or whom?

He closed his eyes. His shrink had told him children had huge imaginations, and that they all had imaginary playmates. Gregory had tried to explain to him, repeatedly, that this had not been a playmate—it had been a demon. A beautiful female demon who had appeared whenever he was least expecting it, causing him to run away and cower in his hiding place in abject fear.

He froze in the act of removing his shirt. Had he just heard someone in the corridor outside?

No, he decided, he had not. Gregory reminded himself that he was no longer that cowardly, frightened child. He was a chief financial officer at Barclays, Madrid, with a beautiful home in that city, and another one in Marbella on the Costa del Sol. And that the shrink, whom he had fired, had undoubtedly been right: she had been a figment of his imagination even if she had not been a playmate. And she had never done anything, anyway. To this day, he didn't know why at the age of three and four she had scared him so relentlessly.

Still, his pulse was accelerated now. He couldn't help hating the house. Already the air felt like it was choking him, it was so dense, so thick, making it difficult to breathe. And even though it was a beautiful night, filled with millions of stars, as far as he was concerned, the night was a chasm of silence and stillness, while the lights remained out, the phones useless, as if they had time-traveled back into the most barbaric of past times.

Images tumbled through his mind, too quickly for him to sort out, but they were all bloody, until he finally realized he was imagining Margarita in an ugly, violent death, and his father before her, run over by a car on the streets of Pedraza.

Of course, he had never seen either his father or his sister-in-law in such a state.

An image of the woman tried to come into focus in his mind. Panic rising, he shoved it away. Even though he refused to see her, he knew who she was—he did not want to recall any childhood demons now. Years ago she had been so vivid he had thought her real. Now he was determined to keep her relegated to the dusty shadows of ancient, unwanted memories.

Something scraped outside his door. Gregory stiffened.

And then he heard it, very distinctly, nails scratching on his door.

And he knew. For one moment, sheer panic overcame him, and he was reduced to a child of three or four years old again.

Cass and Alyssa, their arms filled with pillows and blankets, approached the library, then halted in midstride. About to enter the very same room was Antonio, a sleeping Eduardo, blankets, and a pillow all in his arms.

He turned and looked at them. He had placed several candles in the library, which provided just enough illumination in the corridor for Cass to make out his surprised expression.

She realized he might not be able to see her as clearly, and she called out to him as they came forward. "What are you doing?" she asked quietly.

Now he smiled. "I could ask you the same thing."

"We decided to camp out here." She smiled back.

He continued to smile. "I was going to read for a while."

Cass motioned at the boy sleeping in his arms, her smile fading. Was he also reluctant to leave Eduardo alone?

His smile disappeared. "I did not want to leave him sleeping alone upstairs—even though my brother has a room just down the hall."

Their gazes held as a mutual comprehension formed between them. Cass realized that they had to talk—and frankly. They entered the library and set the children up in their blankets with their pillows in one cozy section of the room, by the sofa, not far from Antonio's massive desk. "How's that?" Cass asked Alyssa, kissing her cheek. Eduardo, who had woken up for one instant, was just inches from her.

"Much better," Alyssa said, yawning, her lids lowering abruptly. Cass watched her fall instantly asleep, a Beanie Baby she hadn't slept with all year tucked in her arms.

She straightened, and found Antonio watching them—watching her. Her heart accelerated abruptly because his gaze was so intent.

Cass didn't move. Everything hit her at once. It was just after midnight, the house was huge and dark, the night silent and still, and she was alone with him. Somehow the two sleeping children did not seem to count. Her heart sped. And she thought, *This is so dangerous.*

And she wasn't thinking about Isabel de Warenne now.

Cass tried to get a grip on herself. It was intimate, but they were both adults, her sister was upstairs, and nothing was going to happen just because they were alone together at such an hour on such a night. Nothing.

"This is an unusual night," he said softly.

"Very." Cass went to stand beside him. "This house is very spooky at night. I don't like leaving Alyssa alone, either."

Their gazes met again, holding for what seemed an interminably long time. He spoke slowly. "Truthfully, I much prefer having guests than residing here alone."

"I don't blame you." She hesitated. "Antonio, is she here? Or are we nuts to think so?"

His gaze drifted over her features, one by one. "I do not have a lot of childhood memories from before my father died. But the one thing I do remember, and well, was a terrible argument I overheard between my parents—here."

Somehow Cass sensed what was coming. "What were they arguing about?"

"My mother was crying. I had never heard her so upset. In fact, the only time I have since heard her as upset was after my father's death. She kept telling my father that she hated this place, that we had to go home to Madrid." He was grim. Cass saw a nerve twitch in his cheek.

"Do you remember anything else?"

He hesitated, his gaze direct. "Actually, I think I do. I think she said, 'I am so afraid.'"

"I am so ready to leap to conclusions," Cass whispered, now looking around at the four corners of the room and then into the dark corridor outside.

His hand closed over hers, briefly, surprisingly. "I know you are. Your imagination is charming."

Her breath caught. She met his gaze and felt the intensity there. She didn't want to move, and she couldn't quite think of a reply. Instead, she said, quickly, "You mentioned that your mother remarried. Where does she live? Could I talk to her sometime?"

He had dropped her hand. "She lives in Sevilla. Her husband died a few years ago. I'm afraid she would not be very communicative. Not about this house, the past, or Isabel." He held her gaze. "Your very name would set her against you."

Cass grew uneasy. She had to come clean about her aunt. "My aunt blames herself for your father's death, Antonio. I don't know why." There, she had said it. And she felt as if a huge weight had lifted from her shoulders.

His gaze flickered. "I would like to speak with her," he said softly.

She could only stare. She did not want them discussing the past. She knew Catherine would incriminate herself.

"But when the phones are repaired, I will call her—and try to get her to speak with you," Antonio said.

He meant his mother. Cass melted a little, inside, unable to look away. "I promise to drop the subject if she gets upset, even slightly," she said, meaning it.

"I know you would never upset her, or anyone, not intentionally."

Cass's pulse accelerated. "Thanks."

"You are a very kind person, Cassandra," he said, and for one moment Cass thought he might reach out to her. But he did not. Instead, he turned away, leaving her breathless.

"This house has a huge history, and I must learn what that history is." He paced back and forth, then paused. His gaze locked with hers. "I have never felt so strongly about anything, Cassandra. So many questions—and the answers are all here."

Cass told herself to focus on the conversation—not the man. "I feel it too," she said, low. "There is something so compelling about your home. It's as if there's a magnet here, drawing us all, keeping us enthralled."

The minute she had spoken, her heart skipped. *She is summoning us all together . . .*

"I need you here to help me," he said.

Cass's eyes widened. She had not expected him to repeat his proposition.

He did not break their interlocked stare. "Have you had time to consider staying?" he asked very softly.

And she heard herself say, "I want to stay." *What am I doing?!* But it was true. She did want to stay. Desperately. And not just because of the enigmatic compulsion of the house—or Isabel. She wanted to stay. Even though she was so scared. She wanted to stay because she was a woman who hadn't allowed herself to feel anything for a man in a very long time, and this man, who had belonged to her sister, was making her feel alive again in ways she had not expected, not wanted, had forsaken forever.

"Then it is settled," he murmured.

His tone was so low and sensuous that Cass remained frozen, staring up at him.

He must have realized that, unintentionally at least, he was coming on to her, because he stepped away from her abruptly. It was hard to tell, but Cass thought he was flushing. And her heart was slamming around in her chest like an out-of-control Ping-Pong ball. She jammed her hands into the pockets of her trousers nervously. Things were on the verge of getting out of hand, she decided, and she *had* to leave on Monday.

But how could she, Goddamn it? How?

She reminded herself that her relationship with her sister was at stake.

That Alyssa might be at stake.

And what if her earlier suspicions were correct? What if Aunt Catherine was right? What if Antonio's mother was right? And what if, dear God, there was a summoning . . . Cass could hardly believe herself. "Antonio, I want to stay, but it's against all my better judgment," she began.

"It is settled," he said with insistence. For he was an astute man, and clearly he saw the internal battle that she waged.

Nothing was settled. Cass hugged herself. She told herself she had two days in which to make a decision.

"If I do stay," Cass said slowly, "maybe we should send the children home with my aunt. Maybe they shouldn't stay here." The moment she spoke, she flushed—hoping he would not think she was trying to get rid of the children so they could be alone.

But clearly the notion never crossed his mind. "Eduardo looks forward to spending the summer with me. It is very important for us." He reached for her. When his hands settled on her shoulders, and it *was* platonic, Cass became dazed. "Cassandra, she can't hurt us." He spoke slowly. "She might make us a bit uncomfortable, but isn't that all in our minds?" His gaze was intent and searching.

Cass thought about everything that had happened since they had arrived. She thought about how the house felt like a magnet. "You're probably right," she said slowly.

"You'll feel differently tomorrow, in the light of day, when we have an electrician here and when the phone lines are restored." He did not release her.

"Yes, I guess so." Cass hoped so—but didn't really believe it for a minute. What was she doing? She was getting in deeper and deeper. He thought she was staying, with Alyssa, they would be working side by side every day, she was in love, he was not, she would undoubtedly get hurt, and badly—like never before. And to hide her thoughts, she looked away.

He touched her cheek. Startled, Cass whipped her gaze back to his face.

"I do need you, Cassandra. Together we can unearth the facts of Isabel's life and learn what has been the cause of this destiny that seems to link our families. We can piece together the puzzle of what happened to her between the age of eight, when she lost her family, and the age of nineteen, when she wed. And then we can find out if she was really tried for heresy, if she was really burned at the stake." His tone was low and hoarse and very seductive, not because he was trying to seduce her, but because he was so impassioned. His eyes smoldered for the very same reason.

"Not fair," Cass muttered. Her pulse had gone sky-high. A brilliant man, a fascinating man, and a lust for the past which they shared. He was capitalizing on it. "And you know it."

"I know it," he said, not removing his hand from her cheek.

They stared at each other.

And Cass thought, *It would be so easy to slip into his arms. Who would ever know?* They had already kissed, and gotten away with it. So easy . . . "You're trying to seduce me," she said firmly. But she did not walk away.

"I am trying to seduce your mind," he said, smiling just a little. "Because you are a woman who must be seduced from the mind, not the body."

He was so very right—and so very wrong. Cass pulled away. She was more than intellectually aroused; her thoughts had veered in erotic directions.

He released her.

Cass walked away, thoroughly shaken.

"Cassandra."

She halted, her back to him. Her tension escalated tenfold.

He turned her around, and the next thing she knew, she was in his arms, and their mouths had locked.

And from that first brushing of lips, something ignited immediately—his hands held her head still and his mouth plied hers. The demand was unmistakable, intense. And Cass was crushed against his chest, enfolded in his body. His tongue was in her mouth. Her hard, tight nipples were knotted against his cashmere sweater, and she clung to him, opening, for more. Their teeth grated. It hurt. But pleasure shot through Cass, emanating from her sex.

Cass felt one of his impossibly hard thighs move between hers, pressuring her labia. Friction swelled her clitoris. Desire, the kind she had never experienced, the kind she had only read about, the kind she had suspected only existed in novels and her own secret fantasies, overwhelmed her. She rode him. Hard.

He spoke to her in Spanish. Harsh words, guttural words.

Cass felt the first tiny explosion, a harbinger of what was to come, and she cried out.

So did he. And then her bottom was in his hands, she was bent backward over an object—a chair, a table, a desk—while their tongues mated frantically and their bodies tried to. His hands were so large that a buttock practically filled each palm. Suddenly he shifted.

And Cass was pressed down flat on her back, and she realized she was on his desk, and something fell to the floor, shattering, and he moved on top of her, and the wonderful, hard protrusion of his manhood was arcing up against her pubis, promising her ecstasy. She managed to think, *Oh my God,* as she spread her legs wide.

He reached for and unzipped her jeans.

Then he palmed her wet, heated sex through her satin panties.

Cass shifted and came, wildly, loudly.

One of the children cried out in his or her sleep.

Simultaneously they shifted.

And Cass's mind leapt into action. "The kids!"

He stood up instantly, lifting her to her feet, and when she met his gaze, she saw that he was as stunned and excited as she. The expression on his face, and in his wide, gold-flecked eyes, was one she would never ever forget.

Eduardo cried out restlessly again.

She did not move, except to zip up her jeans. Her panting seemed terribly loud, her heartbeat thundered in her ears, and Cass worried that she would wake both children as Antonio quickly went to his son, bending over to him and murmuring words of reassurance. She followed his tall muscular body with her eyes. Greed filled her. A greed that was pure and raw hunger. Cass could only stare. She could only think about what it would be like to have him inside of her.

She closed her eyes, swallowing a moan. There had been no mistaking his passion. He wanted her the way she wanted him.

And she had come, for God's sake. She had come and he had only touched her.

When she opened her eyes, he was standing with most of his back turned to her, but a three-quarter moon was visible in the night outside, and moonlight was spilling onto him. Cass saw he was very rigid, his legs were braced apart, and he was still breathing hard. He was still aroused.

He still wanted her.

It was almost unbelievable.

Cass wasn't sure exactly which happened first, and next. For it was in that moment that she thought about the fact that he had been Tracey's lover, but it was also then that she saw him stiffen impossibly, as if snapped upright like a puppet on a string, and he cried out.

Cass looked past him at the window, and her heart dropped right to her feet.

Standing there, clearly framed by the window, backlit by the moon, was a woman with long, curly hair and a pale, oval face.

Her hair was disheveled, her face wild. And it was not Isabel.

Gregory moved decisively to the door, throwing it open. He almost jumped in surprise at the sight of Tracey standing there, smiling at him—instead of the female demon he had half expected.

"I know you will think me awful, simply awful," she said softly, "but I can't sleep. Antonio has broken up with me, and my sister and I are fighting." Her look was soft and plaintive. She held up a bottle of red wine, which until now had been hidden behind the sheer layer of her black dress, through which he could glimpse long, endless, provocative legs.

He knew what she wanted—or at least, he thought she did. Even though she had dutifully ignored him all night, he'd sensed it all along. Antonio had agreed with him, that she was not his type. But she was his brother's lover. *Jesus!* What was he thinking?

He found his tongue. "This is a surprise," he said evenly. He had to send her on her way. He wondered when the last time was that his brother had made love to her.

She shrugged a little, holding up two wineglasses in her other hand. "I really can't sleep," she said. "And you're still awake, too."

She was the most beautiful woman he had ever seen and he was already hard. But he glanced down the black corridor, toward his brother's room. "This is not the best idea," he said.

She stared, the smile gone. "Antonio and I have broken up," she said flatly. "He wants my sister."

Gregory was grim. "You seem to be taking it well."

"I guess we weren't right for one another," she said philosophically. She smiled again. Her eyes went right to his mouth—before sliding down the entire length of his body.

"Your sister has a lot in common with my brother," Gregory agreed, warring with himself. Then, "Tracey, I would love nothing more than to have a drink with you. But not now, not here, in my brother's house. Why don't I take your number? I'll be in London on business in another three weeks. If you are still available, I'll give you a call."

She gave him a look and slipped past him, brushing her hip against his groin as she did so. Gregory was seized with almost violent desire. For one instant he could think of nothing but throwing her down on the bed and burying himself inside of her.

He stepped back, away from her, shocked by the brief, almost insane passion he had just felt.

She sauntered over to the bed and sat down on it. She swung her long legs and smiled at him.

Just a drink. What's one drink? You're a grown man, you can control yourself. The rationalizations sped like lightning through his head.

"It's just a drink," she whispered. "I'm not asking you to sleep with me." She smiled. "I wouldn't do that. I mean, he's right up the hall—with his son."

He drifted toward her, almost against his will, his heart beating hard inside the cage of his chest. "Yes, just a drink," he repeated, taking a glass from her. He poured them both glasses, then set the bottle down, suddenly finding himself sitting on the bed beside her.

She shifted, crossing her legs, the skirts riding up over her knees. He looked.

"Cheers," she said, clinking glasses.

"Cheers," he responded, finding it harder and harder to think coherently. Her perfume was as mesmerizing as her body and face. He could not define the scent.

And she was on her knees, the wine forgotten, spilled all over the bed, coming forward, over him. An instant later, as their mouths touched, her warm, wet loins, which were bare, were riding him as he went down on his back.

Their mouths opened and locked violently. Gregory had no more coherent thoughts.

Instead, he flipped her onto her back, kissing her frantically, shoving up her skirts, palming her wet, throbbing pussy. She reached for and unzipped him and he sprang hot and thick and long into her hands.

She bent to suck him down her throat.

He thrust hard and deep, managing to think that this was as close as he would ever come to heaven.

And then he pushed her back down, knifing into her, while she cried out, her nails raking down his back.

And when it was over, when they both lay side by side, half-clothed, he thought, *Jesus. What have I done?*

He suddenly sat up, reaching over his shoulder to touch his back. *"Por Dios,"* he said, "I'm bleeding."

"I'm so sorry," she whispered.

He looked down, and saw endless legs and rampant sexuality, her skirts twisted around her waist. She lifted one leg, high and higher still, until he could kiss her toe.

"What are you wearing?" he murmured.

Their gazes locked, hers so blue and intense he had to flinch and glance away. "Violets," she said slowly. "My favorite."

THIRTEEN

MIDNIGHT

Antonio whirled and ran from the library.

Cass didn't think twice, she ran after him. Who the hell could be outside on such a night?

Antonio had flung open the front door of the house; he dashed outside into the darkness of the night. Cass paused on the front steps, watching, her mind racing. Antonio had run around the side of the house, disappearing from sight.

She stared. His reaction was surprising—did he know the woman? She began to feel ill. Obviously he did. Obviously he more than knew her. And Cass had a dreadful inkling.

Slowly she walked down the steps, only to see him returning. In the faint moonlight his face seemed ghastly white. "Did you see her, too?" he asked harshly.

"I saw a woman," she said slowly.

"It wasn't my imagination," he whispered, almost to himself. "Oh, God!"

Cass didn't move toward him. He was shaking. A terrible sickness filled her from the inside out. "You recognized her?" she asked.

He glanced at her with absolute bewilderment. He seemed to be in shock. "Yes."

Cass did not want to ask. She said, "Who is she?" already knowing the answer.

His face crumpled. "My wife."

In the great hall Cass paused, hugging herself, nauseous now. Antonio was outside, calling his wife's name. Funny, but she hadn't known her name before; it hadn't mattered. But it was Margarita.

She stared almost blindly into the blackness of the night. A million stars remained overhead. On any other night she would have admired the brilliant sky. The warm summer night. The glinting three-quarter moon. But not now.

This was impossible, wasn't it?

He had been shouting for her, circling the house, for what felt like hours now, and his voice was very hoarse. Cass felt tears fill her eyes. And she thought, *You stupid, stupid, fool. Did you really think he was for you?*

She sank down onto the front steps. He was preoccupied now with a woman who had disappeared eight years ago. The last thing on his mind was the passion they had just shared. And she cried a little.

Suddenly he was standing before her, as pale as a ghost, his eyes circled, red rimmed, the light in them bewildered, desperate.

"Any luck?" Cass managed, wiping her own eyes with the back of her hand and hoping he wouldn't notice her misery and heartbreak.

He didn't even reply. He moved past her, and Cass realized he remained in a state of shock.

And her misery vanished. In that instant it struck her that they were the same. Eight years ago her lover had simply left. And even though somewhere in her subconscious she had already suspected the truth about him—she had already suspected that there were lies heaped upon lies—she just had refused to believe it. Well, Antonio's wife had simply left one day, too. Or disappeared.

Cass stood up and walked inside, after him. "Antonio?"

He seemed startled by her voice, and he turned, finally meeting her eyes. Then he shied away, seeing the front door, which remained open. He went to it, shutting and locking it. She stared at his broad shoulders and back. Then she walked over to him, refusing to debate what she intended, and she turned him around and embraced him. Amazingly, he did not move away. His arms encircled her very loosely.

"Can you talk about it?" she asked softly, stepping back. She was recovering her own composure now. Cass decided there *must* be a reasonable explanation. Was his wife an amnesiac, running around the countryside, lost and bewildered? If only she hadn't seen the woman, too. But a woman had been standing there, Cass was quite certain of it. "Are you sure that was your—" She could not say the word "wife." "Are you sure that was Margarita?"

He glanced at her. "Yes."

He had no doubt. If Cass hadn't seen a woman standing there herself, she would think he had seen a figment of his imagination—that he had seen something he'd yearned to see for so very long now. Suddenly she shivered. If she was worried about Isabel haunting them, what about the possibility that it was his wife? Assuming that she was dead?

Cass wet her lips. "Antonio?"

He turned, and Cass felt the full impact of his expression—it was one of defeat.

"What kind of perfume did she wear?" she asked.

"What?"

Cass repeated the question. "Your wife. What kind of perfume did she wear?"

He looked at her as if she were losing her mind. "Something floral but spicy. I don't recall the name, but it was by Loewe."

Cass. "Was it the scent of violets?"

His gaze widened. "No, it was not. Jesu! Are you thinking we saw her ghost?" he cried.

"I don't know what to think," Cass said softly. She rubbed his shoulder, but he did not seem to notice. "Are you sure it was her? Maybe it was another woman. Look, the house has no lights. Maybe there wasn't even a woman out there at all." Cass didn't think so; still, she didn't know what to think. "You haven't been back here in years. Maybe you saw what you wanted to see."

He just looked at her with an odd expression. "I don't think so. She was so real."

Suddenly he covered his face with his hands.

Cass took his arm. "Let's go back to the library."

He nodded.

And as they walked back inside, Cass was torn. He still loved his missing wife. That seemed so clear. How could she not feel for him? But God, he no longer was even remotely interested in her, Cass. And wasn't that as it should be?

She wondered what it would be like to be loved so much, that way, by this man. She could not imagine it.

And Cass wanted to know what had happened. But now was not the time to pry.

But before they had even reached the library, he said, "There was never an answer. There was never a single explanation. There were only theories."

Cass faltered in surprise.

He entered the library, went straight to the bar cart, and poured himself a shot of whiskey. To his credit, he did not toss it down. He didn't even sip it. He just held it, staring down at the drink.

Cass sucked up her composure and her courage. "What happened?"

"We came for a holiday." He looked at her. His smile was a parody, and it was ghastly. "Actually, it was my idea. I hadn't been here since my father's death when I was four, and I was ready, so ready, to come back, to look at the past, to even look for answers about my father and his life. Margarita was thrilled. She had encouraged me for years to come here. She thought it would be good for me." He finally took a sip of scotch, then set it down with a grimace.

Cass knew better than to speak.

"Two days later, I woke up. The bed beside me was empty. There was a huge thunderstorm. Something was banging downstairs. I wasn't concerned, but I got up to check, and found the front door wide open. Then I was mildly concerned. I closed and locked the door. I found a window here in the library open. It was making all the noise. The thunder and lightning had stopped; it had begun to rain. I went back upstairs expecting to find Margarita asleep in bed. But it was still empty." He paused.

Up until then, he had been speaking matter-of-factly. Now his tone choked. He did not look at Cass. "She wasn't in the bathroom, as I had thought. She wasn't with Eduardo. She wasn't anywhere. She was gone."

Cass stared. "Gone?" So those rumors circling among the students at his lecture had been true, she managed to think.

"Vanished. Without a trace. Never to be seen again."

Cass realized in that instant that they were not the same, not at all. He had adored his wife. He'd had a good marriage. She could sense all of that. And then his wife had simply disappeared.

"She was happy. One of the happiest, kindest people I have ever known. We were happy. She loved me, our son. She did not leave me and my son. She did not run off with a lover. She did not run off to commit suicide. There was no sign of a forced entry anywhere. She was not abducted—and there was never a ransom note."

"My God," Cass whispered.

"She was a healthy, sane individual. There was no history of mental illness in her family. None." He gripped the drink so hard his knuckles turned white.

"I'm sorry," Cass said helplessly.

"But the front door was open. There were a few tracks. Her footprints. Her feet were bare. She didn't take anything. She was in her nightclothes. She left the house and walked away into the night."

Cass didn't know what to say.

His face changed. It wrinkled hideously, turning savage, frightening. He threw the glass with all of his might at the wall. It shattered.

Cass awoke to brilliant sunshine. It was bathing her face, and she screwed her eyes shut, exhausted, not wanting to wake up. There was so much peace in sleep.

Then the events of the prior evening hit her, hard. Immediately she sat up, still groggy, blinking against the blinding light.

She was alone in the library, on the floor, where she had curled up with Alyssa, only to toss and turn restlessly—with fear and dread—until dawn. Now she estimated that it was close to noon. Cass threw off the blanket and got to her feet.

For a moment she did not move. Had they really seen Margarita outside the window last night? She studied the library, and then the countryside that was visible through the windows. In the light of day, her fears of the night before seemed absurd. The day felt amazingly benign.

There was an explanation, she thought. There was always an explanation.

People tended to see what they wanted to see. Maybe Margarita hadn't been in love with her husband, maybe there had been someone else.

Maybe she hadn't been happy. Maybe she had been seriously depressed, but hiding it and doing a damn good job of it.

Maybe there had been kidnappers. Real pros.

Cass sighed. They were probably never going to know the truth. Unless that really was Margarita and they found her again. She recalled how devastated Antonio had been, and her heart turned over, hard.

She realized that she herself was somewhat depressed. Now was not the time to even think about the passion they had briefly found—and as quickly lost.

Abruptly Cass tried one of the lamps, but the lights were still out. She lifted the phone; still no dial tone. Someone would have to drive into a nearby village to call an electrician, buy fuses, and alert the telephone company to their predicament.

She left the library. She found Alfonso in the kitchen, preparing what she suspected would be their lunch, and outside, in the inner courtyard, she saw Alyssa and Eduardo playing hopscotch. Eduardo would hobble with amazing agility through the blocks drawn in chalk on the stone ground. Alyssa was cheering. Cass had to smile in spite of bleak mood.

"*Buenos días, señora,*" Alfonso said with a smile. "*Los niños . . .* they play . . . *bueno.*"

"*Buenos días.* Yes, they do play well together." Cass suddenly realized she was ravenous—she had hardly eaten a thing all day yesterday. "Where are Antonio and his brother, *por favor?*"

His reply was in fluent Spanish, and Cass could only blink.

"Pedraza," he said firmly. "Pedraza."

Of course, the brothers had gone to town. Cass poured herself a glass of fresh orange juice. "Alfonso, have you seen my sister? *Por favor,* Tracey, *hermana mía?*"

"*No he visto,*" he said, smiling.

Cass got the gist and wasn't thrilled. He was offering her an interesting-looking egg dish, which appeared to be a frittata made with potatoes, and Cass smiled hungrily. As he warmed it in the oven, she went upstairs to shower quickly and change. But once she left the entry hall, her steps slowed.

The house no longer felt quite so benign.

There were shadows on the stairs. The air was thick and still. The hairs on Cass's nape lifted.

Cass told herself not to be ridiculous. After all, she rationalized, even if the house was haunted, nothing had actually happened since their arrival; it was hardly a big deal that the lights and the phones had gone out because of lack of maintenance.

Or that they had seen, or thought they had seen, a woman standing outside the window last night, a woman who had disappeared without a trace eight years ago.

Cass quickened her pace. It was a big deal. Just like it was a big deal that her aunt Catherine was coming all this way to Spain.

Upstairs, she fled into her bedroom, refusing to glance around; she quickly gathered up fresh clothes and bolted into the bathroom. She locked the door, then unlocked it. Neither way pleased her. As she waited for the water to warm, she fidgeted, uncomfortable. Finally she began to knead the muscles in the nape of her neck.

Okay. She was a coward. The house was still creepy, even in the light of day.

Cass was showered and dressed in five flat minutes.

Tracey's door was firmly closed. Cass knocked quickly, intending to wake her sister up. She hadn't forgotten how weird she had acted the night before.

There was no answer. Her heart lurching unpleasantly, Cass glanced all around her, but the corridor was empty. Sunlight was filtering in from the opposite end.

"Tracey? Rise and shine." She pushed open the door and blinked.

Tracey was not in her bed. In fact, it was perfectly made up, as if she hadn't slept there at all. Cass knew her sister would not make her bed, and even if, for some reason, she did, she would never do so like a professional housemaid.

She glanced around the room, espying Tracey's shorts along with a G-string and the tank top she'd worn earlier. If Cass had expected to see any clothes thrown around, it would have been the tiny see-through black dress that she'd worn to supper.

Suddenly Cass was alarmed. Tracey wasn't there. She clearly hadn't slept in her bed. If Cass hadn't seen Antonio fall asleep at his desk last night in the library, over a book, his glasses still on, she would have known exactly where—and with whom—she had slept. But this was so odd.

Just like her sister's behavior had been so odd last night.

Cass felt a small bubble of panic. She tamped it down. Tracey was not missing.

A thought struck her. What if it had been Tracey outside that window, not Antonio's wife?

Suddenly she had an image of her earlier that day, sitting beneath the tree, almost catatonic. Cass shivered. And she knew.

Isabel. Isabel was somehow behind this.

She didn't want to have such thoughts, but they had come out of nowhere, so strongly that they were undeniable.

I will be your mother now.

Cass stiffened. She did not know what that absurd statement meant, and she wished she'd never remembered it—or that Alyssa had never dreamed it.

"Damn it, Tracey, where are you?" Cass cried. "I have Alyssa to take care of, and maybe even Antonio. Goddamn it, why do I have to take care of you, too?"

The door closed behind her.

Cass jumped, crying out. She faced the closed door, wide-eyed. "Tracey?"

There was no answer.

"Tracey?" Cass asked, frightened. But why would her sister play tricks on her?

No one answered her.

And in that moment, so much flashed through Cass's mind. Her aunt's warnings. Tracey's odd behavior. Alyssa's dreams. The power going out last night. Seeing Margarita—or someone—outside.

Someone closing the door to the crypt.

Just like someone had just shut the bedroom door, now. Someone . . . *but who?*

Was someone playing tricks on them all? Was someone merely being mischievous?

But who? And why?

Gregory.

Cass stiffened.

He had seemed a decent sort—and he was Antonio's twin brother, for God's sake. She was convinced now that she had imagined the hateful look he had given her. But what if she had not imagined it? Because what she had thought she had seen was utter malevolence.

She reminded herself that he had only arrived last night—but he could have lied. Maybe he had arrived earlier—maybe he had closed the door to the crypt.

Maybe he had messed with her laptop.

But why would he do such things?

And suddenly Cass thought about the way he had looked at Tracey. Surely Tracey had not crept into bed with him—and in any case, surely he would have thrown her out.

Surely he had not seduced her.

Very uneasy, Cass faced the door. Then she swung it open.

She did not know what she expected—Gregory, all smiling charm, or utter hostility; her sister, beguilingly serene, or angrily demanding to know what Cass was doing in her room; Margarita; Isabel.

No one was there. Cass glanced left, then right, and rushed down the hall. She pounded down the stairs, aware that her suspicions might be more than suspicions, they might well be turning into sheer paranoia. But could she truly be blamed if that was so?

A moment later she heard two male voices ahead of her, and suddenly she turned the corner and saw Antonio and Gregory ahead, trooping into the kitchen. She followed them.

"Good morning," Antonio said, setting down a bag of groceries. He met her gaze. His brother set down another bag. "I'm glad you had a chance to rest." He smiled—and it was as if last night had never happened. It was as if he had not been devastated by the sight of a woman who may or may not have been his long, lost wife.

She was ensnared by his eyes while her heart thudded uncontrollably, and even while she was telling herself that the five hundred obstacles that lay between them were for the best—because of her sister and because of Aunt Catherine—she knew she was lying to herself. She was fascinated. Intrigued. Lust filled. Smitten. Hopelessly so on all counts. "I had trouble falling asleep."

"It was a long night." Then, his tone changing, "Fuses. Tonight we shall have lights. Unfortunately, the phone man will not be here until Monday or Tuesday, but an electrician promised to make it this afternoon."

Cass must have shown her disbelief, because Gregory said, "This is Spain, Cass. Here there is *never* any urgency."

"I'd forgotten," Cass said, as Alfonso set the frittata in front of her. She sat down and dug in, her appetite instantly returning, and was rewarded with the best eggs she had ever tasted. "Wow."

"We call that a *tortilla español*," Gregory told her amiably. "Usually we eat it as a tapa, instead of supper."

Cass suddenly looked at him. "Have either of you guys seen Tracey this morning?" She kept her tone light and casual. She did not yet reveal that Tracey had not slept in her bed.

"I haven't seen her since supper." Antonio was busy turning over the package of fuses. He had also stocked up on candles and matches, she saw.

"Nor have I," Gregory agreed with Antonio.

Cass looked at the two brothers. Slowly she said, "She's not in her room. I checked. No one's seen her since last night?"

Gregory seemed alarmed. "I assumed she was sleeping late, as you were."

"She's probably taking a walk," Antonio said, unpacking groceries. "It's a beautiful day."

Cass stood. "Her bed was not slept in." And she looked Gregory right in the eye.

He looked away. Unpacking another bag of groceries.

Cass stared, amazed. He had slept with her sister—she was almost certain—and he was lying now. He was an unethical prick.

"No one has seen her since supper last night?" Antonio asked, motionless. "Her bed was not slept it?"

And his alarm made her turn. Cass thought about the fact that she had been in his arms last night. She was the last person who should be casting stones at anyone, much less Gregory, she realized with a sinking heart. "I don't think so."

Antonio's jaw flexed and their gazes met. In that instant Cass knew he hadn't forgotten or even shut out any of the events of last night. He was merely wearing a facade, but it hadn't been hard to chip away. He spoke sharply to Alfonso, and Cass knew he was thinking about Margarita having vanished once from this very place.

"Tracey isn't gone. She'll show up," Cass said.

His jaw did not relax. He poked his head out the open window, calling to the children. Neither Alyssa or Eduardo had seen Tracey since she had left the dining room the evening before.

Now Cass was trying not to succumb to the panic rising within her. "She'll show up," she repeated.

"I am certain you are right," Antonio said, but his expression belied his words. He did not believe his own assurances; he was also alarmed.

Cass managed a lopsided, fake smile. "She's probably out sunbathing or something."

"Probably," Antonio said.

Cass thought about her sister's flawless porcelain skin, and knew she'd never lie out in the sun in this lifetime—and met Antonio's gaze and knew he knew it too. Suddenly she said, "Earlier I went to her room. Someone shut the door while I was inside."

Antonio looked at her.

She had to glance at Gregory, but he was buttering a piece of toast. She looked back at Antonio, thinking about the crypt, thinking about Isabel. What had he said yesterday? That the most she could do was to make them uncomfortable. That it was all in their minds. "I can't even get on the Web to do any research with the phones down," she said.

"I'll drive back to Pedraza later and impress the urgency of the situation upon the phone company," Antonio replied.

"Give them money," Cass said flatly.

"I did," he returned.

Cass felt eyes upon them both. She looked up. Gregory was staring. And she saw him flush.

"Actually," he said, clearing his throat, "we had a drink together after supper."

Antonio glanced at him with mild surprise. "You and Tracey?"

"When was that?" Cass shot. Thinking about the fact that initially he had lied—that she was right.

"It was about eleven-thirty." He hesitated, glancing at Antonio, but Antonio was putting a carton of milk and eggs into the refrigerator. He sighed. "She said she couldn't sleep. We had one drink—in one of the salons. I haven't seen her since."

Cass stared. She did not believe him. He met her gaze, and this time he did not look away.

There was no reason to doubt him. But she did. "I can't believe this." She was grim, facing Antonio. "It's twelve-thirty. The last person to see my sister was Gregory, around midnight last night. Twelve hours ago. Antonio, I don't like this! Is it possible it was Tracey we saw outside the library window last night?'

He stiffened and paled. "No."

Cass could not look away. She heard herself say, "It was really dark out."

Gregory cut into their conversation, looking from the one to the other. "What are the two of you talking about?"

Cass wet her lips. Antonio walked away from them both. Cass hesitated. "So many strange things have happened since I arrived here the day before yesterday. And last night—"

"Last night," Antonio turned, "I saw Margarita standing outside of the window."

Gregory turned white.

Antonio was with the electrician when Catherine and Celia arrived. Tracey had yet to reappear, and although Cass had spent several hours with Antonio and Gregory in the library, sorting through Eduardo's research material, her worry had been increasing by leaps and bounds. Now she hugged her aunt, hard, thinking, *If only she had not come.*

She is summoning all of us together.

Celia rushed off to find Alyssa, and Cass was left alone with her aunt in the great hall. "How was your trip?" Cass asked, studying her aunt, who looked terribly worn and fatigued.

Catherine, clad in black trousers, a matching blazer, and a man-tailored white shirt, smiled wearily. "At least we did not get lost on the way here." Slowly she glanced around the huge hall with an expression that was a combination of disbelief and perhaps distaste.

"I cannot believe you hired a driver, Aunt Catherine," Cass said, meaning it. "If only I could have picked you up at the airport."

Catherine glanced at her, her expression strange, and she slowly walked to the threshold of the salon and stared inside.

"Aunt Catherine?" Cass asked, worried.

Catherine did not turn. "Nothing has changed," she said hoarsely. "I hated this house then, and I so hate it now."

Cass stared at her. "Is she here?"

Catherine said, "Can't you feel her?"

Cass trembled. "It's her, isn't it, making this place so cold, so heavy, so tense?"

Catherine hugged herself. "I don't think I should have come."

Antonio appeared, in a pair of trousers and a red polo shirt, the electrician beside him with his toolbox in hand. "Lady Belford," he said, his gaze suddenly intent upon Catherine.

Cass stiffened unbearably. It was bad enough suspecting that Isabel was lurking about, that the families were somehow cursed, while being attracted to him and having to deal with her sister and his feelings for his missing wife, but Catherine's secret suddenly felt overwhelming. She prayed they would not get into the topic of what had really happened to Eduardo now.

"Señor." Catherine took his hand. "I am so sorry we are not meeting under more pleasant circumstances. And I do hope I am not imposing."

He stared at her for a moment. "Of course you are not imposing. It is a pleasure to have you here." He hesitated, and Cass could imagine what was on his mind. Then he turned. "Cassandra, there is a room next door to Tracey's. Could you show your aunt to it? I need a moment with the electrician."

"Is everything under control?" Cass asked, not liking his expression.

Antonio met her gaze. "Lightning must have struck the house. The wires are badly damaged. He says he's never seen such localized destruction before."

Cass stared, her heart accelerating, the phrase "localized destruction" filling her mind. "But there was no storm."

"There were storms here a few weeks ago."

"A few weeks ago?" Cass did not have an optimistic feeling. "He can fix it, right?"

Antonio was grim. "Not today."

Cass was disbelieving; the electrician was already outside, loading up his truck. "When will we have lights?" she asked, images from last night tumbling through her mind.

"He will return on Monday," Antonio said. "I'll be back in a moment." He paused, glancing at Catherine. Then he hurried outside after the electrician.

Cass didn't exactly like that look. She turned, only to find her aunt watching her. She smiled, knew it was miserable. "The lights went out last night. The phones went down, too. This is a very old house and it needs rewiring—"

"I hope so," Catherine said, glancing at the duo standing by the utility truck.

Cass stared. What the hell did that mean? "What are you implying?"

Catherine gave her a look. "You know what I am implying. She's here, for a reason, and now we are all here. Where are Tracey and Alyssa?"

Instantly Cass picked up the small duffel bag at her aunt's feet. She had no intention of worrying her aunt over Tracey's whereabouts. "Alyssa and Eduardo are playing out back. What reason? I mean, ghosts stay behind, don't they, because they are unhappy? That's her reason." She did not like the direction the dialogue was heading in.

"Oh, Cassandra," Catherine said, with pity. "She's here for one reason, and that is to wreak revenge on us all."

Cass was left standing in the hall, alone and aghast.

Isabel was here because she wanted revenge? Cass didn't believe it. Not for a New York minute. Ghosts were not capable of thinking or motivation. She had not a doubt.

Then she realized that her aunt had gone upstairs. Up the wrong stairs. To the master wing of the house. To the wing where Isabel's room was.

"Aunt Catherine, not that way," she called. "Your room is in the south wing!"

But Catherine did not stop, and she disappeared on the next landing. *Oh, great,* Cass thought, and she followed her aunt upstairs.

Cass espied her at Isabel's door. She almost called out. Instead, oddly, her tongue felt glued to the bottom of her mouth. She paused and watched.

Catherine hesitated outside the door to Isabel's room and slowly pushed it open. She shivered, and stepped inside.

Cass followed. Her feet felt leaden; still, they moved of their own volition.

Catherine was staring at the room. She finally faced the portrait.

Cass realized she was breathless. She hugged herself—it was so damn cold in Isabel's room. Cold and gloomy and ugly. Cass was stiff with tension; stiffer than any board. "What is it?" she asked softly.

Catherine did not face her. "This is where I stayed."

Cass started. "You used this room?"

Catherine nodded, her gaze on the portrait. "When I first arrived here, it was to help Eduardo finish his research. We had both become obsessed with her." Catherine shivered again. "She had the most tragic of lives."

"We found her headstone."

"The one in the cemetery?" Catherine nodded without turning. "I'm surprised he even brought her ashes back here."

"She didn't die in Spain?"

"Oh, no," Catherine said softly. "She was burned at the stake on Tower Hill in London."

Cass trembled. "But she was here?"

"Briefly, we think. There are letters in the library—or there were— letters from Isabel to her cousin, Rob de Warenne."

Excitement seized Cass. "Letters? Oh, God, what a find that will be!" Then, "Who was Rob de Warenne? Her uncle's son?"

"It was so long ago," Catherine murmured. "But he was a distant cousin, I think, not the earl's son. He was her lover."

Cass froze. "What?"

"He was her lover. If you read the letters, it is so obvious." Catherine swallowed. "She was the last thing I saw before falling asleep every night, and the first thing I saw upon awakening each morning."

Cass was still trying to absorb the fact—or speculation—that Isabel had had a lover.

"Until we became lovers."

Cass stared. Dread replaced all of her enthusiasm. "You do not have to talk about this if you don't want," she tried, her tongue sticking to the roof of her mouth. Because she sensed what was coming—and she didn't want to know any more. Not now, when she had become close to Antonio. Not now, when she would have to lie to him in order to protect her aunt. And she felt almost certain that she couldn't lie to him anymore, not even by omission.

Catherine turned to face her. "What was truly astounding is that we never even pretended to love one another. It was merely lust."

Cass didn't know what to say. "That happens. Let's go. This room isn't the friendliest of places—"

"And the lust turned to hatred, and the hatred to violence and death."

"Please," Cass whispered, her ears ringing. "I don't want to know."

"But I have to tell you!" Catherine cried, her eyes filling with tears. "We'd made love violently and we had fought viciously. I remember thinking about how much I hated him, but I could not seem to summon up the will to leave. I can't even recall why we drove into Pedraza, but I remember hoping, desperately, that once there, we would separate, and I might have the opportunity to strand him."

Cass could only stare. Her aunt was telling her a story about a stranger. Cass found it impossible to believe that they were one and the same woman.

"He was on the other side of the street. The streets in the village are so narrow. And I saw a car turning the corner. I knew Eduardo could not see it. And I called to him, waving him over."

Cass felt like clapping her hands over her ears.

"He crossed the street without looking. One second later—less—the car made impact," Catherine said hoarsely.

Cass felt paralyzed. "I don't think you are remembering what happened correctly."

Catherine hadn't heard her. "But in that short span of time, he realized what was happening, and I saw the shock—and disbelief—the horror on his face, just before the car struck him."

"Let's get out of here," Cass said grimly.

Catherine shook her head. "Of course, I was in shock, too. The moment it had happened, all my hatred was gone—I could not understand how it had come to this—and I held him, but he was already dead, and when I looked up, she was there."

Cass seized her shoulder. "Who? Isabel?"

"Yes. And she looked triumphant."

Cass stared. Her aunt finally met her gaze, staring back. Tears slid down her face.

Then Catherine said, "But maybe I am wrong. Maybe it was a trick of the light, my imagination, I do not know. I was in shock myself. And I had lived with this portrait for almost an entire week." She turned to look at it again. "I hate this house," she said. "I hate her."

Cass couldn't reply. Her mind was racing at the speed of light. Was it possible that Catherine had really seen Isabel? And if so, did it matter? Of course it mattered! Because if she was correct, Isabel had been elated over the death of Eduardo de la Barca.

But that would mean Isabel was more than some lingering energy; it would mean that she had feelings and thoughts.

But it did not mean that she was capable of summoning everyone together.

For that would give her motivation, an agenda.

"You couldn't have seen her," Cass said quickly. "It was your imagination."

"You are probably right."

"I know I'm right," Cass said, grabbing her aunt's arm. And she thought, *Eduardo had been Isabel's revenge.* "You look tired," she began. "Let's get out of here." The sooner the better.

Eduardo had not been Isabel's revenge. No way.

Catherine looked at her. And suddenly her face became distorted: her lips stretched into a grotesque smile, her skin tightened and sagged and tightened again, her face becoming the face of a very young woman, and her eyes, her eyes turned into Isabel's piercing blue regard. "Yes," she said. "Yes, he was."

Cass cried out.

Her aunt—who was no longer her aunt—stood there smiling at her, and it was taunting and malevolent and horrific.

Cass dropped the duffel bag. She was a heartbeat away from fleeing, but somehow she stood there, incapable of assessing how many seconds were passing, and she reached out—and touched her aunt's arm.

And she was looking at Catherine again.

Not Isabel.

"What did you say? I'm sorry, I didn't here you," Catherine said, her color paler than usual now.

Cass could not speak. She had just been faced with an ugly monster, she was sure of it, a woman who was not her aunt, a woman who had been dead for over four hundred years—or had she been hallucinating? Was she the insane one? Was she losing her mind?

"I wish you hadn't come," she whispered, perspiration trickling down her brow. And she thought, *Something terrible is going to happen.*

Catherine bit her lip and suddenly hugged her, hard. "Something terrible will happen, but we are in this together, Cassandra. And it's too late. Too late to stop it, because we are all here, together, in this house, just the way she wants it."

Cass felt as if she were losing all of her composure. She could not face another night again, not without lights, and she was suddenly so scared, her temples throbbed painfully. "No one has seen Tracey since last night," she whispered. "I didn't want to tell you."

"Oh, God," Catherine said. "Not Tracey!" She started to cry.

"Tracey will be fine," Cass said sharply. But she had to face her own doubts—she wasn't convinced, not at all. "In fact, why should we even stay until Monday? As soon as she returns—which will be at any time—we can pack up and leave first thing in the morning."

Catherine nodded, tears slipping down her cheeks. "If you say so."

Cass stared into her eyes and knew that she did not have hope. "There's something else, isn't there? Something else that you haven't told me."

"Yes. Eduardo's own father died of brutal stab wounds while in his early forties."

Cass's heart lurched. "Eduardo was forty-two when he himself died, wasn't he?"

Catherine nodded.

"What are you suggesting?" Cass asked uneasily. But the extent of the tragedy that had continually struck the de la Barcas through the centuries was now glaring. Antonio's father and grandfather had died violently as young men. And . . . Antonio was in his late thirties.

Cass was frozen.

"His wife stabbed him." Catherine looked at her as Cass stood there, jerked from her horrifying thoughts, appalled. "She was found guilty by insanity—and she spent the rest of her life in a mental institution."

Cass looked at her aunt as the scent of violets surfaced beside them, growing rapidly in power and strength. "Antonio never said anything," she whispered. "Aunt Catherine?"

Catherine glanced uneasily around. "Let's leave now," she said, turning to the door.

Cass wasn't about to argue. She thought she could feel the other woman with a sixth sense, standing there, between them, but it was undoubtedly all in her mind—except for the sickly smell of violets; that was real. And her aunt seemed to be aware of her presence, too— because in spite of her words, she did not move, she just stood rooted to the spot, eyes wide, breathing shallowly. Isabel, if she was present, if she was beside them, was entrapping them now in the scent. It had never been stronger. It was overpowering. Cass coughed.

Her aunt was starkly white. Catherine reached for and loosened several buttons on her shirt, fanning herself with one hand. She coughed.

"Are you all right?" Cass managed, coughing again, reaching for her because she looked as if she might keel over at any moment.

Catherine continued to cough, so hard now that she could not speak.

Cass became alarmed. She patted her aunt's back, but Catherine was suddenly choking.

Cass screamed, catching her aunt in her arms as she went down to the floor, her face beginning to turn red, her eyes bulging, her hands on her throat—as if she were being asphyxiated. Cass realized her aunt was having some kind of terrible attack—a seizure, perhaps—and that she needed oxygen.

"Antonio!" she screamed. "Antonio! Antonio!" She did not know what to do. Her aunt could not breathe, her face was turning purple. Cass tore open her shirt. She had never administered CPR, but she knew what to do.

Antonio came running.

"We have to get her to a hospital!" Cass shouted at him. "I think she's having a seizure."

Antonio knelt beside Catherine, who, Cass saw in horror, had stopped breathing. Her face was blue, eyes wide, unseeing. Immediately he began to administer CPR.

Cass watched in abject terror as Antonio pumped her chest and breathed into her lungs, to no avail. *No,* she thought hysterically, *this can't be happening, no, it's impossible!*

And through the haze of her panic and fear, she was vaguely aware of the odor of violets. It was diminishing.

Cass continued to watch Antonio as he tried to force air into her aunt's lungs, praying mindlessly now, over and over, *God, God, God.*

Antonio sat up.

Cass realized then, and she looked from him to her aunt, who lay unmoving on the floor, her face blue and waxen. "Don't stop!" she screamed at him.

He slowly turned to face her, but not before closing her aunt's eyelids. "I am sorry, Cassandra," he said.

PART THREE

ISABEL

FOURTEEN

He had finally come.

Her uncle, the earl, who had exiled her to this place seven years ago, was waiting for her.

Isabel crouched behind a tree, knowing she must go in, but unwilling to move. Her heart beat with excruciating speed. A dozen soldiers wearing the earl of Sussex's colors were swarming about the yard—her yard—all boisterous male camaraderie. Her servants were nowhere to be seen, not that Isabel blamed them. The soldiers looked tired and mean. She had little doubt that they had come from the North. Just weeks ago thousands of rebels had gathered at Sittingbourne to protest high wages and scarce food, and vast forces had been dispatched to overcome them.

"Isabel!" Lady Helen was calling her.

Isabel sighed. She was not very fond of her companion—her uncle had chosen his wife's cousin to attend her years ago, just after the loss of her family. Helen was a shrew, even after all the years they had spent together. Isabel also suspected her to be a spy. She surely reported on Isabel's behavior to her benefactor. Not that there was much to report, for in seven years, living amongst the east Sussex forests and dens, she had become not much more than a retiring country mouse.

"Isabel!"

She could not delay this meeting. She stepped out from behind the tree.

Helen stood in the middle of the yard; she saw her and cried out. "Of all days, today you've been picking berries?"

Isabel squared her shoulders, raised her chin. She was bare of foot, and she gripped her apron so the blackberries would not tumble to the ground. "He did not advise us of his visit."

Helen's dark brows arched. "You will be haughty, as well? Let me remind you, my lady, he is your guardian, but he has forgotten your very existence, until now. Because you be old enough for a husband."

"I have hardly forgotten the facts of my life," Isabel said. She kept her head high as she walked through the milling men and horses, ignoring a few lecherous winks and equally rude suggestions. In spite of her bravado, she was afraid. She had to make a favorable impression upon her uncle. Her entire future depended on it.

Helen swatted one mail-clad arm. "She be Sussex's niece. Mind your manners, lout!"

Isabel hardly heard Helen as she shoved open the heavy front door.

The earl was in the hall, pacing with some irritation, and he was not alone. Two knights accompanied him. Isabel hesitated, for he had yet to see her, engrossed as he was in deep conversation. If only she had a chance to run to her rooms and don appropriate clothing.

The earl of Sussex suddenly halted in midstride. He stared at her and Helen coldly. "We asked for wine. Where is it?"

Isabel curtsied, sinking to the floor. Since the manor where she lived was nothing like Romney Castle—it had originally been built as a hunting lodge—the stones were rough and hurtful beneath her feet and even her nose, which she touched to the ground. She could not quite blame the earl for thinking her a servant. "My lord, I beg your pardon, but I will see to it that wine is brought directly."

"Isabel?" he asked.

Isabel stood, still holding her apron so she would not lose the berries. "Yes, my lord," she whispered, suddenly tongue-tied.

He was wearing her father's garnet pendant on a heavy chain suspended upon his chest. She could not move. Memories she refused to entertain tried to rush at her, and with the worst possible timing, Isabel felt dizzy and faint, and a deep, penetrating pang of sorrow lanced through her being.

"My dear niece," he finally said. His blue eyes were piercing. " 'Tis been far too long. Let me look at you, my brother's lovely daughter."

Isabel did not speak. His words seemed honeyed and false. Or was it her imagination?

But she already knew he did not care a whit about her. The allowance he gave her was generous—she could not possibly spend it, living as she did in the country—but rumor held that he was one of the most powerful men in the realm. Like her own father, her uncle was an adviser to the king. Had he cared for her, he would have allowed her to remain at Romney Castle or he would have corresponded with her, even if just once or twice a year. Not only did he not care about her or her circumstances, she thought, with some anger, she would always believe that her father's death had pleased him. For otherwise, he would not be so powerful or so wealthy.

He was speaking. Isabel realized she hadn't heard a single word; she flushed. "I beg your pardon, my lord, what did you say?"

"I said you are the image of your mother, God keep her in peace."

Isabel could not decide if he meant his words. He undoubtedly lied. From what she remembered, her mother had been the kindest, gentlest, and most beautiful of women. "Thank you, my lord," she whispered. "But you do overly praise me, I think."

Helen jabbed her with her elbow.

"And modest, as she was, I see." John de Warenne waved at her. He was a man of some forty years, with iron gray hair and a darker beard. He stared her up and then down again. "I can hardly believe it. How remiss I have been. More time has passed than I realized; when I last saw you, you were but a scrawny child, all eyes and legs and hair."

Isabel wisely held her tongue. The last time she had seen him had been a year after the funeral, when he had come to take over Romney Castle for himself and plot with Lord Seymour, Prince Edward's uncle, about the succession to the throne, as the king was about to lead an army himself to war in France, against all advice. Isabel had eavesdropped and heard their every word.

Henry had returned after a successful venture, and had lived another three years.

Prince Edward had become England's king after he died.

"My dear niece, I shall spend a day or two here, and we must become reacquainted. But for now, I have urgent affairs to conduct. If you will excuse me?" He smiled, but it did not reach his eyes, and he was already turning to his men.

Isabel was stunned by the abrupt dismissal. Would he not even hint that he might make a marriage for her? Surely he could see that she was almost a woman full grown.

Helen gripped her arm. "Thank you, my lord, and you shall have wine in all haste."

Isabel could not believe her misfortune. They had but exchanged a few mere words. She had to know her future. "My lord," she began quickly.

Suddenly Lady Helen was turning her around. "Not now," she hissed in her ear.

Had they been alone, Isabel would have yanked her arm free. But they were not alone, and as she was half dragged away, her gaze inadvertently caught that of one of the knights. He smiled at her.

She looked away and followed Lady Helen from the hall.

Isabel sank down on the stairs the moment she was out of sight. Above her, Helen faltered, then turned. "What do you do now?" she demanded in a whisper. "Come with me this moment!"

"No," Isabel whispered back, as adamantly.

The men were beginning to speak. Isabel strained to hear. Someone was saying, "And so the escape has failed. She is not in Antwerp as the emperor might have us believe. She remains in Maldon, my lord."

A moment of silence followed, and then an exclamation, from another of the knights. "God's blood!" It was angry.

"Hold, Robbie, hold. We must think carefully now on our course." Sussex.

"What good can come of this?" the knight, Robbie, asked. "A royal princess afraid for her life, forced to such extremes, it is unbearable."

Isabel stifled her gasp with her hand. Dear God in Heaven! They were discussing the princess Mary—who undoubtedly had tried to flee England, but had failed. Isabel crouched lower, tempted to crawl back downstairs so she might eavesdrop with more ease.

"You are too hot, as ever," the earl said. "We must ponder these events." He swore. "Dudley rules the council, the king is a sickly boy, factions conspire every conceivable plot . . . Rob, we shall send Mary a message. A very carefully worded message indicating our concern for her well-being, our displeasure with the tyranny of the council, but we shall not be so bold as to proclaim our loyalty to any particular cause—yet."

A silence fell. Isabel's heart thundered so hard that she wondered if the men in the hall below could hear it. She was also perspiring. What did her uncle plan? Even she believed Mary was Edward's rightful heir—even if she was a Catholic. Why did Sussex not support her completely? What if Sussex allied himself with another cause? Isabel's temples throbbed. She knew she should always ally herself with her protector, but some instinct warned her not to trust the earl—to only trust herself. Not that it really mattered, as she was stuck at Stonehill. Matters of state—politics and conspiracies—hardly affected her.

"My lord, I will gladly bring her the message myself." Robbie was speaking forcefully. "Indeed, I beg you to let me perform this service."

"The roads are guarded. As are the rivers and canals. It will be no easy task, Rob. The council has spies even in her household."

"I must go, my lord."

"Very well. But you must travel in disguise. And only by day—it will be too dangerous for you to travel by night. Leave at dawn."

There was only a silence, but Isabel could imagine the men smiling now. The brief, fascinating interlude of conspiracy was over. Now Isabel could worry about her own future once more. And she thought, *Somehow I must gain Sussex's attention before he leaves.*

And she never imagined that she would—and not in any way that she might have foreseen.

Isabel lingered by the open front door in the hall. The evening was sweet. The air was seasonably cool and exceedingly pleasant, and as it had been a clear and sunny day, the night was filled with winking stars. She had no desire to sleep. Indeed, how could she even think of it? Sussex was in the hall even now, playing cards with that young knight, Robbie, while her own jester played the lute for their entertainment. Outside, the forty or fifty men her uncle had brought with him were lounging about her yard in the makeshift camp they had erected since their arrival, dining around open fires, playing dice, and even flirting with several dairymaids who had appeared from the village and neighboring farms within hours of the men's arrival. Stonehill Manor had never been like this.

Helen had retired, but once her cousin was in her own bedchamber, Isabel had quickly returned downstairs. She had never been more awake. Her mind was in a perpetual race. She knew her future was at hand—if only she could gain her uncle's attention.

"And what huge burdens do you carry, my lady?"

Isabel started at the sound of a familiar male voice. She turned and saw the blond, gray-eyed knight who she had learned was Robbie, the one who would take a message to the princess Mary on the morrow.

His gaze was narrowed with speculation. "You appear so sad," he said.

Isabel was nearly undone, and it was a singular moment in her life. As their glances held, she fought for her composure and she won. Still, she could not smile. "Merely the burden of wondering if you dared to win against my uncle," she said rather coolly.

He stared searchingly, causing Isabel to flinch and look away, and finally he laughed. It was a free and wonderful sound. Isabel started.

His laughter died, his smile vanished. After a long pause, he said, "Your eyes can undo a man, my lady."

Isabel refused to blush. "I do not think so," she said. "Are you always so bold?"

"Only when confronted with a lady such as you. How is it," he wondered, "that Sussex is right and you are so modest? Do you not possess a looking glass?"

Isabel's heart was pumping erratically, in spite of her intention to remain aloof. She was very aware that he was merely being gallant and a flirt; still, there were very few men at Stonehill of her station, and she was not adept at such intercourse. She hoped she was not flushing; her cheeks felt warm. "Of course I do." She knew she must change the subject. "Did you best my uncle in gaming this night, sirrah?"

His regard had become very thoughtful. "I've yet to best Sussex, mademoiselle, but not through lack of trying." And he smiled slightly at her.

It was a very genuine if not tentative smile, and Isabel now wished for him to remain overly bold. "Would it be wise to best your benefactor?" she asked cautiously.

"Perhaps not, but then, I do not profess to be the wisest of men." He smiled again at her. His gaze was serious, searching. "And how do you know he is my benefactor?"

" 'Tis but a guess, Sir Robert." Isabel wasn't about to admit to the conversation she'd overheard earlier, in which Robbie had been determined to carry the earl's banner for him.

"Then 'tis a good guess, my lady, because like yourself, I have no family to speak of other than Sussex, and he is my patron as well as my benefactor."

Isabel's eyes widened. He knew something about her, and she was strangely pleased as well as even more discomfited. "Pray tell," she said, "how you came to be alone in this world."

His smile was lopsided. "You do know we have not been properly introduced," he said, sweeping her a courtly bow. "Robert de Warenne, at your service, my lady, and that I do intend with all of my heart."

Isabel stood very still, his piercing gaze on hers. "De Warenne?"

"It seems we are cousins, but very distant ones," he said wryly. "Come." He held out his arm.

Isabel looked at it. He had long since shed his armor, and wore a dark green velvet doublet that was narrow waisted but full sleeved over a linen shirt with Spanish embroidery winking from the collar and cuffs. His jacket was sleeveless and a paler shade of green, his hose tan. He did not wear an extremely exaggerated codpiece as some of the other men did, which somehow relieved her.

She looked at his hand. It was tanned and strong and ringless.

"I do not bite, my lady," he said, low.

A voice inside her head told her not to go with him, that it would be more than reckless, it would be dangerous. She had no interest in a frivolous flirtation. She had no interest in a genuine friendship. She only wanted to leave Stonehill and find her rightful place in this world. Isabel gave him her hand. No one was more surprised than she.

It was dark out, and a Gypsy had begun to sing, but if anyone noticed them or paid them any attention, Isabel could not say. His hand was warm and strong and overwhelming. The last male to hold her hand had been her brother, Tom.

And suddenly, desperately, Isabel missed her brother and wished he were alive.

Isabel withdrew her hand from his. He glanced at her but did not protest as they strolled across the yard.

"My father was Sussex's favorite cousin—their fathers were brothers," he told her in his warm, rich voice. "My father, Guy de Warenne, was rather impetuous and he involved himself with the wrong faction when I was but a child. I am afraid our late departed king decided he must pay the price of his betrayal with his head." Robert smiled at her.

"Ouch," Isabel said, smiling back a little in spite of herself.

"To make matters worse, Guy was a young man at the time—and he had never married."

She looked up at his handsome face. His features were strong and manly. "Oh, I do begin to see." Robert was a bastard.

He shrugged, as if indifferent to his illegitimacy. "My mother was a widow at the time of their affair, but when she remarried, well, she already had three legitimate brats, and I was a by-blow that could be spared. I was only eight when Sussex accepted me into his household. That was twelve years ago." They paused by the edge of the hill. Below them they could see the Thomson farm, and beyond that, the village and the chapel in the valley. Knee-high grass swept up against Isabel's skirts, which brushed Robert's legs.

"You have done well for yourself, then, Sir Rob. You wear the badge of the Knight of the Garter."

He smiled as he faced her squarely. "I am tireless in my quest," he said. "Had I not been thus, I might still be a servant in the stables at Chiswick."

"You have fought many battles?" Her curiosity carried the day.

"Indeed I have, fair Isabel." His gaze roved over her face. "My first taste of war was with King Henry. We took Boulogne." His eyes never left her. "Only to have that cowardly Suffolk hand it back over to the French." He added, " 'Tis where I won my spurs."

Isabel was rapt. "But you were but a boy."

"I was almost your age," he said quietly. "And are you not a woman?"

Isabel felt blinded by the intensity of his gaze. She could not move, speak, or breathe. She could not look away—and she wanted to, she did. And that tiny warning voice was there—*do not do this, do not begin to care, there is no hope, only danger* . . . Tom's smiling face appeared in her mind. Isabel stepped slightly aside, to put more distance between them. She was breathless. "Perhaps you might bring that fact to my uncle's attention," she finally said.

He studied her. "Why? So he can marry you off to some powerful lord?" he asked roughly as a breeze from the sea swept up the hill.

"I am fifteen, and I cannot stay at Stonehill forever," she said firmly. "I am my father's heir, my dowry is rich, I have much to offer the right nobleman."

"The right nobleman," he said, unsmiling, his jaw hard and flexed. "But not a by-blow, who has had to earn his every penny, his spurs, his single Cornish estate." It was not a question.

Isabel almost gaped at him. Was he angry? Abruptly she turned to leave. "I must go."

He seized her arm from behind. "Why? Because I have the courage to speak my mind?"

"You speak nonsense," she cried, refusing to face him. He was not suitable as a prospective husband. And that would never change.

He whirled her around. "Oh, do I? I dare to be honest. And you? Your answer is to run away."

He was right, but Isabel would never admit it. "If you wish to ask for my hand, then I suggest you speak with your benefactor."

"I did not realize you were so determined upon your rank."

" 'Tis all I have left in the world," Isabel said.

He stared, his face set, then did as she asked. Isabel whirled and began to stride away, back to the encampment in front of the manor, back to the house. Her instincts had been right. She should have stayed away from him in the first place.

"I leave at dawn," he said quietly. "And we might never see one another again."

Isabel halted in her tracks. She could not move forward, though she dearly wished to.

The roads are guarded . . . the council has spies even in her household . . .

She heard him approach from behind. "Do not run away from me," he said. "Isabel, I have been smitten this day, and we must talk."

He had been smitten. And he was leaving on a mission fraught with danger, and even though he was young and strong and clever, what if he failed—what if he did not return? Isabel had learned seven years ago that there was no justice in the world. God often sanctioned terrible things. When she finally turned to look at him, it was to nod, and tears filled her eyes.

He was not for her. But surely it would not hurt to talk; she would never forgive herself if she denied him and he never returned from Maldon.

He touched her cheek. "Do not cry. Why do you weep? I am surely not the cause of your tears!"

Isabel could only cry, trying not to think about her family and Tom, trying not to think about him, but it was impossible. Her father as he strode into the hall at Romney Castle, fresh from a stag hunt, his cloak trailing mud, beaming with satisfaction, her mother rising up to greet him, her belly swollen with the babe that would be born soon after, and die just as shortly, her face alight with expectation and happiness, and Tom, on her father's heels, as dirty, grinning from ear to ear, rushing to Isabel to regale her with tales of his prowess . . . The memories flooded her along with the tears.

Rob pulled her against his chest and held her there. Isabel sank into his arms. No one had held her like this, not man nor woman, in seven years. It felt so good, so perfectly right.

He stroked her hair.

Isabel clung to him, her tears slowly ceasing.

His hands slid down her back.

And for the first time in her young life, Isabel felt desire begin to awaken within her.

His mouth moved over the top of her head, the kisses soft and gentle and bare.

Isabel became still.

She was aware of his mouth on her hair, but even more aware of a huge weight that felt as if it were lifting from her actual body. And somehow her arms had slipped around his hard waist, somehow her face was buried against his strong chest. She could hear his thundering heartbeat.

Slowly Isabel looked up.

"I love you," he said, and he lowered his mouth to hers.

The exultation was so fierce it shocked and stunned Isabel, and then she knew sheer joy, and she said, against his questing lips, "I love you as well, Robert." And she had never meant anything more.

Sussex stared in absolute disbelief. "You what?"

Outside the manor, the sun was rising, casting a pink blush over the hills. Inside, Robert and Isabel stood side by side, not daring to hold hands.

"My lord, I wish to marry Isabel. As we are cousins, I did not think it too unseemly a request." Robert stood ramrod-straight, eyes wide and unflinching. Beside him, Isabel began to tremble, watching her uncle turn beet red with rage.

Sussex gaped at him; then he looked at Isabel. "Be gone," he shouted at her.

Terrified, and suddenly filled with a dreadful feeling, she quickly did as he asked, but not before she flung a blurring glance at Robert, who did not dare regard her. She grabbed her skirts and fled up the stairs, tripping in her haste. Lost in the grip of terror, beginning to panic, trying to tell herself that it would be all right, she crouched on the stairs.

Sussex paced forward and shoved his face within inches of Robert's. "Did you take her?" he demanded.

"I did not," Robert said, two pink spots mottling his tanned face. He stood as if he wore all of his armor, stiffly at attention, unmoving.

Sussex stared, and then he visibly relaxed. "Rob," he finally said, in a calmer tone, "you are young, and I forget what it is to be your age when a comely wench is about. But she is to marry elsewhere when the time is right, as you must know. By God! One day soon she will be a useful tool, for us both! Perhaps even in this damnable coil with Dudley." He had been pacing; now he stopped. "And you, my lad? Have you forgotten your ambition? You have much to do if you wish to make a place for yourself in England, and I know you well know it. Or are you asudden satisfied with a damned pair of spurs?" Now Sussex was angry. "Have I raised you all of these years for naught? I must only snap my fingers to find another sergeant, Rob. That is not what I had in mind for you, and until now, that is not what you have had in mind for yourself!"

"My ambition has not waned," Robert said stiffly. "But my heart has found its true love, my lord."

Sussex raised both brows, stared, and burst into mocking laughter. "True love? There is no such thing. What you feel now has naught to do with anything but the cock that hangs between your legs, and I have no doubt that in a sennight or two, another comely wench will stir more feelings of true love. God's eyes! You have a service to do, my boy, and do it well. Bring back any message the princess cares to give. Heed her well, and glean carefully any conspiracies she might share with you. My future—and yours—depends on it. You shall find me at Chiswick, as I shall leave Stonehill tomorrow. Now, be gone, and no more ranting about *true* love." This last was said in an utterly mocking manner, followed by brief laughter.

Isabel had covered her mouth with both hands, so as not to shriek or scream. She stood up. Robert was unmoving, his face flushed, and finally he bowed and turned away. His strides were hard as he crossed the hall, his booted steps loud, spurs clinking.

Isabel closed her eyes. Dear sweet Virgin Mary, but she had seen the hard, hard look in Rob's eyes. And it was happening again . . .

To love completely, ceaselessly, recklessly, and to have all destroyed and lost.

"Rob!" the earl of Sussex shouted.

Rob halted but did not turn.

"In time you will thank me for preventing you from making a very foolish decision. Years from now, I wager upon it, you will thank me indeed."

Robert left the hall.

Uncaring if her uncle saw, Isabel ran after him.

Robert was pulling on the dark, anonymous brown robes of a traveling friar. His own page had prepared a mount and a pack mule and was in disguise as an acolyte.

Did he intend to leave just like that? Without another word, without even a good-bye? Would he give up then, so easily? Briefly Isabel closed her eyes. *How she hated her uncle. She had hated him from the moment he had first arrived at Romney Castle, a bold and satisfied usurper.*

Robert saw her, but he did not move to her. He was grim.

They clasped hands. Isabel felt the tears forming in her eyes. "What shall we do?" she whispered, his hands hard and warm and strong, covering hers. "Is this good-bye, then? After all we have said and shared?"

"No, for with us, it can never be good-bye." His tone was low and urgent as he led her away from the house. "In spite of what we want, great matters abound, matters that are far bigger than you and I, and I must go now."

"This I well understand. After all, the both if us are but pawns in the grander scheme of things as designed by God and my uncle the earl." She struggled not to cry. Before last night, being married off for a political alliance was what she had hoped for and dreamed of. Now it was the kiss of her heart's death.

"Hush," Robert said. His gaze commanded hers. "Listen to me well."

Isabel heard the urgency in his tone, and slowly she nodded.

"If I can, I will stop here on my way to Chiswick."

The hope rose up inside her breast so swiftly she felt astonished. "I do not want you to fall from Sussex's grace. I have heard he is a dangerous man when crossed."

"I will not fall from his grace, for I will serve him with all of my heart, as always," Robert said flatly.

Isabel stared, recalling the look she had glimpsed in his eyes in the hall, a frightening and hard look, still wondering what it had meant, yet hoping against hope. "Very well."

"Do not fret, Isabel," he whispered, gripping her hands more tightly. He took a deep breath. "I need two or three years, at least. Two or three years in which to advance myself well beyond the rank of knight. Can you give me those few years, my love? *Will you wait for me, Isabel?*"

Their gazes had locked. She began to understand. She began to nod. "Yes. Yes. Of course I will wait for you, Rob." And full realization struck her then. He wanted her to wait for him! Because he loved her . . . "Of course I will wait for you," she repeated more firmly. "I will not become another man's bride. This I vow to you, Rob. I would rather die."

He stared at her searchingly, and then they kissed.

And within minutes, he was on his nag. Crossing the courtyard. Leaving. It would be at least two years before she saw him again— unless he could detour to Stonehill on his return to Chiswick. "Godspeed," Isabel whispered, the tears salty on her lips.

He looked her way one last time as he rode out of the gate.

And it wasn't two years before she saw him again, it was almost five. By then, it was too late.

FIFTEEN

CASA DE SUEÑOS—THE THIRD DAY, 5:00 P.M.

Gregory was growing worried. He hadn't lied when he had told Cass that he had last seen Tracey around midnight. After that one moment of insane lovemaking—if it could even be called that—she had gotten up abruptly, smiled strangely, and left without saying another word. He had been filled with guilt all day.

Gregory felt as if he had betrayed his brother, and it was a feeling he had never had before. Worse, he had the urge to tell Antonio what had happened and to beg for his forgiveness. He would resist that urge, out of fear. Even if Antonio had no feelings left for Tracey, what they had done was terribly wrong.

His brother and Cass had just returned with the authorities; Catherine's corpse had been taken to a hospital in the town of Segovia. In their absence, Gregory had been left in charge of the children and Alfonso—Celia had taken to her bed in a state of grief and shock. Antonio was now downstairs somewhere; Cass had disappeared into her bedroom. Gregory felt so sorry for her.

Now Gregory paused on the threshold of the upstairs corridor, the sounds of the children's voices wafting up to him from the kitchen below, where they were having a late lunch of sandwiches and gooey, melted ice cream. The children hadn't yet been told about Catherine Belford. And the power in the house remained out.

He could not help himself. He walked to the door and pushed it open. He was so oddly compelled. He did not even recall this bedroom from his childhood. And the light inside the large room was dim; it took his eyes a moment to adjust.

Then he saw her—the demon of his childhood dreams.

Sweat poured down his body in streams.

And Gregory was almost in disbelief, staring at the portrait of the woman in the red dress and ruby necklace, the woman who stared back at him as if she were real—as if she were alive. He could hardly think. He only knew that it was her, his childhood tormentor; there was no mistake.

And her eyes, her eyes were so damn vicious . . .

As abruptly as his feet had led him to that room without conscious volition, he backed out, slamming the door, and as he did so, he could have sworn that he heard his name, softly, mockingly, being called him from inside the room.

The urge was to flee downstairs like a coward. Instead, he did not move, furious with himself.

He wasn't a coward—he had jumped out of airplanes, for God's sake. He raced cars. He helicopter-skied. He had even bungee-jumped. And last year he had gone on safari in a politically unstable part of Africa.

His mind began to work, as furiously. Undoubtedly, as a boy, he had seen that portrait, and for whatever reason, it had remained engraved on his mind. And minds were a funny thing. His mind had used that image, coming up with a frightening tormentor instead of an imaginary playmate. He'd leave it to a new shrink to figure out why.

And he had not just heard his name. Of that he had not a doubt.

"Papá! Papá!"

At the sound of Eduardo's alarmed voice, Gregory came to life, straining to hear that Antonio was responding to his son. Instead, Eduardo was calling out again. Quickly Gregory traversed the corridor, hurrying back downstairs. "Eduardo! *Qué tal?*"

Eduardo and Alyssa were sitting at the kitchen table with Alfonso, looking at photographs. Antonio appeared behind him. "What has happened?" he asked. He seemed drawn and tired.

Everyone at the table, both the two small children and the elderly man, looked pale and pinched with shock.

"What is wrong?" Gregory asked, a frisson of unease filtering through him.

Eduardo looked at them both, his gaze wide. *"Dios mío,"* he whispered. "Alyssa's aunt took these photographs, and something is very strange!"

Gregory did not want to know what that was. He did not move as Antonio stepped forward—with obvious reluctance. Gregory watched his brother ruffle his son's hair with a smile. But then his smile died, because Eduardo was shoving a photograph at him.

Antonio was frozen.

Gregory did not want to ask, he did not want to know. "What is it?"

Antonio finally came to life, and he handed him the photograph.

It had been taken in the ruins just down the road. In this photograph a part of the crumbling wall and one tower were clearly visible. And bolts and swirls of light, or electricity, the reddish gold color of actual flames, filled up that frame, as if electrical charges were ricocheting back and forth along the ruined wall.

And clearly visible in the swirling sparks was a figure and a face.

It was Isabel.

Cass lay on her stomach in her bed, unmoving. Her aunt was dead. Catherine was dead, and Cass had cried and cried and cried, and now she was exhausted, and all of her tears seemed spent.

She had never known such a terrible sense of loss before. Such a huge aching emptiness. Such profound, piercing pain. Her heart seemed to be in pieces, and Cass didn't think it would ever be whole again. Catherine had been far more than her aunt, she'd been her mother and her best friend. How could this be happening? How could she have died? How could she really be gone?

On Monday there would be an autopsy.

But Monday was too late.

If only Catherine hadn't come!

She is summoning all of us together.

Alyssa. She didn't know. Somehow, someway, sometime soon, Cass would have to pull herself together and tell her niece the awful truth.

She did not think she could do it.

A hand slipped over her head, into her hair.

And the moment she felt his large palm, she knew it was Antonio, and she glanced up. Surprisingly, more tears filled her eyes.

"I thought you were sleeping," he whispered. "I hope I did not wake you." His eyes were filled with sorrow.

"You didn't," she managed, choking on the two single words.

He hesitated. "I only wanted to check in on you. Can I bring you something? Anything?"

Cass shook her head, then managed to think about poor Celia. "Did you give her the Valium?"

"Yes." He did not have to ask her who she referred to. "She's sleeping now." His gaze held hers.

Amazingly, more tears came, filling her eyes.

"Why don't you take a Valium as well?" he asked softly.

"Do you know what I need?" Cass whispered.

He sank down onto the bed and pulled her into his arms. Cass burrowed deeply there, against his chest, holding on so tightly.

She wanted to weep again, but she had cried all afternoon, and only a few tears would seep out.

Antonio held her, stroking her hair, her back. "I am so sorry," he said.

Cass already knew. She wondered if she could lie in his arms like this forever. The pain, she thought, would never abate, never go away, but she needed him like this. "The children?"

"They are eating melted ice cream, they are fine. We will tell them later, together."

She wanted to ask about Tracey. She did not dare.

He held her.

Cass let him.

And suddenly, abruptly, Cass knew what it was that she wanted, what it was that she felt. Suddenly, abruptly, everything changed. Cass's grief vanished. And in its place was violent desire.

She looked up at him, stunned by the feverish urgings of her body. Their eyes met. And in his eyes she saw the same, identical lust.

Cass didn't think. She reached for his head, her fingers threading through his thick hair, as he gripped the back of her skull, anchoring her in place. Their mouths came together, fusing, and then their lips were open, fusing again, and Cass felt his teeth, grating her gums, and she was fully on her back, spreading her thighs, wide and wider still, and he was between them, and even though they were both dressed, she felt a huge arousal there. Cass gasped, tearing her mouth from his.

"Christ," he said, rising up over her, gripping her jeans, tearing them open.

"Oh yes," Cass said, thrusting her hips up toward his face as he yanked both the jeans and her panties down. And it occurred to her that they were being watched. The sensation was distinct.

But she could not care. He said something in Spanish, something she knew was rough and crude, tossing her legs over his shoulders, his fingers finding and opening her; playing her.

"Eat me," Cass said harshly, an order.

He buried his face between her legs and his tongue was everywhere.

"Oh God," Cass cried, holding his head.

His tongue slid over every inch of her, laving her repeatedly, deliciously, excruciatingly. Cass could hardly stand it. She could not bear the building pressure. She tried to push him away; she tried to pull him closer. Pleasure became borderline, mingling with pain. But he would not stop.

His tongue began flaying her. She wept.

The violets surfaced more strongly; Cass vaguely realized with some distant, functioning part of her mind that the scent had been present for some time.

And Cass was coming. She thought, *Isabel is here,* but his tongue would not stop and she did not want him to and the orgasm was an endless series of spasms that were rocking her body wildly, and had barely died when he said, "I want to fuck you."

He was rising up over her, ripping off his belt. Cass gripped his wrist, hard, her eyes on what she wanted, that one single huge penis, barely contained by his trousers, so close to her face. "No."

His eyes blazed. "No?"

She gripped the waistband of his pants, popping them open. "Come in my mouth," she commanded.

His eyes widened and an instant later Cass was facing every swollen, aroused inch of him. She held his buttocks as he thrust deep, again and again, and when he bucked over her, she sucked harder, swallowing every drop.

He did not collapse. He held her face, kissing her, and Cass kissed him back, still tasting him, tasting herself, their mouths tearing at one another, insatiably, and finally she felt him growing again. "Fuck me now."

"I will fuck you all night." He thrust into her.

Cass clawed his back and shouted in pleasure and encouragement; she wanted more, faster, harder fucking, and she could still taste him, salty and bitter, and his hands, on her buttocks, began to hurt, but the pleasure refused to die; instead, it was building and building . . .

He pulled out. "Turn over."

Cass didn't hesitate, and when he took her from behind, she cried out, pain mingling with the pleasure, indistinguishable, and when his hands found her this time, pulling her open, he cursed, and Cass knew it was because it was so good it was unbearable . . .

They came again.

And this time he collapsed on top of her, and she could not find the strength to move.

Antonio slid off of her. Cass's pulse finally began to slow; her mind began to function, comprehending what they had just done. And suddenly a new tension overcame her.

And with that new tension came absolute coherence and complete comprehension.

Cass froze. The sickly sweet scent of violets was everywhere—they were bathed in it, drowning in it.

She glanced at Antonio, who lay flat on his back, still completely clothed, his khakis open. His eyes were closed and his chest was rising and falling rapidly.

Cass sat up, still staring. And slowly she looked around.

She expected to see Isabel, smiling at them. She saw an empty room filled with lengthening shadows, a room that was cold and ugly.

His lids lifted and their gazes met.

Cass flushed, and had her jeans or underwear been near, she would have covered the lower half of her body. "She's here."

He also sat up.

"Oh my God." Cass suddenly hugged herself. And a chill entered her, freezing her to the bone.

Antonio zipped his pants. "Cassandra."

She stared wildly at him. "Aunt Catherine just died, and you and I . . ." She could not find the right words to describe what they had just done.

"It happened," he finally said, clearly at the same loss as she.

She thought about what they had done. She thought about what she had said. She was aghast, in shock. "I've never done those things before," she managed.

He hesitated. "Some of the things I said . . . I don't know what overcame me."

Cass suddenly jumped off the bed, knowing he was watching her, and she found her underwear and leapt into them. Then she hopped into her jeans. "I don't know what overcame me, either," she cried, aware of the heat in her cheeks. She had never wanted anyone the way she had just wanted Antonio. The intensity of her desire had been so great it had been violent—she had actually welcomed pain. Her temples began to throb.

Antonio was standing. "You are misunderstanding me," he said.

Cass couldn't face him. Aunt Catherine was dead—she and Antonio had practically desecrated her death. What *was* happening?

"Cassandra." He turned her around to face him. "I don't regret this."

She had no choice but to meet his eyes.

"I regret the timing. I am at a loss to explain . . . certain things. But I don't regret making love to you."

Cass stared. "We weren't making love." Love had not been on her mind when they had been in bed together. Sex had been on her mind. No, not sex. Fucking. Animal fucking.

Antonio actually flushed.

"Antonio, I am worried."

"How so?"

Cass took a quick glance around the room; they were alone. "She was here while we were . . . doing it. I am certain."

"Cassandra," he protested slowly.

"She was watching us. I felt it. Didn't you?" Cass cried. "We weren't alone!"

"Cassandra." His jaw flexed. "You are in the throes of shock and grief. I admit to also being out of sorts. But Isabel was not here just now, watching us."

Cass folded her arms. "I would love to agree with you, but I can't. Didn't you smell her perfume? It's gone now—but a few minutes ago this room was reeking of violets."

He hesitated. "No, I did not." He was firm—and grim.

Cass faced him. "Maybe I am confused . . . I wish that were the case. Antonio, there's something I have to tell you."

"What is that?"

"When Catherine had her seizure, or whatever it was, I could barely breathe, also. That damn scent was there—"

"What are you suggesting?" He was suddenly angry. "That Isabel is haunting us—*and* that she killed your aunt? That she has this poisonous scent?"

Cass paled. "I don't know what I'm suggesting!"

"I'm sorry." He pulled her close. Cass stiffened in surprise, resisting him, but briefly, he embraced her before releasing her. "We are all overwrought."

"Yes, we are," Cass agreed unevenly. "But let's look at the facts. My aunt suffered some kind of attack within minutes of arriving here. My aunt, who was your father's lover—who was here thirty-four years ago when he died. Tragically. You didn't tell me your grandfather also died in his early forties—stabbed to death by his own wife."

Antonio paled. "No. I did not."

Cass found it hard to breathe. "How old are you, Antonio?" she asked unsteadily even though she knew.

His eyes widened. "Thirty-eight. What does that have to do—" He stopped.

Cass felt tears coming to her eyes. "I don't want anything to happen to you."

His jaw flexed. "Nothing will happen to me."

"But something is happening here. Your father, your grandfather, now my aunt. And what if Margarita is tied in to all of this?" He paled. Cass didn't regret her words. "I felt Isabel here, moments ago, I am certain—it was not my imagination—and I think she was very pleased, no, satisfied, with this—with us. Antonio. I'm not crazy. My aunt is right. There is a pattern here. We just don't know what it is, exactly." She paused. "My aunt told me that Isabel wants revenge."

He stared. She stared back. He finally said, "Isabel is dead. If ghosts exist, they do not have desires—or ambitions, Cassandra."

Suddenly she was so angry. "So now you are an expert on ghosts?"

He flushed. "Hardly."

"Well, what if they do have desires? Thoughts? Feelings? Motives?" When he remained stubbornly silent, she cried, "Did we really see Margarita last night? Maybe it was Tracey. Maybe it was Isabel herself."

"At this moment, I do not know what we saw last night," he said grimly.

"Maybe Aunt Catherine is wrong," she cried. And then as she recalled that Catherine was dead, tears slipped and slid down her face. "But so far she has been right, hasn't she? She said tragedy strikes when our families are together. Your father is dead. My aunt is dead. And where is my sister? It's almost six o'clock. In a few more hours she will have been gone for twenty-four hours!" Suddenly, to Cass's horror, she began to cry. "I just lost my aunt, I can't lose Tracey, too."

Antonio pulled her into the shelter of his arms. "Tracey will be fine. We will find her. There will be a simple explanation. As for the rest, it is coincidence."

Cass wanted to believe him. But there was a tension in his tone and she looked up, meeting his eyes. "You're saying the words," she said, "but you don't believe in them, either, now do you?"

He did not answer her.

Cass trembled. "There's something you are hiding from me. What is it?"

He stared. "There is a photograph," he finally said. "But I am sure there is a rational explanation."

The search for Tracey began.

They searched every room, every closet, every bathroom, even the dark, cavernous dungeons below. And then they left the children with Alfonso while Cass, Gregory, and Antonio split up to cover the ground around the house.

Cass was trying not to give in to hysteria and panic. But it was past seven o'clock. In two hours it would be dark.

She headed past the garage and cottage, while Gregory took the opposite side of the house, Antonio the Jeep, the better to cover more territory. As she walked farther and farther away from the house, stumbling on the uneven, rocky ground, the sun still high but not quite as bright, she desperately tried to hold back the waves of undulating fear, while her mind wanted to spin and race, conceiving every possible explanation.

This made no sense. Tracey could not have simply disappeared.

And now she was finally beginning to understand what Antonio had gone through eight years ago. Margarita's disappearance had made no sense then, either. How did one live with that kind of unresolved loss? Never knowing what had really happened, not knowing if the one you loved was alive or dead?

Cass resolved not to let her thoughts go there. It was too soon. And Tracey wasn't Margarita. She was a loose cannon. She had been rejected by Antonio. What if she had simply decided to leave?

But Cass could not imagine her sister walking down the road until a passing vehicle came by to give her a ride to civilization.

And tragedy had already struck twice—three times if you included Margarita in the equation. Cass could not shove aside the gnawing fear. Tracey's disappearance was not a coincidence.

Cass realized the house was no longer in sight. She paused, standing on a slight knoll, squinting, the sun behind her, realizing she had been walking for a good hour. Her body was tired, her feet hurt. But then, her body was sore for a very good reason. No—she must not remember what had happened earlier that afternoon. She could still barely believe it.

Had Isabel been watching them? Cass shivered.

She looked around again, afraid that she might be lost. Her heart lurched unpleasantly—she could not deal with being lost tonight, not after all that had happened. And what if she couldn't make it back to the house before dark? She should have turned around earlier, she thought, with a sinking heart. The idea of wandering around in the dark, lost and alone, was distinctly unappealing.

Isabel's taunting image filled her mind.

Cass felt raw fear. "Go away," she muttered nervously. But what if she was right and Antonio was wrong? What if Isabel was a very active presence amongst them? Cass had seen that damning photograph. Antonio and Gregory kept insisting that it was not a photograph of a ghost, that the image was hardly clear. Cass disagreed. The image was clear enough for her.

Just what was Isabel capable of? Could she feel, think, plan?

Trembling, Cass turned to gaze in the other direction from her vantage point. She hadn't found her sister and she was going to have to go back. Just ahead was the ruins of the castle. Huge shadows spilled forth from the crumbled walls and the two towers.

Cass was about to turn around when something caught her eye, and she faced the ruins again, holding up a hand to shield her eyes from the setting sun. Light flashed below the castle walls, a reflection of some sort.

What if it was Tracey? What if it was Isabel?

Cass started to run toward the ruins, which were farther than she had thought. She did not let up her pace, praying the reflection she had glimpsed had been caused by her sister, refusing to think it might be someone—or something—else. In fact, Tracey never went anywhere without her gold Cartier lighter. That could certainly cause a reflection of the light.

She hit the road, running harder now, as the sun continued to sink lower, as the shadows surrounding the ruins lengthened, as the sky blushed pink, mauve. It was quickly turning into twilight, making it impossible to see clearly.

She would have to follow the road back to the house in darkness, she realized, very unhappy with the thought. She had forgotten how quickly the sun set. But at least she could not get lost on the road, even if it meant traveling a longer distance.

Isabel's image flashed through her mind, her eyes piercing and intense.

"Do not think of her now," Cass told herself, speaking aloud. She hated the sound of her own voice. In the desolation of the night, it sounded jarring.

Suddenly she came up short. The electrician's truck was ahead. Maybe it had caused the reflection of light she had seen. For one moment, as Cass stared at the older vehicle, she thought it was parked, and at an odd angle—and then she realized its front end was smashed into the castle wall.

There had been an accident.

Cass broke into a run, and a moment later she was beside the front door. She cried out. The electrician was collapsed on top of the steering column, and the entire windshield was broken. The front of the truck was crushed into itself like an accordion.

"Oh, God." Cass knew he was dead, but she opened the door and touched his neck, looking for a pulse while careful not to move him.

She jumped away from him, having never touched a dead person before, suddenly, violently, wanting to throw up. Cass turned and heaved.

And when the heaves had passed, she sat there on her knees, shadows falling over her, trying to understand how the electrician had gone off the road at such a high speed. She finally got up, thinking that maybe his brakes had failed, or the steering, or maybe he'd simply had a heart attack. And as she stood there debating the possibilities, suddenly the car's radio came on.

Cass jumped in shock and fear as the radio blared, some Spanish disc jockey speaking rapidly, unintelligibly. And as suddenly, the radio went dead.

Cass backed away.

A short, she finally told herself, a short caused by the crash.

The dead man suddenly fell over, to one side. Cass screamed.

She had left the door open, and his head lolled out. Cass met a pair of wide-open, astonished eyes.

And she saw the knife protruding from his chest.

———

Cass couldn't breathe as she ran down the road, stumbling on rocks and ruts. The night had abruptly turned black. She was immersed in what was almost total darkness. She was trying not to think the worst, trying not to think about ghosts and murderers, trying desperately not to become overwhelmed by panic and fear. Of course she was out there by the ruins alone. But nothing in the world could have stopped her from glancing repeatedly over her shoulder—she was terrified.

The electrician was dead.

Stabbed to death.

Her aunt was dead.

Casa de Sueños was already a terrible place of tragedy. But was it also a place of death?

Suddenly the night seemed to sigh.

Cass ran harder, gasping for air, her legs beginning to fail her, until she realized it was only a breeze, sighing through the trees. Wasn't it? And her thighs were screaming now in pain, her calf muscles knotting, cramping; she did not know how much longer she could keep up the pace, but she refused to slow down. She did not dare.

Cass fought to run harder, unable not to think. Ghosts did not stab people. People stabbed people. What if the electrician hadn't fallen out of his vehicle, what if he had been pushed out? What if whoever was responsible for his murder was still lurking about? Finally terror overcame her.

Which was why when headlights suddenly fell over her, her first instinct was to leap off of the road and hide.

But not before she froze, briefly. Trapped in the car's headlights.

Cass dove off of the road. She landed on her hands and knees, sank onto her belly, rocks stabbing her cheek and chin, dirt in her mouth, shaking like a leaf.

A car door slammed.

Cass imagined the murderer, approaching her, stalking her.

"Cassandra!"

Suddenly Cass was on her feet. "Antonio!" she screamed. His tall form was the happiest apparition she had ever seen.

"Cassandra! Thank God!" He ran toward her.

She flew into his arms. He held her, hard.

"Where have you been? Damn it, you were supposed to be back at the house at eight-thirty!" he cried.

She gripped his shirt. "He's dead! Oh, God, he's dead. Antonio, he's been stabbed to death!"

"What? Who's dead?" Antonio held her still.

"The electrician," she cried.

His eyes widened. A moment later she was beside him in the Jeep and they were flying down the road to the ruins. He braked next to the truck, grabbed his flashlight, and leapt out. Cass followed him reluctantly to the corpse.

The radio continued to play.

Antonio cried out.

"What?" Cass whispered, glancing from his shocked expression to the shadows surrounding them.

"That knife came from the house," Antonio said grimly.

Cass paused on the threshold of her room, uneasy because she was the only one upstairs. Everyone else had gathered in the library for a stiff drink before Antonio drove into Pedraza to alert the police about the murder.

The house was cast in absolute darkness; Cass held a candle. She was trying desperately not to think about the dead electrician. At least the house was firmly locked up for the night.

She entered her room, placing the candle on a table. She was aware of a terrible sense of urgency now.

Cass bent and hefted her aunt's duffel bag, about to go through it when the unmistakable scent of violets began to pervade the room. She froze.

It became stronger.

Cass was paralyzed. *I am imagining this,* she tried hopelessly to tell herself. She was not detecting Isabel's perfume. Ghosts, spirits, entities, whatever you wanted to call them, did not exist. Catherine had had a seizure—surely the autopsy on Monday would show that. The electrician had been the victim of some coincidental crime.

She refused to think about the fact that Antonio's grandfather had also been stabbed to death. She refused to wonder if he had died there at the house. She dumped the duffel upside down, pulling out her aunt's things.

Suddenly Cass slowed and stopped. She was unprepared for the monumental and piercing grief, the absolute anguish, that suddenly overwhelmed her, making her feel dizzy and faint. Cass had to sit down on the bed beside her aunt's things.

How could Catherine be gone? If only this were a terrible dream, if only she would wake up, home at Belford House, with everything the way it had been before the viewing of the necklace.

Cass closed her eyes, suddenly nauseous. And what about Tracey, who had disappeared—just like Margarita?

And there in her mind she could see Isabel, so damn clearly. And she was smiling. With hatred, with malevolence.

Cass hated her own imagination.

The electrician's dead, astonished gaze filled her mind.

"Damn you, Cass," she told herself aloud, "cut it out!" No one, she decided, could be better at scaring her than she herself.

The journal was there, amongst her things. Cass stared at the faded notebook bound in tired blue leather.

She picked it up.

Antonio did not know the truth about his father. Was the truth here, in these pages? Should she come clean?

Cass trembled. If there was any chance at all of some kind of friendship or an even deeper relationship developing between them, surely the knowledge that Catherine had lured his father to his death would destroy it. Antonio would never want anything to do with her or anyone in her family if that was the case.

And shouldn't she feel the same way, given all that had happened?

And then, slowly, she looked up.

The lid on her laptop was closed. But the green light blinking on one of the indicators signified that the machine was on.

Cass's heart skipped violently, sickeningly.

She dropped the journal.

She realized that the cloying scent of violets had increased.

Cass could not move. She could not breathe. The scent surrounded her, making it difficult to breathe. She thought she might begin to choke—just the way her aunt had.

Cass finally looked around the room. It was filled with shifting shadows—and it was no longer a place she wanted to be. Then she looked at her laptop, and she looked at the glowing green light. A small voice inside herself told her that she was going to have to get up and open the machine.

She dreaded doing so.

Then she looked cautiously at the door. Had she just heard someone pausing there?

Her heart was pounding with erratic force. "Antonio?" Her voice came out as an unintelligible croak. "Antonio?" she tried again.

There was no answer.

Cass gripped the bed. Someone was out there, she was certain of it—she knew it with all of her being, all of her heart.

The murderer?

Stop it! Cass shouted silently to herself. Abruptly she got up and ran to the laptop, opening it. She cried out.

The DOS prompt was flashing—pointing at three words.

THEY BETRAYED ME.

Cass inhaled, seized with convulsive tremors, stepping back, away.

THEY BETRAYED ME.

No. It was impossible. This was a joke, a terrible joke, and when Cass found out who was the prankster, she would commit murder herself.

Murder. It suddenly flashed through her mind that Tracey might be dead.

"No," she whispered, backing away from the laptop with its unmistakable yet impossible message, slowly turning around in a 360-degree circle. Shadows seemed to dance all around her, leering. But she was alone.

Cass's gaze swung wildly to the door.

The door.

She had to open it.

Cass closed her eyes for an instant, inhaling hard. Of course she had to open it. Because she had to get the hell out of this room. But what if she was right? What if someone was standing there on the other side of the door?

The murderer could be there.

Was it Gregory?

Cass strained to hear as sweat trickled into her eyes. But all she could hear was her own labored breathing, her own deafening heartbeat. *Damn, damn, damn!*

Go to the door.

The words popped vividly, powerfully, into her mind. Cass hesitated. Because she knew that something terrible would happen if she opened that door.

And then she heard it, and there was no mistaking the sound—nails scratching the outside of her door.

It was an invitation and she knew it.

Cass shook. *Go to the door,* she told herself silently. And a voice echoed inside her head. It was not her own.

Go to the door.

Suddenly Cass moved, refusing to think about the consequences, her brain too paralyzed with fear to do so. And she swung the door open.

Isabel stood there, staring at her, unsmiling, and this time, this time she did not disappear.

SIXTEEN

The summons had come a sennight ago, and it had been so urgent that there had been hardly any time to prepare. Isabel had thought that Sussex would never bring her to court, where he was a member of Queen Mary's council. But she had been wrong.

Surely she would soon see Rob.

His letters had ceased well over a year ago.

"London Bridge, my ladies." One of Sussex's soldiers rode his mount up to the litter that carried Isabel and Helen, interrupting her thoughts.

Isabel clutched her small black and white spaniel, Zeus, who kept licking her hands. They were actually there, with London just across the bridge. She inhaled. There had been no explanation for her uncle's summons, but she could imagine why he had finally issued it. Somehow he had recalled her very existence, and he must intend to arrange a marriage for her. Isabel dreaded the prospect.

She did not, could not, understand why Rob had ceased writing to her. In the beginning, when they had first been refused by Sussex, Rob's letters had been both frequent and long, filled with the narrative of his adventures in Scotland, France, and Flanders. His letters had made her smile, laugh, and finally cry, especially the one in which he had shared the good tidings of his appointment by Dudley himself to serve the lord chancellor. Of course, with King Edward's death and then Jane Grey's fall, Dudley had been tried for treason and beheaded; now Queen Mary was on the throne. Her uncle had joined the popular uprising in her support at Framlingham last July, just days before her coronation, as had many other noblemen. Isabel reasoned that if her uncle now served the queen, Rob did, too.

Isabel was trembling, for the excitement of seeing both London and Rob, finally, again, was so overwhelming she could scarcely breathe. "How far are we from Westminster, Sir Thomas?"

"A good hour, my lady, but do not fret. Our journey is all but concluded, and with nary an inconvenience, I might add." He smiled through his beard at her.

"And I shall happily inform my uncle of that fact," Isabel said, her mind racing ahead. She could see the Tower of London across the Thames, to her right, as well as the Tower Bridge. Barges and galleys and small dories filled the river. She was wide-eyed. There was no question, Isabel thought, that she was a country mouse. London with its crowded, narrow streets, filled with horsemen, carters, drays, and other litters, with gentlemen and their servants, with noblewomen, churchmen, yeomen from the outskirts of town, apprentices, beggars, and vagabonds, was the most exciting spectacle she had ever seen. Never mind the stench—she had to keep her pomander near her nose—and never mind the roar of wheels, the clatter of hooves, the shouts and cries of beggars and brigands.

Isabel loved London. It had been love at first sight. She never wanted to go home.

Ahead of her, two gentlemen were engaged in an ungentlemanly fight of fisticuffs. The soldiers at the head of her column swore and shouted angrily at the riders, carts, and pedestrians in their way, clearing a path for her, sometimes with the points of their swords.

" 'Tis the Tower, Helen, look," Isabel said, reaching for Helen's hand. Zeus began thumping his tail. His bug eyes were dark and bright.

"I had not thought to see this sight again," Helen said with a slight smile, following Isabel's gaze.

Isabel knew well enough the role of the Tower in government, and she shuddered and looked away. "And that must be Saint Paul's," she cried, pointing to her left. The cathedral's spires were glorious, majestic, the grandest sight Isabel had ever beheld. Her heart was flipping over mightily. Would she be allowed to remain in town for some time? Oh, but she would beg her uncle on bent knee to stay in London, never mind that summer would soon approach. Isabel had heard that all the nobles and gentry left London in the summer, but Isabel knew she would wish to remain.

And this summer the queen was to marry Philip, the emperor's son and heir. Isabel trembled at the thought—how she would love to attend the wedding!

Rob's handsome image came to mind again, and Isabel's heart lurched. She had rehearsed what she would say to him this entire journey. But surely, once they were face-to-face, there would be no need for any rehearsed speech. Surely, once they met again, all would be well, as before. Isabel hugged her year-old dog, nuzzling her cheek to his long fur.

"Indeed, that is Saint Paul's, and the Tower is to our right." Sir Thomas was smiling at her. "Would you care to go past the Tower, my lady, for a closer look?"

Isabel stared at him. She might be a country mouse, but she was no fool. The Tower was where the country's most powerful political prisoners were interned. More often than not, those imprisoned there ended up without their heads. "Who is in the Tower now?" she breathed, almost afraid to know.

"Sir Thomas Wyatt was executed last week, as you might have heard, but the old bishop of Worcester remains within, John Hooper," Sir Thomas told her.

Wyatt had led a vast rebellion against the queen, going so far as to enter London with his forces. Of course, in the end he had been defeated and seized. Isabel was filled with tension. "A bishop in the Tower? And what are his crimes, Sir Thomas?" She thought the name sounded vaguely familiar but could not place it.

"Heresy, of course. He refuses to give up his evil and corrupt doctrines and confess himself a faithful son of the pope."

"I see," Isabel said slowly. Her mind spun. She was aware that her queen was a devout Catholic, and she was certainly aware that many of the villagers near Stonehill, and even some of her own household, now attended mass. She herself had never thought twice about continuing to worship in the manner in which she had been raised. She was surprised when Helen reached for and took her hand, squeezing it in warning.

Things were not the same in London, Isabel realized then.

"God bless Queen Mary," Helen spoke up firmly. "For saving this country and all the good people in it from such grievous heresy as we have been forced to endure." She nodded emphatically.

Isabel blinked at her companion, who was a devout Calvinist.

"Amen," Sir Thomas said. "Let us make a small detour. Although they cut Wyatt down from Tower Hill to distribute his corpse among the rebels as a warning, enough sinners swing from the top of the hill, and 'tis quite a sight, I assure you."

"They do not remove the corpses?" Isabel asked, shocked.

" 'Tis a lesson for all about the evils of heresy, my lady. A warning not to stray from God's true path."

"Sir Thomas, there is no need to go past the hill," Isabel said, managing a smile. "I am overwhelmed as it is with all that I see as we speak."

"Very well." He bowed from the saddle. "Then on to Westminster, my lady."

Isabel couldn't help thinking about Rob and she bit her lip. "Thank you, Sir Thomas," she said.

Sir Thomas and two of his men led them through the throngs of courtiers in one antechamber after another. Sussex was in conference and could not attend them; they would be escorted to Isabel's room. Isabel was dazed. She had never seen so many noblemen and so many noblewomen in one place, at one time. She could hardly absorb the sight of Westminster itself, with its towering stone walls and high-domed ceilings, with its numerous rooms and stained-glass windows, much less the sight of so much velvet, lace, and satin finery. Jewels flashed everywhere. Isabel glimpsed rings and chains and pendants, rubies and emeralds and sapphires, ruffles and bows and embroidery, and fur. Rabbit, squirrel, fox, mink, and sable lined cloaks and coats. Her head felt like it was spinning. The air was overly warm, too stuffy, and body odor filled each room. As her bewildered gaze went from bejeweled throats to moving mouths, from exaggerated codpieces to heaving bosoms, from tapestry to painting to giant columns and pillars, she wondered if she might faint.

She was relieved that she would not meet her uncle directly.

On an upper floor, miles from the crowded halls below, it seemed, a door was thrown open to a small chamber with one window, one four-poster bed, and a small pallet for Helen. There was a fireplace on one wall, but no fire within, and one small writing desk in a corner of the room. There was no other furniture, not even a chair, not even a single rug.

Helen looked around while Zeus, set down by a servant, eagerly began exploring. "We will adjust the furnishings," she announced. Isabel walked over to the window and smiled. London was sprawled across the skyline, and directly below, she saw a series of small gardens.

"Thank you, Sir Thomas," Helen said, closing the door.

Isabel felt like dancing and lifting her skirts; she did just that. Her spaniel came running to her to attack her skipping feet. "Isn't this glorious, Helen?"

Helen did not answer, and Isabel stopped spinning about, realizing that Helen had found a letter on the writing desk.

" 'Tis for you, my lady."

Isabel already recognized her uncle's wax seal on the missive. Her heart sank. Instantly she scooped up her puppy, holding him so tightly that he began to wiggle in protest.

"Why do you tarry?" Helen scolded, removing Zeus from her arms.

Isabel took the missive, and slowly she broke the seal and opened it. She scanned the page, her heart lurching unpleasantly, and finally she carefully refolded it.

"Well? You seem disturbed. What happens?"

Isabel stared. "He has found me a suitor, and I must prepare myself even as we speak in order that I might receive him."

Isabel prepared for her guest with desperate care. First she sent Helen on an errand that would take her all day. She then quickly soaked her skirts in urine stolen from several chamber pots in adjoining rooms. She blackened two of her teeth with lead, and bribed another serving maid to bring her egg whites, which she mixed with alum to streak her vivid red-gold hair white. The final touch was to take the pits of cherries, ground up finely, and wash her face with them. The effect was to blotch her unusually clear and porcelain complexion.

Isabel was frantic. Surely this ploy would work. But what if Sussex ever discovered it? The mere notion terrified her.

Her uncle's servant escorted her down to an antechamber at precisely four o'clock. Isabel's stomach was in knots, her temples throbbed, and she remained anxious and afraid. The gentleman gave up any attempt at conversation, instead holding a pomander to his nose. He pushed open the door. "Lord Montgomery, my lady," he said.

Isabel did not glance within. "Will my uncle be joining us?" she asked.

"The earl intends to speak with you tonight after the evening's entertainment," the man replied. He bowed and left.

Isabel inhaled, for courage. Then she stepped inside the small but pleasantly appointed chamber.

She already knew that Douglas Montgomery was the second and youngest son of a baron, but as his older brother was sickly, her uncle had informed her that there was little question that he would one day, sooner than later, come into his father's lands and title. He was a widower with two children, she had been told, and he was also a personal friend of her uncle's, which meant that they were allies in this land of ever-changing political winds and alliances.

His back was to Isabel as she entered the chamber, and when he turned, Isabel faltered. She was expecting Montgomery to be older, if not deficient in other physical attributes. But he was tall and broad shouldered and he had hardly reached thirty. His hair was raven black and his eyes blue and piercing. For one instant, as their gazes met, Isabel was stunned by his youth and his appearance.

And in that instant, his eyes widened in shock as he looked at her.

A small voice lanced through her head, and it told her to go upstairs, undo her disguise, and be herself with this man.

Immediately Isabel turned off that terrible, disloyal, and wayward thought, for she would soon be reunited with Rob.

Montgomery had recovered. He strode forward, his face a mask she could not read. He bowed. "Lady de Warenne. Your uncle sings your praises, and I am honored that you receive me."

Even as she clung to her resolve, Isabel found herself torn, and despising what she was doing. She curtsied in return. "My uncle does overly praise me, I think. Good day, my lord."

He straightened, as did she, and their eyes met. His eyes were a deeper, darker blue than Rob's. "I trust your journey was a safe one?"

"Yes, it was, many thanks, my lord." He continued to try to hold her gaze and she continued to try to evade it.

He was now holding his handkerchief somewhat discreetly by his nose. "That is a blessing, then." His smile was brief.

Isabel had to stare. He would stand there, in spite of her odor, which was, she thought, far worse than her appearance, and make pleasant conversation with her. How could this be? Her heart was sinking rapidly. "Have you been at court very long, my lord?"

"I only arrived two days ago. I rarely come to London, my lady, although I keep a home not far from here."

Isabel could comprehend him. He had come to town only to meet her in the hope of finding a new wife. " 'Tis my first visit here, and I am delighted." She smiled. "There are hardly such interesting sights in Sussex County."

His eyes widened; his stare became searching.

Isabel grew uneasy.

Finally he said, "I confess to being confounded, my lady. The rumors of your beauty have preceded you. I had expected to meet with a young woman of but nineteen, with startling red-gold hair and a flawless complexion. Rarely have I ever found rumor to be so . . . ill founded."

Isabel felt herself flush. "Clearly, my lord, I am no beauty, and I am so sorry you have been misled. But rumor is just that, is it not?"

"I did not intend to insult you," he said quickly, actually touching her hand. "Have you been ill recently?"

She trembled, drawing away. "You did not insult me. I possess a looking glass. Of course, I do not ever bother to use it." She could not look at him now. "I am rarely ill."

A silence fell. She stole a glance at him and saw that he seemed torn. Her own confusion returned. Why was she deceiving this man—who was not only handsome, but who seemed strong of mind and manner?

"Lady Isabel . . ." He sighed. "May I escort you to dine tonight? The pleasure would be mine."

Isabel could not believe her ears. "My lord, I have had a tiresome day, and I fear I am unwell. Might we continue this conversation another time?" She was already rushing to the door. "I do beg your pardon, sir," Isabel cried.

And she did not pause to hear his answer, but she knew he stared after her, in surprise and dismay.

Isabel fled into her chamber.

"*What is this?* What is this hideous and foul manner?" Helen cried.

Isabel started, not realizing that Helen was present—not having expected her back for hours.

"Dear God in Heaven, what have you done?" Helen gasped.

Isabel quickly clutched Zeus, who was not offended by either her odor or her appearance. He licked her neck, squirming in her arms.

"I do not comprehend you." Helen continued to gape. "This trick— it is to chase away your suitor while you sent me to the market on a fool's errand!"

Isabel could not think of a reply. She was still reeling from her encounter with Montgomery. Why had he seemed dismayed when she had run from the room? Surely he had been relieved.

"You just see what shall happen when the earl hears about this greatest transgression of yours!" Helen said, hands on her narrow, bony hips now. "You will not get off lightly, my lady, I assure you of that."

"How loyal you are," Isabel said softly.

"I am loyal, more than you will ever know. I have cared for you since you were eight years old, and I want but the best for you, Isabel," Helen disagreed sternly.

"You have a fine way of showing it," Isabel said, stroking Zeus's silky fur, images of Rob—and Montgomery—dancing in her head.

Never before had she regretted giving herself to Rob. It had been the most glorious evening of her life. How could she regret it now?

Montgomery's keen blue eyes, set in his striking face, filled her mind.

Isabel screwed her eyes tightly closed. She had vowed to wait for Rob, and wait she would. She regretted nothing. She loved Rob, with all of her heart, aye, with all of her soul. But . . . if only Montgomery were less kind, less clever, and less striking in appearance. If only he were short, fat, and bald, with rotting teeth falling out of his head!

Helen was grim. "I do not understand you. I see the mulish purpose in your eyes. Mark me well, Isabel. Your uncle clearly has summoned you here in order to find you a husband. Have your brains been addled?" She seemed angry. "I know you are not devout, for if you thought to marry God, that I would understand. You must wed and bear children, Isabel. 'Tis the reason God gave you life—and spared yours when your family died."

"You know nothing of God's will," Isabel said flatly. And she was angry that Helen would even dare to guess God's will and speak of her family in the same breath.

"Lady Isabel." Helen drew herself up. "I suggest you bathe this instant and clothe yourself appropriately, and join his lordship downstairs with the rest of the court for supper and dancing."

Isabel stared. "Tell his lordship I am indisposed, and I cannot join him this evening."

Helen made a sound of incredulity and she turned and marched from the room.

Isabel sat down on the bed, despairing. Now she was openly defying her uncle yet again. But she had no choice—otherwise Montgomery might glimpse her as she truly was. No good, she thought, could come of this deception. And she was afraid.

But perhaps she was wrong. For the next day she was informed that Montgomery had no wish to press his suit, and that he had left court for his home in the north of England. And Isabel could not help feeling a brief and passing moment of sharp regret.

Sussex summoned her to him, not the next day, but four days later at noon.

"A warning, Isabel," Helen whispered to her as they hurried through the many halls of the court.

Isabel's tension, already high, increased. She was dreading this encounter, quite certain her punishment for her deception of Montgomery would be strong and brutal. Sussex was known to be a man of little tolerance; he rewarded his allies generously and dealt with his enemies harshly. He had never been known to forgive a betrayal. Isabel prayed he loved her a little, and that he might show her the mercy he did not show the others fallen from his favor.

"I did not inform your uncle of your treachery."

Isabel stopped. She stared, stunned. "But—"

"The deed was done and there was no undoing it. I saw no reason for you to suffer, as I have every hope you have realized the error of your ways, and may soon suffer enough as it is."

Isabel remained stunned, and she did not reply. *Helen had not betrayed her.*

"I trust it will never happen again," Helen said, low.

Isabel hesitated, then nodded quickly. She would deal with the next suitor when the time came, and not one moment sooner. But dear God, for now she was spared the rod—if not exile back to Stonehill.

"Good," Helen said firmly.

They were following Sir Thomas. Isabel was suddenly detained by a hand upon her shoulder. She stiffened in surprise and turned.

Familiar, beloved blue eyes met hers.

Isabel felt her own mouth drop open, even as her heart skipped wildly. Rob!

"Isabel?" Robert de Warenne asked incredulously.

Instantly, heat flooding her cheeks, Isabel curtsied. The noise of the crowded room had vanished, it was now absolutely silent, and all she could hear was her own thundering heartbeat and her own rapid breathing. She forgot everyone, everything else. Rob. He was here. Finally—*after all these years.*

"Please, rise," Rob said, and then his hands were beneath her elbows and he was lifting her to her feet.

And Isabel took in every one of his beloved features, noting all the changes, and all that was so painfully familiar. He had matured. His jaw had hardened, his nose was straighter now, more full. There were lines at the corners of his dazzling blue eyes. In fact, he was far more striking than he had been as a youth of twenty—for he was a grown man.

He was also gaping at her. "I can hardly believe this encounter," he finally exclaimed. "Isabel, how beautiful you are."

And Isabel met his gaze again and felt tears coming to her eyes. For she saw in his regard all that she needed to see. "Rob." She stopped. And smiling, "Hello."

He smiled then, for the first time—his teeth had remained white and even. "My lady," he said, and he released her elbows to bow. "A sight you are, Isabel." His jaw flexed then and he touched his chest. "My heart pounds as if I am in the midst of battle."

That was when Isabel realized how finely he was clothed. His doublet was gold velvet. Cuffs of French lace spilled from his sleeves. His hose was also gold, but satin. His dagger was bejeweled. A huge pendant lay on his chest, suspended by a thick gold chain; it was either a ruby or a garnet. Isabel noticed that he wore two rings—a sapphire and a pale green gemstone that might have been jade. And there was a badge on his left sleeve. Isabel recognized that it belonged to the queen.

"Rob, we have so much to talk about," Isabel managed, thinking that he had done very well for himself, indeed. And she was overjoyed for him, for them both. For hadn't his lack of means been the issue standing in their way? Surely Sussex would change his mind about their match now.

"Indeed we do," he said, and suddenly he was taking her hand.

A cough sounded behind them. Isabel suddenly remembered that Helen stood there, listening to their every word, Sir Thomas behind her. Dread filled her as she stiffened, and her gaze flew to Rob's. She turned. "Helen, I wish you to meet my cousin, Sir Robert de Warenne. Lady Helen Courtney, Sir Robert."

Robert bowed; Isabel saw how direct and piercing Helen's regard was. Her heart sank—Helen was no fool. "I am more than pleased to make your acquaintance," Robert said, smiling at Helen. Then, to Isabel, "It is Admiral de Warenne now, my lady."

Isabel almost gasped aloud in surprise and pleasure, but she managed to stifle the sound. "You have risen in the world, Rob."

"Yes, I have. The queen rewarded me personally for my defense of Ludgate against the traitor Sir Wyatt." His eyes found hers and they were sparkling.

"Admiral de Warenne," Isabel breathed, loving the sound of his title upon her lips.

"So you fought the rebel forces?" Helen asked coolly.

Isabel looked at her pinched expression and was afraid that she suspected everything.

"Indeed I did, as did many other of the queen's loyal followers." Rob turned to Isabel, arm extended. "I have business with the council, but that can wait. Let us walk in the gardens, for there is so much to say. I am sure you do not mind, Lady Helen?"

Helen was not doing a good job of hiding her disapproval. "Lady Isabel has been summoned to meet with her uncle, the earl of Sussex. We must not keep him waiting."

"Her uncle, my cousin, will not return from the queen's business until much later in the day," Rob said with a quick smile. "You will be waiting here for several hours, of that I can assure you. Thomas, I will deliver your charge safely back to the earl. Come, Isabel," he said, not giving Helen another chance to interfere while Sir Thomas, who clearly knew Rob, nodded deferentially.

Rob knew his way well through the corridors and halls of the royal residence, Isabel realized. She remained dazed as they hurried away from the crowded rooms close to the queen's receiving rooms. She had to reassure herself from time to time that it was really he; she would steal a quick glance at his perfect profile and her heart seemed to burst with happiness. And he would glance at her too, she knew, when she turned her head away.

Sunlight spilled into the vast hall they had entered. Only a few courtiers were passing through, and ahead, beyond the massive columns supporting the high, vaulted ceiling, Isabel saw a small garden filled with flowers and trees.

And she also saw a man of medium build standing with his shoulder against one column, staring somewhat morosely outside.

Rob's strides slowed as they approached. "Don Alvarado," he said firmly. "Good day to you, my lord."

The man, a Spaniard, turned. Isabel had never seen so much finery or such jewels, and he made the rest of the courtiers seem shabby in comparison to his splendor. He bowed. "Admiral de Warenne, good day." His accent was heavy—and difficult to understand. His glance fell upon Isabel.

"May I be of service, my lord?" Rob asked with deference. Then, in French, *"Je voudrais vous aider, s'il vous plaît."*

"Je suis bien, merci." Don Alvarado was glancing at Isabel again.

"Oh, forgive me, I have failed in my manners," Rob said. *"Pardonnez moi."* Rob turned to Isabel. "Alvarado de la Barca, *el conde de* Pedraza, an envoy from Prince Philip, king of Spain, heir to the emperor, betrothed and beloved of our queen."

Isabel curtsied, not really liking the count's stare and wishing for nothing more than to be alone with Rob. "I am most pleased to make your acquaintance, my lord," she said in French, after Rob introduced her.

They exchanged a few words, the count never smiling, his gaze far too intense, until Rob made their excuses and hurried them away.

"It has been a scandal," Rob remarked. "In all these months since the marriage treaty was signed, there was not a single letter or gift from Philip for the queen until Don Alvarado arrived a few days ago."

Isabel's eyes widened as they searched his tanned face. "How rude and ungentlemanly," she said. "The poor queen!" But her pulse was racing and it was not Mary Tudor whom she was thinking of.

"We have all agreed with that," Rob said, rather grim. "It was almost an insult. However"—and his expression lightened—"the count has brought such gifts, I cannot even begin to describe them. Gowns and furs and jewels—the queen did cry in front of her lords and ladies, Isabel, with pleasure and with joy."

"Oh, I am glad," Isabel said, as they entered a small, shady garden. She was only now aware of it. Dear God, they were together, and they were alone.

Suddenly he was staring at her, unsmiling. Isabel became paralyzed, and every single question, every declaration, that she wished to ask and make disappeared. There was only expectation and the sudden, familiar tightness and tension of her body, and her quickening breath. "Oh, Rob," she heard herself say.

He took her hands tightly in his and he held them to his chest. Even through the doublet he wore, the shirt beneath, she could feel his pounding male heartbeat. "This day is most amazing," he whispered roughly. And then he lifted her hands to his mouth and kissed the tops of each one.

Tears came to Isabel's eyes, because the two kisses were so

tender and so gentle, so filled with the unspoken declaration of his love.

"Rob," she whispered, blinking back the tears, wanting to ask him what had happened, why she hadn't heard from him, yet her gaze kept drifting from his blue eyes to his firm, masculine mouth.

"I am, again, undone," he said harshly, and his eyes locked with hers.

Isabel realized what he was going to do before he pulled her into his arms, before his mouth softly feathered hers. And as she sank into his embrace, she knew she was home at last—she knew there had been no errors, no delusions, and she knew she would one day die still loving this man completely.

And then their mouths fused with a hunger fueled by four years of separation. Their lips parted, their tongues met.

They broke apart, wide-eyed and stunned, and Isabel realized she was smiling and crying at the very same time. *Nothing has changed after all.*

"I have hurt you," he cried, aghast, trying to wipe the tears from her cheeks with his thumbs.

"How could you hurt me when I love you so?" Isabel asked, still smiling. He froze.

Isabel stopped smiling. Something was wrong. It was written all over his countenance, it was written there in his startling eyes. "Rob?"

He wet his lips. "Isabel." He spoke her name with the greatest caution. "Do you not know?"

Isabel's heart began to pound and hammer. "Do I not know what, Rob?"

He stared, as if incapable of answering.

"Rob! What is it that I must know?" she cried, a frightened demand. "Surely nothing is amiss, not between us?"

Ron inhaled loudly, released her hands, and turned his back to her. His fists found his hips. His stance was wide, thighs braced hard apart.

And her heart felt as if it were about to begin a hellish descent. "Rob. You frighten me." She walked around him to face him and saw that he had lost much of his coloring. "You truly frighten me!"

"I do not mean to frighten you. But it seems I have forgotten that you have lived at Stonehill all these years." He did not meet her eyes now. "Surely, even there, you receive news of the goings-on at court?"

"Sometimes," Isabel said slowly, breathless with dread. "What has happened?"

"A year ago I married the lady Anne Hammond, a widow and an heiress."

Isabel stared, knowing she had misheard. "What?"

He did not repeat himself, and would not look her in the eye

A year ago I married the lady Anne Hammond . . .

She blinked, surprised to find tears marring her vision. " 'Tis a jest?"

He glanced at her. "No, Isabel, I would hardly make such a jest."

It was not a jest. She remained stunned, in absolute disbelief. A year ago he had married . . .

"Isabel." He reached for her, worry in his tone.

Isabel managed to elude him. Her heart pumped so furiously now that she could not breathe and she gasped for air. "No! Do not . . . How dare . . . Do not!" She backed away, absolute realization beginning, and with that horrific comprehension came an even worse feeling, utter anguish, sheer heartbreak. Isabel felt as if she were a house made of wood, the timbers shearing apart, and with their collapse, the entire solid world, once supported by their weight, came thundering to the ground. And the tears began to fall.

"Oh, God! I never intended this!" Rob cried. "It has been years, Isabel, since we were foolish children making foolish vows!"

Foolish vows, she thought, looking at him, and then she doubled over, racked with pain. She would never survive this treachery.

He had killed her dreams, and now he was killing her.

SEVENTEEN

Cass was frozen with shock, fear, and dread. Isabel did not disappear. She did not vanish or evaporate. She stood there staring Cass in the eye. She was no figment of the imagination, and Cass knew it.

And then Isabel smiled. There was nothing kind about it. It was chilling.

Every hair on Cass's body stood on end, her heart was slamming against the walls of her chest, she felt paralyzed, but somehow she managed to speak. Her words were raw and dry. "What? What do you want?" She had to be dreaming. She had to be losing her mind. This was not real.

Isabel walked past her.

Cass shifted to watch the woman as she paused in the midst of the bedroom, not far from the table where Cass's laptop was. Her back was to Cass. Cass's eyes widened as a comprehension seized her—and as it did, Isabel vanished. What was left in her stead was the glowing computer screen with the three words written upon it.

THEY BETRAYED ME.

Isabel had wanted her to see the message again.

Cass turned and fled the room, not even thinking to grab the candle, and a moment later she slammed into a human wall of flesh. She screamed.

Antonio shook her. "It's me, Cassandra."

"Oh God!" Cass grabbed his hand and dragged him back the way he had come, but even as they fled the length of the corridor, Antonio demanding to know what was wrong, Cass's mind was turning over the stunning incident. She had just been confronted with a woman dead for 445 years. She had just been confronted with a ghost. She had not dreamed it, imagined it. And Isabel's ghost did not seem in the least bit pleasant.

And there was also no escaping another fact—Isabel had communicated with her.

They betrayed me.

Isabel was present. And she was not just a form of abstract energy—she possessed intelligence, and this experience proved it.

Intelligence—and will.

Intelligence—and what else?

Cass began to shake. Who had betrayed Isabel? And why was she singling out Cass for her damnable communication? What did it mean? What did she want? Surely she wanted something!

They were at the top of the stairs. Antonio was demanding to know what was wrong. Cass hadn't even been aware of him confronting her, or their having halted. He was gripping Cass by both arms. She blinked at him as he shouted, "Talk to me!" Then he demanded, "What the hell is happening?"

Cass couldn't speak. A ghost with intelligence, a ghost with willpower, a ghost with an agenda? "Where are the children?" she demanded as another terrible notion struck her. Walls and halls and doors and stairs did not limit Isabel. There was no escaping her—not if she chose otherwise.

And even right now she could be downstairs, preying upon the children.

Ghosts did not stab people.

How the hell could Antonio know that?

"Where are the children?" Cass cried frantically.

Antonio stared. "In the library. With Gregory and Celia. Alfonso isn't feeling well, he has gone to bed."

Cass blinked at him, almost without comprehension. "Antonio. I just saw her."

He started, eyes wide. "Tracey?"

Cass was suddenly sick; briefly she had forgotten all about her missing sister. And now she was afraid that Isabel was tied in to Tracey's disappearance. *They betrayed me.* Did Isabel want vengeance? Was Aunt Catherine right? "No," Cass said, choking, finally looking up at him. "I saw Isabel."

He stared, becoming grim.

And Cass saw the doubt in his eyes. She gripped his shirt. "I saw her. We stood face-to-face, I don't know for how long. But before I saw her, my laptop went on. I went to it and opened it, and there was a DOS prompt—with three words, Antonio. Three words. *They betrayed me.*"

He just stared.

"Are you listening?" she shouted, wanting to strike him. "She communicated with me through my laptop!"

His hands settled on her shoulders. "I want to believe you," he said. "I do. But, Cassandra, ghosts don't type. In fact, in my opinion, ghosts don't do anything other than hover about whatever edifice they are haunting."

Cass was furious. "This ghost does far more than hover, Antonio, this ghost communicates, this ghost is intelligent, this ghost wants something!"

His expression changed. "Why are you so angry?" His hand touched her cheek.

Cass stiffened, about to fling his hand away. She was more than angry, she almost felt enraged and she wanted to hit him. She began to struggle for her composure. *What was wrong with her?* She and Antonio were friends, and more. How could she be so angry with him, almost violently so? Cass stared at him. And as she did, she recalled how violently they had made love just a few hours ago.

And a recollection of Tracey striking her, kicking her, also came to mind.

Cass didn't like it.

"Cassandra? What is it?" Antonio was asking.

Cass didn't really hear him. And the electrician had been stabbed, Aunt Catherine had choked to death violently, and Eduardo had suffered an equally violent death. And what about Antonio's grandfather? "There's seems to be a pattern emerging here, Antonio, one of violence and death."

"Cassandra—"

"No! Your father, your grandfather, my aunt, the electrician!" She was shouting. "They are all dead—they were all somehow murdered."

He stared. "Do not tell me you think Isabel is involved."

"But she's here, communicating to me," Cass said. She glanced past him, down the dark corridor, suddenly trembling—and her mind was made up. "C'mon." She grabbed his hand and half dragged him after her, lengthening her strides. Sickness filled her now, accompanied by dread.

"All right," he said, his flashlight wobbling in his hand as he hurried to stay abreast of her.

In the doorway of her room, Cass paused. But Isabel was not in sight, thank God, and as Cass sniffed the air, she realized that no lingering scent remained. She was gone.

Antonio stepped past her, shining his light on the laptop. The lid remained up, the DOS prompt blinking, but the message was gone.

Gone.

Cass stared in disbelief.

"Cassandra," he said gently.

She knew what he was going to say and she whirled. "No! I did not imagine her, and I did not imagine what I saw on the screen! You're going to have to take my word on that, Antonio!"

He did not respond.

Cass heard herself curse. Then she rushed to the bed to grab the journal—maybe there were answers within it, answers they now desperately needed. "Let's get out of here," she said.

Antonio allowed her to precede him out.

And Cass was in such a rush to leave that she forgot to turn off the computer.

"I'll be right back," Gregory promised the two children and Celia.

Inside the library, it was eerily bright, as a huge fire roared in the hearth. Several candles had also been lit and placed about the room. Eduardo and Alyssa were sitting in their blankets, Eduardo reading a story aloud. Both children looked up as one, alarmed.

Celia sat wrapped in blankets, looking terribly old and exhausted; defeated. Tea that had long since gone cold was on the small table beside her chair. "Señor Gregory, where are you going?" she asked.

He smiled briefly. "The toilet."

Alyssa and Eduardo watched him leave, and then they looked at one another, the book forgotten. For a moment the library was absolutely silent except for the crackling of flames and Celia's long, heavy sigh.

"He'll be right back," Edurado said with a quick smile.

Alyssa looked at him, filled with unease, wishing her aunt Cass would hurry back to the library, wondering what could be taking her so long. Worry overwhelmed her. Her great-aunt was in the hospital, and Alyssa wanted to know what was wrong with her and why nobody would talk to her about it. And where was her mother? Cass kept reassuring her that Tracey had probably rushed off into town, acting without thought, as she usually did, but Alyssa knew something was terribly wrong. Not only could she feel it, she could see it in her aunt's dark eyes. And what was wrong with Celia? She seemed sick. Alyssa had tried to talk to her, but she hadn't even heard her.

"I don't like his leaving us," she said slowly, wishing the fire did not make the shadows dance and lengthen and then shorten along the walls of the room.

Eduardo's smile was frail. "You don't have to worry," he said bravely.

Alyssa folded her legs beneath her, glancing around at the enormous room, the four corners of which were almost completely immersed in blackness. "I wish Aunt Cass would come back. What's taking her so long?"

Eduardo patted her arm. "If she's with my father, they're probably very busy with research."

Alyssa nodded seriously. "My aunt is the smartest woman I know. Smarter even than my great-aunt."

Eduardo agreed. "She is the smartest lady I know, too. And my father is the smartest man I know. He lectures all over the world!"

Alyssa thought that something smelled odd in the room. "I think they like each other," she said. "Your father doesn't like my mother anymore." Suddenly she fell silent, worried all over again. Where was her mother? How could she just leave them like this? What if she stayed away this time for a long time? Alyssa just wanted to know when she would see her again.

As if reading her thoughts, Eduardo said, "Maybe your mother got lost." He patted her knee.

Alyssa frowned, her heart racing. "I hope not!"

"Don't worry. If she did, I'm sure they'll find her. Remember, your aunt and my father are really smart."

Alyssa smiled a little, then she coughed. "What's that funny smell?" It was sweet, like flowers. Yet Alyssa did not like it.

"I don't know." Eduardo reached for his crutches as he glanced at the door. "What is taking my uncle so long?"

Alyssa stood, just in case he needed help standing up. She watched him position the crutches, brace himself, and somehow swing himself up. He was very strong, she thought. Suddenly something slammed behind them.

Alyssa whirled, Eduardo hobbled around. "What was that?" Alyssa cried, staring toward the dark shadows of the far wall. All the windows were closed, the draperies only partially drawn. Outside, there was a three-quarter moon, stars numerous and bright, lighting up the night.

"I don't know. I think something fell," Eduardo said, low.

"I know." Celia spoke for the first time.

The two children turned to look at her.

"This house is haunted," she said.

Alyssa froze.

"Do not say that, señora," Eduardo said, his tone nervously high.

"Can you not feel it?" Celia asked heavily. "Catherine felt it." Celia lapsed into silence, a tear sliding down her face.

Behind them, there was another noise, followed by a loud hissing sound. The children turned simultaneously.

"It's just the fire," Eduardo cried. "*Where* is my uncle?"

"Maybe he's disappeared, too," Alyssa whispered, clutching his hand as he held on to his crutches.

Their eyes met. Alyssa flushed. She hadn't meant to verbalize what she wished she had never heard the adults saying. Her mother had disappeared. She wasn't lost. She had vanished.

Just like Eduardo's mother had, a long time ago.

Did that mean she was never coming back?

"He didn't disappear," Eduardo said nervously, looking the way Alyssa felt—as if he might cry—when a soft tapping sound began behind them.

Alyssa gasped as they all turned, facing the window—and then she cried out.

A woman stood there, her features somewhat indistinct, but her long hair was a wild, moon-colored mass flying about her face and shoulders.

"Mother!" Alyssa shouted.

The woman stared, then stepped back, away, and out of sight.

Alyssa did not think. Her mother had come back! She hadn't gotten lost—she hadn't disappeared—after all. She ran out of the library as fast as she could. "Mother! Wait!"

Celia was standing. "Stop!" she cried. "Miss Alyssa, don't go!"

There was no reply.

Celia rushed after her, moving with surprising speed.

And Eduardo was left alone.

———

Cass and Antonio turned the corner of the hall, guided by Antonio's flashlight, when they saw Gregory walking back toward the library. Instantly Cass's radar went up. Why had he left the children alone—even for a minute? "Gregory!" she called.

He paused before entering the library, and as Cass hurried to him, she realized that something was terribly wrong. And the moment she halted beside him, she saw that her worst fears might be on the verge of being realized—both children were gone. Celia was gone. The library was starkly empty.

"You left them!" she cried. "Oh, God, they're gone!"

Antonio came up behind them. "Don't panic. They're undoubtedly in the kitchen, looking for a snack."

"I only left them for a moment," Gregory said.

Cass rushed back down the corridor, the two men on her heels. She flung open the door to the kitchen, but it was cast in blackness and no one was there. She thought—*I'll kill him if anything happens to the children.* And she meant it.

Cass ran back out, into the great hall.

The front door was wide open.

Cass stumbled, clutching Antonio for support. "You locked that."

"I did. They must have opened it." He walked to the door, swinging his flashlight in a wide-ranging arc. The landscape outside was a mass of shadowy shapes and forms.

"Why would they go outside in the middle of the night?" Cass cried. But she knew. Isabel had something to do with this. Isabel had something to do with every odd occurrence that had transpired since they had all arrived at Casa de Sueños. Because Isabel had an agenda. "Oh, God." She barreled past the men.

"Eduardo!" Antonio cried through cupped hands.

Cass began calling for Alyssa. Gregory joined them, saying, "They can't have gone far. We should split up."

Cass gave him a furious look—this was all his fault.

Antonio touched her. "Cassandra," he said firmly, calmly.

She shook him off. "No! If anything happens, Gregory is to blame."

"They're fine. Nothing will happen." But his eyes flickered with unease.

"I am so sorry," Gregory said, anguish written all over his face. "I never thought they would leave the library. I was only gone for a few minutes—and Celia was with them."

"Celia?" Cass was scathing. "The woman is in shock."

"It's not your fault," Antonio said flatly to his brother. He gave Cass a cold look. "We should split up. I agree."

Cass's temples throbbed with excruciating force. Split up. Divide and conquer. She hated the turn of her own thoughts. "I don't like the idea," she whispered. "We seem to be forgetting something. There's a dead man at the ruins. There's a murderer running around here, maybe even amongst us. And—there's Isabel."

The two men looked at her. Even in the darkness, Gregory had paled. "There is no ghost of that ancestor of ours about," he said, but his tone was hardly firm.

"Oh, no? I just saw her." Cass almost felt triumphant. And a part of herself felt disturbed, and was wondering why she had cast all caution to the winds, why she was so unkind, when unkindness was as foreign to her nature as cruelty or malice. "Whoever murdered him was inside your house, Antonio," she said, unable to stop herself. Her gaze went right to Gregory.

Gregory's face tightened. "I do not like what you're suggesting. Obviously my brother and I are above reproach—and so is Alfonso."

Cass straightened. "Oh, so I'm to blame? Or maybe we should blame a sixty-five-year-old woman—Celia?"

"Did I say that?" he shot back.

Cass stared at him, wondering if he was a deranged murderer. Ever since she had met him, he had been behaving oddly, she decided. Secretively. He was hiding something. "I doubt the electrician stabbed himself—in the chest."

"In the heart," Antonio muttered.

Cass jerked.

"He was stabbed directly in the heart."

"The children," Cass said. "We have to find them." Her tone pitched wildly upward. And then she saw the look the two men were exchanging—and it was a look of understanding which excluded her. "What is it?" she demanded. "What do the two of you know that you are not saying?"

"We don't know anything," Antonio said, walking away and shouting for Eduardo again.

Cass thought she heard something, and she gripped his arm from behind. "Shh. Listen!"

The cry, if it was a cry, was faint.

But Antonio took off like a rocket, around the left side of the house. "Eduardo! Where are you!"

Cass and Gregory were racing after him, and they heard the small, feeble, voice. "Papá! Papá!"

Antonio suddenly bent. Eduardo was prone on the ground, his crutches scattered some distance from him, and his father pulled him hard into his arms.

Cass gripped the boy's shoulder from behind. "Is he all right? Where is Alyssa?"

"Are you all right?" Antonio cried, relief in his tone.

"I fell. She was running so fast—" His voice broke.

"Where is Alyssa?" Cass shouted, fear flooding her.

"I don't know. She ran away, that way, I think," Eduardo said, sounding close to tears.

Cass felt the stabbing of sheer dread. "No."

Antonio stroked his brow, and Cass realized that both father and son were trembling. "Talk to me, little one. Tell me what happened."

Eduardo nodded. "We were reading in the library and then we heard noises. And then we looked at the window, and this woman was standing there. Alyssa thought it was her mother."

Eduardo looked at Cass. "She had pale hair. And Alyssa ran out of the room. Celia ran after her. I tried to follow them, but I could not keep up." Tears filled his eyes. "When I got to the hall, the front door was open, so I went out, but I could not find either of them." His voice rose shrilly.

Antonio stroked his hair, then held him close. "You did the best that you could." Over Eduardo's shoulder, he met Cass's gaze.

Cass was shaking uncontrollably. Had Tracey returned? Had Alyssa found her mother? Or was this some horrible prank? And if it was a prank, who had committed it? The murderer?

Antonio stood, helping Eduardo to his feet. Gregory had retrieved the crutches and he handed them to the boy. Antonio looked at Cass. "Take him into the house. Wait in the library. Gregory and I will search. Do not worry. She can't have gone far. We will find her."

Cass felt a tear begin to slide down her cheek. "I want to come, too."

He leaned toward her and kissed her mouth, briefly. "Please stay with my son. He is upset. Just make sure to lock the front door when you go back inside."

Cass wanted to refuse. She looked at Eduardo's pale face, his eyes brimming with tears, and suddenly, savagely, she cursed her sister, wishing she were dead.

Cass sat with Eduardo, her arm around him, staring blindly at the fire, praying for Alyssa's safe return. Tears kept coming unbidden to her eyes; she was sick with fear and dread. And she was using all of her willpower to refrain from interrogating Eduardo, who remained terribly upset.

Catherine was dead, Tracey was missing, and now Alyssa was gone, too? Cass felt as if she were on the verge of complete madness.

She closed her eyes to fight tears of real panic and fear. Isabel was behind everything. She had no doubt.

It was hard to think clearly now, but Cass knew she had to try. What if she were Isabel? What if she had been this young woman orphaned at eight, and burned at the stake twelve years later? After being forced into a marriage that had to have been loveless, with a foreigner, while forsaking any chance of true love?

I would not be sad, Cass thought. *I would be pissed off and angry.*

Cass froze. Anger, fury, rage, wrath . . .

They betrayed me.

Isabel wanted revenge. There was no other conclusion. But why prey upon her family as well as the de la Barcas?

They betrayed me.

"This is all my fault."

Eduardo's whisper interrupted Cass's whirling thoughts. "Of course it's not," she said quickly, but she could not smile. "Your father will find Alyssa in no time at all."

Cass glanced at her watch. Fifteen minutes had gone by. She could not do this. She could not sit there like a lump of lard while the most precious thing in the entire world to her was in jeopardy. But in jeopardy how?

Cass had to grapple with the very worst notion, a notion she did not want to face. If Isabel could send a message to her on her laptop, was she capable of other physical acts?

Cass closed her eyes, sick to the very pit of her stomach. Surely she was not capable of sticking a knife into a man's chest.

Antonio's grandfather had also been stabbed . . .

"Cass," Eduardo whispered, just as the sound of footsteps reached them.

She jumped up as Antonio and Gregory appeared, entering the room—Alyssa in Antonio's arms, holding on to his neck like a little monkey. "Alyssa!" Relief briefly immobilized her, and the tears began to fall in earnest. "Thank God," she choked.

Antonio smiled at her as he let Alyssa down to her feet. "She was scared and hiding in the bushes," he said lightly, as if nothing had happened at all.

Cass met his gaze, saw a warning message there, and understood he did not want to further frighten the children—there was something he wanted to tell her. She embraced her niece, hard. Alyssa clung to Cass's neck. Her little body was warm and real; Cass rocked her.

Then, "Don't you ever run off like that again, do you hear me?" Cass cried. "Or you will be grounded for the rest of your life!"

Alyssa nodded, her eyes red and puffy from crying. "I'm so sorry, Aunt Cass. I don't know what happened. But I thought I saw my mother and I had to go find her." Tears welled.

Cass hugged her again. "That's okay, sweetie." Had Alyssa seen Tracey? She did not dare ask now. "I think you and Eduardo should get into those blankets for a good night's rest." Now she was inspecting Alyssa from head to toe. She had a few scratches on her arms and one on her cheek, from a bush, Cass thought, and her hair was a wild mess, but other than that, she seemed fine. But what had actually happened?

And where was Celia?

Slowly Cass looked up—into Antonio's grim countenance.

"Will you stay here? All night?" Alyssa asked anxiously.

"Promise," Cass said, stroking her hair. She managed a smile and prayed it was cheerful and reassuring. "C'mon, guys. Into those blankets, let's go. Tomorrow's another day." She just prayed they would all get through this night without any further incident. But she did not think it likely.

The children were tucked in, and then an eternity passed as Cass waited for them to fall asleep so she could talk seriously with Antonio and his brother. When they both appeared to be out like lights, Cass hurried over to the two men, who were seated at Antonio's desk with scotch whiskeys. "What happened?" she whispered.

Antonio met her gaze. "She implied that there was a woman outside, not her mother, a woman who frightened her terribly and caused her to hide. I convinced her it was her imagination and that there is nothing to fear."

"Isabel," Cass breathed.

"That woman is not here," Gregory cut in tersely. "Jesu! I am tired of hearing about her."

"Oh, she is here," Cass said flatly. "Antonio doesn't believe me, either, but I saw her. She is haunting this house, but it's worse than that." Keeping her voice low, Cass said, "She wants vengeance on this family."

Gregory stood up, drink in hand, swilling half of it. Cass realized he was as white as a sheet—a very unnatural pallor for a man with a golden complexion and a Costa del Sol tan. "What is it?" she asked uneasily.

He cursed. "I vote that tomorrow we pack up everything and everybody and leave."

"And what about Celia?" Antonio asked quietly.

Gregory cursed again.

Automatically Cass reached for and found Antonio's hand. He was flesh and blood, strong, a man, and she felt instantly comforted. Their gazes locked. "Please, please, do not tell me that something has happened to Celia."

"We cannot find her. Not at night, in the dark, anyway." He was more than grim. "I'm going to wait until the morning to drive into Pedraza and call the police. I don't want to leave you alone here with the children tonight."

Cass stared, trembling. "So you admit that something terrible is happening here, and that one by one we are all falling victim to tragedy?"

Antonio took a swig of his drink. "Let us assume, for one moment, that you are correct. That Isabel is present, that she sent you a message. What should we deduce from those two facts?"

"She is intelligent and capable of a certain amount of willful action," Cass said promptly.

"This is nonsense," Gregory cried. "There's a murderer on the loose. That is a fact. All the rest is nonsense."

Cass faced him furiously. "Is it nonsense that your father died—and it was not an accident? Is it nonsense that you grandfather also died—brutally, tragically? Is it nonsense that Antonio's wife disappeared while here? That my sister has vanished? That the electrician is dead—murdered? And now Celia is gone, too?" She faced Antonio, who had risen to his feet. "Did your grandfather die here?"

Antonio nodded, eyes riveted on her. "What do you mean, that my father's death was not an accident?"

Cass squared off. "My aunt killed him," she said.

Gregory had gone to bed. Cass had thought he hadn't seemed very happy about going upstairs to sleep alone, but she had not suggested that he sleep in the library, and his set face had told her that his macho pride was dictating his decision. That was fine with her.

Antonio sat at the desk, hunched over it, reading Catherine's journal. Every time Cass heard him turn a page, she would turn to look at him, wanting to go to him and hold him. But she did not.

She was afraid now of his rejection. She was afraid of what he might find in Catherine's journal. She was afraid they would never be able to recover from the fact of Catherine's guilt—if it was a fact.

Cass was praying that her aunt had been mistaken.

But there was no time to agonize now. There was too much work to do—and she kept feeling that there was not enough time in which to do it. It was already eleven o'clock. She was going through the books, files, and folders crammed into the bookcases, looking for a clue—any clue—that might help them understand Isabel so they could fight her. But how did one fight a ghost?

What Cass knew about the supernatural was based on television talk shows and dramas, movies, popular fiction, and maybe the occasional New Age self-help book. It boiled down to one bottom line. Ghosts were supposed to be laid to rest; instead of haunting people, places, and things, they were supposed to go to the "light." But how did one send a ghost off to Heaven—or hell?

Antonio suddenly closed the journal with a thump. Cass whirled, a biography of Queen Mary in one hand, a biography of her sister, Queen Elizabeth, in the other. The shelves were filled with medieval history books and the biographies of famous historical figures, most of it pertaining to the subject of Spain and the Spanish, or Europe. But Cass was finding more and more works on Tudor English history—and specifically for the period of time when Isabel had lived. Cass could imagine why.

Antonio sat slumped back in the chair, his second scotch in hand.

Cass walked over to him. "Are you all right?" she asked uneasily, afraid to touch him.

He turned to look at her. "They were having an affair."

"I'm sorry," Cass said, wishing to know more.

He rubbed his temples. "Your aunt was filled with guilt. So was my father. They both, I think, never stopped loving their respective spouses.

But that did not stop them. I do not understand what actually happened . . . how your aunt and my father actually crossed the line. They did not understand, apparently, either."

Cass swallowed, thinking about all that her aunt had said. "Did she eventually come to despise him?"

"Yes."

Cass stiffened. That was not the answer she had hoped to hear.

He stood abruptly and walked over to the children, bending over his son to rearrange the blankets. Cass found herself moving to stand behind him. "Do you think my aunt killed him?" she managed. "Purposefully?"

He faced her. "I do not know, Cassandra. I just don't know."

"Are there any clues in there about Isabel?"

He stared. "They were both obsessed by her."

"What?"

"The two of them came here to work side by side uncovering every aspect of her life. They were both obsessed—to the point where my father called your aunt Isabel and she imagined herself to look like her ancestor."

Cass suddenly stared. "Antonio, you and I . . . we are here, working side by side, doing the exact same thing."

"I know."

He dreamed of fire, and in the midst of the flames, she was always there, leering at him, the demon woman from his childhood. Gregory tossed restlessly, perspiring, even though he slept in nothing but a pair of briefs. *Wake up*, the creature in his dreams whispered. *Wake up*.

He did not want to wake up, but he did not want her there, either, in his dreams, with that beautiful yet ugly face. How could a woman so beautiful be so evil? he wondered.

Wake up.

Gregory's eyes shot open and he was suddenly, abruptly, awake.

And he knew he was not alone.

He stiffened in fear, then saw the woman standing at the foot of the bed, a shadowy outline in the darkness of the night-blackened bedroom.

"Gregory?" Tracey whispered.

Realizing that it was Tracey, not that creature, Isabel, he shot up. "Tracey! Are you all right?"

She came forward and was sliding into the bed; he gripped her thin shoulders as her moon-colored hair fell over his hands and wrists. "I think so," she whispered hoarsely.

He dropped his hands, throwing his legs over the side of the bed, groping almost blindly for matches and the candle on his night table. When the candle was lit, he held it up and met her pale blue eyes. "Thank God!" he cried, cupping her head with one hand. "Thank God. What happened? Where were you?"

She just looked at him. "I'm fine. Please hold me now."

He realized she wasn't fine. There was a bruise on her face the size of a baseball. Her T-shirt and shorts were dirty and torn. And was that blood he saw specked on her clothes? He froze.

"Please," she whispered again.

He set the candle down and pulled her into his arms, thanking God that she was alive, because secretly he had believed her to be dead. Just like he *knew* Margarita was dead. He knew it with his heart and soul— with all of his intuition.

Tracey was thin but warm, wonderfully warm and alive in his arms, and she was trembling. He stroked her hair and her back. And the moment her body responded to his in the timeless way of male and female, he became aware of her that way, too.

He was instantly erect.

She smiled against his cheek, then they turned their heads and their mouths met and mated almost immediately. As Gregory moved over her, his tongue in her throat, it crossed the back of his mind that this was so insane.

She found and stroked his penis, and he could not wait. He tore her shorts off, the G-string with it, and frantically his hands moved over her pubis. An instant later he was driving deep within her, and they were both crying out.

Within moments, it was over. Tracey's orgasm felt violent to him, and he came immediately. Too late, he had forgotten a condom again. Too late, he had also forgotten to ask her if she was using birth control.

Damn it, he thought, suddenly so sated he was unable to move.

She laughed.

The sound was odd and he stiffened, rolling to his side, looking at her.

Isabel smiled at him.

Gregory leapt from the bed, staring in absolute horror at the reddish-haired woman from his childhood nightmares who lay half-naked in his bed.

"Get out," he screamed.

Isabel laughed again.

EIGHTEEN

Midnight

The ravine was covered with brush, and she crunched down, amidst the myriad branches, praying the brush and the night would hide her.

She could hardly breathe—never had she run so far, so fast, in such terror. But she did not dare make noise, even now; panting harshly, she was trying to hide the sound. She was terrified.

Above, on the cliff from where she had fallen, she could hear the occasional scuffing of shoe upon stone. Or was it wind upon branches?

Did it matter? She was going to be discovered.

Rocks and stones dug into her shins and knees. Her fingers clawed the hard dirt ground. She tasted dirt, and fear.

And she tasted blood. There was so much of it. It was her own.

They worked side by side, removing books, browsing through them, placing each in distinct piles by subject and time period. Folders were added to the piles. The night was terribly silent.

And it was dark. The fire had died down to the merest of small flames.

Cass wished it were later; she wished the sun would come up. She no longer enjoyed the nighttime; she had become afraid of the dark. She glanced at Antonio. He remained very disturbed. What else had he read in Catherine's journal? What wasn't he telling her? "Antonio?"

He looked at her, a book in his hands. "Yes?"

"Something has been bothering me the more I think about it. Isabel did not communicate 'he' betrayed me. She used 'they' betrayed me."

He leaned one shoulder against the bookcase. "Assuming you saw what you saw."

Her temper flared. "I saw what I said I saw. And if Isabel did not communicate those words to me, then someone else around here is a rotten prankster. And then that would mean there is also a murderer on the loose. And who would that be?" When he did not answer, she said, "Hasn't there been too much coincidence? God, my aunt is dead!"

He reached for her. "I believe your aunt had a heart attack, but there does seem to be a terrible amount of coincidence. We are doing exactly what it was that my father and your aunt were doing—obsessively digging into Isabel's life." He met her eyes. "And we also crossed the line."

Cass was motionless, loosely in his embrace. Then she stepped away. "Yes, we did." She was trying not to feel hurt about his phrasing; it was impossible.

"History repeating itself," Antonio said softly.

Cass hugged a book to her breasts. Catherine and Eduardo had become lovers, and she and Antonio had become lovers. "I've already wondered about this. There is one thread that seems to connect everything."

"And what is that?" He was intent.

"Violence. What we did was violent, or at least, I think so. Your father, your grandfather, my aunt—they all died violently. I mean, even if Catherine died of natural causes, I was there. It was brutal. A car accident—if it was an accident—is violent. The way Tracey hit me—"

"She hit you?" He stared. "Why didn't you tell me sooner?"

Cass was grim. "She didn't mean it. She flipped out. She was not herself."

He absorbed that. "So what are you suggesting? That Isabel, who also died violently, has somehow spread this contagion?"

Cass started. She hadn't considered Isabel's death in the equation, but Antonio was right. "I don't know, Antonio," she said. "But you are a de la Barca, and I am a de Warenne. The two families, involved again. Aunt Catherine seems to have been very right." Grief stabbed through her. She wondered if it would always be that way.

"What about the electrician? Why has he been murdered? He is neither a de la Barca nor a de Warenne. He was an innocent bystander. Maybe his death is coincidental."

"I might buy that—except he was stabbed with a knife that came from *this* house." Cass sighed. "I'm having enough trouble trying to understand why she hates my family, too."

"Sussex forced her into the marriage to Alvarado." Antonio shrugged. "Human beings are so complex. What motivates you might not motivate me. Isabel might have hated her uncle for the simple fact that he arranged the marriage."

"Maybe, on some other subconscious level, she hated him because he took her father's place."

"Maybe."

"So who are 'they'? Sussex and her husband?"

"We are jumping to conclusions," he said, but he smiled.

Cass smiled back. "Yes, we are." They had begun to enjoy themselves. Her smile faded. Now was not the time for pleasant debate. Her aunt was dead, Tracey and Celia missing—just recalling that made her sick inside—and Isabel was lurking about. Cass almost thought that she could feel her listening to their conversation. "We have to find out what happened to Isabel. Because then we can figure out what it is that she wants." She turned back to the book she held in her hands.

He stopped her. "We may be giving Isabel far too much credit, Cassandra. I still cannot fathom a ghost with an agenda."

Cass stared back. "I truly hope you are right. But I know you are wrong. History *is* repeating itself. " She glanced down at the book she held—a study by different authors on the reformation. "We have to figure Isabel out, find out what she wants—and give it to her—or stop her, if it is us that she wishes to destroy," Cass said grimly, flipping open the book. As she did so, a piece of paper fell to the floor.

Before she could retrieve it, Antonio grabbed her arm. "You have this amazing imagination," he said harshly. "But now you have gone too far!"

She met his gaze. "There is a pattern, damn it, and we both know it."

"Nothing is going to happen to me, or to you, or to anyone else," he said firmly. "We will find Tracey and Celia, and all will be well."

Cass straightened. "What if we can't find them?"

He hesitated. "Tomorrow we will bring in the police, and tomorrow I want everyone to leave."

Cass did not move. "I do not like your tone."

"I have not finished my work here. I will stay."

Cass could not believe her ears. "You can't stay here alone!"

He turned away, but not before she saw just how determined his expression was.

Cass stared at his back. How could she leave if he remained behind? She began to tremble. A disaster, she thought, it would be a disaster waiting to happen.

Or another tragedy.

"She's setting us up," Cass whispered. "Divide and conquer."

"Nonsense," Antonio said sharply.

"You cannot stay here alone," Cass said grimly. "I can see it in your eyes. It's her. Isabel. You won't leave because of her. You've been playing the devil's advocate, but you believe. You believe everything I've been saying!" she cried.

He crossed his arms. "What is that paper which fell out of the book?"

She felt furious. *Stubborn man!* She bent down to pick up the slip of paper. It was a carefully folded page. The moment she opened it, she realized it contained more of Edurado's notes.

"What is it?" Antonio asked too sharply.

"I recognize your father's handwriting," Cass said, "but I still can't read Spanish." One word did jump off the yellowed page at her. *Sussex.*

Antonio took the page. He squinted against the dark. "This says, 'Farmer, pages five hundred sixteen to five seventeen, Grantham, pages twenty-two to twenty-three and two hundred eight, Sussex.' "

Cass blinked at him, immediately aware of excitement stirring within her. "I just saw those books—one of which, at least, is Mary Tudor's biography." She bent over one pile, sorting rapidly through, and came up with the two books. "Which pages in Farmer?" she asked.

"Pages five sixteen to seventeen," Antonio asked, squatting beside her.

Cass scanned a long page. "I need more light." She rushed over to the fireplace, Antonio beside her. "This is about Sussex's appointment to Mary's council shortly after she became queen. It mentions here that he did not join her cause until the very last minute, just days before her coronation. Of course, he was not the only nobleman to do so." Cass felt disappointed. "There is nothing new here."

"The Grantham. That is a biography of Queen Elizabeth, I think."

Cass ran back for the other book. "Twenty what?"

Antonio told her the pages and Cass found them. She said, "Well, here we go. Sussex was also appointed to Elizabeth's council, just days after her coronation." She looked up at Antonio, then turned to page 208. "And he was accused of treason at the end of the first year of his reign." Cass was perplexed.

A silence had fallen over the room.

It was so deep and yawning that Cass was jerked out of her speculations, suddenly worried, suddenly uneasy—and afraid. The dread in her increased impossibly. She glanced up, but both children continued to sleep peacefully. Just behind her, the fire was dying, reduced to a few of the tiniest flames.

Cass handed Antonio the book and let him read the entire page, suddenly chilled to the bone. Something was going to happen before the night was out—she felt certain of it.

Something was going to happen now.

Antonio looked up and their gazes met. "Is that significant?" she asked in a whisper. She kept glancing warily around. "Am I somehow missing something? Grantham goes on to say Sussex did escape with his life—although he lost his title and his lands. This was well after Isabel's death." She continued to whisper.

"He was a man of political expedience—a political survivor," Antonio said. "For most of his life, it seems. He changed allegiance to support Mary, then did the same to support her sister. But such political creatures were hardly unusual at the time."

"No, they weren't," Cass said slowly. "I guess what this means was that he was not a man loyal to any cause or conviction. He was loyal to himself." She turned, but no one was standing behind her. Isabel did not stand behind her.

Antonio stood. "It is odd, don't you think, for him to have married his niece off to a Spaniard?"

"Yes, it is. What are you saying?" But even as Cass spoke, she suddenly knew, and could not believe she hadn't grasped this before.

They stood unmoving, staring at one another. One single candle continued to burn, not far from where the children slept. Cass could hear Antonio's breathing. It was rapid and shallow now.

The violets surfaced, rapidly.

"She's here," Cass said. She wanted to reach for his hand. She could not move.

Antonio slowly turned and scanned the room.

Suddenly the page containing Eduardo's notes, which she was holding, burst into flames. She cried out, dropping the burning paper, backing away. Antonio raced over to stamp on it repeatedly. And then the fire was out.

Ashes remained on the carpet, a small scattering of ashes, with just a few small sections of the charred page.

Motionless, Cass stared at the ashes, then she looked up at Antonio. He was as white as a ghost.

"Ashes," Cass said. She looked around everywhere, expecting Isabel to materialize at any moment, and then what? Then what would she do? And what if the children awoke and saw her? What if she turned on them? She had set the page on fire. What else could she do?

The silence remained vast, absolute, and the scent of violets began to rapidly diminish.

Cass realized she was shaking like a leaf.

Antonio stood motionless, staring back at her, wide-eyed. Cass knew he was realizing the exact same thing. He inhaled, hard. "Sussex," he said. "The note she burned was about Sussex."

"She hates, him," Cass whispered. "We were right."

"He used her," Antonio said, his tone returning to normal now. Their gazes locked.

"And she is letting us know it," Cass finished.

London—July 28, 1554

They were married at Westminster Cathedral on July 28, 1554.

In the bishop's hall, Isabel sat beside her groom at the head of the longest of four dining tables, where course after course had been served. She remained dazed. Had it only been a month ago that Sussex had informed her of the count of Pedraza's desire for her hand? That interview felt like it had happened a lifetime ago.

Isabel was only vaguely aware of the revelry around her. On a raised platform, Queen Mary and Philip sat side by side, above Isabel and her husband, dining from plates of solid gold, while the groom, the bride, and all of the guests dined on pure silver. All around Isabel and Alvarado de la Barca, Spanish and English lords and ladies ate and drank without pause—beer, ale, and Spanish wines were on the table, and thirty or forty courses had been served. There was dancing, too, but it hardly went well, as the Spanish did not know the dances of the Englishmen. Isabel barely noticed the awkwardness, the sulking, the boisterous good cheer, the noise, the laughter, the queen and her consort, who had yet to be crowned king.

And even had she noticed, she would not have cared. There was naught that she cared about. Not even her future as a countess of a faraway land.

And no amount of scolding from Helen had managed to make her care.

Isabel became aware of Alvarado, who was feeding her morsels of pigeon and partridge, which she dutifully accepted, even though her stomach was threatening to discharge its contents. He then offered her wine from his own silver goblet, and she forced down a sip. She knew she should at least attempt a smile; she could not. Someone not far from her at her table whispered, "How frightened she is, poor dear." Was she frightened? How could she be frightened? This was probably a dream. A poorly conceived dream.

And then she espied Rob sitting farther down the table, with Lady de Warenne.

Isabel stiffened in shock. It was as if ice water had been thrown upon her, and suddenly the dreamy quality of the day vanished. She felt herself swallowing, she tasted the heavy red wine, and she could hear the deafening noise of laughter and conversation in the hall. She stared. His wife was a comely young woman with very dark hair and pale skin. Rob stared straight ahead, not looking her way.

And suddenly Isabel wondered, *What have I done?*

And the words whispered again and again in her mind.

Haunting . . . taunting.

She trembled, seized with sudden panic and fear, her husband's thigh pressing against her own now. Had she actually become this man's wife? She could not recall the Catholic ceremony. She could not recall preparing for the wedding. Her panic increased. She could not remember a single outstanding day in the past month, just as she could not recall the long interview with her uncle when he had presented her with de la Barca as a suitor.

Suddenly she looked directly at the man sitting next to her.

He wasn't much taller than she. He was very dark of skin, almost ebony of eye, and neither attractive nor homely. But he rarely smiled. And looking at him now, Isabel felt sheer terror.

She was wearing a silver gown, encrusted with thousands of tiny white pearls and hemmed with rubies and sapphires. For the first time since she had been dressed that morning, Isabel realized how heavy the dress was. But the weight of her gown was nothing like the weight of her own sudden, absolute despair.

I shall die, she thought, *and soon.*

But it will not be soon enough.

Suddenly a huge noise filled the hall, shocking Isabel once again, and she realized that as one, the wedding guests were standing, as was her husband. Their cries of ribald encouragement filled the hall. Isabel felt her husband's hand upon her shoulder, and immediately she looked up.

He smiled at her, slightly, the first time he had ever done so.

Isabel could not smile back. She realized that dinner was over, and that she and Alvarado would be escorted back to the chamber they would share for the next few days, as custom demanded. She could not move.

And she felt Rob's eyes.

Without conscious volition, Isabel met his gaze for the first time in months.

His regard was blinding in intensity. She stiffened, and quickly she looked away.

"Rise, my sweet, rise," her husband commanded softly in the language they were using to communicate—French.

Isabel found herself on her feet, an image of Rob's expression competing with images of a huge four-poster bed draped in cloths of state. *Oh, God.* How would she be able to receive Alvarado? How?

And what if he realized she was not a virgin?

Isabel suddenly remembered that Helen had hidden a pin in the folds of her gown. Somehow Helen had known the truth. Isabel began to shake.

And the crowd was rushing them from the hall.

In the darkness he caressed her bare breasts, her waist, her hips.

Isabel lay unmoving, shivering, eyes tightly closed. Rob's image and memories of their love and passion refused to leave her be.

He spoke to her in Spanish, his voice deep and thick with lust.

Isabel hardly knew what he said, but she heard her reply—a choked sob.

"Do not be afraid," he whispered, moving over her.

Isabel tensed, for he was hard and ready, and she could not reply. How could this be happening? How? What had she done, she wondered, for God to punish her so?

He entered her, not abruptly, but in stages, with difficulty.

Isabel cried out, because he was hurting her.

More Spanish followed, the words low and meant to soothe.

Isabel could not relax. Tears streamed down her face. Too late, she realized the terrifying vastness of her mistake. Too late, she realized she still loved another man.

"I am sorry, I am sorry," he said, and then he was straining in her, again and again. This time Isabel felt the dams burst, and she wept, without control.

A high sun streaming through shutters that were only partially closed awakened Isabel.

And in that same singular moment, the realization struck her rudely that she was now, truly, the count of Pedraza's wife.

The despair washed over her, again and again. Isabel opened her eyes reluctantly, with dread. She saw that his side of the bed was indeed empty. She closed her eyes in relief, wishing for nothing more than the sanctuary of sleep. But she was awake now, and for the moment, nothing would change that.

English tradition demanded they remain within their chambers alone together for several days. Isabel bit her lip to keep tears from filling her eyes at the very notion.

She finally sat up, brushing her eyes with her fingertips, yearning for Zeus or even Helen. It was done. She was wed, and to a powerful and fine nobleman. She must accept her lot in life. She must make the best of it. She must please Alvarado, her husband, until death did part them.

Isabel slid from the bed, her heart so heavy, then glanced down at the blood left on the sheets from the many pricks she had given to her fingertips. Her husband had not even bothered to check the bed for signs of her innocence. Bitterness welled up inside her.

Rob had said he'd married a widow and an heiress. She had assumed his wife to be older, a hag. But she was young and pretty, and Isabel felt sick just thinking about it.

Do not do this to yourself, she tried, but her own silent plea had no effect. All she could think about was that she did not want to be this Spaniard's wife, no matter how fine and noble he was, and how she truly hated Anne de Warenne.

Abruptly Isabel stood, and naked, she went to the robe already hanging on the wall hook. She slipped it on, went to her trunk, and lifted the lid. She hesitated, her pulse going wild, then dug deep into the midst of the trunk, finally extracting a thick volume of poetry.

Her heart slammed as she held the book to her chest.

Quickly then, she hurried to the bed, sat down, and extracted the three letters she had hidden within the tome—all three missives sealed and unread, all three from Rob.

She stared at the seals. He had been trying to communicate with her ever since he'd confessed to his marriage. But she had not been able to send the letters back, their seals unbroken, or to toss them into flames. Thus she had kept them.

She was trembling. In the past, the voice of reason had warned her not to keep the letters—and not to read them, either. Now, not daring to think, Isabel used her nail to slit open one of the letters.

She read, "My dearest Isabel, I offer you my most sincere felicitations regarding the great occasion of your betrothal to Alvarado de la Barca. I can conceive of no more worthy alliance for you than this, such a great and fortunate match. My dear cousin, thoughts of you remain with me always, filled with cousinly devotion. So much time has elapsed since we last spoke, and I entertain so many regrets for that lapse, that I pray you will agree to receive me before the nuptials. Forever your most loyal and devoted cousin, Admiral Robert de Warenne."

Isabel stared at the letter in her hand. The page was shaking violently, but no, it was not the page, it was her own hand.

What did this missive mean?

Isabel could not breathe. *Cousinly devotion . . . no more worthy alliance?* Was this a jest?

But he had suggested they meet. Before her wedding. But why? To offer her more hearty, merry congratulations? Or for another reason?

Cousinly devotion. Was that what he now felt?

What if he still loved her? What if he'd wanted to meet with her to tell her that?

She read the letter again. He had signed it, "Forever your most loyal and devoted cousin." What did that signify? Did it signify anything?

And suddenly she was seized with determination—to meet Rob, forthrightly, and to demand what his professions of loyalty and devotion meant. If he no longer loved her the way he once had, then she must know, and she must know it now. Because, dear God, she thought she still loved him.

The outer door to their apartments scraped open and booted footsteps sounded.

Isabel froze. But only for one instant, and then she slipped the opened letter, its envelope, and the other two inside the book, and as she slammed it closed, the footsteps grew louder, approaching. Isabel saw the broken wax seal on the bed, besides her hip. As Alvarado stepped through the doorway of the bedchamber, she moved to sit upon the pieces of crimson wax, the book clutched tightly in her hand.

He was studying her.

Isabel stared at him, her heart thundering with fear, thinking, *If he finds these letters, he will know all and I am doomed.*

"Isabel?" His regard became searching. "Are you ill?"

Isabel smiled then, the strain of her deception a crushing weight upon her. "I feel weak," she whispered.

"You did not eat last night," he said, his gaze going from her face to the book she held in her hand.

Too late, Isabel looked down at the volume, her heart pounding so loudly, surely he could hear, and then, slowly, she looked up and met his eyes.

He came forward, unsmiling, and before she could take another breath, he took the book from her. Briefly he glanced at the title. "Poetry?" His brows lifted and he laid the book on the table where a tray had been laid out with bread, meats, cheeses, and ale while she slept. He shook his head. "I detest that brew. Do they not know I drink only wine?"

Isabel leapt to her feet, trying not to look at the book on their breakfast table. Did a piece of parchment protrude from the pages? "I shall make certain, my lord, that from now on, wine is served with your every meal," she said quickly.

He faced her, eyes warm. "You please me very much, Isabel," he said.

She wished she blushed. But she felt as if there was no color at all in her face—just as she felt as if no warm blood ran in her veins. She was so cold, so terribly chilled. "I am glad," she said softly.

The light in his eyes changed. "I had thought to share some bread and wine with you. But looking at you, faced with your beauty, it moves me to other thoughts."

Isabel did not move. She could not.

He came forward, and as he slid his hands over her arms, her gaze moved over his shoulder to the book that lay upon the table. "My thoughts move me to begetting an heir," he said, low.

Isabel lifted her gaze to him, smiled, and said, "Those are my thoughts exactly, my lord."

HAMPTON COURT—AUGUST 4, 1554

The rain fell heavily.

It fell with a hard, staccato sound, echoing the beating of Isabel's heart. She stood just beneath a row of pillars, out of the downpour, a small garden before her, which she made no attempt to enter. She kept the hood of her cloak pulled up overhead. It disguised her face.

Every single moment that passed was torturous, an entire eternity, it seemed. She knew Rob had received her carefully worded message. There was no one she could trust except Helen, and she had sent her companion on the errand of seeing it safely delivered directly into his own hands. But would he even deign to come?

Her temples throbbed, her body was stiff with an unbearable tension. He was her cousin, she told herself, of course he would come.

A noise behind her made her whirl, but it was only a pair of courtiers passing through the palace. Isabel looked away before they might glimpse her face beneath the hood, but they paid her no mind, engrossed as they were in their own low, private conversation. She had recognized one of them, the queen's chancellor, John Gardiner. Oddly, he made her skin crawl with unease.

"Isabel?"

She whirled again, this time to see Rob standing in the rain, the hood of his crimson cloak thrown carelessly over his head. His blue gaze was brilliant.

Their gazes locked and her heart turned over, telling Isabel all that she needed to know. She had been wed less than a week. Two days ago they had moved into their apartments in the palace. Her husband was searching for nearby lodgings, and just yesterday he had presented her with a magnificent ruby necklace, set in three tiers, for she had so pleased him, he said. But dear God, nothing had changed. Rob moved her as no other man ever could.

He threw off his hood and came swiftly forward, beneath the vaulted row of pillars. "How fare you, Isabel?" he asked, his gaze searching.

Her smile felt tremulous. "Very well," she lied.

His gaze did not cease in its vigilance. "So marriage agrees with you?"

Another lie came from her lips. "My lord is a very fine man. I am honored that, of all prospects, he chose me."

"The court talked of the match for weeks before the wedding," Rob said, unsmiling. "How scandalous it was, de la Barca marrying for love."

"I am sure it was a scandal," Isabel said, looking away, hearing the bitterness in her own tone. Her husband had married for love. Rob had not, and now they were both wed to others.

"Isabel." There was something in his low, hoarse tone that made her meet his regard once more. "I feared you might never speak to me again."

And the fear was there in his eyes, she realized. "You are my cousin," she said. "Indeed, your letters reminded me forcefully of that."

His eyes widened in surprise. "I cannot pour out my heart on a page of vellum," he said quickly. "Dear God, there are spies everywhere."

She stared. "You mean, you wrote as you did for fear of a spy reading your words?"

"Of course," he said urgently.

Her mind was spinning, and joy was cresting in her breast. "Rob, whose spies?"

He laughed then, but abruptly, the sound short and harsh. "Good Christ, every lord of consequence has spies. Your uncle, the prince, Noailles, Gardiner, Paget, perhaps even your husband."

Isabel paled. "My husband might spy upon me?"

Rob stared. "You belong to him now, Isabel. He is smitten with you. I think he would guard you well. I would—if I were him."

Isabel trembled. "You would?"

"I have thought of nothing but you since we last met," he whispered roughly. "And now I torture myself every day and every night, thinking of you in that Spaniard's arms. Do you love him?"

She felt her body sway forward, toward him. "No."

He took her hands. "Do you still love me?"

Isabel wet her lips, ignoring the voice of caution, which told her to dissemble now, or at least avoid his question. "Yes."

He closed his eyes, a sound escaping from his chest, and then his blue gaze was on her, filled with urgency, and he was pulling her against the wall, where the shadows were dark and deep. His hands cupped her elbows, large, warm, strong. "I must find some small measure of solace then, from that thought."

Isabel felt his thighs pressing against her legs, they stood so closely together. "Rob, what would you have written had you been free to speak your heart?"

His gaze moved over her face, feature by feature. "That jealousy devours me, that I regret all, that I still love you, and that I cannot bear the notion of never having you again."

Isabel trembled. "I would write those very same words, were I free to do so," she whispered softly.

His eyes blazed and somehow she was in his arms, somehow his mouth was on hers, firm, demanding—unyielding.

He broke away first, glancing around in all directions. "This is far too dangerous."

"Have we been seen?" she cried, shivering. She was astounded by her body's urgency and wanting. She needed this man desperately, beyond all reason, all sanity. It might be madness, but it was a madness she embraced.

"No, I do think so. Your hood slips." He reached for the edge and pulled it back over her face.

Isabel's heart continued to pound heavily in her breast. "What do we do now, Rob?"

He was grim. "Either we must never see one another again, or I must yield to temptation, Isabel."

She stared, frightened and stunned. "I cannot," she finally said, "give you up."

His eyes were hard. "Then meet me. There is an inn. The Wolf and Boar. 'Tis just a few miles from the palace, on the road to London."

She continued to shake as she realized where this rendezvous would lead. He was asking her to betray her husband and break her wedding vows. Could she do so?

But how could she not?

"I will meet you, Rob," she said. And it was a decision that changed her life.

"And where have you been this day, might I ask?"

Isabel winced. The last person she wished to see now, other than her husband, was Helen. "I have been wandering about the palace, exploring the many different rooms and meeting some of the ladies present," she said, smiling but avoiding Helen's eyes.

Within her breast, her heart was singing. She had just left Rob's bed an hour past, and *nothing* had changed. Her body felt glorious, as did her heart, her soul. And she could not stop herself from recalling his every caress, his wicked tongue, and the strength of his manhood. She could not stop recalling how it felt to lie, sated, in his arms, against his chest. She would die, she thought, if anything ever happened to him. She knew she could not live without him. Not ever.

"Indeed? And why is the hem of your gown crusted with mud? Why is your cloak soaked through?" Helen asked, hands on her narrow hips. "And why do you seem so pleased, like a kitten in the cream—when these past days you have been of an exceeding ill humor?"

"My gown is stained because I foolishly decided to cross the palace by one of the gardens," Isabel said brightly. "Helen, I do not overly care for your questions."

"I only seek to prevent you from reckless behavior," Helen snapped. "I am worried about you, Isabel. How is your cousin, Admiral de Warrene?"

Isabel stiffened while her heart plummeted. "I would hardly know, as he has yet to respond to my letter," she said sweetly. "I am wet and dirty and I must change." She hurried past Helen, into the antechamber of their suite, but Helen was on her heels.

"Your uncle wishes a private word with you, and he says you must go directly to his apartments."

Isabel faltered as she opened the trunk containing her gowns. *There are spies everywhere.* Did Sussex know of her treachery already? No! It was nigh impossible.

"You are pale. Do you now become ill?" Helen asked, taking a red velvet dress from her hands and shaking it out. "This needs pressing."

"There is no time, I must meet my uncle," Isabel said. She gave her back to Helen so she might undo the buttons there. Her fear did not lessen. Every noble of consequence had spies, Rob had said. And did that include her husband?

Isabel suddenly faced Helen, clad only in a chemise. "Helen, would you ever betray me?"

Helen stared, Isabel's soggy dress in her hands. "That is a most odd question."

"Please, answer it." Isabel met her gaze.

Helen did not look away. "We have been together since you were eight years old, or have you forgotten that?"

"My uncle placed you with me."

"Aye, he did. For he was intelligent enough to know that a wayward girl such as you needed a firm hand like mine."

They stared at one another. Helen spoke first. "Isabel, heed me well. Do not do anything to endanger all that you have so suddenly and fortuitously gained. Alvarado de la Barca treasures you. How fortunate you are."

"I would never jeopardize my marriage," she said, too lightly.

Helen stared, then said, "Good." And she turned away to retrieve the dry red velvet dress.

It was only when she was on her way to her uncle's chambers that Isabel realized Helen had never answered her question.

Sussex was alone at his desk, a quill in hand, his expression grim and filled with concentration, when Isabel was shown into the chamber. Her own face, she thought, must be pale white, and she was wringing her hands nervously. The moment he heard her footfall, he set the quill down and looked up. And he smiled.

Relief washed over Isabel. *He does not know,* she thought, her knees suddenly weak.

"My dearest niece," he said, standing. "We have hardly had the chance to speak since your wedding." He moved around his desk and kissed her cheek. "But how you glow. I see your husband agrees with you."

Guilt assailed Isabel. "I am most pleased with my lot in life, my lord," she said demurely, keeping her eyes on the floor.

His gaze slid to her throat. "I have heard he gifted you with a magnificent ruby necklace, one worth a king's ransom," Sussex said.

Isabel wore several simple gold chains and a locket that had belonged to her mother. "Yes, he did. 'Twas a most generous gift."

"You do well, Isabel, to please your husband so." Sussex met her gaze, then turned and strolled back behind his desk. When he faced her, he was not smiling. Isabel tensed.

"Sit down," he said quietly. "There is a matter I wish to discuss with you."

Immediately Isabel obeyed, once again filled with dread. Did he know of her rendezvous with Rob after all? Her uncle was a master at playing with people. Isabel knew she could never outwit him. That she must never even try.

"What we now discuss shall remain forever in confidence between you and I," Sussex said, his gaze piercing. "Do you comprehend me?"

Isabel wet her lips, nodding. Her palms had grown clammy and wet. She was frightened.

"Good. I have taken care of you for many years, Isabel, and never have I asked aught of you."

Isabel could only nod. Where did he now lead? Did he know?

"The time has come for you to do your duty to me. Without hesitation, reluctance, or any other hindrance of emotion, except for that of loyalty and devotion."

Isabel went cold. Those were Rob's words . . . Was it a coincidence? "What is it that you wish for me to do, my lord?" How stiffly her lips did move.

Sussex leaned toward her, hands on his desk. " 'Tis simple, actually."

Isabel nodded fearfully.

"Your husband advises Philip. I wish you to become informed of all the matters which he and the Spanish king discuss, and you shall pass that information to me, privately, aye, even secretively."

Isabel stared, stunned.

Rob's words echoed . . . *There are spies everywhere.*

"You wish . . . you wish for me to *spy* upon my husband?" she managed, shocked.

"I do not wish to put a name upon your duty," Sussex said coolly. "Nor do I wish for you to think about what you must do. Government is a vast and weighty affair, of which I am a part. Should the queen die, grave issues face the land. I must remain prepared. Thus, learn what they discuss, what they plan, their policies, and convey all to me and only to me. Do you understand?" He was standing, towering over her. And he was not giving her a choice.

Isabel nodded, and it was difficult to speak. "Yes, my lord." She began to tremble.

"Good," the earl finally said. "You may go, Isabel."

Isabel stood so quickly that her chair scraped rudely back. She could hardly breathe, but she curtsied slightly—and rushed from the room. Never had she been more eager to escape anyone.

But his eyes remained upon her—she could feel them, hard and cold and so very ruthless and frightening.

And once outside the door, once in the common hall, she collapsed against the wall.

First Rob's lover, and now this.

She was to become Sussex's spy.

NINETEEN

Cass wasn't sure what woke her up, but she was suddenly yanked out of a disturbing dream. One moment, she lay cuddled up with Alyssa on the floor, her heart pounding, telling herself it was only a dream, and then in the next moment, she thought about her confrontation with Isabel last night and her frightening message. She thought about both Celia and Tracey having disappeared, and suddenly she remembered that her aunt was gone.

The sound of a mug or coffee cup being set down made her open her eyes. Shoving her hair out of her face, she slowly sat up.

Antonio was awake, sitting at the desk, a cup of coffee steaming beside him. He was bent over something, reading avidly, his glasses slipping down his straight nose. Cass studied him. It was impossible not to admire him; he was such a solid, brilliant, attractive man. She sighed. What would happen once this nightmare was over? Once they left Castilla? Cass didn't dare think ahead.

Neither one of them had gotten very much sleep last night. They had begun researching Sussex's life in the hopes of finding out more about Isabel, until Cass hadn't been able to keep her eyes open. She vaguely recalled crawling into the blankets with Alyssa and instantly falling asleep.

They should all leave Casa de Sueños. Staying was dangerous—Cass was certain of it. But they had to find Tracey and Celia first. Cass could not leave without her sister and the elderly woman whom she had known for most of her life.

And there was no way she would leave Antonio behind.

Antonio had yet to notice that she was awake. Cass could imagine that she looked like a wreck. She was debating getting up when he turned. "She had a child. The same year that she died."

Cass started. "Isabel had a child?" she gasped, all worries about her appearance first thing in the morning now gone.

"I found a passage in one of my father's books, and it is marked." He hesitated, smiling. "Good morning." His gaze slipped over her.

Cass had slept in her jeans and a tank top. She knew her hair was in snarls. She flushed. "I'll be right back," she said, standing and fleeing the room.

In the light of day, the house wasn't as bad as it was in the dead of night, she thought as she raced into the nearest bathroom to brush her teeth and wash up. But it was not quite benign. There was a stillness now which she was acutely aware of. It was almost as if it were the lull before the storm.

Barefoot, she raced back to the library. Antonio handed her a mug of hot coffee, his smile brief but warm.

Their hands touched slightly. As Cass sipped the sweet, hot coffee, she thought that no matter what was happening, the attraction that she felt for him was somehow stronger than ever. But was it real? Or was it merely a part of Isabel's master plan? Assuming she had one?

Cass hated the notion. But her aunt and Eduardo had never intended to become lovers, and look at what had happened—and where it had happened. Cass was scared.

"Alvarado was at Mary's court." Antonio picked up a volume and opened it to a marked page. "My father found this entry. The chapter here is devoted to Mary's marriage to Philip. Alvarado was in the service of the emperor. His title isn't mentioned, but it says, 'Only one Spaniard was allowed to attend Philip, Count Alvarado de la Barca, throughout the meal.' And then, later in this book, there is a reference to the Count of Pedraza's pregnant wife. It is in the context of a section describing Mary Tudor's supposed pregnancy."

"So Isabel was pregnant. But did she ever have the child?"

"I wonder if the child was conceived out of wedlock," Antonio said.

Cass froze. "What would make you think that?"

"Because there is no child on our family tree. Had the child died, even as an infant, it should have been included."

"Unless it was never born."

"I suppose it is just a feeling I have."

They regarded one another, sipping their coffee in silence. "What are we going to do?" Cass finally asked. She heard the note of helplessness that had crept into her own tone.

"We must alert the authorities about the electrician's murder. And we must also find your sister and Celia."

Cass set her mug down. Then she slowly glanced around the library, just as she saw the children stirring. "Doesn't it feel unnaturally still this morning?"

"Yes, it does. I noticed the moment the sun came up." Their gazes held.

"We didn't imagine what happened last night, Antonio."

Before he could respond, Alyssa wandered over, yawning. "Good morning, Aunt Cass."

Cass tousled her dark hair. "Why are you up so early? It's not even seven yet, sleepyhead."

"I don't know." She yawned again as Eduardo hopped forward on his crutches. "Do you think they have cereal here?"

"I don't know." Cass smiled.

"We have cereal," Eduardo said. "Come with me. I'll show you where in the kitchen."

Cass watched the children wander out of the room in their pajamas. When she looked away, it was to find Antonio regarding her with a strange intensity. Cass's heart skipped. What did that look signify? He said, "If Gregory will go into Pedraza to notify the police, then you and I can stay here to search for your sister. As soon as we find her, you and the children will leave."

And Cass thought about Tracey again. A sick feeling overcame her. Fear overcame her. "I have thought about it. Isabel wants vengeance on your family because she was forced to marry Alvarado when she loved someone else, and she wants vengeance on my family because Sussex somehow used her as his political pawn."

" 'Vengeance' is a very strong word, Cassandra. Especially when you are attributing the desire for revenge to a ghost. I just cannot draw that conclusion from what has thus far happened. What if Isabel is present, and harmless, but a madman is also present—a madman who is a murderer? That at least makes sense."

"You saw her set that paper on fire. All that was left was ashes." Cass shuddered at the symbolism. "And now you're forgetting all of the past. I'm beginning to think she stabbed that electrician," Cass added, low. There. She had finally said it. She had finally uttered her very worst fears.

"Cassandra." He was firm. "Ghosts do not murder people."

"Maybe this one does."

"If she is capable of murder, if she wants revenge, then why hasn't she done away with me by now?" he asked pointedly.

Cass was still, not knowing what the answer was.

"Do not tell me you think she is playing a game of cat and mouse with us, as well?"

The idea hadn't occurred to her. But now it made too much sense. "We have to find Tracey and Celia and get the hell out of here," she cried.

He reached for her hand. Cass was acutely aware of his touch. She looked up, meeting his gaze. Neither one of them looked away.

An urgent need to be in his arms, to be held there, overwhelmed her. It wasn't the same violent, insane need she'd felt yesterday, when they had coupled like animals in her bed, just hours after her aunt's death. It wasn't violent or mindless; Cass felt how deeply she was falling in love with him, and it was stunning. She managed to tear her gaze away.

He stood up, knocking over the coffee cup, which was empty. Neither one of them noticed. Cass was motionless. Inches separated them.

"Come here," he said roughly, and the next thing she knew, she was in his arms, and he was holding her, hard, against his tall, strong frame.

"Good morning," Gregory said.

Cass moved away from Antonio. Hostility toward his twin surged within her. *What great timing,* she thought. And the extent of her own anger and disliking surprised her.

"So are we ready to lock up the house and go back to Madrid? We can stop and notify the police of Tracey's and Celia's disappearance, and the murder, on our way back to the city."

Cass turned, about to protest.

"You notify the police," Antonio told his brother. "Cassandra and I will search for Tracey and Celia. They can't have gone far. Hopefully we will find them by the time you return."

"Are you mad?" Gregory asked in disbelief. "We should all leave now. Let the police find them. They're professionals."

"I won't leave without Tracey and Celia," Cass said with heat. "I am not abandoning my sister and my friend. And I am not abandoning Antonio, either."

Gregory faced her. "Who said anything about abandonment?"

"But that's what it is," Cass said coldly. Then she looked at Antonio. "And once we find Tracey and Celia, you're leaving, too."

"I have work to do here," he said firmly. "I cannot leave. Not now. Not yet."

There *was* so much more to do there at the house, and a part of Cass more than understood him—a part of her wanted to stay behind with him. Just the two of them, working side by side, unearthing the truth about Isabel's life.

As Catherine and Eduardo had done.

"No." Gregory was harsh. "Damn it, Antonio, that dead woman is haunting this house—and she's been here since we were children. She is evil. I am sure of it. No one should stay."

Cass blinked at him in surprise. "You've certainly changed your tune."

He ignored her.

Antonio folded his arms. "Did something happen, Gregory?"

Gregory was grim. "Not really."

He was lying. Cass knew it. But why would he lie, and about what? And why did he have a glimmer of guilt in his eyes?

What was going on with him?

Cass stared. He avoided her eyes. She reminded herself that he was Antonio's brother. His twin. But appearances could be, and often were, deceiving. Still . . . that did not make him psychotic, a madman, a murderer.

She turned and wandered to the window, not knowing what to think. And suddenly she wondered if she should try to communicate with Isabel.

Cass blinked. She had been gazing out the window, but paying very little attention to the view. Now she stared at Gregory's car, parked some distance away, but clearly visible in profile. "Oh my God. Gregory—your car!"

Both brothers ran to her side. From what Cass could see, Gregory had two flat tires.

Suddenly chills covered her entire body—and Antonio must have had the same inkling, because simultaneously they turned and ran.

With Gregory on their heels, they raced out of the room and to the front door. The BMW was parked right in front of the house. All four tires were flat.

"*Por Dios!*" Gregory cried, running around the car. "My tires have been slashed!"

Slashed. His tires had been slashed. All *four* of them.

Cass suddenly knew. She knew before she ran to the garage. The doors were closed, but there was a side door, which she wrenched open. And inside the garage was the Jeep, its four tires slashed, and her rental car—in the exact same condition.

Both men paused beside her.

Slashed. With force and anger, with hatred, with intent.

With an agenda.

They were stranded.

Everyone remained stunned. Cass's mind had gone numb. It was Antonio who finally spoke—after glancing beneath the hood of the Jeep. Wires were wrenched apart and mangled. "I'll have to head for town on foot," he said grimly. "But I intend to hitch a ride."

Cass had a horrible premonition of Antonio being waylaid by some deranged killer, waylaid and stabbed in the back. And what did all of this have to do with Isabel? Surely Antonio was right. Ghosts did not stab people, they did not slash tires or mangle wires. Whoever had done all of this was flesh and blood, a real live human being.

But Isabel had left a message on her laptop, Isabel had set fire to Eduardo's notes . . .

"Someone has purposefully stranded us here. Don't go. It isn't safe." She reached for him; he did not shake her off.

Someone . . . or Isabel?

Cass could not help herself. Her mental calculations were subconscious—but there were four adults present at the *casa,* and two children. She did not include Tracey and Celia, who were missing. Alfonso was not strong enough to murder anyone or wreak such havoc on the cars. She trusted Antonio implicitly. She stared at Gregory, thinking, *Dear God. Is he the one? Is he psychotic?* What if he secretly hated his brother? What if he was a deranged killer hiding behind the facade of good looks, good family, and professional success? Even hiding behind the facade of Isabel herself?

Gregory looked from her to Antonio. "I'll go. I'm in better shape than you, I can run most of the way."

Cass felt her pulse, already erratic and high, accelerating. She did not want Antonio to go, but she did not trust Gregory, not for an instant. Not anymore. She wondered if her fear and panic were blinding her, making her irrational.

"No," Antonio said sharply.

Cass moved closer to him. "We have to talk," she whispered. "Please."

He shook his head. "I will put on running shoes—"

"I'll go," Gregory said with some heat. "You should stay here with your son, Tonio."

Cass faced him. "So which is it? You can make better time—or he should stay with Eduardo?" Her words came out with a caustic ring.

His stare was cool. "Both."

Antonio stepped between them. "I'm older. I will go."

Gregory looked at him in disbelief. *"Oh, perdón, el conde!"*

Antonio grimaced. "If you choose to see it that way, so be it." He shrugged and started out of the garage, his strides long and resolute.

As Gregory raced after him, Cass felt her heart sink with fear and dismay. She knew something terrible would happen on the road to Pedraza, she just knew it.

"Then let's draw straws," Gregory said.

"No."

"Antonio, there is safety in numbers. You have a son—"

"He's right." Cass ran up to them, panting as she hurried to stay abreast. "Just let Gregory go, please, Antonio. Eduardo needs you."

Antonio halted and looked at her. She could see the conflict in his eyes. Finally he nodded. But he turned to his brother. "I want you to be very, very careful," he said. "Trust no one. There is a killer nearby. A killer who had stranded us here for a reason. Perhaps he will offer you a ride. Trust no one, Gregory."

Gregory seemed pale. He nodded tersely. "Do you think I do not already know this? I will leave immediately."

Cass gripped Antonio's hand to prevent him from following Gregory back to the house. When Gregory was out of earshot, she looked at Antonio, not quite able to get out what she wished to say.

"What is it, Cassandra?" His gaze was piercing.

"I know he's your brother," she began slowly.

"No." The one word was like a whiplash. "He is more than my brother, he is my twin, and do not ever forget it." Anger etched all over his face, he shook her off and stalked after his brother.

Gregory had left.

Another search had begun.

Cass and Antonio were rapidly approaching the ruins of the old castle, having decided to stick together. As Gregory had said, there was safety in numbers. They had been searching for a full hour, and neither Tracey nor Celia was anywhere to be found.

Cass was grim. Any hope she had seemed to be slowly, steadily disintegrating. Now the two towers jutted out of the dry, brown landscape, and the gleaming blue vehicle was catching the sunlight where it was crashed into the wall. Cass glanced at Antonio. "You don't think they might be around here?" She did not want to go anywhere near that dead electrician again.

Antonio did not reply.

Cass glanced at him. There was something on his mind, something he wasn't sharing with her. Or was it just that he was as worried as she over everything that was happening?

They paused. "I'll go check the ruins to see if anyone is there," Antonio said. "You stay here. I'll be right back."

Cass nodded, watching him go. A few minutes later, he returned. "No luck?" she asked, already knowing the answer.

He shook his head. "Let's start back to the house. We'll take a different route," Antonio said grimly.

The sun was high and hot, and they started back rapidly, in silence. Cass couldn't think. She only knew that she was beginning to unravel— when she had to keep her composure for a few more hours, just until the police arrived, for the children's sake.

For her own sanity's sake.

"Cassandra. There is something I haven't told you."

She tensed. She did not like the tone of his voice or the look in his eyes. "I thought so."

"My father went insane just before he died," Antonio said too calmly. "And so did your aunt."

"What?!" Cass knew she had misheard him.

"They both went insane in the days before my father's death," he repeated, this time less calmly.

Cass stared, disbelief giving way to something else, a suspicion, an inkling that she could not quite finger. "Are you *certain*, Antonio?"

He met her gaze as they walked along the rutted road. "It was horrible," he said finally. "His behavior was filled with hatred and anger, and it was directed at your aunt—but it made no sense, none at all."

The mere mention of Catherine filled Cass with grief.

He touched her back gently. "She was also incoherent with the same anger and hatred, Cassandra. You should not read the journal."

Cass didn't want to. She wanted to remember her aunt with all of her wits and dignity intact. And then she thought about the slashed tires.

Slashed . . . with hatred and anger.

Cass stopped short.

Antonio also paused. "What is it?"

"The moment I saw all of those slashed tires, I just thought, whoever did this was so angry, so hate filled. There seems to be so much anger and hatred present now, Antonio."

He stared. "Like my father and your aunt?"

Cass nodded, and suddenly it all fell into place.

He had paled. He, too, understood. "The way we made love. Violently. Unnaturally. I have never tried to hurt a woman before. I wanted to hurt you."

Cass trembled. "I have been having these feelings of hatred and anger—ever since we arrived. Toward Tracey, toward Gregory. Feelings that are so intense they frighten me. Feelings that are not me."

He stared at her. "I have, too," he said. "They come out of the blue. And disappear as abruptly."

Their gazes locked.

"Are you thinking what I'm thinking?" Cass whispered.

He stared, wide-eyed. "If you are right . . ." He inhaled, hard. "When I first saw her portrait, she seemed so sad."

"But it's changed," Cass whispered. "It *has* changed."

He nodded. "Jesus. If you look at her portrait now, you can see the anger and hatred in her eyes."

She plucked his sleeve. "And there is malevolence there, and, I think, belligerence."

"I have noticed," he said grimly.

Their eyes met and held.

"And she has enough energy to start fires, send a message," Antonio said grimly.

"Does she have enough energy to slash tires? To stab someone?" Cass asked fearfully. Already suspecting the answer. And it was no.

"That is not what I think," Antonio said.

"Her anger is the contagion," Cass whispered.

"And it is poisoning our minds," he said.

The walk seemed endless; her feet began to hurt. It was unbearably hot out, and Cass was covered with sweat. Her T-shirt and shorts were sticking to her like a second skin.

They sank down on a flat rock to rest and sip water from a sports bottle Antonio carried. Their shoulders brushed.

Cass went still. So did he. And their eyes met.

Cass could not help herself. She was falling in love and they had this one brief moment to themselves—when God only knew what would happen next. "Antonio?"

His gaze moved to her mouth. "Cassandra, you are the most desirable woman," he whispered, and his tone was rough.

Cass met his eyes. "Is she poisoning our minds?" she whispered.

He was pulling her toward him. Cass was breathless with need and expectation. "No. Not now. Not like this," he said, kissing her gently.

A moment later Cass was on her back and he was kissing her hard and touching her everywhere. And when their loins settled the one against the other, soft against hard, heat against heat, she gasped, because he was already hugely aroused.

He pulled her T-shirt and bra over her head, tossing them aside. His next words were in Spanish, but Cass did not have to understand them to decipher their meaning. He wanted her as desperately as she wanted him. She closed her eyes as he nuzzled her breasts and she began to tremble.

He began sucking one nipple.

She could not stand it, this, him.

"Oh, God," Cass said, and she needed to feel him buried deep and hard, massive and thick, inside of her.

Their mouths locked. He palmed her hard. Cass ripped open his shorts. They fell to the grass, Antonio tugging her shorts and panties down her hips. An instant later he was thrusting into her; as instantly, Cass was coming.

And this time there were no damned violets.

And when he collapsed, it was to cry her name—a sound that Cass knew she was never going to forget.

Antonio rolled onto one elbow and Cass was able to look at him.

Their gazes held. "It's not because of Isabel," she whispered. "This isn't because of her."

He flipped onto his back, still breathing hard. "I want to make love to you. Slowly. For hours and hours. Not like this—on some flat, dirty, ant-infested rock."

Desire surged again, immediately. "You do?"

He turned back to face her, pushing her hair out of her face, tucking it behind her ear. The gesture was so gentle, so tender. "Of course I do." He leaned forward and they kissed.

This time it was slow, soft, lingering—endless. Somehow he found a bed of grass and he moved on top of her, somehow she wrapped her body around his. Their tongues flirted before mating. Their hips picked up an ancient, tireless rhythm. And when he entered her now, it was slowly, with excruciating care.

Cass let him show her all the possibilities. He let her eagerly learn.

Antonio found her clothes, handing them to her. Cass tried not to look at him. The sun was at its apex now, it had to be noon—they had made love all morning. Cass did not know what to think; she was dazed.

If she had been falling in love with him before, now the deed was done. She would never be able to walk away from this man, not after what they had just shared. And what they had shared had been love, not lust—Cass had never been more certain of anything.

Isabel had not been with them, poisoning their minds.

Cass finished dressing. Guilt began to make its insidious presence known. Tracey and Celia were missing; Gregory was hitchhiking his way to the nearest town. Isabel remained a threat to them all. And Cass had just experienced the most incredible morning of her life.

Antonio was waiting for her. Cass was surprised yet again when he took her elbow firmly in his hands as they walked past the cottage, toward the garage and house. His touch now did crazy things to her, reminding her of what they'd shared, what they could still share, and of what she really wanted from him. Cass wondered if they might ever share a future.

She wanted to hope, but just then, faced with the looming presence of the house, and the sight of Gregory's BMW with its four flat tires in the drive, the prospect seemed dim.

"Everything is so quiet," Antonio muttered, breaking into her thoughts.

Cass glanced up, shivering because he was right, the stillness was eerie, unsettling, even laden, and she gazed past the BMW, at the front door of the house, and then she glanced back at Gregory's car—and she screamed.

Tracey was sitting in it, and she was dead.

Cass heard herself screaming again and again.

Antonio grabbed her, trying to hold her, trying to prevent her from going to her sister, who was sitting slumped over the wheel, immobile and unmoving, her long hair a funny, dark, tangled mass.

"Let go!" Cass screamed savagely, striking him, and she broke free of his grasp, already knowing what that horrible color was—it was the color of old, dried blood.

She wrenched the door open, saw the scratches on Tracey's legs, the cuts on her arms—both hands gripped the steering wheel. Her hair was a snarled mass, and her clothes were also terribly stained—with blood. "No!" Cass reached for her.

And to her shock, Tracey's body did not yield or fall into her arms. It remained stiff with resistance—impossibly so.

Cass stopped breathing; and then she shoved Tracey's hair away from her face, saw her wide, unblinking eyes, but she also saw the vapor of breath coming from her parted lips, and then she saw how white her knuckles were—and the almost imperceptible rise and fall of her chest.

"Tracey!" Cass threw her arms around her, but Tracey did not budge.

"Cassandra!" Antonio shouted from behind her.

Cass barely heard him. "She's alive! Tracey, what's happened, Tracey!" Cass wept, caressing her, stroking her, holding her, trying not to think about the blood.

What happened?

And Cass felt her sister soften in her arms. Her body relaxed in waves, until Tracey was in her embrace, trembling wildly, uncontrollably.

Cass took her by her shoulders, intent on getting her out of the car, when Tracey slowly looked at her—her eyes huge and vacant, like the sightless eyes of a blind person. And Cass was terrified.

"I . . . want . . . to . . . die," Tracey said.

TWENTY

DAY FOUR—NOON

Unlike most Europeans, he worked out regularly, and ran several times a week in El Retiro Parque. Gregory had left the villa at a jog, but after an hour had gone by, he was tiring, and now, another hour later, he was walking, but briskly. The two-lane highway he was on was completely deserted, and the fact that it was the weekend did not help. The road ran now through high, rolling terrain, wooded hills sloping upward on the other side of the road, a shallow ravine on his right. The nearest town, the walled medieval village of Pedraza, was perhaps forty kilometers from the house, most of the going uphill. If he could sustain his current pace, even if no one came along to offer him a ride, he would make it in two more hours or so.

He was determined to sustain the pace.

He was so close.

But God, it was so hot.

And as the sweat trickled down his face, burning into his eyes, he could not stop thinking about the horror of turning in bed to Tracey and being greeted with Isabel de la Barca's chilling smile instead.

Chilling, taunting . . . haunting.

He had imagined it. Either he had imagined Tracey turning into a replica of the dead woman, or he had dreamed up the entire episode of sex.

The latter was far more likely, he told himself firmly. But his sheets had smelled of sex that morning, very distinctly, in a way that could not be produced by a wet dream.

Gregory did not want to think. But there was nothing else to do. His gut remained tight and curled with fear, with panic, and with the worst of premonitions.

Someone was going to die. He just knew it, the way he'd always known it, ever since he was a small boy hiding in terror from the demon of his dreams. The demon who he now knew was no demon, no figment of the imagination, but a goddamned ghost—and the proof was right there in that photograph Cass had taken.

And even as he hurried on, chills broke out over his entire body.

Now he wondered whether Tracey had returned last night. If so, why had she then disappeared? Of course, he had screamed at her like a lunatic, and she had bolted from the room. Had he chased her away? Or had he been in the throes of an incredibly real dream? A dream brought on by his own cowardice, his own worst fears?

If only he had never seen that photo—then he could tell himself that this was all a weird obsession left over from his childhood.

But far more than childhood nightmares were at work at Casa de Sueños, he thought grimly. Catherine Belford and another man were dead. Two women were missing. And *she* was somehow to blame.

The moment he thought that, he denied it with all of his being. That ghost was haunting them, but ghosts did not murder people. Ghosts did not slash tires. Ghosts did not destroy wiring. Ghosts were nothing but formless energy. When had anyone *ever* died at the hand of a ghost?

Reflecting light broke into his musings. Gregory suddenly realized that something was ahead of him on the highway—and he blinked.

And for one instant he made out a man, approaching slowly, and he blinked again, halting in his tracks—afraid he was hallucinating.

But he was not. For as he caught his breath, he saw a man on a bicycle, pedaling slowly, steadily, toward him.

Exultation filled him, and with it, hope. Gregory ran forward, waving frantically, calling out, *"Hola, señor! Hola!"*

The man was actually a teenaged boy and he cruised to a stop, his gaze hardly suspicious, as there was no crime in these parts. Gregory produced his wallet, ripped out a two-thousand-peseta bill, and handed it to him, explaining that he needed the bike.

There was no negotiation to be had—the boy could buy another bicycle for five or six hundred pesetas—and as Gregory climbed onto the seat, he felt a wave of relief. For he had been afraid, in the back of his mind, that somehow he would be prevented from making it to the police that day.

He took off, riding hard. He estimated that he would reach the town in less than half an hour now, and he smiled as he glanced up at the sun—he would be speaking to the local gendarmes well before noon. *Por Dios.*

The horn blared behind him.

Gregory almost lost his seat, the horn was so loud and so close behind him, when he had been alone on the road all morning. He slowed, glancing over his shoulder—and saw the huge twelve-wheeler truck bearing down upon him.

His heart slammed wildly; the horn blared again, two huge headlights and an even larger, shining metal bumper bearing down at eighty or ninety kilometers per hour upon him.

The idiot, Gregory thought, his pulse rocketing with sheer fear. What was he trying to do, run him off the road?

Gregory veered onto the very narrow dirt shoulder, which was no more than eight inches wide, felt the blast of heat from the truck's engine, heard its roar, directly behind him, looked back—and saw the driver's face in the windshield, just meters away.

He screamed.

The driver was a woman.

And as the truck continued, swerving onto the shoulder of the road, *swerving toward him,* Gregory jerked hard on the handlebars, the bike hit the rocky ground beside the road, and then a huge tire brushed the bike. And he knew.

He knew as he flipped upward, high into the air, still astride the bike, and then as he came down, the bike wrenched from his hands, he knew as his body hit the side of the ravine, pain exploding everywhere, almost at once, and he knew as he flipped again and again, picking up speed, tumbling down the cliff, that this was the end.

He landed hard on rocks, in a trickle of water at the ravine's bottom. And just before he lost consciousness, he thought, *This is what she has always wanted, ever since I was a boy.* How could he have ever had doubts? She had won.

Cass was already frightened; now her sister's words made her terrified.

"Cassandra, let me help."

Antonio. Eagerly Cass slid out of the car. "She's hurt. She badly hurt." Her heart would not slow. Every racing beat was filled with pain and dread.

Antonio reached into the car and lifted Tracey into his arms. Tracey clung to him, burying her face in his shoulder.

"I'll take her up to her room," Antonio said grimly.

Inside . . . her room . . . the children. "God! I don't want the children to see her like this," Cass cried as they hurried toward the house.

"I am in absolute agreement," Antonio muttered darkly.

With shaking hands Cass unlocked the front door for Antonio, and followed him as he carried her sister upstairs. On the landing, she rushed ahead of them; the bedroom door was open. As Cass glanced into the room, it occurred to her that something was wrong, but she dismissed whatever her mind was trying to tell her, because the first order of business was cleaning Tracey up. "Put her in the shower," she told Antonio, and he nodded in agreement.

As Antonio set her down on her feet in the claw-footed bathtub, Tracey continued to hold tightly on to him for support. She continued to tremble and shake, and she kept her eyes squeezed shut. Cass turned on the faucets, adjusted the water temperature, then picked up the shower hose. And as she directed it over her sister, she felt violently sick.

The water mixed with the dried encrusted blood on her clothes, and ran red in the tub beneath her feet.

Cass fought not to vomit. She quickly stripped her sister but it was too late, for her white tank top and shorts were already turning pinkish red. And Cass inhaled.

Her legs were scratched everywhere, but that was nothing compared to the huge bruises on her torso, and then Cass glimpsed her breasts. A series of thin red lines radiated across them. Cass's gaze slammed to her arms. The same thin red lines were slashed across the undersides of her wrists and forearms.

As she held the hose over her sister, she turned to look at Antonio, knowing her shock was there in her wide eyes. His eyes were as wide as hers felt, as wide and as grim. Cass found herself shaking her head. Those cuts—whoever had done that to her sister, he had used a knife. Oh, God. *What had happened?*

"I'll do this for you," Antonio said firmly.

"No! She's my sister," Cass shouted, and then hated herself for screaming at him when he was trying to help, and none of this was his fault—or was it? Maybe it was even her fault. Tracey had run away because she was unstable, but the growing attraction between her and

Antonio had added to her fragility. Had they triggered her disappearance?

Guilt choked Cass.

And she wanted, desperately, to convince herself that all was well, that she was in no way responsible for what she was now seeing, but her mind had shut down, and there were no mental arguments for her to make.

And then she grabbed the shampoo and washed her sister's hair, the activity a refuge. But she could not stop telling herself that she could have prevented what had happened to Tracey. It was something she would never forgive or forget.

Cass realized she was crying.

"Please go and let me finish," Antonio whispered.

Through her tears, Cass looked at him. His tone had been amazingly kind, incredibly gentle, filled with empathy and compassion. But it was too late. This was the last straw. Cass didn't think that they were ever going to be able to go forward in the future, not after this singular moment in time.

"I can't leave her," she said hoarsely.

When Tracey was as clean as possible, they wrapped her in a towel and Antonio carried her to her bed. Cass sat down beside her, but Tracey's eyes were already closed, and as Cass covered her with a blanket, she felt hot, fresh tears gathering in her eyes, and they began to fall, steadily, in earnest and in torrents.

He touched her shoulder.

Cass shook her head. She could not speak.

Which was fortunate, because if she could, she would tell him to go away.

His hand remained until she shrugged him off. She didn't want him comforting her. After a silence, he said, "When you need me, I will be downstairs. I am going to get the children and Alfonso."

Cass did not reply, and she didn't look up as he left the room, either. But what she did do was cover her face with her hands and weep.

"Cass?"

The whisper was low and somehow pitiful; Cass jerked and met Tracy's own tear-filled stare. Instantly she reached out to stroke her brow, her cheek, and then take her hand. "I love you."

Tracey blinked at her as tears slipped down her cheeks. "Alyssa. Is she all right?"

Cass stiffened. "Of course," she began, but then she realized she hadn't seen Alyssa since earlier that morning. She recovered her composure, forced a smile, even as tears made it hard for her to see clearly, and she said, "She's fine."

"Tell her I love her," Tracey whispered.

Cass was frightened. Her sister had endured some kind of horror, but she was not the kind of person to talk this way. "You can tell her yourself when you feel up to it."

Tracey shook her head. "No. No. Don't bring her here. Please don't."

Tracey was growing distraught. "Fine," Cass said, realizing that Tracey was right. The condition she was in would only frighten Alyssa. She continued to hold her hand tightly. "Tracey, please, tell me what has happened—who did this to you?!"

Tracey stared at her. "I don't know what happened," she finally said.

Cass stared back, in dismay. "How . . . how can you not know?" But even as she spoke, the word *shock* went through her mind, followed by *trauma* and *amnesia*.

"Everything's a blur," Tracey whispered, more tears falling. "I'm so tired. How did you find me?"

Cass stared. "You came back," she finally said. "You were in Gregory's car."

She looked at Cass with bewilderment in her eyes.

"Do you remember leaving the house?" Cass had to ask.

Tracey hesitated, then nodded. "Yes, I do. I was so angry. So incredibly angry. At you."

Cass felt as if she had been struck. She had to close her eyes. "I'm sorry," she choked. And she was. God, she was. Now she regretted every moment spent with Antonio. What had she been thinking?

"I don't want to be angry. It scares me," Tracey whispered.

Cass stroked her brow again. "You don't have to be angry now. You're here, and safe. I'll take care of you, Trace, I promise. I promise," she repeated firmly. And she meant it.

"I'm scared," Tracey said hoarsely, again.

Cass met her gaze. "Don't be scared now," she finally said, forcing a reassuring smile which was a monumental lie. Then, "Why are you scared? Because you can't remember what happened?"

Tracey blinked at her. It was a moment before she spoke, and when she did, her words were so low it was hard for Cass to understand— she had to lean closer in order to do so. "Something terrible is hap-

pening," Tracey said. "I don't understand anything . . . I don't understand myself."

Cass stared.

Very afraid—and refusing to let her mind go where it logically
wished to.

But she had to ask. Too much was at stake. Lives seemed to be at
stake. "What is happening?"

Tracey shook her head. "I don't know," she cried.

In a way, Cass was relieved she hadn't answered, but then Tracey
lifted both arms so Cass could see the horrific series of tiny red lines
slashed across the undersides of them. "I didn't want," she began, and
she wept.

Cass reached out and gripped her hands. "What happened? You remember something—who did that to you?"

Tracey shook her head.

"You didn't want what?" Cass cried, crying again.

"I didn't want to do it," Tracey cried. "It was like there were two of
me. I hated myself and I had to do it, I hate myself so much, but I
tried so hard to stop myself, but my left hand couldn't stop my right
hand, and I watched myself do it, and there was so much blood and it
hurt so much and I couldn't stop."

Cass remained thoroughly shaken and ill to her very core as she paused
on the threshold of the library. The scene she was greeted with was
quaint, the two children playing Junior Monopoly on the floor, Antonio
seated on the couch beside them, a stack of books next to his hip, one
open in his hands. Cass stared blindly. The cozy scene hardly registered.
Her sister had inflicted those terrible wounds on herself. It was, she
knew, some kind of psychological disorder. But she did not know the
name.

What was happening to Tracey?

She had never done anything like this before. Cass was certain. Could
such a disorder surface so late in a person's life?

Cass closed her eyes. The *disorder* had surfaced there, at Casa de
Sueños. Another strange and terrible occurrence that just could not be
explained . . . or could it be explained?

Could Isabel's anger be so powerful that it could infect a person so
greatly that she would behave irrationally, insanely, dangerously, the

way Tracey had? Even to the point of hurting others—of hurting oneself?

"Cassandra." Antonio saw her and shut the book, standing, but at the same time Alyssa also espied her and leapt her feet, rushing over to her. "Aunt Cass! My mother's back!" she cried with obvious relief.

Cass smiled down at her, sliding her hand over her back. "Yes, she is, and right now she's taking a good long nap." Cass was shaking. She just could not stop.

Alyssa regarded her very seriously, far too seriously for a seven-year-old. "But what happened? Where has she been?"

Now the truth was a way out. "She can't remember, Alyssa," Cass said gently. "Sometimes people lose their memory for a short period of time. It's a kind of sickness, which goes away, and it's called amnesia." Cass sat down so no one would notice her uncontrolled trembling.

"Amnesia," Alyssa repeated quietly. "Can I see her?"

"Not now. But she asked about you before she said anything else, and she told me to tell you that she loves you," Cass said.

Alyssa stared and instantly realized that Cass was telling the truth. She flushed with pleasure. "I was so scared. I thought I might never see her again," she whispered. "Like what happened to Eduardo with his mother."

Cass stared, Alyssa's words searing themselves onto her mind. Tracey had returned, so there was no obvious link between the two vanishings. Or was there? What if Isabel was behind *everything*? What if her energy was so powerful that it had affected everyone, Antonio's grandmother, who had stabbed her husband to death, Catherine, who had lured Eduardo in front of a car after becoming his lover, Margarita, who had disappeared, and now her own sister?

And what about herself and Antonio? What about Gregory?

Cass still didn't know what it was that he was hiding, but she felt fairly certain that it was not significant. He had not been involved in Tracey's disappearance—Cass could now safely assume that he had not been involved in any of the events that had happened in the past four days.

Cass tried to tell herself that she had no hard evidence, that it was all speculation, but she was not convinced. Because even now, she sensed that Isabel was near.

Too close.

Alyssa skipped back to Eduardo, and Cass found herself meeting Antonio's gaze. He walked over to her and she found herself standing;

he put his arm around her, and they stepped into the hall. "How is she?" he asked.

Cass pulled away. She fought hard, but her eyes grew moist as she told him what Tracey had said.

"She needs to be hospitalized," he said tersely. "Immediately. Thank God Gregory went to the police."

Cass looked at him. "I guess that's where all that blood came from," she whispered roughly.

He put his hand on her shoulder. "Cassandra, that amount of blood did not come from those cuts and scratches. I assure you of that."

She pulled away from him again. "Oh, so now you are a doctor? Or some kind of forensic expert?" she asked so shrilly, both children stopped playing Monopoly in the midst of a roll of the dice in order to stare at her. She managed to lower her voice. "Just what the hell are you implying?"

He stared. "I haven't implied anything. What is it that you wish to say?"

"Nothing," she ground out, whirling.

He caught her by her arm and whipped her back around. "Someone stabbed the electrician."

"Don't." Cass had never used such a tone before. It was filled with both warning and raw fury. *She would protect her sister at all costs.*

He dropped his hand. "We should not be fighting. I do not want to fight with you. Cassandra. God, I am in—"

She knew he was going to tell her that he was in love with her; she knew it the way she knew the sun would set in just a few more hours and that Isabel would return.

She cut him off. "Are we fighting?" She was cool, even as her composure continued to spiral downward into a mass of hysteria and fear. "I hadn't noticed."

"We are not to blame for what Tracey has done to herself," he said, his gaze steady and earnest, attempting to hold hers.

Cass avoided eye contact. *Bullshit,* Cass thought. "I never said we were."

He stared.

Cass turned away, aware that she was putting a huge, insurmountable wall between them. She folded her arms across her chest, wishing it were not so hard to breathe.

And also wishing that deep within her breast, her heart weren't hurting so much.

And he did not move; he did not walk away.

Cass finally said, "How long will it be before Gregory reaches Pedraza—assuming he has to walk the entire way?"

"I would say he is just about there," Antonio replied very quietly.

Cass had to look at him, because the dignity in his tone was her own undoing. She didn't want to hurt him. But what they had done to Tracey was insufferable and he was hurt.

"I have stumbled across some information about our ghost," he said, his gaze roaming over her features.

"I'm not sure I care right now," she lied.

"What if Isabel has poisoned Tracey's mind, too?" he asked, and it was not a question.

Cass stared. His adept mind was already drawing the same conclusions that she had. "She hasn't."

Antonio looked at her, and Cass thought she saw pity in his gaze.

"She hasn't poisoned Tracey in any way," Cass cried.

Antonio turned away, and when he faced her, he said, "I found two letters, Cassandra. Just moments ago. The letters your aunt mentioned. One is from Isabel to her cousin, Robert de Warenne, the other from Robert to her. Apparently they were lovers, and they corresponded while Isabel was pregnant, and here, at Casa de Sueños, in Spain."

Cass stared, her mind slowly absorbing and turning over the information.

"She was miserably unhappy," Antonio said. "But there is something else."

"What?" Cass asked.

He looked at her. "Why would the letter Isabel sent to her lover in England be here, in Castilla, among the de la Barca possessions?"

Gregory must have reached Pedraza several hours ago, so where were the police?

They had actually packed up half of his father's notes and books, and had had lunch, too. Keeping busy seemed to be their mutually agreed upon if unspoken goal. They had also searched briefly for Celia, to no avail. Now Cass kept glancing at her watch. It was 3:00 P.M. She had a distinctly bad feeling.

Antonio also glanced at his watch, then looked up, and their gazes met.

"I don't want to worry you, but where is he?" Cass asked.

"He should have been back by now," Antonio said. Abruptly he sat down at his desk. "Something has happened."

Cass almost touched his shoulder before she thought better of it. Instead, she crossed her arms protectively over her chest. "These things take time."

"No. Something has happened. Why did I let him go? Why didn't I go myself? It was my responsibility."

Cass sighed harshly. "I'm going to go upstairs to check on Tracey," she said. She'd done so every hour—Tracey remained deeply asleep.

Antonio nodded, not glancing at her.

Cass fled the library. She couldn't handle much more now. She was overloaded and acutely aware of it.

But what if Isabel was not yet through with them?

Her tension escalated and it was unbearable.

As she stepped into Tracey's room, she saw that Tracey was still asleep, but her expression wasn't relaxed. It was filled with distress. She was tossing restlessly, making plaintive sounds, clearly in the midst of a terrible dream.

Cass sat down beside her, stroked her hair. "It's all right, Trace. It's just a dream."

Tracey gradually quieted, but Cass decided to sit with her a bit longer, and as she did so, she found herself glancing around the room, wondering what it was that was bothering her.

And then she knew. The clothes Tracey had worn the day of her disappearance were in a pile on the floor. They were not the clothes Cass had stripped off of her in the shower.

Cass stood. That meant that Tracey had returned, unbeknownst to anyone, in order to change. Didn't it? But why? And how was that possible?

Cass found herself reaching for the clothes. Maybe she was making a mistake. But the short white shorts, the tiny pink top, Tracey had worn those clothes to the crypt, had been in them when they had fought in the great hall, and when she had run out of the house.

Cass tossed the shorts down, perplexed, and as she did so, something rolled out of a pocket. She thought it was a coin, turned back to her sister, now soundly asleep, then did a double take. A thin, delicate gold chain lay on the floor, the smallest gold cross with a tiny diamond in its center attached to it.

Cass stared, incapable of movement, stunned.

She retrieved it, recognizing it, sickening deep in her gut. The chain was Celia's. She wore it every day; she never took it off. Cass was certain it was hers.

Cass couldn't understand why Tracey had the chain; in fact, it was very hard to think right now, much less clearly, she was so upset. Cass gripped her head. "Stop," she whispered to herself. "Think and be rational!"

There had to be an explanation for that chain. Just as there was an explanation for the blood on Tracey's clothes—just as there was an explanation for the murder of the electrician.

Cass began to tremble. Despair overcame her. Suddenly it felt as if there was no way out. She loved Antonio, but she could not have him, not now, not after this. She had wanted to protect Catherine; instead, Catherine was dead. How could she protect Tracey? How?

And then the fragrance of violets filled the room. Quickly. Becoming overpowering in its intensity. Cass was aware that she was shaking; her knees had become useless, and she sagged against the bed. Isabel was there. And Cass had not a doubt that she would materialize at any moment.

Cass did not move, waiting, helpless, terrified.

The odor was so strong that she could not breathe. Cass began to cough and choke, tears started to slide down her cheeks. Tracey even coughed as she slept. Suddenly Cass felt as if she might strangle for lack of air, just as her aunt had been asphyxiated, and she could not stand it, she needed air, and she rushed from the room. But the hallway was also filled with the sickeningly sweet stench.

Cass clutched her throat, unsure of what was happening now.

Images of her aunt, convulsing on the floor, turning blue from lack of oxygen, filled her head.

And as her eyes closed, as she choked and choked for lack of air, the image of her aunt changed, and Cass saw herself, as if she were up high on some perch, looking down from an aerial view, and she watched herself choking to death, and then she was prone on the floor, her face turning blue.

Darkness cloaked her.

Cass fought her way up through the thickness of it. And when the blackness turned to gray, when there was light, she opened her eyes, expecting to find Isabel standing there, staring down at her.

But no one was there. And Cass realized that she was lying on the floor, on her back, panting harshly, staring up at the ceiling.

The corridor was very still and very silent.

Her breathing was obscenely loud in comparison.

And then Cass saw her.

Standing a few steps away, by the wall.

Isabel.

Cass tensed. Waiting for a knife to flash, almost certain that Isabel would stab her to death just as she—or someone—had stabbed the electrician to death, just as Antonio's grandmother had stabbed her husband to death. Fear made it hard to breathe all over again.

But Isabel just stood there. Her stare was brilliant, blazing, and then she turned and walked down the hall, toward Cass's bedroom.

Cass began to breathe. The scent of violets was rapidly diminishing. She gulped down fresh air, again and again, until the scent was almost gone.

Cass managed to climb to her feet. She felt shaky and disoriented. But she hadn't imagined what had just happened. She had suffered an attack just like her aunt, she had come very close to death, and she had just seen Isabel. Isabel, who had allowed her to live.

And she had gone down the hall, into Cass's bedroom.

Cass staggered against the wall. She stared toward her room—the door was closed. Cass thought she had seen Isabel walk through it, but she wasn't sure.

She didn't want to move. Not unless it was to flee back downstairs. But somehow her feet moved in the opposite direction and she started down the hall, her heart pounding now in sheer dread, not wanting to do what she must do, incapable of stopping herself from forward movement, using the wall for support, staggering against it. At the door she paused, afraid.

Isabel would be on the other side. And then what?

Cass again found it hard to breathe, but this time it had nothing to do with asphyxiation—it had everything to do with panic.

Open the door.

The voice was there, inside her head, loud and clear, a command.

Open the door.

She found herself reaching for the knob. Even though she wanted nothing more than to run away, as fast and as far as possible. Even though she knew that it was Isabel, there inside her mind, whispering to her.

Open the door.

Cass obeyed, pushing the door open.

Isabel was not present. Her bedroom was deserted.

Cass buckled against the doorjamb. *Thank God!*

And as she sighed hugely in relief, she saw her glowing computer screen.

And even from a distance, she knew words were there, and she understood.

Isabel had left her another message.

Cass did not, could not, move.

She had no idea how long she stood frozen in the doorway, staring at the screen of her laptop, at the tiny white letters illuminated there, from a distance that made it impossible to see clearly. She finally started forward, one foot after the other, slowly, numbly, dumbly, in a state of dread.

Cass halted—then reached out to grip the desk for support.

I AM YOUR SISTER NOW.

TWENTY-ONE

And when will you tell his lordship the truth?"

Isabel's temples throbbed. They had remained in their rooms at the palace after all, and she sat in a high-backed chair, to ease her back, which ached constantly these days. Her eyes closed. How she wished that Helen would go far away. She had become a nag and a shrew, and outwitting her was never an easy task.

Helen handed her a cold compress for her temples. "Is there a reason you do not wish to tell your husband that you are with child, Isabel?"

Isabel did not meet Helen's gaze. "I have waited to be certain I am truly bearing his babe," she said coldly. Abruptly, she stood. At her feet, Zeus did so as well. He had grown fat these past few months, eating too many leftover scraps.

Helen made a sound, half snort and half disbelief, and walked away. Isabel was relieved. And tears filled her eyes.

Her belly did not protrude in her clothes, not yet, but when she was naked, she could see a new firmness and swelling. She had not had a single monthly time since her marriage, so she might very well be four months pregnant. Isabel's stomach lurched.

A chamber pot was nearby and she used it, retching uncontrollably. When the spasms had passed, she remained on her knees, crying, until Zeus's warm wet nose touched her cheek.

Instantly she sat on the floor, pulling him into her arms, hugging him tightly. *What if the child was Rob's?*

Oh, how foolish could she be, to take a lover before getting an heir! What if the child had Rob's blue eyes and blond hair?

Perhaps, she thought, inhaling raggedly, Alvarado would never know. Her own eyes were blue, her hair neither red nor gold, but some unusual shade in between. He might never know—they all might never know—until the child was well grown, and bearing some distinct resemblance to either man. Her temples felt as if they could split her skull in two.

"Oh, Zeus," Isabel whispered, stroking his silken head while he regarded her out of wide, worshipful eyes, "what did I do?"

But it was far too late for regrets, and how could she regret her love for Rob, which remained stronger than ever? She had yet to tell Rob, but she had seen the look in his eyes last night, when he had covered her small belly with his large hand, exploring its new firmness. And when he had looked up, the question had been there in his unwavering regard, for Isabel knew him so well now—and she had looked away.

Rob, who had just fathered a stillborn boy and whose wife had died during the birthing. Rob, who had no heir, not even a bastard one.

Before she could dwell on her dilemma anymore, Helen reappeared in the bedchamber. " 'Tis time for you to go down to sup, Isabel, or should I send the count a message that you are not well enough?" Disapproval remained in her tone and her eyes.

Isabel bit her lip. Helen knew that she had a lover, Isabel was quite sure. There had been too many afternoons to count when Isabel had reappeared in her apartments, dreamy eyed and smiling, unable to think of anything but Rob, with Helen scowling at her. If only she had been a bit more discreet, she thought, in despair. Isabel stood up.

"Do not move about so suddenly," Helen scolded. "You must be careful, Isabel."

Isabel waved at her. "I am more than careful. No, I will go down." She smiled wanly. She was not joining her husband because she wished to do so, but because it pleased him, and she was terrified now of falling from his favor.

Isabel did not hurry as she moved through the many halls and corridors of the palace. She had long since become familiar with the manner of life at court. She nodded at several gentlemen as she passed, while ignoring the loud argument transpiring between a group of Spanish courtiers and their English counterparts. The foreigners and Englishmen were fighting, often violently, every single day. In fact, her husband frequently complained about the treatment of his people, not to mention the court, the food, the drink, the entertainment, and just about everything else English.

Thank God he did not complain about her.

"Countess?"

The voice was familiar, yet it was not. Isabel faltered, glancing at a throng of men striding toward her.

Vivid blue eyes found and held hers. Isabel suddenly realized that she was face-to-face with Douglas Montgomery, and she faltered. She had not seen him since she had deceived him when he had come to court to press his suit for her hand.

He strode forward, his gaze never leaving her face, and he bowed.

Isabel was stunned by his presence, and more than that, she finally realized that her heart thundered hard in her breast. But dear God, what must he think of her? "Lord Montgomery," she managed.

He straightened, and now his gaze slid quickly over her face before returning to her eyes. "Yes. I see I made such a singular impression upon you that you still remember me."

Isabel realized, too late, that he was referring to the horrid deception she had practiced upon him, and she flushed. "My lord, I hardly know where to begin. I do apologize for my behavior when we first met—"

"I knew you were in disguise," he said.

Isabel just stared at him, at a complete loss.

His smile was slight. "I was very insulted, but that is all in the past now, is it not? You have long since been married, as have I."

Her heart continued to thunder—Isabel could not understand why. "I truly did not wish to insult you, my lord."

"I have no wish to dwell on the past. The future is what interests me—as does the present." His gaze locked with hers.

Isabel understood and she could not quite move. She ensnared him still. And she could not help feeling absurdly pleased.

"I wish to congratulate you on your marriage," he finally said after a long and awkward silence.

Isabel knew she blushed. "And I, on yours."

He smiled then. "Have you heard? My wife is with child. We expect the babe to come in May." His eyes were lit with pride.

She remembered her own state—and dilemma—and her smile faded. "That is wonderful, my lord."

He took her hand again. "The strangest look of worry—or was it sorrow?—has just passed through your eyes, my lady. What could possibly cause you such grief?"

Isabel was taken aback. She wet her lips, casting about frantically for a reply. "You mistook me, my lord, for I hardly worry over much these days."

"Then I am glad, but I know what I have seen."

Isabel stared. The urge to confide in him overcame her, and she had to tell herself not to be a fool. "Then you do know more than I," she said, as lightly as she could.

Suddenly he tucked her arm in his. "Let us stroll. Will you walk with me, my lady?"

She glanced at him. She should go on about her affairs, but it was too pleasant to see him again after all this time, and she nodded as they began to walk. "Yes, please."

"How do you find life at court?" he asked.

"I find it interesting and entertaining," she said. "Do not forget, I was rather a country mouse until my uncle recalled my very existence."

His gaze was warm. "I doubt you were ever a country mouse. You are too clever and too beautiful."

She slowed. There was no mistaking that his words were a compliment. But she was not discomfited, not in the least. She was oddly elated. And as she met his searching regard, she felt amazed. Why, he is so upright, so proud and so sincere, and as handsome as Rob. How had she failed to notice when he had come to court as a suitor?

Suddenly she wondered if she had made a terrible mistake. As suddenly, dismayed, she cut off her thoughts. "What brings you to court?" she asked quickly.

"In truth, I thought it time to see you again," he said quietly, no longer smiling.

Isabel halted. Their gazes had locked and she could not move.

" 'Tis not exactly what you must think." He gripped her arm. "Since that day we first met, when you tried to trick me with that wretched disguise, I have not been able to forget you. In truth, I think I am somewhat smitten." His smile was self-deprecating. "But that is not why I have come to speak with you."

She regarded him with growing unease. If he was not here to flatter her, then why was he present? "I do not understand."

He was so dark of eye, so dark of countenance. "Isabel. There are so many rumors, rumors I have not believed, but now we must speak of them."

She faced him, suddenly frightened. "What rumors? Oh—rumors of the king's desire to go to war in France? The queen is pregnant, you know." She knew she spoke so quickly that her words were jumbled. "The king will never leave until after the babe is born, well into the spring."

He gripped her arms. "Rumors abound about you, Isabel, rumors I have not believed. But I have met your husband. I have met the admiral. And I see the pain and conflict and worry in your eyes. Dear God, I understand now, everything, including why you rejected me— but you play a dangerous game."

Isabel could not move. His words caused her to reel, almost blindly. "What . . . rumors? I know not of what you speak!" she cried, too loud, her tone high and out of pitch.

He tightened his grip. "The court talks about you and Admiral de Warenne, my dear."

Isabel stared at his dark, handsome face. She wanted to say, *He is my cousin.* She could not form a single word.

The court talks about you and Admiral de Warenne.

No! It was not possible! Her vision blurred, the hall around her darkening.

"Do not faint," he said, throwing one strong arm around her. Before she knew it, he had lifted her into his arms, was striding across the hall, while she fought the blackness, thinking, *The court talks about you and Admiral de Warenne*, and then she was being lowered onto a stone bench in a small garden where the air was damp and wet with mist. "Breathe deeply, no, do not sit up," he said firmly.

Isabel lay on the bench, breathing rapidly, shallowly, his words an ugly, terrifying refrain in her mind. When she opened her eyes, they blurred with tears, and his handsome, concerned face was there.

"If the world knows of your liaison, it is only a matter of time until your husband does, as well," Montgomery said.

She stared, and suddenly she was holding his hands tightly, shaking her head. She should lie, deny everything; instead, she was crying. "How could they know? How could anyone know? Except, mayhap, for Helen . . ."

His regard was piercing. "Does it matter how they know?"

She struggled to sit up; instantly he put his arm around her to aid her. "I love him," she heard herself whisper.

"I know you do."

There was something in his tone that made her gaze lift to his.

His smile was twisted. "Life is incomprehensible, is it not? Even after my thirty-two years, even after all that I have witnessed, and lived through, I still fail to understand God's will."

Isabel could only agree, silently. Did the entire court know? *Oh, God! He has to be wrong!*

"De Warenne is a fortunate man," Montgomery said.

She met his gaze. "Do not, my lord, say anymore," she finally said.

But his next words were not what she was expecting. "And he is not worthy of you."

"Do not slur him out of your jealousy!" she cried.

"I do not deny my jealousy, but I speak the truth. For if he loved you, he would not place you in this position." Montgomery remained grim.

"Do not speak of what is not your affair."

"But you are my affair, Isabel. I did not mispeak when I said God's will is strange and incomprehensible. Otherwise there would be but one woman in my heart—my wife." He stared. "You must be careful, Isabel. Trust no one. There are so many petty jealousies here, and there are spies everywhere."

She stared. "I understand." She realized he was going to leave, and oddly, she was not ready yet for him to do so.

"Should you ever need to reach me, you can leave a message at Carew Hall. The manor is on the Thames, and my servants are trustworthy. I will not turn my back."

Isabel felt more tears rise up, along with a confusion she could not comprehend, and an equally incomprehensible, accompanying fear. She nodded. "Thank you, my lord. That is an offer I may one day accept."

"I pray you will never have to," he said.

"Yes, Isabel? There is something you wish to say?"

Her husband was working late, as always, dealing with matters of diplomacy and state. Isabel hesitated before his desk, Montgomery's dark image instantly coming to mind. He had been haunting her thoughts ever since their unexpected encounter earlier that day.

"Do you have a moment to spare, my lord?" Isabel asked nervously. Thinking, *The whole court does not know.* Montgomery was wrong. And Alvarado surely had no suspicions at all. Otherwise she, Isabel, would sense something to be gravely amiss.

They continued to converse mostly in French, although he had picked up a small amount of English, and she could get by rudely in Spanish if need be.

He was waiting. His face was a mask that was impossible to read, but then, he had never been a very expressive man. Isabel met his gaze for one instant, and in that instant she thought that his eyes were cold and hard. She looked away, terrified, thinking, *Sweet Mother Mary, he knows!*

His hand closed on her arm. Isabel had not seen him stand. His touch made her flinch. "Is something amiss, my dear?"

Breathlessly she met his gaze, only to look away, afraid he would see her guilt.

"What do you wish to speak of, my dear?"

Isabel managed to think. His tone was not unusual, she realized, for it was somewhat kind, quite level, and also slightly patronizing. She must have imagined the cool light in his eyes, and only because Montgomery had so distressed her. She had nothing to worry about. She and Rob had been overly cautious; they had been most discreet. Isabel finally faced him. She still could not look him directly in the eye. "I am with child, my lord."

For one moment his expression did not change—for one moment Isabel was frightened again—and then he smiled. "I have hoped for this day," he said.

"And I," she replied, a terrible lie.

"No wonder you have been at once pale and flushed, with appetite and with none," he said, guiding her to a chair and urging her to sit. "When might we expect the child?"

Isabel smiled at him. Her heart beat like a caged butterfly against the walls of her chest. "I think in five or six months, my lord. I have yet to see a physician. I wished to speak with you first."

"How thoughtful you are, as always, Isabel. Again, you please me to no end. Is any man more fortunate than I? So you think the child was conceived soon after we were wed?" he asked.

"Soon after we were wed," she whispered, incapable of breathing normally.

He nodded, smiling, then turned and moved to a table where he poured two glasses of white wine. "We must toast the unborn babe, Isabel, and we must toast you, my beautiful, clever, loyal wife."

Isabel accepted the glass with a trembling hand, trying to decipher an innuendo in his words and finding none. Montgomery had also called her clever—Alvarado meant nothing by it. They drank to the babe's safe delivery, and her own quick conception of the child. They drank to the event of a son. The wine went down like vinegar, causing Isabel's insides to curdle.

She had always wanted a child, but not like this. Never like this. Her heart was so heavy. The extent of her betrayal was finally sinking in.

How had she come to such a terrible place in time? When once she had been innocent and trustworthy, filled with dreams of hearth and home, husband and duty and love? At least he did not know. Surely if he suspected, he would kill her now.

Alvarado finished his wine and smiled at her. "The time has come, my dear."

Isabel froze. "What time?"

"The time has come for you to go to Spain. My son shall be born in Castilla, as I was, and my father and grandfather and his father before him." He raised his empty glass in a salute. "You shall set sail as soon as the physicians complete the examination and assure me that all is well."

Isabel was stunned. Eyes wide, she stared at him in sheer disbelief. Leave court? Go to Spain? Now? But . . . How could she leave Rob?

"I will join you as soon as my duties here are done, hopefully before the child is born," Alvarado said.

Isabel remained stunned. No, she could not go. She could not. "I am so happy here, my lord, we are so comfortable—"

"You will leave within the week, of that I assure you," he said. "Begin your preparations now." He walked away.

Their conversation was over.

December 24, 1554

My dearest Rob,

My heart so aches for home and all there that I hold dear. Oh, Rob, there are not words enough in the English language for me to describe to you my loneliness and anguish. This land is a cold and barren place. It is a hateful place. It will never be home. Nearly two months have passed since I set foot on these foreign shores, and I am so afraid I will never be allowed to return to England, that this horrid land will be my burial place.

I despair, surrounded by servants whose tongue I cannot understand, with only Helen to comfort me, and the child that grows apace in my womb. Even the doctors who come are strange and foreign and I cannot comprehend them. I suppose their nods and smiles mean that all is well, but my sorrow is so great I cannot care. I miss all the times we have shared. It is all that I dream of. You are always in my heart and in my thoughts. Not a single minute, hour, day goes by that I do not think of you, yearning desperately to return home. This cold and ugly house with over-solid stone walls has become my prison, my husband, my gaoler.

Please advise me. I await your correspondence eagerly.

Your loving and devoted cousin, eternally yours,
Isabel

February 21, 1555

My dearest cousin,

Too much time has passed since last we spoke. I recollect our many conversations, with both sadness and joy, and with longing, and look forward to many more. How fare you, dearest Isabel? I have heard here at court that all is well, and I cannot tell you how that pleases me. I hold your health and happiness and that of the unborn babe close to my heart, as always.

There is much news to impart. The queen is well as her time grows near, although Philip is eager to go to war in the spring, and she is a bit melancholy knowing that. And there is concern, too, for the country itself, should the birthing not go well, and even questions regarding the throne. But I do not want to dwell on that, even though those matters occupy my thoughts night and day.

Protestant rebels still afflict the land everywhere, and the cause of peace was not helped when Bishop Hooper did meet his fate. He was, at long last, condemned to the stake for his heresy, with several other heretics. The burnings have encouraged the rebels, especially in the Southeast. My dearest cousin, how I wish you were here to share with me the worries I bear. Our country is divided now, far worse than before. Lutheran against Calvinist, Anglican against Catholic. The other day I came across two ministers stoning a priest. The ministers were promptly arrested, but the priest, an old man, was already dead. Dear God, how have we come to such anguished times? I see no end to the conflict, for passions run ever too high on all sides.

I do not mean to darken your hours with such foreboding, but always, you were the one I could share my most private thoughts with. Old customs do not die easily, it seems.

I eagerly await tidings from Castilla.

God bless you and the child,

Your devoted, loyal, and most loving cousin,
Admiral Robert de Warenne

TWENTY-TWO

Cass stared at the computer screen, refusing to comprehend the message, and as she did so, the screen blinked and darkened and brightened again, and suddenly it was filled with words, without any punctuation.

I AM YOUR SISTER NOW I AM YOUR SISTER NOW I AM YOUR SISTER NOW
I AM YOUR SISTER NOW I AM YOUR SISTER NOW I AM YOUR SISTER NOW I

Cass began backing away, slowly, step by step, her heart pounding in her chest, so forcefully she thought it might tear her rib cage apart, and then she turned and ran.

She ran as if pursued, barged into Tracey's room, and froze in midstride. She wasn't sure what she had expected to see, perhaps Isabel lying there in Tracey's bed, but Tracey slept there, as peacefully as an infant.

Oh, God, she thought, backing away.

An image of her computer screen remained engraved upon her mind.

An image of those terrible words.

In the hallway she glanced wildly around, but Isabel wasn't present, and then she dashed down the stairs. She had to find Antonio. Tracey was in danger now—everyone was in danger, Cass thought, panicked.

And as she rushed into the library, the first thing she saw was that the children were not present. Antonio was standing on a stepladder, removing books from a higher shelf.

"Where are the children?" she cried, aghast.

He almost fell off the ladder, and then he came more carefully down. "Cassandra." He gripped her shoulders, his gaze piercing. Cass realized she was trembling. "What happened?!"

She grabbed him. "Where are the children?"

"Alfonso took them outside to play. They need some air and some exercise. They are fine."

Cass shook her head vehemently. "No. I want them here, with us!"

He continued to hold her, searching her eyes, her face. "What has happened?" He spoke slowly, calmly.

"I had an attack—just as Aunt Catherine did. I couldn't breathe, I was choking—choking on her goddamned perfume!"

His eyes widened impossibly. "But you are all right." His arm was around her now.

Cass continued to shake. Her tongue felt like it was tripping over her words—she had never spoken more rapidly. "I followed her into my bedroom. There's a message on my laptop—a new message." Cass felt violently sick. What did that message mean? She refused to understand it.

"What did it say?" Antonio asked tersely.

She glanced at him, because she thought she had heard fear in his voice—for the very first time. Fear. She was so terribly afraid now. But his expression was calm—a mask of iron composure—and God, she needed him now, calm and strong and rational. But he was afraid— she had just seen it—and now her own fear escalated with sickening force. "Follow me," she said harshly.

They pounded up the stairs. Cass was not surprised to see that this time nothing had changed on her laptop—the fourteen-inch screen remained filled with that one, horrific message, repeated endlessly: I AM YOUR SISTER NOW.

Antonio stepped closer and stared.

Cass hugged herself. "I don't understand. I can't understand. I will not understand!"

It was like there were two of me... my left hand couldn't stop my right...

Antonio looked at her, reaching for her at the same time. Cass slipped out of his reach. "No," she said, shaking her head.

Antonio stared at her. "Is she telling us that she has possessed your sister, or that she is your sister?" he asked quietly. "I believe there is a vast difference."

It was like there were two of me ... my left hand couldn't stop my right ...

Cass wished she had never heard those words! She was filled with horror, with dread. She was going over the edge of a cliff, free-falling—and helpless to stop herself. She even felt dizzy. "What is the difference?" she finally whispered—and it was a horrible capitulation to the truth.

This time he took her hand, clasping it firmly to his side. "If she has some degree of control of your sister's mind, there is hope. Of reaching Tracey—and driving Isabel away."

Cass could not look away from his gaze. "Is there hope? Is there? She made someone kill the electrician. She made your grandmother kill your grandfather. She made Catherine lure Eduardo to his death!"

"She is so angry," he said quietly. "But anger can be managed, even defused."

Cass stared. "Managed? Defused? Are we going to play shrink with her? She's a ghost, Antonio. She's dead. And pissed off. In a very big way. And I don't have a clue as to how to deal with her! Maybe she will not be satisfied until we are all dead, every single one of us!" Cass realized her teeth were chattering.

"Do not think the very worst," he said sharply. "We must remain strong—mentally. Because her anger contaminates those who are not strong enough to resist it. Do not succumb to hysteria and panic, Cassandra."

And there was a warning in his tone. It was frightening, too.

She seized his arms, helplessly thinking, *Tracey is not strong. Tracey is weak.* "Tracey is the perfect prey, isn't she?" She was shaking.

"We should lock Tracey in her room—or even tie her up—for the moment," Antonio responded flatly.

Cass stared in more horror. "Maybe you are right," she finally said. She was nauseous now. "You think she killed the electrician, don't you?"

"If Tracey was involved, she was not herself," he said firmly.

Cass backed away. He thought Tracey guilty of murder—it was clear, there in his eyes. "Maybe it was Gregory," she flashed. "He's hiding something ..."

Antonio started. "That is what you think?!"

"I don't know what to think!" she shouted.

"My brother was not the one who reappeared after a mysterious and prolonged absence, covered in blood," he said angrily.

For an instant Cass and Antonio stared at one another, with a sudden, frightening comprehension. They were furiously arguing—they were falling prey to Isabel, too.

"Come on," Antonio shouted, grabbing her hand. And they rushed through the house and to the courtyard—but the children were laughing, playing outside in the sunshine, supervised by Alfonso.

Their gazes collided. They turned and dashed upstairs.

Tracey was gone.

The blackness began to lift.

And as it did, his mind, like a long-defunct engine, slowly, painfully, tried to click into gear and grasp some coherence.

Suddenly there was pain, so much pain, and there was absolute confusion—he did not understand what was happening, or where he was.

And then came total comprehension. He had almost died—but he was not dead.

Gregory did not move, totally conscious now, focusing on the pain shooting in huge waves through his right shoulder. Nothing had ever hurt like this. And then there was the pain in his knee, sharp, endless stabs of it, and the excruciating pounding in his head.

And he was lying on his back on the hard, stony ground.

But he was alive. Gregory slowly opened his eyes, squinting, and found himself looking up at the bright blue sky, the thick cumulus clouds, and the strong Spanish sun.

And then he recalled exactly what had happened, right down to the last harrowing detail—the truck that had purposefully driven him off the road and over the cliff. His labored breath caught. But surely, surely, Isabel had not been behind the wheel. Surely he had been imagining that.

He suddenly closed his eyes, breathing hard, with fear, with panic. Whom was he fooling? She wanted him dead. She had been toying with him ever since he was a small boy, only now her games had become deadly serious—her games had become life and death. He did not know how a woman dead for more than four centuries could drive a tractor-trailer, but she had somehow accomplished this feat. And this time she had almost won.

He gritted his teeth, and as he tried to sit up, sweat burst out all over his face and chest, and the pain in his shoulder was so terrible that he almost fainted. He rode out the waves of blackness, grimacing, refusing to pass out—not daring to. He was afraid she would come back.

He was finally sitting up, unable to breathe because of the pain, and clutching his right shoulder with his left hand. He decided that he had dislocated it. He was going to have to push it back in.

But before he could even think of anything else, Gregory glanced around. No one was in sight.

Relieved, he managed to stand, and when he was upright, pain shooting through his knee, he saw a tree, not much larger than he himself was. He limped over to it, inhaled hard, then jammed his right shoulder against the tree. As he did so, he heard a pop, and the pain was nearly gone.

Jesu, he thought, standing there, sweating buckets and shaking like a leaf.

He waited until the nausea had passed, then glanced at the ravine. It wasn't terribly steep, and he would eventually be able to climb out, but given the condition of his knee, it might take all day. Suddenly he thought about his family stranded at Casa de Sueños and his heart lurched with dread. Isabel had isolated him, nearly getting rid of him— did she think him dead? What did she intend for those left at the villa? He was sick at the thought.

Then he saw the bike.

It lay a good dozen yards from where he now stood, and even from this distance, he could see that the handlebars were bent. If the tires weren't flat, he might just be in luck. An image of the two children playing so innocently in the library, followed by an image of Isabel with her malevolent blue eyes, filled his mind. Gregory hobbled as quickly as possible to the bike. His head started to hurt even more; he touched the back, felt the stickiness, knew it was blood.

Whatever was happening, he would have to ignore it, he decided grimly.

The bike was, miraculously, mostly undamaged. It was dented, the front bars twisted, but both tires had air. Almost exultant, Gregory lifted it up.

Then, as he started at an angle up the ravine, limping and going very slowly, each step a difficult feat, he glanced up at the sun.

It was late. He had been unconscious for several hours. Not a good sign, medically speaking; he probably had a concussion. Now he had a choice to make.

He could ride back the way he had come, and be back at the villa in half the time it would take him to get to town. Or he could continue with his mission.

But he was already feeling weak and faint. He could hardly walk; the distance to the road seemed almost insurmountable. His knee continued to protest every step, and he could feel something wet—blood— trickling down his neck. His heart beat from the effort like a jungle drum, uncomfortably, threateningly. Suddenly Gregory knew he would never make it to Pedraza. And he wasn't sure he could make it back to the house, either. But at least it would be downhill all the way.

He did not want to turn back.

But he did not want to die.

Hand in hand, Cass and Antonio hurried back down the stairs. They burst into the great hall, Cass immediately dropping his palm and racing to the front door, which she swung open. She had only one thought—where was Tracey?

And the first thing she saw as she opened the door was Celia. Celia staggering toward the house, her glasses askew, her hair disheveled, her dress dirty, torn, and stained with blood.

Cass cried out, rushing down the front steps.

Celia saw her and began to run. She started to cry.

Cass embraced the older woman, hard. "Are you all right? What happened!" she cried.

Antonio reached them. "Celia, let me help you." He put his arm around her.

She looked at Cass with wide, frightened eyes. "Miss de Warenne, oh, Lord save us all, you cannot imagine what has happened." Tears fell.

Suddenly Cass was afraid to hear what she had to say. "Let's get you inside. You're hurt." Celia had a huge gash on the side of her head, crusted with dried blood, as well as numerous scrapes and cuts. She was also limping.

"There is a terrible demon about," Celia cried as Antonio helped her up the front steps. "We're being haunted, but she is evil, and she tried to kill me."

Cass slammed the front door shut behind them.

Celia could not stop talking. "We saw your sister in the window, and then Alyssa ran out of the house. I did not even think twice and I followed her. It was the most horrid thing! I kept calling for her and she would cry out, and I followed her cries, going farther and farther from the house. And then I saw this woman—I knew, Miss de Warenne, I knew, in that one terrifying moment, that she was not from this world." Celia was trembling.

Cass could hardly think. But she glanced at Antonio, who met her gaze. She knew what he was thinking. Alyssa had not been far from the house when he had found her. Celia had been purposefully lured away.

"She smiled at me and it was hateful." Celia started to cry again. "I turned and began to run. Oh, Miss de Warenne! I have never seen such meanness, such hate!"

Cass couldn't speak. She put her arm around the older woman.

"She followed me! And I tripped and fell over a cliff, hitting my head, hurting my ankle, almost losing consciousness. And she started calling my name. Soft whispers. Soft but clear. I don't know! Maybe they were in my head. Maybe they weren't real. But they sounded real. It was so real!"

"I know," Cass whispered, trying to comfort her. "I know."

Celia did not hear. "I hid. I did not know what else to do. I hid all night at the bottom of the ravine in the brush. And when the sun came up this morning, she was gone." Celia sank down in the chair at last. She covered her face with her hands. Her hands were shaking. She was shaking.

"Her name is Isabel. We know about her," Cass said, stroking her shoulder. "She wants vengeance on my family, and on the de la Barcas, too." But she was thinking about the fact that Isabel had not used Tracey to lure Celia away. She had used Cass's own greatest weakness—her concern and love for Alyssa—to lure her outside. Cass glanced at Antonio and their gazes met. She knew he understood, too. He was grim.

Celia wasn't through. "That is not all! I woke up—only to find myself sleeping beside a dead woman!"

Cass stiffened. "What?"

"I was sleeping next to a corpse. A very old, rotten corpse—mostly a skeleton, in rags." She wept anew.

"Oh God," Cass whispered, hugging her again.

"How did you know it was a woman if it was so decomposed that it was a skeleton, the clothing mere rags?" Antonio asked.

Cass started. Antonio's tone was filled with tension. Instantly she understood. He was wondering—or hoping—or fearing—that the corpse might be his wife.

"The jewelry. She had a beautiful engagement ring on as well as a wedding band."

Antonio did not move and he did not speak.

Cass straightened. "Antonio? Did Margarita wear an engagement ring and a wedding band?"

He looked at her. Blindly.

And she knew the answer was yes. Cass realized she was sick inside—in her heart. She could not stop now to think and understand why. "Celia, do you know where this ravine was? Could you find it again?"

Celia pointed toward the north. "There's a dry stream bed, maybe a kilometer past the garage. I followed it back to the house."

Antonio, Cass saw, had broken into a sweat. And she thought, *There are still three hours or so of daylight left.*

"Alyssa?" Celia asked, reaching for Cass's hand. "Is she all right?"

"Yes, she's fine. Antonio found her within minutes of your having run outside."

Celia slumped back in the chair. "Thank the Lord. There is mercy after all."

The children. Cass looked at Antonio and knew he was wondering the same thing. She hurried to the doors that opened onto the courtyard, and saw the two children sitting on a stone bench with Alfonso, the children in the midst of a discussion which she could not overhear. "Hey, guys," she called as cheerfully as possible. "Time to come inside."

She turned. "Antonio? Why don't we quickly run down that dry stream bed and see if we can find the ravine where Celia saw—" Cass stopped in midsentence as Tracey stepped into the hall, a half-eaten sandwich in her hand.

She froze.

I am your sister now.

Beside her, Cass felt Antonio stiffen, as well.

Tracey halted in midstride when she saw them.

Cass's heart began to thunder. She quickly took in her sister's appearance. She had put on a white button-down shirt, left open over a small tank top and faded vintage jeans. The sleeves of the shirt hid the hideous scars on her arms, and the rest of her clothing hid the cuts and bruises on her body. Her long hair wasn't brushed, but it was clean, and just pleasantly mussed. Her eyes were wide, bright, and while her face seemed gaunt—she was too thin now—nothing really appeared amiss. Or did it?

Cass looked into her blue eyes again. It crossed her mind that Isabel's eyes were also blue—but at once paler and brighter, somehow.

Paler, brighter, and malevolent.

"Hi," Cass said, her heart still deafening to her own ears.

"Hi," Tracey said, looking now at Antonio and then taking a bite of her sandwich.

She seemed normal. Cass glanced at Antonio—their eyes met briefly—and she studied Tracey again. "I should have guessed you'd be hungry." She could not force a smile.

"I'm famished," Tracey said with a small smile, taking another huge bite.

Cass realized her fingers were crossed. "How are you feeling?" she asked slowly, with trepidation and with dread.

"Exhausted," Tracey said. "But better, I think."

Cass began to breathe easier. "You should rest."

"Yes, I think so, too." Tracey ambled closer. "Why are the two of you staring at me?"

"I'm sorry," Cass said quickly, and to reassure herself more than anything else, she touched her sister's shoulder, but she was solid, real, and very thin—she was Tracey. "Want some company?"

Tracey swallowed and said, "I'm going to rest. I'm really fatigued. I've never been this tired." Then she smiled at Antonio. "Maybe we can speak later."

He nodded. "That would be fine."

Tracey stared at him searchingly, then glanced at Cass, as if sensing something had happened during her absence. But Cass was sure she hadn't given any indication of what had transpired between her and Antonio—surely she was merely paranoid now. Guilt suddenly raised its head when it had lain dormant for so long. Tracey then smiled at them both and walked up the stairs.

Cass and Antonio stood side by side, staring after her, almost holding their collective breaths.

On the third or fourth step, Tracey paused, turning to glance at them, her expression harder to read now.

Cass realized she and Antonio were touching—shoulder to shoulder and hip to hip. She gave Tracey a reassuring smile, but it was undoubtedly ruined because she jumped away from Antonio at the very same time.

Tracey smiled slightly in return, continued upstairs, and disappeared from view.

Cass sagged against him. "She's fine. She is not possessed. She is totally fine."

"Cassandra." He stepped away from her. "I am going to look for that ravine. You stay here with everyone until I get back."

She was instantly alarmed. "I'm going with you, Antonio. Everything is fine right now, Tracey is fine. We just have to be back before dark."

He did not answer her. He was already striding away, through the hall.

Cass ran after him.

"What if we write stories? I like writing stories. We had to write our own books this year in second grade," Alyssa said. "We even published them."

"Can I write my story in Spanish and then translate it for you?" Eduardo asked. The two children were sitting in the library while Alfonso made them an early dinner. Celia slept on the sofa, beneath a heavy wool throw.

Alyssa liked that idea. She smiled at Eduardo. "I'd like to learn Spanish. In school we're learning French, but now that we're friends, I wish it were Spanish."

"I could teach you," Eduardo said, his hazel eyes brightening.

Alfonso entered the room with a tray. *"La comida, pequeños,"* he said.

"Our dinner," Eduardo said eagerly. "I am so hungry. Are you?"

"Yes." Alyssa smiled back. She hated his country home, but at least she had a new friend—and maybe even a boyfriend. Then she saw a flash out of the corner of her eye.

Her heart felt like it had stopped. Alyssa whirled—and saw her mother standing in the doorway.

Alyssa stood abruptly. Her instinct was to rush to her, but then she remembered what had happened when she'd seen her mother in the window, and she froze. Her heart beat so hard. "Mother?" she whispered hesitantly.

Tracey smiled at her. "Hello, darling."

Alyssa blinked again and again. It was her mother—this was not an illusion. This was not her imagination and this was not a ghost.

"Señora?" Alfonso had just set the tray down. *"Puedo ayudarle?"*

And Celia had awoken. "Tracey?"

Tracey did not seem to hear either of them. She continued to smile at Alyssa. Alyssa's small, answering smile vanished. Was something wrong? Her mother was fine, wasn't she? Alyssa stared at Tracey, who still seemed to be the most impossibly beautiful, impossibly glamorous woman in the world. "Are you feeling better now, Mother?"

"I am just fine." She looked at her daughter. "Alyssa, come with me. Just come."

Alyssa fully intended to obey, but for some reason her feet would not move, refusing to obey her brain.

She was aware of Eduardo slowly getting up, crutches in hand.

"Alyssa, come with me," Tracey said again.

"What . . . what is it that you want?" Celia was sitting up, her tone hushed.

Tracey did not even look at her.

"Señora, Celia wants to know where you wish to go." Eduardo spoke as if Tracey needed a translator.

Tracey turned, unsmiling. Her eyes were very bright. "I want to speak with my daughter."

"*Señora. La comida. Ahora.* Dinner. Here." Alfonso smiled brightly. "With the . . . childs."

"I don't want to eat dinner," Tracey said.

Celia stood unsteadily. "Tracey? Are you all right?"

Alyssa suddenly found it hard to breathe. Her mother was speaking oddly. Her expression was odd. Her eyes were odd. Even her smile was odd.

Tracey did not answer. She smiled. "Let us go, Alyssa."

Alyssa could not move. Something was wrong with her mother. Terribly so. Alyssa did not know what to do and she was frightened.

"Did you hear me?" Tracey asked.

Alyssa nodded. "Maybe we should all stay here, together," she whispered, pleadingly.

Eduardo hobbled to stand beside her, and Alyssa felt her heart fill with gratitude.

Celia said, "Tracey, you seem exhausted. How about a bite of supper?" Her smile was brief, weak.

Tracey glanced at her as if she had just noticed her presence for the very first time. Then she turned to her daughter. "Alyssa," Tracey said. "Terrible things are going to happen. Come with me now."

Celia abruptly stepped forward. "Tracey."

And Alyssa was suddenly frightened of her mother. Why was she acting this way? And now she kept seeing, in her mind, that other woman—the ghost. The one she dreamed about—the one who had followed her outside. And what did she mean? What terrible things were going to happen? "I don't want to go," Alyssa whispered.

Alfonso stepped over to Tracey, smiling firmly. He held a bowl of soup in his hand. *"La sopa. Ahora."*

"Do not interfere," Tracey shouted, abruptly striking him across the face.

Alyssa was so shocked—and terrified—that she could not even scream as the bowl of soup went flying out of his hand, the old man falling. He landed on the floor, hitting his head with a loud thump. Celia was the one who cried out.

"Alfonso!" Eduardo gasped.

And she wanted to run to him, because he did not move and his eyes were closed and Alyssa was afraid he was dead. But it was Celia rushing forward, kneeling beside him.

Alyssa was afraid her mother had killed him.

"Alfonso!" Eduardo was hopping over to him also, his expression one of alarm.

Suddenly Alyssa heard Tracey moving—fast and hard, her strides determined. Alyssa cringed as her mother grabbed her arm. "I told you to come with me. How dare you disobey?"

I'm sorry, Alyssa wanted to say, but she was crying now, terrified of her own mother, who had hurt and maybe killed the kind old man, and she could not get the words past the sobs choking her.

"Don't hurt her," Eduardo whispered.

"Come . . . with . . . me," Tracey gritted, pulling Alyssa across the room.

"Tracey! Let her go. Please!" Celia cried.

Alyssa did not want to go, and she balked. Her mother dragged her step by step to the door. "Please," Alyssa sobbed, "don't make me go." And she felt herself wetting her pants.

Tracey shook her once. "Didn't you hear what I said?" she cried.

Alyssa nodded, her eyes glued to her mother's beautiful, ravaged face, aware of the tears streaming down her cheeks, and her heart pumping in huge, terrifying bursts. Where was Aunt Cass? She prayed she would appear.

"Let her go," Eduardo cried, hobbling after them. "Señora!"

Tracey adjusted her grip on Alyssa and pulled her with even more force from the room.

"No!" Alyssa cried. She struggled, but it was so useless. Her strength was no match for her mother's. "Eduardo! Celia!" Glancing backward through her tears, she saw their wide, white, frightened faces. "Don't leave me! Please! Don't leave me!"

Celia seemed paralyzed. But Eduardo set his crutches beneath him and hobbled furiously after them.

Alyssa realized her mother was dragging her through the downstairs of the house. Her expression was stretched so tightly, her face seemed to have become a taut clay mask, and her eyes blazed blue. And it struck Alyssa's dazed and shocked mind that something was more than wrong with her mother, but she did not know what. And the next thing she knew, a door was being opened.

Alyssa was confronted with a yawning hole of darkness.

From behind, she was pushed.

Alyssa screamed as she fell down and down, tumbling and tumbling, finally landing in a heap at the bottom of a very narrow flight of steep, slick stone stairs. "Mother!" she whimpered.

There was no answer.

Alyssa cringed where she had landed, afraid to move. "Mother!"

Tracey did not reply. Instead, a door somewhere above slammed shut—the sound resounding and final. And it was followed by a click.

"Mommy! Don't leave me!" she screamed.

TWENTY-THREE

For the hundredth time, Cass glanced at her watch. It was almost eight o'clock.

"We'll never find the ravine," she called out. Antonio had climbed out of the dry stream bed and was walking up a slight hill. "We have to turn back." She glanced over her shoulder. The house was no longer in sight and the light was finally fading. She knew now by experience that within another forty-five minutes or so, if not less, it would be dark.

They had to go back. Cass shivered. But not because it was cold. She did not know what horrors the night would bring, but Isabel was on the loose, and she could not leave the children alone. She must protect them at all costs.

Antonio suddenly cried out.

Cass jerked, to see him scrambling over the top of the hill, disappearing from sight.

She ran after him. When she reached the top of the knoll, she saw Antonio below in a rocky ravine, and there was no question as to what he was standing beside.

She hesitated. He knelt slowly to the ground.

Oh, God. This was it. Had they found Margarita after all these years?

Suddenly Cass was torn. A part of her was hoping that the answer was yes, but another part of her was fearing such an answer, too.

She told herself that it did not matter. Antonio needed closure, but whatever his response to it might be, it did not affect her. Their lives had been wrecked by the complications Isabel had brought to them all. There was no chance now of ever going forward. Besides, she didn't even want to. Not now, not anymore.

She had a sister to take care of, and her niece. She would have no time to focus on anything or anyone else.

"Cassandra," he said hoarsely.

Reluctantly she started down the steep, rocky side of the ravine. There was no stench—because there was no flesh. The bones were dusty and dirty, but clean.

He wasn't moving. Cass approached him from behind. She knelt beside him. Her gaze was instantly drawn to tatters of peach-colored fabric, and then she saw the sparkling solitaire diamond ring.

Antonio stood up. Cass glimpsed his expression, and she knew they had found her. She straightened to her full height.

"We have to go back." He started climbing back up the ravine.

Cass hurried after him. Without thinking, she grabbed his arm from behind, detaining him. "I'm sorry."

He finally looked at her. His expression was a mask, impossible to read. "So am I." He pulled free and started climbing to the top of the knoll again.

Cass stared after him. What the hell did that mean? Did he still love her? And why was she jealous?

A tendril of air wafted around her, like the caress of a breeze, or hair.

The slightest sweetness seemed to emanate from the ground beside her—violets.

Cass's pulse went wild. Isabel was about to materialize, she thought frantically, and she broke into a run—as if she might outpace her. She caught up to Antonio on the way down the other side of the hill, as they hit the stream bed. Cass scanned the area breathlessly. There was no one about, Isabel was not about. Had she imagined that touch?

Had she imagined that scent? She sniffed and could not decide. Briefly, Cass closed her eyes.

She was unraveling, she thought. *Fear would be the death of her.*

Cass's eyes flew open. She wished she had never had such a thought.

Antonio was marching resolutely back the way they had come. Cass started and had to run to catch up to him. As she did so, she saw how impossibly impassive his face had become. She could not help herself; compassion filled her. "Are you okay?" she asked, hushed.

"No."

Her temples, which had probably been throbbing for hours and hours, suddenly felt explosive. "It's not your fault." She had to run alongside him to keep up with him.

He whirled, and she was confronted with raw rage, the likes of which she had never before seen—not in anyone. "*Not my fault?!* She begged me to go home! She *begged* me, Cassandra. *Voices.* She heard voices in the night. She said she had dreams. Not dreams, nightmares. A woman, whispering, threatening her. Threatening her life. She was so damn terrified and I laughed at her fears! Because my work was more important than listening to her, understanding her, and returning to Madrid. So do not tell me it was not my fault! And in the future, goddamn it, mind your own fucking business."

Cass recoiled as if she had been shot.

Antonio whirled and strode away.

She could not move. She felt as if she had been blasted by a rifle—with both barrels. *Mind your own fucking business?* So this was what their friendship had come down to? Hadn't he told her, just hours ago, that he was in love with her? What was happening to them!

Antonio stumbled and came up short.

They looked at one another. Cass imagined her eyes were as wide and as frightened as his.

"It's her," Cass whispered. "She's doing this. It's *her* rage. Not yours. Antonio—she's poisoning *your* mind."

He stared. And then, "We have to get back to the house."

They ran.

"Mommy, Mommy!" Alyssa wept. "Please come back!"

But Tracey was gone, and Alyssa knew it. Then she froze as she heard a movement above her on the stairs. She began to shake violently, wondering what was up there—a rat? a snake?

She reminded herself that snakes were not inside houses, not even old ones like this, as more tears slipped helplessly down her face.

And Alyssa knew what was up there. It was a ghost.

No, not a ghost—*the* ghost.

The evil woman from her dreams, the one who kept telling her that she was her mother now, the one who had chased her outside last night.

Alyssa shivered and trembled and peed in her panties again.

Something crashed down several steps.

Alyssa screamed, jumping farther away from where she had landed on the stone floor, her back hitting the wall.

"It's me," Eduardo whispered, and his voice echoed loudly around them.

"Eduardo!" Alyssa cried, overcome with relief. She realized it was a crutch—or both crutches—that had fallen down the stairs.

"Are you all right?" he asked, a quaver in his tone.

"I'm so scared," Alyssa replied, and then, as she recalled her mother's almost maniacal expression, more tears fell. How could her mother have done this to her? Why had she done this? There was no one, no one, not even her aunt Cass, whom Alyssa loved more than her own mother. But her mother didn't love her. Her mother didn't want to be her mother, which was why Aunt Cass had raised her.

Did her mother hate her? Did her mother want to kill her? Was that why she had put her in this black place beneath the house? So she would die? So Tracey could be free to be beautiful, travelling all over the world and posing in magazines with new boyfriends?

Alyssa's heart felt like it was being ripped apart inside her small body.

Eduardo was coming slowly down the stairs, thump by careful thump. Alyssa suddenly stiffened even more.

"Don't come down, you'll get hurt," Alyssa cried. "Do you have your crutches? How did you get in here?"

"I have . . . one . . . of them," he panted. "I ran in . . . before she . . . closed the door."

Alyssa's eyes were beginning to adjust to the darkness, and while the room they were in was utterly dark, she could just slightly make out a darker shadow not far from where she stood. She was still afraid to move. "Do you think there are rats and mice down here?"

"I . . . don't . . . know," he panted, still thumping down the stairs. "But . . . they will . . . be afraid . . . of us, too."

Alyssa sucked up her courage and inched forward, almost blindly, until her foot struck what she knew was his crutch. "Wait," she whispered, her voice echoing. "I found your crutch."

She retrieved it and crept forward, on all fours and using her hands now, until she came to the stairs. "Where are you?" She groped for the second step.

"Right here," he whispered from above her.

Alyssa extended the crutch, and was rewarded when she felt him take it from her. Then she hurried up to where he was standing. She hugged him, hard. "Thank you," she whispered, "for not leaving me alone."

"It's nothing," he said nonchalantly. He hugged her even harder back.

"No, it's not. You are a hero, Eduardo, a brave hero."

She felt him smiling. "Where are we?" he asked.

"You don't know?" She was dismayed. "But this is your house."

"I've only been here once before—and I don't even remember that time. This must be a part of the dungeons," he said, low.

Alyssa knew all about dungeons—she had grown up in England, after all. What if there were dead people down there with them? She trembled. "Why did she do this? Why did she do this to me?" She heard her own voice break on her last words.

"I don't know. But don't worry." Alyssa knew he was smiling bravely. "They will find us. You'll see. My father and your aunt are so smart. They will find us right away."

Alyssa hoped he was right. "But what if they don't?" she whispered. "What will happen to us then?"

Eduardo did not answer.

Alyssa knew it was because he had no answer to make.

Once again, the front door of the house was ajar—when they had deliberately left it closed. Cass and Antonio exchanged glances, hurrying into the house and then down the hall. They both heard Alfonso groan at the same time.

They rushed into the library. Antonio cried out just as Cass saw Alfonso sitting on the floor, with Celia, who was holding a wadded handkerchief to his head. He was so white she thought that he might pass out at any moment. Celia was equally pale. And the rest of the room was empty. The children were gone.

Cass rushed past Antonio. And even as she spoke, she knew she should not be accusing them—she knew, somehow, that Isabel was to blame—but the words spilled forth of their own volition. "Where are the children?" she cried furiously. "Why aren't they here?"

Alfonso shrank away from her, beginning to explain, babbling in the language she could not understand.

Cass moaned, holding her head, pacing, her pulse exploding in her chest, too many horrible images of the children to even count wildly tumbling through her mind. As Antonio sank down beside the older man, Celia cried, "Miss de Warenne, it was your sister!"

Cass whirled. "What?!"

Celia was so grim that something inside Cass sickened with dread. "She came in here and asked Alyssa to go with her. When Alfonso tried to bring her a bowl of soup, she struck him down. I begged her not to go, to stay here in the library with us. She did not even seem to hear me. Alyssa did not want to go with her, but she gave her no choice." Celia seemed about to cry. "The little boy ran after them, bless his soul."

Cass's heart stopped. When it started again, she could not breathe. "She would never harm her own daughter."

Celia inhaled, hard, as if about to speak. But she was not given the chance.

"She is not Tracey anymore!" Antonio said, his eyes flashing. "You do not know what she is capable of."

Cass backed away. "You saw her twenty minutes ago. She was fine. Fine. Damn you." She started for the door; he caught her wrist, whipping her back around.

"She isn't fine. She lost her memory and someone killed that electrician. Just like someone killed my wife!"

Cass trembled and pulled free. "Tracey certainly had nothing to do with your wife's disappearance and death." She felt a savage satisfaction as she uttered the words, a satisfaction that she knew was somehow wrong.

"She almost killed my valet," Antonio raged. "He's bleeding and he will need stitches!"

Cass had no answer for that. "I'm sure the children and Tracey are in the kitchen or the courtyard. I'm going to find them." She ran for the door.

"Miss de Warenne!" Celia cried.

Cass didn't want to hear whatever it was the Celia had to say. Ignoring her, she ran into the hall. She could hardly think, her thoughts were jumbled, incoherent, crazed.

Antonio caught up to her. She did not stop. "Alyssa! *Alyssa!* Where are you?" she shouted.

He grabbed her wrist, whipping her around. "Listen to me!" he shouted.

"Let me go! I have to find my daughter!" Cass realized the slip of her tongue but could not care less. What mattered was finding Alyssa now. That was all that mattered. Tracey would never harm her. Not even with Isabel preying upon her. Alyssa was her daughter, for God's sake.

But Antonio had seized both of her arms and he held her immobilized. "Stop, Cassandra. I am sorry. *I am sorry!*"

"We don't have time for this," Cass said, but she did not pull away. She was about to begin crying. She could feel the tears burning her lids.

"No. We must make time. Listen. She is trying to divide us. I can hardly think clearly. I keep seeing Margarita and I feel such despair and such rage . . . We must not let her come between us. If there is any chance of ever resolving this, we must stand strong, together. *Do you understand what I am saying?*"

Cass felt a tear slip down her cheek. She somehow nodded, even though she was dazed, numb. "She's dividing us," she whispered. "Divide and conquer."

"The way she divided me and my wife, your aunt and my father, my grandfather and grandmother!" He was shaking her.

And Cass met his gaze. "Tracey wouldn't hurt Alyssa . . . would she?"

He cupped her face in both of his hands. "I believe Isabel is far stronger than your sister will ever be. Cassandra. Listen carefully. I love you. I need you. We need each other. Don't leave me now."

Cass did not move, her heart hurting, pounding, and she stared into his eyes.

"Trust me," he said.

Cass's brain felt so strange, it felt dazed, numb, almost incapable of all rational thought, almost incapable of anything but hysteria and panic, yet she knew he was right, she did, and she started to nod.

And his expression changed.

His lips pulled back into a menacing snarl, or an equally menacing leer. His face stretched and tightened, the skin became alabaster-smooth, and his eyes blazed blue with hate.

Cass screamed.

"Cassandra?" It was Antonio holding her, shaking her, now. "Cassandra! I need you! Be strong! Don't let her get to you! Can you understand me?"

She stared at him, one single refrain echoing inside her mind. *Trust me.*

Cass somehow pulled out of his grip. She stared in shock and fear, waiting to see some resemblance to Isabel there in his face, his eyes. *Trust me.*

"I have to find Alyssa."

"Good." He nodded, satisfied. "Let's split up. Downstairs or upstairs?"

"Down." Cass did not wait for him to reply. She could not get the image of him grotesquely becoming Isabel out of her mind. She could not wait to escape. She turned and ran into the great hall, all the while calling for her niece. *I love you. I need you. Trust me.*

She could not.

It was a trap.

The children were not downstairs, not in the courtyard, not in the cottage, the garage, or even hiding in the cars. If only Antonio had already located them upstairs. Cass, standing just outside the front of the house, turned slowly around in a wide arc, not wanting to leave any stone unturned. Her glance settled on the chapel.

It was the only place she had yet to search. A square structure two stories high, it had a red-tiled roof and it was attached to the house. Cass stared. The outer door had been stoned up centuries ago, although Cass did not know why. There were only two windows on the second-story level, both dark stained glass, with a cross in the center of each window. A huge cross had also been engraved on either side of what had once been the front door.

Cass felt the hairs on her nape prickling. She slowly walked back into the house. The chapel could be entered only from an inside door.

As Cass reached for the rusted iron handle on the door, it clicked in her mind that something terrible was going to happen, that she should not open the door. But Cass inhaled, and slowly she swung it open.

Nothing in the world could have prepared her for the sight of her sister, on her knees, praying in front of the altar.

The chapel was ablaze with hundreds of small red candles, and incense that was sweet and cloying, incense that was floral, incense that was unmistakably the fragrance of violets, was burning. Cass was paralyzed.

And Tracey was murmuring aloud, words Cass could not understand or distinguish. Was Tracey praying in a foreign language?

Was she praying in *Latin*?

Cass blinked at stared at her sister again, who was now genuflecting.

Tracey did not have a single religious bone in her body—or so Cass had thought.

I am your sister now.

Cass was afraid. She could not seem to move. Here, then, was proof of their worst suspicions and fears.

Tracey stood up.

"Trace?" Cass managed, a raw whisper, standing with her legs widely braced, ready to run.

Tracey whirled, eyes wide, clearly taken by surprise.

Cass remained dazed. Her mind just would not work; it was as if someone had pulled a switch, shutting it down. "Are you all right?"

Tracey stared at her. Cass did not recognize her sister's eyes—even though she was determined to. "Tracey. What are you doing?" How casual her tone sounded to her own ears.

Tracey stared. "I am praying."

"Since when? I thought you were an atheist." Cass could not move. She took in the entire scene again, the few rows of ancient, tired, scarred wood pews, the smooth, uneven stone floors, the altar with it burning candles, the huge crucifix above. *I am your sister now.*

Cass felt violently ill.

"I am not an atheist," Tracey said, her jaw tightening. "Do not accuse me of atheism. I have never been an atheist. Jesus is the eternal Savior."

Cass could only stare, trembling. She finally said, carefully, "Are you now a Catholic?"

Tracey stared back. "No. I have never been a Catholic." Her chin lifted almost belligerently. "But this place will do. It is a house of God."

I am your sister now. Was Cass speaking with Tracey—or Isabel? "It will do for what?" She could not smile, not even uneasily.

Tracey looked at her with one arched brow. "Maybe you should pray," she said quietly. "It might bring you *peace.*"

Cass began to shiver. "Where did you find the incense?"

"The incense?" Tracey looked around, then gestured at the altar. "It was there." She smiled.

Cass did not smile back.

Suddenly Tracey came forward. Her strides were swift, assured. "I'm finished now."

Instinctively Cass stepped back, keeping herself just out of her sister's reach. Their eyes met and held. "Do you know where the children are?"

"No, but I am sure they are safe."

Cass let her sister walk out of the chapel first. "Where did you take Alyssa earlier? And where is Eduardo?"

Tracey paused in the corridor. "They are safe."

Cass's pulse accelerated. "But where are they? How do you know they are safe?" she begged.

"I know."

"Is it because you are Isabel?" There—she had done it. And Cass braced herself for the worst possible answer.

Tracey finally looked at her. She said, "All has changed, has it not?"

Cass did not move. She could not. She was, in fact, sweating. "What?!"

"I am speaking about you and Antonio."

Cass went rigid. "I don't understand," she said, trying to buy time.

"I think you do understand. You are his lover," Tracey said, her eyes unwavering. It was not a question.

Cass almost choked. Was she talking to Isabel—or wasn't she?

"And you're my sister?" Tracey laughed.

Cass gripped her own head. Sisters. This was her *sister*. Not some damnable ghost. She was speaking to her *sister*. Her temples were throbbing, loudly, like drums, there inside her brain. It hurt. "We're just friends," Cass whispered. "Trace, I love you. I do. I never meant to hurt you. I would never hurt you deliberately. And there's nothing between me and Antonio, there can't be. There just can't be." And there was so much guilt.

But he had said, *I love you,* just minutes ago.

Tracey looked at her as if she did not believe a single word and then she walked away.

Was Isabel in possession of Tracey?

And if so, where did Tracey end and Isabel begin?

Cass stood beside the fire, which was roaring now, hugging herself. The children had vanished. They were nowhere to be found. Tracey had not told her where they were—if she even knew. And Cass wasn't sure that she did know, because she was so strange now, as if in a limbo, caught between her own self and Isabel.

Antonio had used a first aid kit which he'd located in the kitchen to bandage the huge gash on Alfonso's head. The older man was conscious, but lying on the sofa and terribly weak. His head must hurt terribly because he was moaning softly. Celia was also hovering over him, holding his hand. Her maternal instincts were always strong, and she had made a rapid recovery from the mental state she had been in earlier the moment she had seen that Alfonso was hurt.

"How could you have let her get away!" Antonio said angrily, pacing.

Cass felt dazed. She stood by one of the windows, staring out into the night. "That's not fair," she began. Now they could not find Tracey. By the time Cass had followed her into the great hall, she had been gone. A quick search of the house had yielded no results.

"My son is gone! My son and your niece. *That* is not fair!" he cried.

How surreal it had all become. Cass felt removed and detached from herself. And she still could not decipher the conversation that she had had in the chapel with Tracey. Whom had she been speaking with? Isabel or Tracey? Or both?

"She just walked away. I'm sorry. But she said they were safe."

"And you believe her? Tell me again, everything that she said," Antonio said, standing in front of her, blocking her way.

"We've been over this ten times," Cass said, aware of becoming angry. "I don't like being interrogated. I don't like being yelled at."

"She knows where the children are," he returned grimly. "But you let her just walk away!"

"So now it's all my fault?" She was in disbelief.

"Did I say that?" he returned. "How I ever involved myself with that insane woman, I just cannot even begin to fathom it!"

She stiffened. "She is not insane," she said dangerously. "You yourself agree, it's Isabel who is controlling her."

"How can you defend her after all she has done?" He whirled. "Damn it. Where is Gregory?" He paced.

"I can defend her, I will defend her, because she is my sister."

Their gazes locked.

He eyed her. "I think she has gone to wherever it is that she has hidden the children."

"She doesn't know where the children are," Cass insisted.

"And you believe that?" he mocked.

The urge to strike him was sudden, vicious, and overwhelming.

"Don't try it," he warned dangerously.

And just as Cass was about to give in to the urge to hit him, hard, with all of her anger, words he had spoken earlier echoed in her mind. *I love you. Trust me.*

What was she doing?!

"Oh, God," Antonio whispered, in anguish. "Cassandra—"

"She's doing this to us! She is making us hate one another!" She gripped his hand.

He pulled her close. "This is my fault, for I know better. I don't hate you. But the moments of hatred are so pure and so strong. Jesu!" He glanced around, waiting, and wondering, Cass knew, if Isabel would appear. A long moment passed. Isabel did not materialize.

But Cass knew she was present, not far away, watching them. "Antonio," she said, low, still holding his hand. "I can feel her."

"I can feel her, too. She is toying with us."

"But why?" An image of Tracey on her knees, praying before the altar, filled her mind. An image of her serenely denying all knowledge of the children's whereabouts followed. She tightened her grip on his hand. "I have had enough," Cass suddenly flared. "I want to try to communicate with her."

His eyes flashed. "Communicate? Or negotiate?"

"Both," Cass replied unsteadily. She would do anything, even sell her soul to Isabel herself, to get the children back, and safely.

Something banged outside.

Cass almost leapt out of her skin. In unison they whirled, facing the direction the noise had come from. It sounded as if someone or something had crashed into the front of the house.

Another thud sounded, hugely, perhaps against the front door.

"What in God's name is that?" Antonio demanded.

They exchanged glances. "I don't have a clue," Cass whispered. Isabel? Tracey? The wind?

There was no wind. Spain's central plateau was hot and dry in the summer.

Antonio started determinedly forward.

Insanely, Cass wished he were armed. She ran after him. "Stop." She gripped him from behind. "What if we are all wrong? What if a murderer is out there—a real live person, someone armed? You don't have a weapon."

"Your sister might be out there—and she is the most likely murderess I can think of," he replied.

Cass recoiled. "She is not in her right mind."

"And does that justify her sins?" he pressed, striding down the hall.

"Are you now a judge and jury? Are you even the law?" Cass said bitterly.

"I will protect my son—and your family, and you, Cassandra—in whatever way I must."

"Then go answer the fucking door," Cass said coldly.

He turned and answered the door.

And the moment he opened the door, something dark rushed into the room. Cass screamed.

An instant later the something became a someone—Gregory, dark and bloody, crashing prone to the floor at his brother's feet.

Cass cried out again. And she realized Gregory was terribly hurt—his forehead was gashed, and blood had stained one side of his face and his shirt. His clothes were torn and dirty. Antonio dropped down beside him, lifting him into his arms, cradling him.

Cass's heart resumed its beating, erratically. She glanced past the twin brothers, at the open front door—into the yawning chasm of the Castilian night. She didn't think twice. Malevolence filled the night. She ran to the door and slammed it closed, bolting it.

As if bolting it would keep Isabel away.

Then she turned to face the brothers. *What has happened?* "How badly is he hurt?"

"His head is bashed front and back," Antonio said hoarsely. And he held him hard against his chest.

"I'll get the first aid kit," Cass said. *Isabel.* Could Isabel have done this? They still didn't know just what she was physically capable of.

The kit remained in the library. Cass did not wait for Antonio to answer, she ran through the house. And as she ran, it crossed her mind that Tracey wasn't in the house.

No. Tracey could not have done that. Absolutely not.

Cass felt the urge to vomit. Her stomach was so sick. The first aid kit was on the floor beside piles of books. Cass faltered. So was her laptop. But she couldn't ignore Gregory. Without a word, she delivered the kit to Antonio and returned to the library, drawn to her laptop.

Her pulse began a slow, heavy, dreadful pounding, Cass glanced from the laptop to the windows. It was night now. The sky was dark and slick, gleaming black, with very few, very distant stars. Cass shivered and walked over to the laptop, powering on.

Her pulse increased. A message. A negotiation. A plea. How the hell should she proceed?

What did Isabel really want?

Cass cringed. She was certain she wanted vengeance. But that was not the answer she wished to receive.

Cass watched as her Word program came on. She started to choose an oversized font, then realized it did not matter. She typed out the words.

ISABEL. WHAT DO YOU WANT?

Cass hesitated. Then she highlighted the phrase, copied it, and keyed in the function paste—again and again, until her screen was filled with the question.

"Miss de Warenne?"

Cass ignored Celia. It was do or die. Maybe even literally. She had to speak with Isabel, really speak with her, just the way hostage negotiators spoke with kidnappers, but she was only a fiction writer, and a coward to boot.

And the night was only just beginning. The clock in the corner of the library was just striking 10:00 P.M.

ISABEL. WHAT DO YOU WANT? Cass typed again.

"Cassandra," Celia cried with urgency and desperation.

Cass's gaze flew from her screen to the older woman. But Celia wasn't even looking her way. She was gazing beyond Cass, at the doorway.

Slowly Cass turned.

Tracey stood in the doorway, staring at her, her blue eyes brilliant, piercing. "Yes?" she said.

And Cass knew it was Isabel.

TWENTY-FOUR

LONDON—JUNE 3, 1555

London with its many towers, spires, and rooftops came into view as the Flemish ship bearing Isabel, Helen, and her infant son moved up the Thames. The waters were sluggish and black, the air was thick and wet, it was unusually hot out, and Isabel had already heard that the sweating sickness had come yet again to London. But the city was the most wondrous sight she had ever beheld, and as she stared past the Tower Bridge to Saint Paul's graceful spires, tears filled her eyes. Home. She had come home at last.

"I never expected to see the city so soon, and not under these circumstances," Helen said quietly.

Isabel's pulse pounded. She did not reply. Helen only knew half of the truth. Isabel bent to kiss the head of her son, Philip, named in honor of the Spanish king and Queen Mary's husband. She was afraid.

"I hope your husband will forgive you, Isabel," Helen admonished.

Isabel looked at her grim expression. Helen thought Isabel had left Spain to surprise her husband, bearing the gift of their child. But she was wrong.

Isabel had run away—and she never intended to return.

The ship was sliding into its berth. Isabel kissed Philip again, who slept peacefully in her arms. He had been born easily, awakening with a howl—and he was pale of complexion, his hair so blond it was almost white, his eyes brilliantly blue. Isabel had never loved anyone the way she loved her child. When she looked at him, the most wondrous feeling, a blending of joy and love which made her feel as if she might take wing and fly off into the sky, filled her breast. And when she looked at him, she also saw Rob.

Alvarado, should he ever glimpse the child, would instantly know the truth.

"Well?" Helen said, "We must make inquiries and find out where the court now resides. We must not set a single foot in the city with so many dead about."

"The court is at Oatlands," Isabel said nervously.

"Good. I will make arrangements for a litter and horses," Helen said.

She had turned away. Isabel caught her arm. "We are not going to court, Helen," she said quietly.

Helen blinked. "I beg pardon?"

"You did hear me the first time. We are not to court." Isabel stared.

Helen's hands fisted on her hips. "And what monkey mischief are you about now, Isabel?"

"We are to Carew Hall. We are to Lord Montgomery."

Helen stared at her as if she had spoken Latin or Greek.

"I am leaving my husband. Do not say one word! My decision is final, and Douglas will help me." But even as she spoke, Isabel was aware of precisely what it was that she was doing—and of the price she could pay. Her husband was not a lenient or even a kind man. He would never forgive her this treachery. He would seek to somehow punish her for it.

But Isabel had no choice. The child was clearly not his. And she needed Rob, desperately. She needed him as her lover, her friend, and the father of her son. Surely he would keep them both safe—especially as he was now a widower. He could hardly turn away his mistress and the mother of his child.

She assumed he was at court. But she did not dare seek him out there—for her husband would be there, as well. She needed a go-between.

Montgomery had said if ever she needed a friend, he would be there.

She needed a friend now.

Helen stared, aghast. "You have lost all of your wits," she said finally. "And I beg you, do not do this!"

Tears filled Isabel's eyes. "Helen, he will take one look at Philip and know the truth."

"Not if you convince him that your son resembles you!" Helen cried. They had never discussed the issue of Philip's paternity, just as they had never discussed Isabel's affair. But Isabel was certain that Helen knew all.

Isabel now stared, because she had never seen her companion so agitated—her mouth was actually trembling, as if she might weep real tears. "I cannot live my life with him. I cannot live in that cold, inhospitable land, in that dark, dreary, melancholic house, growing old, not just in age, but in humor, in my heart. I cannot stand being surrounded by servants who despise me because I am a foreigner, servants who do not understand a word I say. I cannot bear waiting for him to return, waiting to please him, to bear him another son, when I cannot even tolerate his touch. Not when it is another that I love. And does not Philip deserve to know his real father?"

Helen reached for the railing. She had paled considerably. "Philip's father is Alvarado de la Barca. You destroy yourself," she whispered. "May God have mercy on you."

"Isabel?" Montgomery came striding into the hall of the manor house he had inherited from his first wife, eyes wide. He halted at the sight of them all, his gaze on Isabel.

She could not look away from his mesmerizing eyes, not for a very long moment, and in that moment her pulse seemed to riot uncontrollably. Isabel was nearly paralyzed.

He recovered first, coming forward, his gaze now slipping to Helen and the baby, and then he bowed over her hand. "Countess, what a surprise. I thought you to be happily in Spain—in your husband's lands." He looked up, his gaze searching.

Isabel felt like weeping. "I beg a word with you privately, my lord."

His blue eyes moved over her face, slipped to her beautiful blond child once again, and he nodded. He took her elbow firmly. "Come with me."

A moment later he was closing the door to a small chamber, and they were alone.

Isabel's heart continued to beat with undue force. It was so hard to speak.

He studied her. "I am afraid of what happenstance it is that brings you to me," he finally said quietly.

"You told me once, not long ago, that you would be my friend if ever I was in need," she replied breathlessly—desperately.

He nodded, grim. " 'Twas a vow I made, not just to you, but to myself. I do not break my word, Isabel."

He was an astounding man, Isabel thought wearily. A fine, honorable man. "My husband does not know that I am in England."

"I suspected as much." He came forward, gripping her arms, worry etched all over his strong face. "Isabel—"

"I have run away," she cried.

He paled.

She just stared at him, beginning to tremble, an image of her beautiful child there in her mind. "I fear for my son's life, dear God. I fear God will punish him for *my* sins. I fear my husband's wrath when he sees Philip. I fear to become old and haggard, unloved and alone, I fear so much, Douglas . . . I fear to die in that horrid land and to remain there for all eternity!" And it was a plea.

Somehow he moved closer, somehow she was in his strong, solid, oddly familiar embrace—as if he had held her this way, intimately, as lovers do, many times before. But of course, he had not. "No, do not fear," he murmured, as Isabel became aware of his height and strength and even the warmth of his body.

"I cannot go back," Isabel whispered. Her skirts were crushed against his thighs, his arms were hard around her back, and suddenly their eyes met. And she knew. She knew as surely as she knew the sun would set that night that he would kiss her, and he did.

For a brief eternity, his lips plied hers, soft and tender, and then suddenly they stepped apart.

Isabel stared at him in shock.

His expression was hardly stunned. It was grim.

She backed away. Her hand found her mouth. "I . . . I came here to beg a favor," she heard herself whisper roughly. "I came here to beg you to get word to Rob."

He laughed harshly, once. "I suspected so."

"The child—"

"Is de Warenne's," he finished for her. "Isabel, you play with fire. You must not continue this deadly game. De la Barca will never forgive you your treachery."

"And that is why I have run away!" she cried. "That, and I cannot live without love, having found it once. Can you not understand?"

"Did you find love with de Warenne?" he asked angrily.

She did not like his look or his tone. "Of course I have."

He stared, jaw flexed. There was so much anger in his eyes, on his face.

"Why do you look at me that way? Why?" She was growing frightened.

"I want you to return to your husband. Mark me well, Isabel—I, who love you unselfishly. De la Barca will hunt you down if you do this, and no one, not even I, will be able to protect you from his wrath."

She shivered. "How can I return? How? The child is obviously Rob's. And Rob will protect me—he will protect us."

"You will lie through your teeth," he nearly shouted. "You will love him and lie to him, and convince him the child is his!"

Isabel shrank away, for she had never seen him in such a temper.

He paced. And when he faced her, he had recovered his composure, but barely and with difficulty. "Isabel. I am afraid he will kill you for this. You must go back to him."

She hugged herself. "He will kill me if I return, even if I lie, slowly, minute by minute, hour by hour, day by day. I hate Spain! I hate the Spanish people! And his touch." She shuddered. " 'Tis Rob I love and need," she implored.

He strode to her. And suddenly he was shaking her. "When will you awaken? When?" He was shouting again.

"I do not comprehend you," she cried. "And you are hurting me!"

He released her. But his fists remained clenched. "Rob de Warenne serves no master but himself. Yet to do so, he must be very clever. Your husband serves the queen's husband. Can you not understand? De Warenne will never risk his neck to keep you and the child!" He was shouting at her again.

"You are wrong," she said, tears falling. "You are wrong."

He turned away, but Isabel had glimpsed something in his eyes, and she rushed after him. "What is it that you know that you do not tell me?" she cried.

He slowly turned, but did not speak.

Panic filled her, and with it, an inkling. "Douglas?" She could barely utter his name.

"He has a new mistress, Isabel."

OATLANDS—JUNE 5, 1555

She lay in his bed, ravaged. Her mind refused to think. There was only the heartrending pain in her breast, a pain she had been living with for the past two days.

In the antechamber outside, she heard Philip begin to cry, but she could not get up. The hungry cries ceased. Isabel heard Helen hushing the child, and in her mind's eye, she could envision her companion rocking her son.

Rob has a new mistress.

Her grief knew no bounds; it was unbearable.

"My God, what is this?" her husband exclaimed in the antechamber.

Isabel's entire body stiffened with tension. He had come; the games would now begin.

The games she would play for the rest of her life.

Isabel wanted to die.

They were speaking, her husband and Helen, but Isabel hardly heard. She must recover all of her composure now, all theatrical abilities, for she must deceive her husband and deceive him well. Her son's life and future were at stake. And that was why she would live—and outwit her master now.

His heavy, heeled footsteps sounded. Isabel knew he paused on the threshold of the bedchamber, and she opened her eyes, sitting up slowly.

He stood there, staring, a resplendent figure in a burgundy velvet waistcoat that was bejeweled and embroidered. His eyes were wide; he did not smile.

Isabel smiled. "Surprise, my lord," she said softly—seductively.

He remained motionless.

Isabel slipped from the bed, clad in a low-cut crimson gown gilded with gold thread. Her bosom was mostly bare, her waist nipped in to impossible dimensions. And she had bathed in her favorite fragrance—violets. The scent seemed to fill the room.

His gaze slid over her. "Indeed, this is a surprise," he said, in heavily accented but precise English.

Isabel was surprised. "My lord, how well you speak," she cried—as if with delight.

"I have been at court for long enough," he said flatly.

Isabel moved toward him. "I have come bearing you the greatest gift a lady might bear her lord," she said, moving into his arms. "Have you seen your son?" And she pressed against him, smiling.

His hands closed on her shoulders, and it went through Isabel's numb, dazed mind that she was succeeding in yet another deceit. He said, "And is it my son, my dear?"

It took her a moment to comprehend his words, as she had been rising up onto her toes to kiss his cheek. She blinked.

"Did you not hear me?" he asked, dangerously low.

Oh God, he was aware of the truth, of her betrayals and treachery, of her adultery. Isabel's instinct was to step back, away from him, but she did not do so, overcoming a sudden, vast revulsion for the man she had married. Indeed, she pressed closer to him. "Of course, my lord. What kind of question do you ask? Do you jest now, about our son?" she said, coyly, batting her lashes at him. When her pulse had found a new and frantic beating, one filled with a real and awful fear.

He released her so abruptly that she stumbled and would have fallen had she not landed against the wall. He disappeared, only to reappear with pages of vellum in his hand. He shook them at her. "Is it my son?" he demanded, his eyes as black as a thunderstorm.

She was unable to comprehend what he was doing—and what it was that he held. "Of course," she said, and she smiled. "How could you doubt me?"

He smiled at her, but the smile was merciless, and he read, " 'My dearest Rob, My heart so aches for home and all there that I hold dear. Oh, Rob, there are not words enough in the English language for me to describe to you my loneliness and anguish.' " He looked up at her, dropped her letter to the floor, and read anew. " 'My dearest cousin, Too much time has passed since last we spoke. I recollect our many conversations, with both sadness and joy, and with longing, and look forward to many more. How fare you and the child, dearest Isabel?' "

Isabel stared at him, stunned. He had her letters. He had Rob's letters. The implications were only just beginning to sink in.

He strode to her and flung the page filled with Rob's carefully scripted handwriting into her face. "Should I continue, dearest Isabel?"

He had intercepted her letters. He had stolen Rob's letters. She began to tremble, and she was truly afraid.

"I did not believe it, you know," he said savagely. His entire body was shaking. "The rumors of you and him. My beautiful wife, cuckolding me, not behind my back—in front of my face. I did not believe any of it, not even when I saw the way de Warenne would watch you—for so many of the courtiers would watch you as he did, Isabel, my beauteous wife. But then, then I saw this." He bent and grabbed the letter she had written to Rob on the eve of last Christmastide. "And then I saw his letters to you! Speak, goddamn you, speak!"

He was shouting, he was enraged, but Isabel could not move, not even to save herself from his wrath.

"Will you not speak?" he screamed.

Tears came—and fell. "I have loved him since I was fifteen," she whispered.

He struck her. So hard that she knew he had shattered the bones in her face, and she fell, sobbing, to the hard stone floor.

In the antechamber outside, she heard Philip begin to cry.

And above her, she heard Helen plead, "My lord, have mercy on her, please."

"Get out!" Alvarado shouted.

The kick to her ribs took her by surprise, and she curled over, overcome by waves of excruciating pain. But he was hauling her upright to her feet. "Is the child mine?" he shouted at her as she staggered in the throes of dizziness.

"No," Isabel heard herself say.

He backhanded her another time across the face and Isabel was knocked anew to the floor.

"Whore," he shouted down at her, and then she heard him move, whirl, leave. The door slammed shut behind him.

Isabel began to weep, as much from the pain as from the fear.

"Oh God." Helen knelt over her, her hands soft.

Isabel cried out.

"Oh, God! Let me get compresses, oh, Isabel!" Helen leapt up and was gone.

Philip was howling now.

Philip. Her son. Rob's son.

No, not Rob's son, never his son—only hers. She had to get up, she had to go to her son, and together they must flee—for their very lives.

Isabel tried to push herself up onto her hands and knees. But the pain in her middle was so intense that she cried out instead, and then the waves of blackness came.

Isabel fought, and failed.

The darkness fell, and it was a brief blessing.

OATLANDS—LATER THAT NIGHT

Can you hear me? Isabel?"

Isabel heard Helen, but her voice was so odd and so distant. And then there was the pain, so much of it. Her face throbbed, but that was nothing in comparison to the burning agony in her rib cage—and that within her breast.

"Isabel, sweet, please, can you hear me?"

Helen. Oatlands. Montgomery . . . Rob had a new mistress and her husband had discovered the truth. Isabel was suddenly awake. *Philip!*

"Thank God," Helen cried.

Swimming in pain, Isabel looked up at her frantic companion. "Philip! Where is he?"

"Shh," Helen soothed, stroking her brow. "He is asleep in the next room."

"No!" Isabel tried to sit up, but the moment she moved, she was so dizzy she began to wretch. And that was so painful she wept.

"Be still! The doctor says you have broken ribs. Please, be still," Helen begged.

The pain would not ease. Isabel rode wave after wave, eyes screwed shut, all the while desperately aware of the fact that she must seize her son and escape Alvarado and his wrath. But how? When she was so wounded she could not even rise from her bed.

Montgomery.

She met Helen's gaze. "Go to Douglas, now. Tell him what has passed. He must help me and my son—we must run, now, tonight." Even speaking cost her dearly, and she was panting for breath through the fierce, unrelenting pain.

Helen, bless her soul, did not argue, for once. Instead, she was on her feet. "I do not want to leave you," she said. "But there is no messenger we can trust."

"Go. Go now," Isabel cried. And tears streamed down her face.

Helen nodded, hesitated, then left. Isabel finally heard the outer door slam. Thank God. Within hours, Montgomery would be at court, and Isabel knew he would move heaven and earth to rescue her.

Rob's image came to mind and a new pain was added to all of the old ones, and with it, for the first time, a deep and profound regret.

How foolish she had been.

Banging sounded on the outer door.

Isabel tensed, wide-eyed, as the banging increased and a servant rushed to answer it. She could not quite see all the way across the other room, but she heard many men entering, their booted footfalls loud, swift, approaching. Isabel stiffened even more, suddenly no longer aware of the terrible pain she was afflicted with. Every instinct she had told her to be afraid. Dread filled her.

And a soldier wearing the chancellor's badge appeared on the threshold of her chamber, surrounded by his guard.

Isabel sat up.

"In the name of God and the pope, you are hereby under arrest," he said.

"Arrest?" And even as Isabel managed to utter the word, his men swarmed around her bed, and she was being removed from it.

"Arrest! In God's name, for what?" And even as she cried out, she was being pushed to her feet, and suddenly her arms were forced behind her back, manacles locked on.

"You have been charged with the most heinous crime of all, the crime of false and treacherous beliefs, the crime that is against God," the soldier told her grimly.

Isabel gasped. Unable to comprehend what was happening . . . She was being charged with heresy? "This is a terrible misunderstanding," she cried as the soldiers propelled her across the room. The pain stabbed through her, repeatedly, like a knife. "Where are you taking me?" No one bothered to answer her—or even look at her, for that matter, as they dragged her out.

"Please, where are you taking me!" she screamed as she was wrestled through the last doorway.

And the sergeant in charge finally answered her. "The Tower," he said.

TWENTY-FIVE

Her mother did not want her. Her mother did not love her. Her mother wanted her dead.

Alyssa almost wanted to die.

Tears slid soundlessly down her face, even though she was trying so hard not to cry. She was so cold and so afraid. If her mother didn't want her to die, then why had she locked her and Eduardo in this horrible black place? Then why hadn't she come back? It was so hard to keep the tears at bay. Her heart had never before hurt like this. But now she understood why Tracey never came home.

Mommy, Mommy, she kept thinking.

"Alyssa?" Eduardo's whisper was a sudden hiss in the dark night.

"Yes?" Trying not to allow tears to creep into her voice. She wanted to be braver, like Eduardo, but she wasn't brave at all. She was only seven years old, and she wanted her aunt desperately.

Aunt Cass would come. Alyssa was sure of it.

Alyssa knew she would hug her forever when she came for them.

Eduardo took her hand. "Are you strong enough to try calling for help again?" he asked. Alyssa heard the note of anxiety in his voice.

"I'll try." But Alyssa didn't think she could shout anymore. They had shouted and shouted for help, for what seemed like hours and hours, at the top of the small, narrow staircase where they sat huddled together now. No one had answered their cries. Her throat hurt badly; it was raw and dry, as if she were really sick.

"This time they'll hear us," Eduardo said with a confidence Alyssa knew he did not really feel.

And the tears began again, and this time they would not stop.

Alyssa wept.

"Please don't cry," Eduardo pleaded. "They'll find us soon."

How could this be happening?

What if they were never found?

Was this what had happened to Eduardo's mother?

"I want my aunt Cass," Alyssa sobbed. "But they're never going to find us and we are going to die!"

Cass could not move.

Stunned, she stared at her sister standing on the threshold of the library. And it somehow clicked in her shocked brain that she had just tried to communicate to Isabel, and now Tracey was there.

Tracey had responded. Not Isabel.

Because they were one and the same.

"Yes?" Tracey said again, and it was a question.

Cass shivered. "Isabel?" she asked cautiously.

"Yes. What is it that you want?" Tracey's eyes, which seemed oddly unfocused, went from Cass to Celia and back again. She did not look at Alfonso.

Cass shot a glance at Celia, saw her tear-filled eyes and the fear on her face. Alfonso had passed out. "Where are the children? What have you done with them?" Cass asked as cautiously as before.

"I told you. They are safe."

Cass stared, trembling. *I told you.* "But where are they? Please! Please tell me."

"I cannot." And Tracey smiled.

The smile was cold, chilling. Goose bumps broke out all over Cass's body.

Tracey turned to walk away.

At any other time, Cass might have run after her and gripped her from behind. She did not do so. She did not even move. "What do you want?" she asked hoarsely as Tracey moved through the doorway. "What is it that you want?!"

Tracey faltered. Slowly she turned back to Cass. Her blue eyes were brilliant in their intensity. "I want that which is fair and just."

Cass felt her gaze blurring, her knees knocking together at the very same time. Sickness, dread, swamped her. She could hardly stand. "We all want justice. We can have justice. We can. Tra—Isabel. Do not involve the children! Please!"

But Tracey—rather, Isabel—wasn't listening; she was leaving the room.

"We must find peace!" Cass cried. "There has to be peace, Isabel, *peace* between the two families! Please!" she sobbed.

Cass realized she was gripping Antonio's desk for support, watching her sister walk away, down the hall, through her tears. Should she follow her? Would she lead her to the children?

Cass began to shake uncontrollably. "Isabel!" she screamed. "Do not go!"

Tracey glanced back at Cass, once, without pausing.

Cass sank onto the desk, her mind spinning uselessly now—like a car spinning its wheels in the mud.

She wanted justice.

Cass was afraid of what that meant.

Celia cried out.

"What is it?" Cass inhaled, turning.

"The computer," Celia whispered.

Cass turned, stared. A message blinked at her from the screen.

PEACE IS DEATH.

Cass found Antonio standing over his brother, eyes wide, face set, legs braced. Tracey faced him.

Cass was breathless and desperately thinking. *Peace is death.* She did not have to dwell upon the meaning of Isabel's message. She wanted—intended—to kill someone, if not them all.

"What's going on?" Cass asked, breaking the silence filling the great hall. Gregory, she saw, was conscious and alert, his pupils dilated, his eyes too wide and focused on Tracey.

Antonio did not move or speak. His gaze was hard, and also directed at her sister.

Cass was sweating. "What happened?" She was terrified. Because she had to face the facts. Tracey was not herself. She was under Isabel's control. It seemed more than likely now that she had hidden the children and murdered the electrician. And Cass did not dare wonder what she had done with the children. Not now.

Cass was shaking. Antonio had murder in his eyes, and Cass knew she had to protect Tracey, yet somehow they had to destroy Isabel, too.

And they still did not have a clue as to how to do so.

Tracey's back was to Cass. Cass heard her say, "He's alive." The statement was just possibly surprised, and it interrupted Cass's thoughts.

Cass's inside curdled.

"My brother is very much alive," Antonio said harshly.

Cass moved past Tracey, giving her a wide berth and aware of her extreme caution, to stand next to Antonio.

Bits and pieces of all of her recent conversations with Antonio flooded her now, including the one in which they had agreed that Isabel was trying to divide them in order to conquer them. Cass glanced at Tracey, but she saw no expression at all on her masklike face. Cass stiffened. Did her sister's face seem different? Fuller, less gaunt? Her eyebrows thinner, more arched? But that was impossible!

Antonio bent to his brother now, who tried to wave him away.

"I'm fine now," Gregory said. "Exhausted, but fine."

"You are not fine," Antonio said, cleaning the gash on his forehead. "A maniac ran you off the road. You were almost killed!"

Cass glanced at Tracey's impassive face. Now, looking at her, she thought she could see a resemblance to Isabel—which she had never seen before. She began to shake, told herself she was imagining it. And suddenly she recalled another piece of the puzzle. Hadn't someone told her that Catherine had begun to resemble Isabel in the days just before Eduardo's death?

She was trembling. She stole another glance at Tracey. Goddamn it. She did look somewhat like Isabel. Even her hair seemed reddish now. Was it a trick of the light? Or a trick of her own mind?

Cass reminded herself that Isabel preyed on people's minds.

Antonio was putting an ointment on the gash on Gregory's forehead. "Is that what happened?" she asked, watching.

Gregory looked at her. "It's worse than that. But you won't believe me, I don't think." He glanced at Tracey again. "Is she all right?"

Cass hesitated, her gaze going to her sister. Her lips seemed narrower, her nose straighter, her eyes wider apart. Something inside Cass was crumbling. Maybe it was what was left of hope.

"She's fine," Cass lied, her skin prickling with unease. Tracey wasn't fine, but just where did Tracey end and Isabel begin? What if Tracey was completely gone—what if there was nothing left of her at all? And what would Antonio do if he knew about their conversation in the library? Cass couldn't trust him anymore. "What else happened?"

I love you. Trust me.

Cass forced the memory aside.

Gregory suddenly shoved at Antonio. "Ouch, damn it!"

Antonio's reply was terse and foreign.

"It was Isabel. She tried to kill me. She was somehow behind the wheel of the truck that drove me off the rode," Gregory said.

Cass stared.

"I don't think a woman who died in 1555 would know how to drive," Antonio said grimly. "Shall I bandage your knee?" he asked. "It might help."

"I think it will be better after some rest," Gregory said. "I only know what I saw," he told them both defensively. His gaze was on Tracey again.

Cass was no longer watching the brothers, she was staring at Tracey.

Coolly, with extreme composure, Tracey met her gaze. There was a knowing light in her eyes.

Antonio said, "Maybe it was your mind playing tricks on you. Or maybe Isabel was playing tricks on your mind."

"And some madman drove me off the road?" Gregory asked sarcastically—angrily.

Cass had been squatting, and now she rose to her full, if diminutive, height. "What do you think?" she rasped.

Tracey stared. That odd, nearly smug light flickered in her eyes. She said, "I do not drive."

"No. You do not drive. But others drive, don't they?"

Tracey smiled. "Others drive," she said softly.

And Cass knew. She had taken over the truck driver's mind.

"Who are you?" Cass demanded. And she was acutely aware of the two men watching them, listening to their every word. But she could not seem to contain herself.

"You know who I am."

Cass backed up. Her heart hurt her, it beat so hard. "You're not my sister, are you?"

"I am your sister," Tracey said with another small smile. "Now."

Antonio lunged to his feet.

Cass realized what he was about, saw him coming, and tried to grab him and detain him, but she might as well have tried to stop a locomotive. He shoved her aside, so roughly that she fell to her knees, hard. And he grabbed Tracey by the arms, shaking her.

"What have you done to the children, you bitch?" he roared.

Tracey's eyes changed. They paled impossibly, brilliantly, blindingly. And she flung him away.

Cass cried out as Antonio hit the floor. How did her sister have the strength to jettison a six-foot man who weighed close to two hundred pounds? she wondered, stunned. And the answer was obvious. Her sister's energy knew no bounds—it was supernatural.

Antonio was enraged as he climbed to his feet. Mouth tight, jaw flexed, he launched himself at Tracey. Too late, Cass screamed at him. "Stop! You will kill each other!"

And he lunged at Tracey.

But Tracey remained on her feet, and it was stunning. The momentum carried them both backward, toward the door leading to the courtyard. And then they were in a hand-to-hand struggle, Tracey holding her own, remaining upright, with a superhuman effort. Antonio could not seem to wrestle her into submission or down to the floor. He could not even force her hands down and behind her back.

Tracey raked her nails down his face, leaving a bleeding set of claw marks.

Cass looked wildly around for a weapon, aware of Gregory climbing unsteadily to his feet. There was only the first aid kit, and as she grabbed the box, its items spilling, she watched Gregory charge her sister and his brother.

Later, Cass could not say whether the act was contrived on Tracey's part. But as Gregory rushed the pair, Tracey moved aside, taking Antonio with her. And Gregory ran headfirst into—and through—the glass doors opening onto the courtyard.

Cass screamed as the glass shattered upon impact and he cried out, lurching onto the ground on the other side, like a man on fire—except he was covered with blood and glass.

Antonio broke free of Tracey, his attention diverted. Cass saw blood everywhere.

And then, from the corner of her eye, she saw Tracey picking up a long, lethal-looking piece of glass. Lifting it high.

"Antonio!" Cass screamed in warning.

Using the shard as she might a knife, Tracey plunged it into Antonio's back.

His eyes went wide in shock and surprise, and then he keeled over, face-first.

Cass stood frozen, and her gaze locked with Tracey's.

Tracey dropped the glass, gave Cass one hard look, and turned and fled.

Cass moved. She ran to Antonio, using both palms to cover the wound on his back. "Tonio?"

"Gregory," he gasped.

Cass held him, still covering the wound with her hands, then she let him go, tore her T-shirt off, and used that wadded up, holding it tightly to the wound. "Let me take care of this first," she cried. And she realized that if he died, she would never, ever be the same because she loved him with all of her heart.

He lay facedown on the floor, but his head was turned to one side, his eyes screwed shut. They opened, filled with pain. "I'm fine," he gritted. "Let me up. I'll kill her."

Cass went rigid. "No! That's my sister—even if she is possessed— and you are not going to kill her!"

"She's taken the children," Antonio shouted, and then he shut his eyes again, gasping.

Cass put more pressure on the wound. Her temples throbbed, there was a ringing in her ears, and she could not think clearly. But what if the children were dead? Clearly Isabel wanted to kill Antonio and his brother. Did she want to kill Tracey? Did she want to kill Cass? Cass closed her eyes hard.

Peace is death.

"How are we going to stop her?" Cass whispered in despair. Her heart felt as if it were being wrenched in half. She was so afraid for Tracey. But she was even more afraid for the children and for Antonio.

Antonio did not answer.

Cass blinked back hot tears and looked down at him. He had passed out.

She froze. And she was suddenly enraged. She needed help, Goddamn it, she did. How could he pass out now? Damn him!

And then she felt tears, and she regretted her thoughts, her anger, but it was all Isabel's doing, Isabel was infecting them all—and she had been doing so ever since they had first arrived at Casa de Sueños. Or was it since Tracey had come home to Belford House with Antonio for the black-tie affair?

And just how bad was his wound? And what about Gregory?

Carefully Cass lifted her T-shirt, but it was sticking to the wound as the blood clotted, which she prayed was a good sign. There were a few bandages left. She would bind the wound tightly, leaving her T-shirt in place, she decided frantically. And then she would confront her sister.

No. *She would confront Isabel.*

A few minutes later she had bandaged Antonio's back. Cass hurried over to Gregory, but he was so badly cut everywhere, including his handsome face, that she didn't even know where to begin. She only knew one thing. Isabel had done something with the children, and Isabel had possessed her sister. She didn't want to leave Gregory, not like this, but she had no choice. Isabel had to be stopped. The children had to be saved.

And Cass was very afraid. Everyone present at Casa de Sueños had been hurt by Isabel—except for herself. The odds seemed to indicate that she would soon become Isabel's next victim.

Somehow there had to be a way to outwit her. Outwit her and destroy her.

Cass slowly stood, straining now to hear, trying to overcome her own violent trembling and her equally violent fear. But the night in the courtyard was resoundingly silent. There weren't even crickets to break the silence. Not an owl, not the whir of a fan, the crackle of the fire in the library, nothing.

Just the silence of the vast Castilian night.

She wet her lips. Her pulse was in overdrive. Every fiber of her being was on alert. This was, she knew, the worst moment of her life.

A goddamn nightmare come true.

And she stepped back into the house, standing just inches away from Antonio, straining to hear something, anything.

More silence greeted her. It was vast, absolute.

"Where are you?" Cass said aloud. But her voice was a mere whisper.

"Where are you?" she tried, louder now, her own pulse deafening. "Where are you?!"

There was no answer.

Tracey had disappeared down the corridor leading to the bedrooms she and Cass had used. Cass looked around. Before she went down that corridor, she needed to arm herself. Because Tracey had supernatural strength.

Cass finally picked up a long, thin shard of glass, wrapping one end with what was left of the bandages. Her heart continued its drumlike beat. She refused to think about what she might have to do to defend herself. She started down the corridor, quickly leaving the lighted hall behind. Alfonso had not bothered to place any tapers in this end of the house—just her damnable luck.

Every doorway made her slow and then pause, waiting for Tracey to jump out at her from behind.

Cass squinted at the stairs. She was afraid to go up, afraid of what might greet her there, afraid of what—and whom—she would find.

The library was directly across the courtyard, and because of the fire roaring in the hearth there, it shed some light. Cass started up the steps, and she could only think, *Afraid, afraid, afraid.* The fear was overwhelming.

On the landing above, she stopped. "Tracey?"

There was no response.

Cass swallowed. Her own bedroom was to her left, at the end of the house. To her right, just ahead, was Tracey's bedroom and another, unused room. What should she do? Where had Tracey gone?

While Isabel might be able to walk through walls, Tracey could not. She could not have simply disappeared.

Cass suddenly heard a floorboard creak—and the sound came from her own bedroom, which she had not entered since yesterday. She froze.

And then she walked to the door, which was ajar, afraid of what she would find on the other side.

She pushed it slowly open, holding the glass tightly in her hand, behind her back, prepared to raise it and use it if need be.

A yawning blackness greeted her, illuminated only slightly by a few faint stars just outside the bedroom windows.

"Tracey?" Cass tried. Her unease grew. Her every instinct told her that Tracey was inside. "It's me, Cass. I don't want to hurt you. I want to help you."

"Then why are you holding that glass?"

Cass jumped away in shock and fear. Tracey had spoken from behind her, so closely that Cass had felt her breath on her neck. She whirled, glass raised. Tracey stood on the other side of the threshold of her room now, and their eyes met and held.

And Cass realized those were not her sister's eyes. For in them there was no uncertainty, no vulnerability, no emotion, nothing that resembled any humanity at all.

"I want to help," Cass croaked.

Tracey did not seem to move, she did not even seem to breathe, and Cass saw the resemblance to Isabel now; it was there, all right, and not just in her mind. It was as if Tracey's features were slowly changing, bit by bit, the way a great actor's face changes in response to different roles, and suddenly the door slammed closed in Cass's face.

Between them.

Cass cried out, leaping away, only to stand trembling not far from the bed in the center of the room. She was in shock. And just as she was trying to assimilate what was happening—Tracey had obviously slammed the door closed, even if she hadn't seen her move—she heard it lock.

Her eyes widened, and she thought, *No. This is impossible.*

Cass ran to the door and wrenched on it, to no avail. It was firmly locked.

A window slammed behind her.

Cass whirled, but she remained alone in the bedroom; Tracey had not walked through the wall, she was absolutely alone, and surely the window had not slammed closed. And just when she was determined to believe that, another window slammed closed, right in front of her very eyes, followed by another, and another, in rapid succession.

TWENTY-SIX

The Tower—June 8, 1555

There was a small, narrow, barred window high up on the wall of her cell, and as the light inside her prison changed, Isabel was able to track the passage of time. Only two days and nights had passed since her incarceration, but those two days felt like two full years. Seated on the cold, dank, urine-fouled floor, on a pallet that had not been changed in what seemed like years, Isabel held her face to her knees, no longer in a state of shock, but in a state of raw fear.

She had been charged with heresy. Why? How?

She trembled, ill within herself. Had Rob's letter not told her of the burnings of heretics? But surely that would not be her fate.

Many Protestants such as herself outwardly conformed to the queen's faith, and were left alone. In face, she suspected her uncle, Sussex, of being just such a hypocrite. Why had she been singled out for arrest and prosecution?

Alvarado's furious image came to mind and suddenly a weariness that made her feel a hundred years old settled upon her. Her husband was a devout Catholic. He hated her now. Had he a hand in this?

And what of Philip, dear God? What was to become of her son?

Isabel moaned to herself, tears slipping down her face. If she could spare her son Alvarado's wrath, she would gladly die.

Footsteps sounded.

Isabel sat upright, gasping from the pain caused by the abrupt movement. Her broken ribs resulted in ceaseless agony; a blazing fire inside her torso. But now the pain dimmed in comparison to her fear and desperation.

This was a terrible mistake. This could not be her fate. Surely the man—or men—approaching would free her and rectify this terrible situation.

It was midday—the sun outside her window told her that—but nevertheless it was dim with shadow in her ward, and she squinted toward the two men approaching. Did she see clerical robes? Her heart began to sink—and then it soared as she recognized the second man.

Douglas Montgomery gripped the bars from outside her cell, paling as their gazes met. "What has he done to you!" he cried.

For one moment, as Isabel stared at him, her entire life played before her eyes. Too late, she regretted everything—her childish lust for Rob, her refusal of Douglas, her marriage to Alvarado, and her decision to see Rob and continue their affair after her marriage began. She stared at Douglas, saw the love and fear in his eyes, and something flared inside of her.

And with it came an ugly realization. *I have loved the wrong man,* she thought.

Oh, God, I have loved the wrong man, the wrong man has sired my child, and had I chosen differently, this man might have been my lord, my husband, my life.

Tears filled her eyes, burning with the bitterest of regret.

"Douglas," Isabel whispered, trying to hold back the tears.

"How badly are you hurt?" Douglas demanded, gripping the bars so tightly his knuckles turned white. "I will make certain a doctor attends you today."

Isabel slowly got to her feet, cutting off her own cries of pain. She gripped the bars, their hands touching. The effort to stand and walk cost her dearly.

"You are hurt," he whispered, agonized. Through the bars he cupped her cheek.

His touch was a touch she had never before felt, not like that, and inside, with the pain and fear, there came exultation and relief. *I love him,* she thought wearily, eyes closed. *And I will die loving him.*

Her gaze lifted and their eyes locked. "Thank you, Douglas," she whispered.

"For what? I have yet to accomplish what I must do. You will not burn, Isabel." His eyes darkened. "Your husband is behind this. He has betrayed you. Not only does he know of your affair, he suspects you of further treachery, he suspects you of being a spy for the English."

Isabel felt as if she could take little more. "Sussex is my master, and he charged me with the task of spying on my husband. But the information I passed on before I left for Spain was not of grave consequence."

"Does it matter? De la Barca's love has turned to hate. He holds the ear of the king of Spain. Philip holds the ear of the queen. De la Barca is determined to rid himself of you, and what better way than to accuse you of heresy?"

Isabel gripped the bars. "Oh, God. Then there is no hope?"

He slid both hands through the bars to hold her face. "You must repent. Confess your sins and repent, because that is the only chance you have to be spared the stake. I will have Sussex's ear tonight. Together we will move the queen to our cause. Do you comprehend me, Isabel?" And there were tears in his eyes. "Dear God, she is a woman, and she is just, and if anyone might comprehend this impasse, it is she."

She nodded, but she had met Queen Mary once—and seen her many times. She was more than frightened, because if any woman was like a man, it was the queen, who, in spite of her small size, was strong of will and burning with intelligence. She was also burning with devotion to her cause—Catholicism. And Isabel recalled their single meeting very clearly. The queen had not cared for her at all. "Do I confess to my affair with Rob?"

He was grim. "De la Barca has proof, does he not? And the entire court knew of your affair anyway. Do not dissemble. Beg for God's mercy, the church's mercy, and the queen's."

Isabel stared at his beloved face. The air above her felt so heavy, it seemed to be crushing down on her shoulders from above. And she was too weak—and too tired—to hold it up. How easy it would be to let that heavy, deathly weight push her down, to sink to the cold hard floor, and just let God's will bury her alive. "She does not like me," Isabel heard herself say.

Montgomery cursed. And then he leaned forward and kissed her.

Isabel slid her hands through the bars, until she had gripped his arms, and as they kissed, even with the iron bars pressing into their faces, what had begun as something tender and fraught with fear and regret became something else, something wild and wonderful, but oh, so bittersweet. When they parted, tears shone in his eyes as well as hers.

"We will get through this, you and I," he said. "I swear this, Isabel. You will survive."

She believed that he would try. But she was terrified that he would not succeed. And she was afraid to even speak her own worst fears aloud—as if that might help them to come true. "I am frightened for Philip. Douglas, what will happen to my son?"

She saw a dark light pass in his eyes. "Mayhap the boy can foster with me—or even with Rob. I imagine de la Barca will not be too eager to raise the child himself. But let us first see you freed, my dear, and then we will deal with what is to become of your son."

Isabel nodded. "Douglas? Before you go. If there is no mercy, if I am to die, will you vow to me, upon the Bible, that you will make certain Philip is safe?"

He grabbed her hands through the bars. "Do not even speak of such an event! And, Isabel, you need not even ask such of me. I would protect and care for your son the way I do you."

Isabel cried then, helplessly, because she trusted him completely.

WESTMINSTER HALL—JUNE 12, 1555

As Isabel entered the chamber of the court, her steps slowed and she glanced around.

The chamber was filled to overflowing with noblemen and noble-women who had come to see her tried for the gravest crime of all. Ahead of her, at the far end of the room, stood three bishops, including the chancellor, John Gardiner. The queen was not present, but Isabel had known she would not be, for she was still confined and awaiting the long-overdue birth of her child.

Isabel felt faint, her knees were weak, and she thought the air too warm, too stuffy—it was so hard to breathe. Panic gnawed dully within her. How had her life come to this moment in time? What was she doing there, being tried for heresy? Being gawked at like a caged bear in a circus? Her dizziness increased, as did her fear. The crowd was bloodthirsty, she realized. And it was her blood that they wished to spill.

Her gaze suddenly found Helen and she stumbled, unable to con-tinue forward.

Helen's eyes were red and swollen from weeping, her face was grotesquely pale, and she began to weep loudly again.

Isabel felt her own tears slip down her cheeks. She looked at the woman who had been her companion since she was an orphan of eight, a companion she had never trusted and never really liked, and suddenly she realized just how erroneous she had been in her assessment of the woman. Helen could not stop sobbing. Her tears were filled with grief.

Isabel realized that Helen loved her, that she was, in fact, a dear, trustworthy friend. "Helen?" she whispered.

"Have strength," Helen cried. "Oh, Isabel, have strength, and beg for the court's mercy."

"Get back there," one of the guards said, shoving Helen back into the throng that was pressing forward to stare at Isabel.

"Philip?" Isabel cried as two soldiers propelled her along, past Helen. "My son! Helen?"

"He is fine," she cried. "Admiral de Warenne came and took the child into his care the day that you were arrested."

Isabel clapped her hand over her mouth to cut off her cry of relief.

The soldiers were hurrying her down the aisle. A number of lords stood in the front row, and when they turned so they could watch her approach, Isabel espied her uncle, the earl of Sussex, amongst them. And standing directly behind him was Douglas Montgomery.

Her heart turned over, not with fear, but with the most profound emotion of all—true and eternal love.

Their eyes locked.

He was extremely pale, but he managed a smile, and in that smile Isabel saw and felt all of his fear and all of his hope.

"Isabel de la Barca."

Isabel had come to a stop before a chair, which she was rudely pushed down into. At the booming sound of her name, she looked up. The chancellor stood before her.

"You have been charged with heresy. If you confess your sins and repent, the court will have mercy on you. Fail to confess, fail to repent, and know that you will suffer death by fire—and God's eternal damnation in hell."

Isabel stared up at him. Her heart thundered in her breast. "I confess."

"What? Did you speak? Speak now, lady. What is it that you say?"

Isabel heard the chancellor very clearly, but suddenly she was seeing her uncle's masklike face—and he avoided her eyes. She glanced past him at Douglas, who nodded at her, his expression strained. It was then that Isabel realized that Rob had not even bothered to come to witness her trial of life and death.

"You must confess your sins, here and now, and repent your unfaithful ways if you wish for the church, this court, God, and the queen to have mercy upon you."

Her glance found her uncle again. The usurper. But instead of seeing him, she saw her mother, on her knees in prayer in her private—and secret—chapel, her priest performing the mass. Isabel could even smell the sweet incense, she could hear Father Joseph as he droned on in Latin as clearly as if he spoke now, in the court chamber. And her petite, beautiful mother, so earnest in her devotions, was so vivid and so real that Isabel was quite certain that, if she lifted her hand, if she did reach out, she would touch her flesh as she knelt there in the knave of the chapel at Romney Castle. Tears filled Isabel's eyes.

The chancellor was speaking again. Isabel also thought she heard Helen's sobs.

She closed her eyes, envisioning her father then, strong and robust, entering the hall after a hunt, beaming with pleasure. And then he was hugging Isabel, who was but a skinny, six-year-old child, and whispering in her ear how proud of her he was, of his little countess, and Isabel was laughing and promising him that he would always be proud . . .

Her father, who had allowed her mother the freedom to worship as she pleased. Her father, who had loved her unconditionally, and who had himself been a devout Anglican.

Her father, who had given her her faith, her name, and her station in this world.

Isabel began to cry.

It felt like only yesterday that she and her brother, Thomas, had sat in the front pew with their father to worship and pray. Only yesterday . . . but it had been at least twelve frighteningly long years ago.

Isabel blinked back her tears and stood up unsteadily, reaching back for an arm of the chair with which to support herself. It was only then that she realized the chancellor had been shouting at her, and that the crowd had been murmuring loudly in shocked tones. She stared at her uncle.

The usurper. The liar. The master of games of deception, of treachery, and of power.

"You only married me to my husband so I would spy for you," she said, quietly but clearly.

Sussex's eyes widened. And suddenly the crowd was silent and straining to hear.

"But then, there was never any love, was there, for your brother's daughter? I was but another pawn, to be played and used to suit your nefarious schemes," Isabel said bitterly.

"Quiet," the chancellor commanded. "There is to be no conversation with the witnesses present. I ask you for the last time, do you confess to your sins? Do you confess to being a wayward and unfaithful daughter of the one true church, of the pope, and as such, of the queen herself?"

"I confess to being a fool," Isabel said, and the exhaustion she had been living with for days, weeks, years, overcame her then as she turned to Douglas, with a weary smile that was only for him—and it was then that she saw Rob.

He had entered the chamber unbeknownst to her, and now he stood beside Douglas, staring at her, his expression wide-eyed and grave.

And Isabel looked at him and saw nothing to endear him to her. He was hardly as handsome as she had once thought. His face, in fact, seemed weak in comparison to Montgomery's. His cheekbones were not nearly as high as she had once recalled. His chin hardly as pronounced, his jaw hardly as wide. And now he avoided her eyes.

She took in every inch of his appearance, and what she saw was a slender man wearing silk and velvet, embellished with satin and fur and too many ostentatious jewels. She looked back at his face again, and she saw the ravages of time, and then, when she finally glimpsed, briefly, his blue eyes, in their pale, watery depths she saw nothing but lies and self-absorption and grand, unfettered ambition.

And how quickly he did look away.

Isabel smiled at Douglas, trying not to cry and knowing she failed, aware that he was silently begging her to consider what she must now do. In her heart she gave him the rest of her love—what little she had been holding back—and she faced the chancellor. "I confess to having lusted for a man not worthy to wipe the dust from the floor where I now stand. I confess to betraying my wedding vows with the reckless naïveté of youth. I confess to spying for my uncle, the earl, against the better judgment of my heart, my mind, and my soul, and I confess now to loving a strong, brave, and truly noble man, far too late, with too many regrets." Her smile was brief. "And yes, I repent."

"Isabel," she heard Douglas say, anguished.

"You do not confess to the sin of straying from the one true faith?" Gardiner was demanding as the crowd broke into mutters and murmurs of amazement.

Isabel stared at Gardiner, who was rather red of face, so flushed was he with his fanaticism. She glanced at her uncle, and saw only the ruthless promise of vengeance there. She glanced at Douglas, and realized he was crying. And she watched Rob leaving the court chamber, his strides hurried, his face grim and turned down.

She glanced over to her husband. His hatred had not lessened, but that was fine. For she hated him as well. She would never forgive him for how he had abused her, and for what he was now doing to her.

"Speak up now before this court condemns you to death by burning," Gardiner shouted at her.

"I confess to worshiping God as my father did before me, with true faith, true belief, and true devotion. I confess to always worshiping God in this way. I confess to the desire to worship this way for the rest of my lifetime, whatever that might be. I have nothing more to repent," she finally finished. And her pulse was deafening to her own ears now.

Gardiner stared at her in disbelief.

Sussex made a sound.

Douglas cried out, and Helen screamed, "No! Isabel, beg for mercy!"

"I beg," Isabel said, her breath choked in her lungs, crying again, "to be released from this hypocrisy, this sham, this utter pretense, of that which is this life."

Gardiner exclaimed, "So be it. Tomorrow at noon you will suffer the stake." And he strode past her, from the room.

Isabel was on her knees. "God forgive you," she said to Gardiner's back, "your sins, and God forgive me mine."

TOWER HILL—JUNE 13, 1555

Isabel stared at the fagots of wood carefully placed about her legs and feet. As she stared, she watched two men adding kindling to the pile. Her hands were tied behind her back and she was bound to a stake.

A crowd had gathered to watch her die. Men, women, and children, lords and ladies, merchants, gentry, yeomen, apprentices, servants, and even monks, friars, and priests encircled the pyre where Isabel was, and they jeered at her loudly, profanely, calling her "whore," "heretic," "Spaniard," "bitch," and worse. Their curses and cries only made her more numb, more dazed. Isabel felt as if she had been drugged.

One of the men stoking what would become her funeral pyre suddenly touched her legs. Isabel flinched.

"Believe me, you want this, milady," he said almost apologetically.

Isabel saw the sheep bladders he held in his hands.

"Filled with gunpowder," he told her. "Otherwise you'll live while your body burns to a crisp."

Her heart suddenly skipped and then it seemed to beat as if it were a living thing. Isabel watched him attach the bladders to her thighs.

"Oh, God, have mercy," she heard herself whisper. And suddenly she was afraid. "God have mercy," Isabel cried.

Soldiers ringed her pyre. They had appeared from nowhere. Isabel stared at their unmovable faces, and it dawned on her that the time had come. She was about to die.

And she watched one of the two men light the kindling encircling her feet.

The flames hissed and caught.

Terror overcame Isabel. "Oh, God," she screamed. "I don't want to die!"

Too late, too late, she realized she did not want to die, and not like this, for she was a coward, and as the fire rushed along the kindling, she thought about her child and Douglas—she would never see Douglas again, never see or hold or kiss her son, never watch him grow to manhood. "I repent!" Isabel screamed as some of the faggots burst into flames.

The crowd hissed and jeered and booed her, and Isabel knew no one had heard. Worse, she felt the heat touching her heels, her toes. It was so hot . . .

"I repent!" she screamed at the soldiers, but if they heard her, or cared, they gave no sign.

And then she felt the fire as it scorched her toes—and then all of her feet.

Isabel screamed and screamed.

And suddenly she saw the horseman riding through the crowd, wielding his sword, cutting down those in his way. She saw his blazing blue eyes and his curly dark hair and she screamed for Douglas, again and again.

He had come to rescue her, and as her flesh burned, she felt the surging of hope.

"Isabel!" he shouted, driving his steed forward.

And simultaneously two arrows pierced him front and back, but still he rode toward her.

He was going to die because of her, and Isabel knew he must not die—because she loved him and because he was too good and honorable to die and because he must care for her son. But there was no way she could stop him, and then another arrow found its mark and he fell from his horse, which wheeled and galloped away.

"No!" Isabel screamed. "Douglas!"

And then she screamed again, because the fire was burning her feet, and she felt the heat on her legs, then her gown caught, and it went into flames.

She was engulfed.

Isabel stared and suddenly she saw Sussex there in the crowd. Behind him she saw Rob and de la Barca. And someone had dragged Douglas away from the pyre; he was sitting up, he was alive.

And the terror was gone. There was only the pain of hell, indescribable, and through the haze of the flames, there was red, red rage.

"Remember this! All of you!"

The hell worsened, but there was more. And she cried, "I will never let you forget!"

The bladders exploded.

For one split second Isabel felt her limbs tearing away from her body, and then she felt nothing at all.

TWENTY-SEVEN

CASA DE SUEÑOS—MIDNIGHT

The two last windows in the bedroom slammed shut in such quick succession that it was almost simultaneous. And then there was silence.

Cass was paralyzed. She stood unmoving, bathed in sweat, her heart thundering in her ears, stunned and afraid.

The silence did not abate.

Now Cass could only hear her own deafening heartbeat.

Slowly she inhaled, struggling to see. She was reminding herself that Tracey could not walk through walls—but Isabel could. And then Cass moved.

Without thinking, she ran to the closest window and tried to heave it upward. Her intention was to leap out. But even as she struggled to lift it, the locking lever snapped around in front of her very eyes, clicking into place.

Cass cried out and backpedaled, and then stood in shock as the levers on all the windows in the room snapped into the lock position.

Locked in. Isabel had locked her in.

The question was, why?

To hurt her, isolate her, what did it matter? Isabel intended to destroy them all, and right now Antonio and Gregory were badly wounded and as vulnerable as infants. Cass no longer cared how Isabel was accomplishing her feats. All that mattered was that she was capable of real, live action—action meant to destroy them all.

Cass panted, facing the door, expecting to see Isabel materialize at any moment. The door remained closed, a paler shadow in the shadowy room. Cass had to get out.

Then it clicked in her mind that possessed or not, Tracey stood outside that door, Tracey, her sister.

"Trace!" Cass cried, rushing to the door and wrenching on the knob, to no avail. "Trace? Can you hear me?"

"I can hear you," Tracey replied very calmly.

"Please, Tracey, you have to fight her, you have to fight her and help me. Let me out!" Cass cried, her cheek against the wood, a wetness streaming down her face. "Please, Tracey, please!"

"No."

Cass stiffened, hating her sister's strange, detached tone, which was so goddamned final. Then she banged on the door, once, with despair. "Tracey! Tracey, snap out of it! Get that witch out of you! Please, Trace, please!"

There was no answer.

Cass choked back a sob, an image of Antonio lying unconscious on the floor assailing her, and suddenly she was even more terrified. She could not let anything happen to him, she could not! "Tracey!" she screamed, beating on the door.

A whoosh of air sounded behind her, loud and stunning.

Cass whirled, her spine to the door, expecting to see Isabel. Instead, she saw a fire sparking in the fireplace. And before her very eyes, she watched it rapidly grow in size. Within three seconds, two tiny match-like flames had become a full-sized, roaring fire.

Cass was trying to understand how this had happened, what it meant, when the fire became so strong that flames began licking the sides of the marble hearth. She was mesmerized, thinking marble could not burn—when suddenly flames leapt across the space between the hearth and rug, and instantly the Persian rug was aflame.

"Tracey!" Cass screamed, turning, beating on the door. "Let me out, please, I beg you!"

"No."

Cass sank to the floor, sobbing, despairing, her entire life flashing through her eyes. Their mother's funeral, tea after school with Aunt Catherine, hours and hours spent alone in her bedroom, lost in a good book; Tracey and her boyfriends, one after the other, Cass watching, wishing, from the sidelines, until there was Rick Tennant. Cass remembered holding Alyssa in the hospital just after her birth, when she was red faced and funny looking, and as clearly, suddenly, she recalled the very first time she had laid eyes upon Antonio, when he had first walked into the lecture hall at the Met, clad in a black sport jacket, a black turtleneck, and black slacks, his notes under one arm.

Oh, God. What had happened to Alyssa and Eduardo? And what about Antonio, who was unconscious?

"What do you want?" Cass sobbed. "Isabel, damn you! *What do you want?*"

"You know what I want," Tracey said very calmly from the other side of the door.

And Cass did.

The heat of the fire behind her was so intense it was starting to burn her bare back. Cass jumped to her feet—but there was nowhere to run.

Isabel intended to burn her alive.

Just as Isabel had burned to death.

Tracey had the feeling she was on a train, one speeding along at hundreds of miles an hour, uncontrollably, passing stop after stop. She wanted to get off. She wanted the train to stop. But the train wasn't even slowing down, and there was no way she could get off.

It was like a dream. A horrible, frightening dream that refused to end. The kind of dream where you had to run or you would die, but your feet refused to obey the commands of your mind and would not move, bringing death close and closer still. Was she dreaming? Tracey wanted to wake up.

Was that Cass, her sister, screaming at her? Begging for her help?

But her voice sounded far away, and anyway, it was only a dream, wasn't it?

A dream—the night—that woman—Isabel.

Cass's cries for help continued. Tracey stared blankly at the door as the odor of burning wool assailed her. She should open the door, she somehow thought. Instead, her body turned and her feet moved and she began walking downstairs.

No, Tracey thought, suddenly touched with a surge of panic. *I must go upstairs, I must let Cass out.*

No, she replied to herself. *Everything is fine, you must go downstairs. Peace is death.*

Peace. Tracey closed her eyes briefly as she entered the corridor, which was nearly black. Peace is death. How she wanted peace.

"Tracey!" Cass screamed from upstairs.

Tracey stumbled even though her legs refused to stop carrying her forward. More panic filled her—she wanted to turn around and go back upstairs.

No. Everything will be fine. Trust me, Tracey heard herself think.

Tracey wanted to trust herself. She wanted peace. God, she did. Then why didn't she trust herself? Her legs would not obey her mind anyway. She could not seem to stop her body's forward motion just like she could not get off the train . . .

Trust me . . . Peace is death . . .

There was calm in the mantra. Tracey reached the great hall, the panic subsiding. She could do this, she could. As long as she trusted herself.

Yes. Trust me.

The words washed over her, a soft, seductive whisper.

The tapers that had been left burning in the hall had all gone out except for two, and most of the hall was in shadow. Tracey stared at Antonio, lying on the floor. He appeared to be dead. Then she stared toward the shattered glass door, at Gregory's equally prostrate form.

A part of her mind managed to think. *What a shame.* And with that thought, as her hand tightened on the knife, as her body moved forward again, toward that door, the panic came.

No! I don't want this!

Trust me . . . Peace is death . . .

The panic ebbed. Tracey stepped outside.

Gregory moaned. And he heard himself as he did so. The sound was huge, laced with pain, and he could hardly believe that it had come from himself.

Jesus. He hurt more than before, everywhere, and he couldn't seem to see. He blinked his eyes furiously, and just when he could finally focus—on a few distant stars overhead—he remembered everything and he literally choked on his own breath. And when he could resume breathing, it was hard and fast, with real, abject fear.

No. With real, abject terror.

He'd gone through the glass door. How badly was he hurt? He did not want to die, goddamn it. No, goddamn Isabel.

And where was she now? Why was he still lying outside on the stone floor of the courtyard? Gregory stiffened with dread.

Blood was interfering with his vision, he realized. He had a cut—or cuts—on his forehead and temple that were bleeding profusely. Gregory automatically tried to wipe the blood away. Where the hell was everyone? Why had they left him like this? Panic sharpened his breathing to an impossible, razorlike edge.

He used his left hand to smear away the blood, and he tried to lever himself slowly into a sitting position. He was overcome with waves of undulating darkness and he gave it up quickly, but it was some time before the need to faint diminished. *Fuck.* He was in really bad shape.

When he'd taken some control of his breathing, when his pulse beat a bit less frighteningly, he twisted his head around so he could see into the house. He froze.

Antonio lay facedown just inside the shattered door, his back and upper torso bandaged, the linen stained red.

Oh God. What happened? Gregory wondered frantically. And where was Cass?

Help. He had to help his brother. He could not let Antonio die.

Gregory moved onto his side, panting with the effort, sweating with it, his vision blurring again. He got onto his stomach and slowly, painstakingly, he began to crawl toward the house.

Within inches he collapsed. But he refused to give up, intending just to take a moment to collect his strength, when he felt that he was being watched.

Instinct told him it was Isabel. Every hair on his nape rose. And he looked up.

Tracey stood just inside the shattered door, watching him.

Relief overcame him and he collapsed again. "Tracey." He thought that his whisper was inaudible. How he needed her now. He had never been happier to see anyone.

He felt her coming, more than he actually heard her, and he twisted so he could look up. "Thank God. Tonio?" he asked.

She paused, standing above him. "Everything will be fine," she said. "Trust me."

And there was something in her blank expression, something odd and eerie, or something in her tone, equally strange, that made him tense with growing dread and a new inkling—one he did not want.

She smiled.

The woman of his nightmares smiled and lifted the knife.

Gregory knew it was the end. "No!"

He tried to twist away as the metal flashed down, but the moment the knife went into his flesh, slicing through muscle and bone, he knew he had failed and that it was too late.

She stabbed him again.

Antonio had been fighting to come out of the darkness for some time. For somehow, somewhere, in the back of his unconscious mind, he felt an urgency, a knowledge, an awareness, that would not let him go.

He had to wake up. The stakes were too high. The stakes were life and death.

But the blackness was thick and soft, and so terribly comforting. It would be so easy to succumb to its embrace, to succumb, to drift, to forget . . . to die.

But the images were there, twisted up inside his brain.

His beautiful son. His dead wife. His injured twin brother. The little girl. Cassandra . . .

He must swim through the shadows and face even greater darkness, and slowly, painfully, he did so. And as the blackness began to abate, the pain began, and with every incremental step back into the light, the pain grew and intensified. Suddenly Antonio was conscious.

And with the consciousness came complete and stark recollection.

Tracey was Isabel, and he must destroy her before she destroyed them all.

Antonio opened his eyes and for one moment he had to fight to see, because many of the tapers left in the hall had burned out. And when he could see, he saw her shadow, not far from where he lay. Turning his head, shifting ever so slightly, he saw her standing not far from him, her back to him, staring out into the night.

No, not into the night, but at his brother, who lay injured in the courtyard, unable to defend himself.

He had to get up, he thought with panic and the first seeds of rage. Before she did the unthinkable.

And as Antonio struggled to sit up, he saw her move out of the corner of his eye.

He froze, head whipping around, and saw her stab his brother in the back with a knife.

Adrenaline gave him the speed, strength, and agility he might not have otherwise had. He lunged to his feet, never taking his gaze from Tracey, watching her wield the knife a second time, and he did not pause to think. He launched himself at her.

And she realized he was coming too late. Just before he hit her with all of his strength and the full force of his two hundred pounds, she glanced back and saw him. Tracey went flying past Gregory, Antonio on top of her.

And as they hit the ground, Antonio seized her wrist and hand—the one holding the knife. Instantly he was met with a force far greater than his own. And he recalled, belatedly, that Tracey was not Tracey, that she was superhuman now, and her strength far surpassed his own.

She snarled at him and tore her hand free from his, raising the knife with the obvious intention of plunging it down into his face.

Antonio jerked aside and the knife sliced past his ear and neck, into the hard stone floor beneath them.

And he looked up into a pair of the most hate-filled, vicious eyes he had ever seen. Eyes that held no compromise whatsoever.

He found her small throat with both of his large hands and he began to squeeze.

Her eyes went wide with surprise.

Satisfaction the likes of which he had never before felt filled him. Rage fueled him. He would strangle her to death and love every minute of the horrific deed.

She dropped the knife, gripped his wrists, and tore his hands away from her neck.

Antonio was again shocked by her strength. Shocked—and afraid.

She smiled at him once, briefly, savagely, and the next thing he knew was that she had a rock in her hand and was about to smash it down on his head.

Antonio reached for her wrist as he tried to roll away. A moment later he felt the blow, the pain, and then there was only darkness.

Cass beat out the last of the fire with the last of the pillows, and when the only flames left in the room were the ones dancing in the hearth, she collapsed to the floor in a heap. She was shaking with utter exhaustion. Every muscle in her body felt limp and useless, her back burned, and her lungs were raw and hurting from the smoke. She lay on the warm wood floor, eyes closed, incapable of movement.

But there was no time to rest.

Antonio was downstairs with his brother, the both of them defenseless, Tracey and Isabel had to be stopped, and dear God, the children had to be found.

Cass somehow sat up. She continued to tremble with exhaustion.

But she had at least put out the fire, saving the house.

Cass got to her feet, gulping down air, continuing to tremble. She did not know what, exactly, awaited her downstairs. But before she went down to fight Isabel, she needed a weapon.

Tears filled her eyes. How was she going to fight Tracey—who was Isabel? Even if she killed her very own sister, that would not stop Isabel.

Cass couldn't stop shaking. She could not kill her own sister. Even knowing that Isabel intended to kill her—using Tracey to do so—she could not kill her own sister.

Cass didn't know what to do.

If only she could reach Tracey, somehow.

She went to the door, then realized it was locked and that she could not get out that way. Grim, she found the first object at hand—a small, heavy brass clock—and she threw it at one of the windows, which opened over the courtyard. The glass broke.

Trying not to think now, she wrapped a pillow around her arm and cleared the window frame of all remaining glass. Tracey had to be stopped. Cass felt tears sliding down her cheeks. *Oh, God.*

She glanced over the sill. The first thing she saw was a series of drainage pipes, running perpendicular to one another. One ran parallel to the ground, and Cass wondered if it would hold her weight; the other was vertical, and ended maybe eight feet above the ground.

Cass's heart skipped a beat as her gaze went from where the drainage pipe ended to the floor of the courtyard below. It was a long way down, but even from where she stood, she could see the two crumpled forms below, and there was no mistaking Gregory and Antonio.

Cass's heart lurched with dread, and then she acted.

Furious, she swung herself over the windowsill, and gripping hard, she lowered herself until her feet touched the parallel drainage pipe. As her weight intensified on the pipe, she felt it buckle. But Cass had no choice.

She let go of the sill, the pipe cracked, but Cass was launching herself at the perpendicular section, and somehow she was hugging it, and even as that sagged dangerously, she was sliding down hard and fast, and then the pipe broke, taking her with it.

Cass landed hard on her rear and back, and for one moment, lay still.

But there was no time to lose.

She rolled over, lunged forward, and before she reached Antonio, she saw the blood pooling below his head. Her heart stopped.

I will die if he dies.

"No!" Cass sobbed, reaching him. She cradled him in her lap, gasping for breath through her tears and the fear and the shock.

The fear was a fire inside her, burning its way out, destroying her from the inside out—and the anguish was unbearable.

Cass thought she was going to die, too.

And then she heard a child's voice.

The children.

Cass was immobilized, straining to hear above her own pulse and her own breathing. Had she heard a child's voice?

Suddenly she was on her feet. That sound—which she had not imagined, damn it—had come from inside the house, not far from the great hall.

The children. She had to save the children. Cass ran into the house, into the hall, mindless of the glass at her feet. She did not pause, racing back toward the grand salon and the corridor leading to her bedroom upstairs. She had just turned the corner when she saw Tracey. Cass halted in her tracks.

The hidden door was open now, in the middle of the corridor, but it was made of the same stone as the walls, and Cass never would have realized it existed in a million years. Tracey's back was to her, but Cass heard her say, "You can come out now."

Cass's knees began to buckle with relief; she realized that Tracey, under Isabel's control, had hidden the children, and now was letting them out. But why? And then she saw Alyssa emerging from whatever was behind that door, dirty and disheveled and clutching one arm, but very much alive. Tears blinded her.

Eduardo was hobbling out, too.

"Aunt Cass!" Alyssa shrieked, spotting Cass and racing pell-mell to her.

Cass caught her in her arms, holding her tightly, so tightly, knowing she had never loved anyone or anything this way—except Antonio, who was dead. She wept, for whatever Alyssa had gone through, for Gregory, and for Antonio. And she wept for Tracey, too.

"Don't cry, Aunt Cass, I'm fine, I really am fine," Alyssa whispered, her own tone thick with unshed tears.

Suddenly the hairs rose on every inch of Cass's body and she froze,

Alyssa in her arms, her face against her soft, dark hair. Slowly Cass looked up.

Tracey stood before her, beside Eduardo, staring at her with that unblinking, demonic gaze.

Cass pulled Alyssa behind her. "Eduardo, come here," she said softly, her heart pumping furiously.

Eduardo did not hesitate. He hopped past Tracey, who did not move, coming to stand behind Cass, beside Alyssa.

"I would not hurt the children," Tracey said.

Cass breathed hard, with difficulty. "Tracey, can you talk to me?"

"I am speaking to you," she said.

"No. Isabel is talking to me. I want to talk to Tracey—my sister." She smiled. "I am your sister now."

"No. You are not my sister, and I want my sister back," Cass said, her pulse pumping even more furiously now. Her cheeks felt hot, burningly so. "I want my sister back."

"You are alive," Tracey said, her eyes glowing.

"I am alive. Why do you want to kill me? Haven't you done enough?" Cass cried.

"You killed me," Tracey said, with anger. "All of you."

"No. I did not kill you. I had nothing to do with those who betrayed you. Was it Sussex? He was a powerful man, surely he could have prevented your death. Was it your husband? Was he the one who accused you of heresy—was he the one who wanted to see you suffer that way? Or was it even Rob? Was it your own lover and the father of your child who truly betrayed you?" Cass cried, drenched with sweat, the odor of her fear thick and heavy about her.

"They all betrayed me, Sussex, Rob, de la Barca, may God damn them forever," Tracey said, her eyes cold and unblinking.

Cass absorbed that even as she said, "Tracey! Where are you? Why aren't you fighting her? She going to kill us both if you don't fight her, damn it!"

"I am Tracey," she said, and she raised the knife.

"Run!" Cass shouted without turning to the children, and as the knife came down, Cass dodged it, miraculously.

Tracey's expression hardened with rage and she gripped Cass's arm, her strength shocking and unbelievable. Cass knew she could never overpower her sister while she was in Isabel's control. As Cass struggled to wrench free Tracey raised the knife again, and it was poised to plunge into Cass's throat.

Their gazes met.

"Don't, Tracey, don't!" Cass cried.

Tracey smiled.

The shot sounded just as a hole blossomed red on Tracey's arm. Cass gasped, stunned, as Tracey let her go, staggering backward, the blossom growing rapidly, and then she fell back, against the marble table on the wall.

Cass turned and saw Antonio reeling on the opposite threshold, holding a small gun, his face and chest covered with blood. *He was alive.* Cass was overcome with relief. But it was short-lived.

"You cannot . . . kill me," Tracey gasped, clutching her arm and leaning against the table.

Cass stared, her dazed brain trying to function. They could physically kill Tracey, but that would not destroy Isabel. Suddenly instinct made her whirl; Antonio had raised the gun and he was pointing it at Tracey. "No!" she shouted. "Don't shoot her!"

His gaze veered to hers, filled with rage, hatred, and fear, and then his eyes softened and he lowered the gun.

Cass leapt to face her sister. "Tracey," she said urgently, rapidly. "You have to talk to me. Talk to me, your sister! I love you! Please, Tracey, get rid of her!"

"You cannot . . . kill me," Tracey gasped, hunched over, her arm continuing to bleed, the blood seeping through her fingertips.

"Tracey, I know you're there," Cass cried, daring to step closer to her. Tracey was physically hurt, so maybe she would no longer be useful as a vessel for Isabel. Cass prayed. "Tracey, remember when Mommy died? And we found Dad asleep in his favorite chair—crying in his sleep? Remember? We went upstairs and hugged each other and cried, too. We were so scared."

Tracey met her gaze. And Cass thought she'd reached her, because there was something startled in her eyes, but then she said, "You cannot . . . kill me."

"I don't want to kill you," Cass cried, frustrated, desperate, despairing. "I love you, you're my sister!"

"No," Tracey panted, looking at her. "No. *I* am your sister now."

Cass knew she was failing. "I love you and I want you back!" she cried. "*I love you.*"

There was an eternity of silence. Then, "No . . . don't . . . love me," Tracey whispered raggedly, her eyes closing.

For one heartbeat, Cass froze. Then she said, "I know I was jealous of you, because of your beauty, all the guys, and then, damn it, I'll admit it, I was jealous because you're Alyssa's mother and I'm only her aunt, but I'm human, okay?" Cass realized she was crying. But she prayed—hoped—she was finally getting through to her sister. "But that doesn't mean I don't love you. I don't want you to die!"

"No. Don't . . . love . . . me . . ." Tracey said, a harsh cry, as she slumped to the floor, clutching her wounded arm.

Cass inhaled hard. She had somehow reached her sister after all. "I do love you," she said hoarsely. "I love you so much that I won't let Tonio kill you. And I won't let Isabel destroy you, either."

Tracey sagged against the wall. "So . . . much . . . pain," she whispered.

Was her sister coming out of Isabel's power? "Tracey?"

"Two . . . of . . . me . . ." she gasped.

"Fight her," Cass screamed, rushing to her and helping support her so she could stand upright.

"Cassandra, don't go any closer!" Antonio shouted from the other side of the hall.

But Cass ignored him, her arm around Tracey. "Fight her. For me, for Alyssa, we all love you so much."

"Two . . . of . . . me . . ." she said, opening her eyes, her gaze meeting Cass's. And briefly it was lucid, and it was Tracey.

"Fight! Fight that bitch," Cass ground out.

"Can't," Tracey gasped, and even as she spoke, Cass realized what was happening. Tracey's fingers on her left hand, holding her wounded arm, were stiffening and whitening with the tension. Clearly a part of her was trying to hold the injured arm—another part of her was trying to release it. And Cass instantly realized why.

Because Tracey still held the knife in her right hand, which dangled at her side.

Cass stared as Tracey's left hand twitched and slowly began to open. She looked down and saw that her grip on the knife was tightening at the very same time.

And Antonio must have seen too, because he shouted, "Get out of the way!"

He was only yards away, having come across the hall. Cass didn't look back at him. She would not move away—giving him a clear shot at her sister.

Tracey had to vanquish Isabel. Cass would not think about the consequences if she did not.

Tracey slowly moved her left hand away from her right arm. Tears were streaming down her face, mingling with perspiration.

"Fight her, Trace, you can do it," Cass whispered, wondering if the blade was going to be used against her.

"Too much pain," Tracey whispered, and suddenly her right arm was dangling free, and in the next instant she had raised the knife high.

Cass stared at the bloody tip. Her heart stopped. It crossed her dazed mind that this was it. She had lost. Isabel would win after all. She was about to die.

And what happened next happened in the slowest of motion, as if all time had ceased.

Tracey looked Cass in the eye, and Cass watched as she pushed the knife down.

Not into Cass's breast.

Into her own breast.

TWENTY-EIGHT

Cass could not scream.

She could only stand in shock and stare down at her sister.

"Mother," came an anguished whisper.

Cass whirled, to find Antonio holding both children, but Alyssa was struggling to break free of the circle of his arms. Tears covered her white, frightened face.

Cass took one last look at Tracey, then rushed to her niece, pulling her into her embrace. As she did so, briefly her gaze met Antonio's. Everything she'd ever hoped to see in his eyes was there—concern, compassion, love, strength.

"Is she dead?" he asked.

Cass thought so. But it struck her that she did not know for certain, and even as she realized that, she heard Antonio moving past her. Cass stroked Alyssa's hair, murmuring reassuringly to her, holding her hard.

But now she began to wonder, where was Isabel?

"I don't understand," Alyssa whispered. "Is that woman gone?"

"I'll explain, one day," Cass whispered, but she stiffened, glancing at Antonio, who was kneeling beside Tracey. Was Isabel gone? Could it be possible?

Of course she wasn't gone, Cass thought instantly. She knew it the way she knew the sun would rise tomorrow.

"She's alive, but she needs a doctor, soon," Antonio said, standing.

Cass released Alyssa, weak with relief, but it was short-lived. They had no way of getting an ambulance or getting to a doctor. She glanced warily around the dimly illuminated hall. Where was Isabel? Cass sensed she was near. The air felt heavy, dense, dark, and ugly, and it was pressing down on Cass almost unbearably. And it almost felt as if the pressure were coming from the inside out—which made no sense at all. Cass's shoulders felt so rigid from the pressure and the tension, she wondered if they would snap.

Her instincts screamed at her that they were in the eye of the storm. That the worst had yet to come.

"We have no power, no phones, no transportation," she said slowly, moving toward Antonio.

His gaze sharpened. "Cassandra?"

"There is no physician here," Cass said. And even as she spoke, even as she met Antonio's gaze, and wondered why he was looking at her that way, she heard herself and was confused by her own words. They did not sound right. They sounded . . . odd.

"We need to bandage the wound. I'm afraid to remove the knife." He stared. "Gregory needs a doctor, too. I'm going to have to go for help."

Cass found herself staring at her sister, lying in a pool of her own warm, red blood. She felt ill, violently so, but something else was happening, because a part of her did not feel ill at all. A part of her felt satisfied. Terribly satisfied.

Peace is death.

"I'll remove the knife," she said, and before she knew what she herself intended, she was kneeling beside Tracey, who did not even appear to be breathing, and she was reaching for the handle of the knife.

"No!" Antonio shouted, grabbing her arm before she could pull the blade free of her sister's chest.

Cass flung him off unthinkingly.

And she watched him fall backward, onto the floor. And she was so oddly surprised at her own strength, but then she realized he was wounded; that would explain why he was so weak. Still, she hadn't meant to hurt him. She wanted to call out to him, but her mouth would not open, nor would it form the words she wished to say.

Peace is death. Trust me.

Cass froze, about to withdraw the knife, only vaguely aware now of Antonio, who was telling her not to take out the knife, that removing it might be worse for her sister, and he was calling her name, again and again—but he sounded so far away.

The scene in the great hall had become surreal, Cass thought. Was this really happening?

Peace is death. Take the knife. Do what you must do to find peace.

Isabel, Cass managed to think, her sister's white, nearly lifeless face swimming in and out of view. "Isabel," she muttered, her mind, curiously sluggish, trying to hold on to that thought. Isabel had returned.

Isabel was stalking Cass now.

And Cass seemed to be above the room, looking down on everyone there. Antonio staring at her, the two children cowering together by the wall, her sister dying on the floor in a pool of her own blood. And Cass just standing there, poised to wrench the knife from her sister's breast.

Antonio was rushing her from behind.

"Cassandra!" Antonio was shouting.

And he was grabbing her.

Hardly even aware of what she was doing, Cass twisted free of him—and watched as he was hurled backward again, this time landing hard on the floor.

And she wondered how she had ever accomplished such a feat.

Sobs reached her.

Distant sobs—as if from another world, another unearthly plane.

Death is peace. The voice inside her head was so warm and soothing, mesmerizing. There was comfort in the refrain. Vast, unthinkable comfort.

But the children were crying.

Cass blinked and saw Alyssa crouched down beside the marble table, staring at her, crying, Eduardo next to her, holding her, also in tears.

The children, she thought. *I have to save the children.*

"Cassandra. Don't let her do this. Cassandra. Look at me. Cassandra. Can you hear me? Look at me!" Antonio cried, gripping her by her arms again.

His face was inches from hers, and Cass met his eyes, even as her body flexed, even as she intended to throw him off of her, damn him for his interference.

Kill him.

The savage, brutal thought formed itself inside her brain, and for one heartrending instant, Cass wanted to take the knife from her sister's breast and plunge it into Antonio's chest. In the next instant, she looked into his eyes and felt his pull.

I love you. Trust me.

Peace is death. Kill him.

Images flooded her confused brain. Images of him lecturing in his black turtleneck, while she sat perched at her small desk, eating up his every word; images of her and Antonio side by side, staring at and discussing the ruby necklace; images of his face alight with intellectual excitement; images of a look, a smile; images of him touching her naked body, eyes wide, intent; images of him above her, while inside of her. *I love him*, Cass thought, staring, their gazes locked. *I love him, I love the children, I love them, I do.*

"Cassandra," he said. "You're stronger than Tracey. Fight her. Fight her, now. Please," he cried, on a sob.

Peace is death! Isabel screamed again and again.

And Cass felt the pain, inside her head, black and burning, an endless vortex, tearing roaring ripping her brain apart.

But she loved him. How could she kill him?

"I love you, damn it," he cried, his grip tightening on her arms, hurting her. He was shaking her.

Cass relished the pain then, hoping it would detract from the spinning blackness in her mind, the blackness and confusion. Isabel's face loomed there, in her mind's eye, smiling, taunting, malevolent. Cass pushed Antonio away. "Go away," she cried.

Antonio stared. "No. No. I will not."

Cass shook her head, Isabel before her, her mantra echoing in her mind. She could not clear it. *Peace is death . . . kill him. Now.*

Cass broke into a sweat. She was shaking wildly, she realized. Her hands were clamped over her ears. She felt that if the noises inside her head did not stop, she would go deaf—or insane.

Peace is death peace is death kill him kill him trust me.

"No!" Cass screamed.

"Cassandra!" Antonio shouted.

Cass clutched her head, harder now, and it was spinning, spinning furiously, making her dizzy, making her insane. She felt like tearing her head off of her own shoulders, to stop that damnably seductive voice, to stop the pain.

"Cassandra! Don't do it!" Antonio screamed.

Cass heard him, and she heard the children crying and she did not understand. *Kill him kill them all trust me . . . I love them,* she swore silently, and she saw the two huddled, terrified children, and then she saw Antonio, as white as a storybook ghost, and then she looked down, at her sister's bloody chest—and at the knife in her own hand.

KILL THEM ALL.

Cass stared at her hand, clenching the knife, and she felt Isabel, behind her, on her, inside her, and she thought about how she loved them, so much, and she felt Isabel's hatred and fury, wrapping itself tighter and tighter around her, and Cass began to strangle for lack of air, her body felt as if it were being crushed in a vise, and Cass looked at the knife.

KILL THEM ALL.

I . . . love . . . them . . . she thought, sobbing.

And she watched the knife clatter to the floor.

She stared at it, a bloody metal blade, somehow lying at her feet, then watched as her own body also fell, slowly, in slow motion, to the ground, crumpling beside the knife.

"Cassandra," Antonio rasped, pulling her into his arms from behind.

The pain, the black vortex, a huge black hole inside her mind, spinning ceaselessly, ceased.

In that one singular moment, Cass felt a blessed blankness, a dark emptiness, and then there was light.

Inside her brain. So much light.

And Cass felt the encircling warmth of his arms, his chest, and she heard his drumming heartbeat beneath her ear. "Am I . . . okay?"

"I thought I'd lost you," he cried against her hair. And he held her hard against his chest.

And there was silence.

The sun hadn't even risen when the first ambulances and police cars arrived.

Cass stood by herself outside, wearing a light wool sweater, her hands in the pockets of her jeans, watching the activity all around the house. A half dozen policemen were walking around, talking to one another grimly in their native tongue, appearing stunned and shocked. The looks they were exchanging were almost comical.

The paramedics thought her sister would live. Tracey and Gregory had been brought by stretcher from the house and loaded into an ambulance that would take them to the closest hospital in Segovia hours ago. Alfonso had been treated by paramedics inside, on site, as had Antonio. Apparently about an hour after he had left the house in search of help, a trucker had picked him up, and using the CB radio, they had called for help.

She was grim. No one would believe their story. Tracey would probably wind up in a mental institution. Would there be a criminal trial first? Would she be accused of murdering the electrician?

And these cops did not look up to the task at hand. They had probably never seen much more than a fistfight or a case of domestic violence, Cass thought. She doubted there were lab technicians anywhere at hand to analyze the "crime" scene. Maybe that was for the best.

The sun was higher now.

The day was stunningly clean, stunningly beautiful, and absolutely benign.

Isabel was gone. Cass had not a doubt. But for how long?

She couldn't help wondering if it was forever. This day was different from the days before. It was a quiet day, but not absolutely silent. Cass could hear far more than the hushed voices of the *policía*, she could hear a soft sighing breeze, the barking of someone's dog, and a chirping bird. Periodically a police car's radio would cackle.

The quiet day felt almost lazy; the unbearable, remarkable tension that they had been living with ever since arriving at Casa de Sueños was gone.

It was almost as if a huge storm, which had been brewing, had swept violently through the area, leaving in its aftermath reduced barometric pressure and fresh, cool, clean air.

"Señora?"

Cass looked up. A policeman was approaching her, and he was holding her laptop, which was open. Beyond him, she saw Antonio standing on the front steps, one arm in a sling to relieve his shoulder where he had been stabbed from behind, speaking with another officer, who Cass thought was in charge. They had yet to exchange more than a word or two since he had returned—and since the police had arrived.

His gaze found and held hers.

Cass smiled.

He smiled back, then turned to the policeman he was speaking with.

Cass's heart lurched a little; she told herself not to think about what lay ahead for them both now. She was exhausted. Overwhelmed. So much had happened in just a few days. But . . . what would happen now?

"Señora, forgive my English," the policeman said. "But we found this in the library. *El conde* has said it belongs to you. In the moment you may keep it, but in the future, perhaps, we will need it as evidence."

Cass almost smiled. She hid her expression. Evidence of what? She was right. These cops were out of their league. Which might bode well for her sister. "It is mine."

"Would you translate, *por favor*? What does the computer say?"

Suddenly Cass stiffened. And she felt the chills sweep over her entire body. "May I?" she asked, with trepidation.

He handed it to her.

Cass's heart stopped.

Her Word program remained on. But the question she had written to Isabel was gone. In its place was one single, concise sentence, and it was even marked with a period.

I WANT TO GO HOME.

"Señora?"

" 'Here lies Isabel de la Barca. A heretic and wanton woman. God save her soul. May she rest in peace,' " Cass whispered aloud.

The sun was up. Cass stood staring at Isabel's grave. Isabel wanted to go home.

She sensed him first, before she heard him. A song began in her heart, and it was distinct. Cass didn't turn. But when he stepped beside her, she slipped her hand into his. Tears suddenly filled her eyes.

They had gone through so much. And now what?

"She wants to go home," she said.

He freed his hand and slid it around her shoulder. "Would it not be appropriate?" he asked. "To bury her in England, where she belongs?"

Cass turned to him and their eyes met. "There's a cemetery at Romney Castle," she said. "I am sure we can get permission to bury her there."

"I will help," he said simply.

She melted all over. "The children?"

"They have just awoken, and Celia is taking them into Pedraza for a huge breakfast. Courtesy of one of the police officers."

Cass nodded. She knew she had to sit down with Alyssa and try to explain everything. It would not be an easy task. "Maybe we should join them," she said. For the first time in days, she was aware of having the beginnings of an appetite.

"Maybe," he agreed. "But I would rather stay here, alone, with you, in spite of how hungry I am."

In that moment Cass knew what she wanted—there was no more

denying it, not even to herself. She slipped into the circle of his arms. "So would I," she whispered against his hard, strong chest. Then she leaned back to look up at him. "I think she's gone," she said. "I think she is truly gone. Everything feels so different today."

"I think she is gone, too," he said. Their eyes held. "Her anger burned for centuries. Today, I think, it finally burned out."

Cass's eyes suddenly filled with tears. "I know what Tracey went through. It was so hard. I almost killed you—and everyone. She was so strong, Antonio. But—how can I blame her?"

He smiled and stroked her hair. "Bless her guilty soul," he whispered. "Bless them all. But . . . Cassandra, you did not come close."

She smiled up at him, relishing his belief in her. "God, the sun feels so good today. Doesn't it?"

"Yes, it does," he said. "But you feel so much better, Cassandra."

Cass met his gaze, no longer smiling, filled with a new tension. "What happens now, Antonio?"

"We gave our statements to the police. They think we are all certifiably insane." His smile was wry. "Your sister will never go to trial, Cassandra, if that is what you are thinking about."

"She murdered the electrician." Cass could no longer deny it.

"As much as I hate to speak this way, the good news is that the electrician has no family. I am hoping to use my influence to have this matter simply, quietly, disappear."

Hope filled her breast. "How is that possible?"

"These are village people," he said. "They are old-fashioned and superstitious. There are already so many rumors about my family and the cloud of tragedy hovering over us. If we stick to the truth, we may frighten everyone enough that the case will be shelved as unsolved.

"And if not, Tracey would be diagnosed as mentally incompetent to stand trial," he said. "Any lawyer would tell you that."

"I'm afraid," Cass admitted. "For her. But if she is institutionalized, maybe that wouldn't be such a bad thing. God, Tonio, she has been severely traumatized by all of this." And Cass closed her eyes. They had all been traumatized by Isabel.

"You have an expression I am very fond of. It is called 'to roll with the punches.' And that is what we are all going to have to do now, Cassandra."

Cass knew he was right.

"If it is any help," he said softly, "I have far more influence in Castilla than I have ever let on. I feel confident that all will end well ... for her, for everyone ... for us."

Cass froze. "Us." A word she had never dreamed of hearing, not from anyone—and not from Antonio de la Barca—until recently. "There is an 'us,' isn't there? Isabel brought us together that first time, but—"

"Most definitely there is an 'us.'" He cut her off, his gaze direct. "And I do not believe she ever brought us together; you intrigued me from the moment we first met."

Cass was thrilled. And coyly she said, "At the Met?"

He laughed. "So now you are pushy? But if you wish to know, even though I had not yet come to terms with the loss of my wife, I was very aware of you, even then. Beauty and brains are an irresistible combination, you know."

Cass's elation knew no bounds. Then her smile faded. "And what if we wish to forget this terrible time?"

He shook his head. "Could you? Could you ever forget this? Could you ever forget *her*?"

Cass saw Isabel as she had last seen her, with murderous rage, and then she thought of the woman who had been betrayed by her uncle, her lover, and her husband. A woman who had lost her entire family at the age of eight. "I don't want to ever forget her. What happened to her was a terrible tragedy ... a grave injustice," she said. "No, I don't want to forget. I only want to put the past where it belongs, in the past. And I want ..." She stopped.

"What?" he asked.

Tears blurred her eyes. "I want a chance," she managed. "I want a chance to see if this is real."

"So do I," he said solemnly.

Their gazes met. Cass could hardly believe this was happening. And as he took her hand, he said, "I need a vacation. When are you going to invite Eduardo and me to Belford House?"

"A vacation?" she whispered, hope soaring.

"And you need a vacation, as well," he said, as sternly as if he were her doctor.

Cass laughed. The sound was light and carefree and it echoed around them in the brilliantly sunny Castilian summer day. "Will you and Eduardo come home with us to Belford House?" Cass asked formally.

He slowly smiled. "I thought you would never ask," he said.

EPILOGUE

ROMNEY CASTLE—THE PRESENT

The castle was above the small cemetery, set higher up on the hill. Cass walked slowly up the path to the graveyard, fighting the gusting December wind. She wore a fleece-lined anorak, but the chill from the windswept sea still went right through her. A wool cap covered her hair. The sky was heavy and bleak, threatening inclement weather.

She was holding two bouquets of white roses in one hand. She pushed open the cemetery gate.

Her pulse picked up its pace. Cass wove her way through the headstones, which were centuries old and now as familiar to her as the back of her own hand. She had to pause then—she always did.

In the midst of the many darkened, weathered headstones was one that simply read, "Philip de Warenne, born May 10, 1555, died February 1, 1608."

Isabel's son. Her lover's bastard. She had been shocked when they had found him there, buried at Romney—but his father, Admiral de Warenne, was also there, so it should not really have been such a surprise.

Cass knelt and laid one bouquet at the foot of his grave. Then she stood.

One headstone dominated the large cemetery now. It was not centuries old, it had been erected but four months ago. She approached slowly. The stone was white marble, unstained by tears or time, and as tall as she. It was surrounded by smaller, weather-stained headstones, and Cass paused before it. Even the earth in front of it was freshly upturned, the small plot of sod green and lush. And a bouquet was there, of withered red roses.

> Here lies Isabel de Warenne de la Barca
> Born ? 1535 Died June 13, 1555
> Daughter of Ralph de Warenne earl of Sussex
> Wife of Alvarado de la Barca count of Pedraza
> A woman who suffered the gravest injustice
> God bless her soul and may she rest in peace
> Now and for all time

Cass felt the tears fill her eyes. It was always this way. She could not visit Isabel's grave without becoming overly emotional—and more than a year had passed since those few days in Castilla.

Days she would never forget.

There were mornings when she awoke and still missed her aunt terribly. But wasn't there an expression, "When one door closes, another one opens"? She would always miss Catherine, always love her. But she had never been happier.

And Tracey had not been charged with any criminal offense. She had, however, admitted herself into a private London hospital that specialized in alcoholism and drug addictions. Tracey was now an outpatient. She hadn't had a drink since Spain—and she was also being treated for depression.

Cass laid the fresh flowers down beside the withered ones.

Below, a car's horn sounded.

Cass jumped, because she had driven up to the castle's car park by herself, but even as she turned, she knew.

A black BMW had ignored all the signs forbidding cars from going any further, and it was parked just below the cemetery gates. Cass watched as the front door opened and the man got out. He was wearing a black sport jacket—he must be cold—and tortoiseshell glasses were slipping down his nose. She knew he was smiling at her.

Her heart turned over, hard. She hadn't seen him in weeks; she wasn't expecting him for another day. Eagerly Cass started down the path, waving.

He waved back.

She flew into his arms.

After they had kissed for a very long time, they pulled apart and her husband tucked stray strands of hair back beneath her wool cap. "Hello, Cassandra," he said.

"You told me you were coming tomorrow," she said. A few fat flakes of snow were starting to fall.

He helped her into the car. "I lied." He smiled.

Cass smiled back as he shut the door, and when Antonio had settled in the seat beside her, they drove down the hill, away from the grave, away from the castle where it had all begun, and back to Belford House.